Pride *and* Prometheus

ALSO BY JOHN KESSEL

Pride *and* Prometheus

JOHN KESSEL

SAGA PRESS

LONDON SYDNEY **NEW YORK** TORONTO NEW DELHI

SAGA PRESS

AN IMPRINT OF SIMON & SCHUSTER, INC.

1230 AVENUE OF THE AMERICAS, NEW YORK, NEW YORK 10020

SAGA PRESS and colophon are trademarks of Simon & Schuster, Inc.

For information about special discounts for bulk purchases, please contact Simon & Schuster Special Sales at 1-866-506-1949 or business@simonandschuster.com.

The Simon & Schuster Speakers Bureau can bring authors to your live event. For more information or to book an event, contact the Simon & Schuster Speakers Bureau at 1-866-248-3049 or visit our website at www.simonspeakers.com.

Also available in a Saga Press hardcover edition

Cover design by Sonia Chaghatzbanian; interior design by Irene Metaxatos

The text for this book was set in Cochin.

Manufactured in the United States of America

First Saga Press paperback edition November 2018

2 4 6 8 10 9 7 5 3 1

Library of Congress Cataloging-in-Publication Data

Names: Kessel, John, author.

Title: Pride and Prometheus / John Kessel.

Description: First edition. | New York : Saga Press, [2018]

Identifiers: LCCN 2017023614 (print) | ISBN 9781481481496 (eBook) | ISBN 9781481481472 (hardcover : acid-free paper) | ISBN 9781481481489 (pbk)

Classification: LCC PS3561.E6675 P75 2018 (print) | DDC 813/.54—dc23

LC record available at https://lccn.loc.gov/2017023614

For Karen Joy Fowler,
who told me to write it

"But my dearest Catherine, what have you been doing with yourself all this morning? — Have you gone on with *Udolpho*?"

"Yes, I have been reading it ever since I woke; and I am got to the black veil."

"Are you, indeed? How delightful! Oh, I would not tell you what is behind the black veil for the world! Are not you wild to know?"

"Oh! yes, quite; what can it be? — But do not tell me — I would not be told upon any account. I know it must be a skeleton, I am sure it is Laurentina's skeleton. Oh! I am delighted with the book! I should like to spend my whole life in reading it. . . ."

". . . when you have finished *Udolpho*, we will read *The Italian* together; and I have made out a list of ten or twelve more of the same kind for you."

"Have you, indeed! How glad I am! — What are they all?"

"I will read you their names directly; here they are, in my pocketbook. *Castle of Wolfenbach, Clermont, Mysterious Warnings, Necromancer of the Black Forest, Midnight Bell, Orphan of the Rhine*, and *Horrid Mysteries*. Those will last us some time."

"Yes, pretty well; but are they all horrid, are you sure they are all horrid?"

—JANE AUSTEN,
Northanger Abbey

"I agree with you," replied the stranger; "we are unfash-
ioned creatures, but half made up, if one wiser, better,
dearer than ourselves—such a friend ought to be—do not
lend his aid to perfectionate our weak and faulty natures."

—MARY SHELLEY,
Frankenstein; or, The Modern Prometheus

ONE

When she was nineteen, Miss Mary Bennet had believed three things that were not true. She believed that, despite her awkwardness, she might become interesting through her accomplishments. She believed that, because she paid strict attention to all she had been taught about right and wrong, she was wise in the ways of the world. And she believed that God, who took note of every moment of one's life, would answer prayers, even foolish ones.

Thirteen years later, below the sea cliffs at Lyme Regis, among the tangled driftwood and broken shale exposed by the retreating tide, Mary found a flat stone plate that, when broken open by a tap of her hammer, revealed four Devil's Fingers.

"Mr. Woodleigh!" she called.

Three days of rain had softened the cliffs above Pinhay Bay, and a recent avalanche had scattered heaps of shale across the stony beach. Behind her the early March surf broke continually upon the shingle. Seabirds cried. A cold offshore wind rustled the stunted trees on the verge of the cliff above. Mary's hair came loose from her bonnet and fell into her eyes; she brushed it away with the back of the gloved hand that held the hammer.

At her call, Charles Woodleigh, bent over the rocks some twenty feet away, raised his head. "What is it, Miss Bennet?"

"See what I've found!"

He laid down his hammer and came to stand beside her as she crouched over her discovery. In the face of the stone plate were four slender conical shells, the shortest an inch or so, the largest, completely intact, at least four inches. It looked not so much like a finger as the point of a spear. She rubbed her thumb over the hard, smooth surface, whose color ranged from rusty brown to dark gray.

"Lovely," Woodleigh said. "I believe you have discovered something, Miss Bennet."

"I have!" Mary said.

The rock containing the fossils was roughly a foot across. Together they pulled it from beneath the rubble and placed it into her canvas satchel. It was not so heavy, but Mr. Woodleigh carried it toward the dogcart they had left at the foot of the road, where his man Daniel and Alice, Mrs. Bennet's maid, waited. As they approached, Daniel saw them, hurried over, and took the satchel, carrying it the rest of the way.

Woodleigh had him set it on the floor of the cart. The gravity with which Alice had taken her duties as chaperone was evidenced by her staying with Daniel rather than braving the blustery seashore. Now she was all concern. She tucked the lap robe around Mary while Mr. Woodleigh told Daniel to take them to the inn.

"A very lucky find, indeed," Woodleigh told Mary as they rode back to town, his feet resting on her discovery.

The rear seat of the cart faced backward, and as it bumped up the rutted path, their view of the bay expanded. The tide would soon cover the beach where they had spent the last hours. The sinuous masonry of the Cobb, the famous seawall, embraced Lyme's small harbor and its fishing boats. Below the Promenade the beach lay devoid of the bathing machines of summer. The high street pitched steeply up from the harbor, not half so busy as it would be in that season. Daniel maneuvered their cart around a man waiting anxiously with a groom alongside a chaise and four. Under the overcast sky the town lay steeped in twilight. Some servants could be seen at the fish market and butcher's shop, while men in work clothes came out of the ironmonger's. Outside the Assembly Rooms, a boy was lighting the lamps at each side of the entrance.

At the King's Crown Inn they dismounted. Woodleigh sent Daniel to stable the horse and cart; Mary allowed the shivering Alice to hurry indoors while she stopped at a table set up outside the inn. On the table were displayed baskets full of Dudley Locusts, verteberries, and several such Devil's Fingers as Mary had discovered. A large, flat stone leaning against a table leg showed the skeleton of some ancient fish. A girl of perhaps fifteen years of age, wearing a well-worn dark green wool dress and an unadorned bonnet, minded the table. Her ungloved hands, which she kept crossed before her, were rough, her knuckles red. This was the celebrated Mary Anning, the girl the locals said had survived being struck by lightning as an infant, and who had acquired such a reputation for her ability to find fossils that enthusiasts from as far away as Edinburgh frequented her stall.

Mary had made her acquaintance earlier. Mary Anning was shy around her betters, but at moments her intelligence broke through their difference in station. Mary wanted to tell the girl what she had found, but hesitated, and in a moment Woodleigh arrived. A basket on the table contained a dozen Devil's Fingers. Woodleigh selected one. Mary Anning's hopeful eyes watched his every move. He addressed the girl.

"You ask a shilling for one of these? Yet this lady has found several herself this very day."

Mary Anning's eyes met Mary's, a glimmer of excitement in her gaze. "Did you go where—"

"Excuse me?" Woodleigh interrupted. "I believe I asked you a question."

"Beg pardon, sir. The lady asked me how she might look for such as these and I told her."

Woodleigh nodded. "Yes, indeed. It's remarkable that there are any left to find, since you deprive this beach of antiquities the moment that they appear. Those of us who study fossils can only travel here at great trouble, on certain occasions, while you have the Blue Lias cliffs at your disposal every day of the year."

Mary set her satchel on the edge of the table, opened it, and showed the girl her find. "I think this must have been exposed by the recent fall."

Mary Anning studied the plate. "These is very fine."

"They are not really fingers, are they?" Mary asked.

Woodleigh said, "No, Miss Bennet. These are the horns of some ancient sea creature."

Miss Anning said, "They comes from some sort of cuttle-fish."

"I doubt that very much," Woodleigh said.

The girl did not argue the point.

Woodleigh surveyed the fossils laid out, including one very fine example of what the locals called a "snake stone," a spiral shell rather like that of a nautilus. Woodleigh haggled with the girl until she agreed to sell it for two shillings.

Mary Anning wrapped the snake stone in brown paper while Woodleigh pulled the pittance he had offered from his purse. From their conversations, Mary knew that the girl's family depended on the meager earnings from such sales for their living. Upon entering the inn, she ventured to speak to Woodleigh about it.

He shook his head. "Your kind heart speaks well of you, Mary. The girl has no learning, yet she presumes to correct her betters. She is unwilling to do work more fitting to someone of her station, and lucky to get what we give her."

"But Mr. Woodleigh, you know this is the girl who discov-ered the fossilized crocodile that was the talk of the Geological Society."

"It was no crocodile. It was an ichthyosaurus."

"Which she discovered. Doesn't she deserve some credit for that?"

"Would we say the beggar who finds a sovereign in the gutter earned it? She could not pronounce 'ichthyosaur' if her life depended on it."

Mary wished he would not be so uncharitable. In areas

unrelated to his enthusiasm he seemed an amiable man, but at these moments he presented himself in the worst light.

"I believe I will retire until dinner," she said.

He looked worried. "Shall I carry your fossil up for you?"

"I will carry it myself."

Mary returned to her room in an ill humor. From her first conversation with Mary Anning, she had felt that her kinship with the odd girl went beyond their given names. Mary Anning was half her age, a Dissenter, and desperately poor, yet they shared an interest in these unwomanly studies. Such affinities were not visible to Woodleigh. He was right, she supposed: friendships outside one's class were ill-advised, and when Mary was younger, she would never have considered otherwise.

Charles Woodleigh was forty-three, the middle son of a prominent family of Devonshire, who had read the law at Lincoln's Inn. In London he had dabbled in Tory politics, made a success in some Irish enterprise, and retired to Exeter to pursue his interests. One of those interests was the study of fossils, which he had commenced in his youth as a member of the Askesian Society. He was a regular visitor to Lyme and its famous fossil cliffs. There, at the Assembly Rooms, Mary had been introduced to him. It soon became apparent that unlike anyone she had ever met, and certainly no one in her family, Woodleigh was delighted by her interest in fossils.

Mary was flattered by his attentions. He was a pious man, and had asked her to sit with him at the local service last Sunday. She had noted how well he sang the hymn. Above all he loved talking about his collection, and she was a ready listener. When they discovered their mutual enthusiasm, Mary dared to think that, if it were possible for a man and woman to spend all of their days speaking of fossils, their acquaintance might lead to some more permanent connection.

Mrs. Bennet and Kitty awaited Mary in their rooms.

"There you are," said Mrs. Bennet. "My Lord, your dress is nothing but mud! You must get out of those clothes immediately. We are to dine this evening with Mr. Woodleigh."

"I know, Mother. I just left Mr. Woodleigh."

Mary hoisted her satchel onto the table. She removed her cloak and undid the ribbons of her bonnet, took it off, and set it beside her discovery.

Kitty was already dressed in the gown she had bought the day before. "What is that?" she asked.

Mary began to open the bag. "I found this on the shore. It's—"

"Oh, dear, it is wet!" Mrs. Bennet exclaimed. "See, you have soiled the tablecloth already."

Mary took the bag from the table and set it on the hearthstone, her enthusiasm only slightly dampened. She opened it to display the stone plate and her fossils. The faint light of the coal fire flickered over its surface. "See! Four of these creatures trapped in this single stone. They have been called Devil's Fingers. Mr. Woodleigh maintains that these are horns of some sea creature, but I believe, and my belief is seconded by the young woman who sells fossils in the street, that they are the remains of some form of cuttlefish."

"You have spoken with some girl in the street?" Mrs. Bennet said.

Kitty bent over the slab. "Cuttlefish?"

"They have also been called thunderstones: some people

believe that they are created when lightning strikes the earth." Mary warmed to her subject. "But that is not likely. In fact—"

"And you found these yourself!" Kitty brightened.

Mary was pleased. "I did. I—"

"How wonderful! I am certain that Mr. Woodleigh was properly impressed. Perhaps now that you have accomplished what you set out to do in Lyme, we could move on to London?"

"But we were to be here for another week," Mary said.

"Mother, must we remain?" Kitty said. "One might attend a hundred balls in Lyme in March and not meet one person of consequence."

Mrs. Bennet had not spared a glance for Mary's fossils. "Now, my dear, you know that I share your opinion of the society of Lyme, but we don't want to harm Mary's chances with Mr. Woodleigh. Patience. We'll be in London soon enough."

As if struck by lightning herself, Kitty fell into a chair near the hearth. "Mary, is this proper? You've always spoken of the risks women take by associating with men." Kitty turned to Mrs. Bennet. "Yet she spends hours with Mr. Woodleigh on her own, without a chaperone."

"Alice was with me."

"Alice no doubt spent her time flirting with Woodleigh's servant."

"With men undeserving of our trust, what I've told you is true," Mary said. "Mr. Woodleigh is not such a man."

"No, Mr. Woodleigh is too interested in your thunderstones to present any danger, I suppose. So I shall wilt here in this dank town until he departs." Kitty coughed theatrically, caught her breath, and continued, "Maybe we can get you to sing for Mr. Woodleigh. If anything might drive him back to Devonshire, that would."

Mary colored. She tried to speak, but nothing would come.

Mrs. Bennet did not seem to have understood Kitty's thrust. "Kitty! You should be half so accomplished as Mary."

Kitty would not meet Mary's eyes. Mary picked up her satchel.

"I must dress," she said. "Perhaps you should send for Alice, Mother—to clean up after me."

Mary retreated to her room, closed the door, and leaned against it. She searched for some witty rejoinder she might have made to Kitty. Over the years she had come to understand how much she served as a source of amusement to her sisters, and had thought herself well defended. How cruel of Kitty to remind Mary of Netherfield Park. Thirteen years, yet it seemed the pain lay ready to be reawakened at the least notice.

Mary was neither a beauty, like her older and happily married sister Jane, nor witty, like her older and happily married sister Elizabeth, nor flirtatious, like her younger and less happily married sister Lydia. Awkward and nearsighted, she had never cut an attractive figure, and as she had aged, she had come to see herself as others saw her. There was no air of grace or mystery about Mary, and no man—not even Charles Woodleigh—ever looked upon her with that sort of admiration.

So she had applied herself to the pianoforte from early youth, had taught herself to sing, and had studied harmony. She became by far the most accomplished of the Bennet sisters, quite vain in her regard for her own abilities.

Until that evening at Netherfield. All of Meryton was gathered at a ball thrown by Mr. Charles Bingley, a newcomer to town on whom Jane had set her sights. At the ball Elizabeth was asked to play, and after she had done so, Mary, eager to demonstrate her skills — she had studied much harder than Lizzy, and was far more adept, everybody said — had sat down to the instrument, played, and sang. Quite well, she thought. She took the silence with which she was greeted as a sign of the revelers' rapt attention. Lizzy caught her eye and shook her head slightly, but Mary could not imagine what she intended.

Mary sang a second song, and was about to assay a third when Mr. Bennet stepped to her side, put his hand gently on her shoulder, and said, "That will do extremely well, child. You have delighted us long enough. Let the other young ladies have time to exhibit."

At that, Mary looked up to see — to actually *see*, for the first time in her life — the faces of the gathered people, and a veil was lifted. Written on these faces was amusement, indifference, even annoyance. Lizzy's expression was one of agonized embarrassment. Mary realized that she was at best a figure of fun, and the closer the relation of the observers to her, the more a cause of shame.

She rose from the pianoforte, her hands trembling, and spent the rest of the ball sitting in a corner. The evening ran on past midnight, and the candles burned down to stubs, and Lizzy spoke with Mr. Darcy, whom she would eventually marry, and Jane danced with Mr. Bingley, whom she would marry — while Mary felt as if she had fallen into a pit that had opened up in the beeswax-polished floor of Netherfield Hall.

Mary had never played again in public. She had managed to hide her shame to the point where, she was sure, no one in the family understood how great a blow she had suffered. To them it was a minor incident, no different from a dozen other purblind things Mary had done that illustrated how poorly she understood the world.

From that day on she began to notice how nobody in the family listened to the things she said. When she discoursed on morality, the likely response was silence or a hasty move to some other subject. Even Lizzy and Jane, the kindest of her sisters, never engaged with her. Lydia, who never listened to anyone longer than half a minute anyway, did not bother to hide her indifference, and Kitty had always followed Lydia's lead.

Looking back on those moments, Mary felt the justice of their indifference. Any person of sense would discount her store of shopworn quotations and banal advice. To think of how smugly she had pronounced on any number of matters that she in truth knew nothing about filled her with shame. Mary discovered herself to be a great ungainly goose, putting herself forward too much, unaware of how other people took her. In reaction she withdrew into her books, her piety, and lately her fossils. Better to hide one's thoughts than risk making a fool of oneself. At home, after Lydia, Jane, and Lizzy were gone with husbands and families of their own, she had only Kitty to depend on.

Over the last ten years Mary had imagined that she and Kitty had found some bond in their approaching spinsterhood, but here, at the least sign of advantage, Kitty had cut her to the quick. As Mary dressed for dinner, all she could think about was that she was alone, had always been alone, and unless Mr. Woodleigh made her an offer, always would be.

When they descended to meet Woodleigh, they found the inn in some turmoil. A young woman who had stopped there the day before with a party of visitors from Uppercross had fallen from the Cobb. Witnesses of the accident said she had lain as if dead. She was being attended to in the home of Captain Harville, only recently settled in Lyme. Rumor had it she was engaged to be married; now, if she were to survive, she would likely be an invalid for the rest of her life.

At supper, Mrs. Bennet expounded upon the risks taken by young women who moved outside their proper sphere.

"Mother," Kitty said, "this girl hurt herself because her fiancé failed to catch her when she jumped from the Cobb."

"No well-bred young lady should trust a man to catch her if she goes leaping from public landmarks. Such pastimes, my dear, are inappropriate. I hope you will not be jumping off things anytime soon."

"Until I have a fiancé, Mother," Kitty said morosely, "I will avoid every instance of jumping."

Kitty saw no prospects on the horizon. At twenty-two she had been proposed to by Mr. Jonathan Clarke, the prosperous owner of a butcher's shop and rendering works in Matlock, not far from Pemberley, Darcy's estate. But Mr. Clarke, though personable, was a tradesman, and he took snuff. Kitty had declined his offer. She'd never gotten another. Mr. Clarke's business had prospered: he was now a man of considerable import in Derbyshire. Every spring, when she invariably encountered Clarke and his wife in London, and then again every summer at Pemberley, Kitty was reminded of her mistake.

"Mr. Woodleigh, are there dangers to your fossil hunting?" asked Mrs. Bennet.

"There are rock slides. The Undercliff itself is the result of a collapse all along the line between Lyme and Axmouth. And of course we must beware of the tides; people have been washed away to sea."

"Washed to sea!" Mrs. Bennet exclaimed. "Mary, I forbid you to go back there. I had rather see you with your nose in a book than out in this foul weather waiting for a landslide, with me unable to think for fear that I shall never see you again."

Mary said, "I am a cautious person, Mother."

Mrs. Bennet sailed on regardless. "Of course, Mr. Woodleigh, this does not mean that you and Mary may not study your bones together in some proper drawing room. Mary is an accomplished performer, you know."

"Is that so?" Woodleigh said brightly. "Delightful. In her modesty she has said nothing of it. I confess, I have never met a young lady who takes such an interest in natural philosophy. Has Mr. Bennet schooled all his daughters in the sciences?"

"Mr. Bennet spends his days among his books," said Mrs. Bennet. "He has left the education of the girls to me."

"Mary is the queen of the library," said Kitty.

"Father lets me read from his collection," Mary said. "And when we are in London, I buy many books."

"Yet it is more common, I believe," Woodleigh said, "for young ladies to study the foibles of their neighbors than natural philosophy."

Mary found herself unable to hold her tongue. "Miss Wollstonecraft wrote that it is only because women are allowed no scientific study that they concern themselves with rules of behavior. In my youth I was one such, intent on propriety. I find I can better spend my time studying nature. Perhaps someday, through science, we shall understand the first causes of our behavior."

"Yes," Kitty said. "I am sure that the soul lies hidden inside some rock."

"Miss Wollstonecraft?" Woodleigh said. "Wasn't she married to that Jacobin, Godwin? When I worked in Mr. Pitt's government, Godwin's traitorous pamphlets caused us no end of trouble. Propriety is not something she, with her natural children, ever took account of. Miss Bennet, I hope you have not taken anything that atheist wrote to heart."

"I am no atheist," Mary said. "I find the hand of God everywhere in nature. Do you not?"

Mrs. Bennet, out of her depth, nonetheless understood a challenge to her domestic authority. "We have no atheists in the Bennet family, Mr. Woodleigh."

"I beg your pardon."

"And Mary, that's enough talk of women radicals."

"I'm sorry, Mother."

Mrs. Bennet smoothed her napkin. "I forgive you, my dear. And you as well, Mr. Woodleigh. Now where is that servant? We called for a pudding, and have seen no sign of it."

The rest of the dinner proceeded in subdued spirits. Woodleigh, as if abashed that he had scolded her, attempted to conciliate Mary. Mary appreciated his effort, but as she sat there, she considered how a day that had dawned so auspiciously, her mind engaged and her heart light, off to explore the Blue Lias cliffs with a man who seemed to appreciate her, had since the moment she had discovered her fossils become a series of blows to her heart.

At the end of the meal Woodleigh excused himself, saying that he needed to make an early night of it in preparation for his return to Exeter. He insisted that they allow him to pay for the dinner. He thanked them for their excellent company and promised Mary, if she might allow it, to write her. And with that he was gone.

The three women retreated to their rooms.

Mary felt confused by the contradictions between Woodleigh's thoughtfulness and his callousness. Life was a mystery, and the content of another's heart a riddle. She wished Kitty were right, and the soul might be discovered by breaking open some rock.

Erasmus Darwin, in *The Temple of Nature*, asserted that life arose spontaneously all the time, and rather than an affront to God, this was a tribute to him as the Cause of all Causes. Every day dead matter gave birth to living things, and every day living creatures surrendered the spirit that animated them to again become dull matter. The border between life and death was permeable in both directions.

Mary was alive. She had been alive since the moment her father and mother had animated her substance and God charged it with a soul. But one day her soul would depart and her body decay. Her flesh would fall away, and her bones would harden into stone. Perhaps someone might crack open a mass of shale a thousand years hence to find her and explain the meaning of her existence.

Back in the room that Mary and Kitty shared, as they let down their hair and brushed it out, Kitty apologized to

Mary for calling back the contretemps at Netherfield. "The moment I said it I could see that I had hurt you deeply. I have been so cross lately, and you do not deserve such treatment. Please forgive me, Mary. I hope you will forgive me."

Mary said that it would be unchristian for her not to forgive.

Kitty embraced her. "You are the best of sisters. I am sorry that Woodleigh is leaving so soon."

Mary said that men would do as they pleased.

"Do you wish to continue here in Lyme without him? Aunt Gardiner would be so happy to see us in London, even if we were to come sooner than planned. If you think it is right, we might ask Mother about it tomorrow."

"Why wait for tomorrow?" said Mary. "Mother is not yet asleep. You should go to her now."

"Oh, do you think so? I shall!"

The look of joy that crossed Kitty's face raised such contradictory emotions in Mary's breast that she was glad Kitty rushed from the room before her expression betrayed them. Assuming that Kitty would notice at all.

TWO

When I saw the ocean for the first time, I despaired. How was I to cross it? It was too vast. It had existed for eons before my creation, and would exist long after my dissolution.

For weeks after Victor had agreed to create a bride for me, he had lingered at his family's home in Geneva. I lurked outside the Frankenstein villa. I would creep silently below their window, careful not to alert their dog. Through a gap in their drapes I watched his aged father, his remaining brother. I studied his beautiful cousin, a woman so fair that simply watching her move broke my heart. His Elizabeth. My hearing is finer than theirs, so even when I could not see them, I heard her comfort Victor on the death of his little brother William, the disgrace and execution of their servant Justine Moritz. Through gloom that their eyes could not penetrate, I read his father's careworn expression.

In the month and a half after Victor and I met on that mountainside above the glacier, as far as I could tell, he did not touch the scientific apparatus locked away in trunks in their attic.

I remember sprawling below a tree one August night, impatient for him to begin constructing my companion; inside me anger warred with melancholy. Moonlight broke through the clouds. I smelled the earth of the forest floor. The leaves above rustled, and I heard the *whooo* of an owl. The summer air felt the way I imagined a caress might feel. Fit habitation for gods. In these woods I had strangled William. The locket I had found encircling his neck, containing the picture of another beautiful woman, I placed into the apron of Justine, a third lovely woman, thereby assuring her death for the murder of the boy.

In my wooden darkness I brooded over Elizabeth's figure in my mind. She was hardly larger than a child, but she was no child. Her shoulders and neck stirred something in me that I could not explain. Her hair curled around her face in ringlets, pulled back behind one ear by a comb.

In one of the books that I read while lying last winter in the hovel beside the De Laceys' cottage, there was a description of Eve, the first woman:

> She, as a veil, down to the slender waist
> Her unadorned golden tresses wore
> Disheveled, but in wanton ringlets waved
> As the vine curls her tendrils, which implied
> Subjection, but required with gentle sway,
> And by her yielded, by him best received,

Yielded with coy submission, modest pride,
And sweet, reluctant, amorous delay.

I would have been content to sit and watch his Elizabeth for the rest of my life, should she allow me to do so. I did not think I could survive being permitted to touch her.

But of course that could never happen. Long before I could have put any of these emotions into words, I'd had that proven to me many times over. The sheer mass of my body frightens them, to be sure, but other men tower over their fellows and still find a place in the world. I have studied my reflection in still water. There is no obvious flaw in my countenance. My hair is thick and luxuriant, my brow noble. One might object to my cloudy eyes, my pale skin, or my dark lips—but I believe the trouble lies not in my difference from men, but in the too slight distance between them and myself. The very fact that I look so like them, when clearly by some token of my bearing, my expression, the way my lips or eyebrows move, I am not human, damns me. They look, and they see that something is *wrong*. I am some demonic semblance of a man. A monster.

Despite what I could observe of all that went on inside the Villa Frankenstein, I could not read what went on inside Victor's mind. With all his intellect, and despite his vow to me, he yet struggles to do me justice. Within the space of a few moments on the mountain, after I had told him my story, I saw him twice vacillate between sympathy and hatred. Who knew what he might be planning or not planning, how faithful he was to his pledge? It no doubt depended on the last person to whom he had spoken.

I was considering how I might remind him of his promise

when, with a great fuss, Victor left the villa in a coach loaded down with those trunks of scientific equipment. Eavesdropping at the stables, I discovered that he was bound for England by way of Strasbourg, where his friend Henry Clerval would join him. I determined to follow.

And so I had pursued Victor all the way down the Rhine. This trip, which took him a month, making leisurely stops to visit the towns along the way, had taken me three.

It was near the end of November, in the middle of the night, that I stood despairing on that verge of the sea. The moon's silver light glittered on the ocean swells that advanced, growing until each wave crested and broke. Black and white and gray. The sound, continuous, rose and fell. I smelled salt and sea wrack.

I was hungry. There was no nearby orchard or vineyard to raid, and in this flat, featureless landscape no woods where I might surprise a rabbit, raid a nest, or find nuts, ferns, or snails.

I skirted the shoreline until I found a road. At a crossroads, a signpost told me I was headed toward Rotterdam, and some miles on I came to an inn with a dock. All the windows were dark. Beside the inn was a ramshackle stable where the horses stood sleeping in their stalls. One of them smelled me, lifted his head, and nickered. When I touched his forehead between his eyes, he shook away my hand and stepped back. The feed trough was empty. My stomach ground against my backbone.

At the end of the row of stalls I found a room full of riding gear: saddles, bridles, and halters hanging from pegs. Nothing to eat; however, from one of the pegs I took a great brimmed black leather hat.

I continued along the river. More buildings arose, closer

together, and soon I was in the city. I reached the waterfront. I had seen boats on Lake Geneva, and on the way down the Rhine, but nothing like the great wooden ships that towered over the quayside, water gently lapping their sides. The smell of rotting vegetables led me to a refuse heap beside a bake house, where I made my repast from carrots too far gone for them, but not for me. A scrawny dog nosed its way into the alley, stood watching long enough for me to take five breaths, then walked away.

My encounter with old, blind De Lacey in the cottage had shown me that, if they could not see me, men might converse with me on a basis of mutuality, even sympathy. In the time since, I had avoided human beings, but in order to find Victor I would have to interact with them. So my work would be to make sure that they could not see me clearly.

I might trust my new hat to obscure my face, but the rags I wore were inadequate: I needed clothing that would make me appear at least plausibly human. I would also have to obtain some of the copper and silver pieces that I had come to realize were the foundation of civilized human interaction.

Farther into the twisting waterfront streets, past warehouses and pens full of livestock, I came upon a district where people were still abroad. Light shone out the dirty windows of a tavern, and music drifted from the door. Through the window I spied men and a few women sitting and drinking while an old fellow played an instrument, squeezing it back and forth between his hands as he sang in German or Dutch, neither of which I understood.

I withdrew to an alley. I waited. Over the course of some time a number of people passed, none suitable to my purpose.

Finally, as I could detect the faint signs of morning, a large man came staggering down the street. I took one step from the alley and yanked him into the shadows. Before he could even yelp, I knocked his head against the wall and he dropped to the filthy pavement.

His chest still rose and fell. I stripped off his clothing, put it on, and left my stinking rags across his prostrate form. His trousers strained at my thighs. His boots were just large enough for my feet. His greatcoat, pinched at the shoulders, would serve. In his pocket I found a purse containing some coins, and even more valuable, a pair of large gloves and a muffler.

It was unlikely that Victor, even if he had come this way, was still here. By now he and Henry must be in England. It was my task to pass that impassable ocean. But men had been crossing such seas for millennia, and I was a man—or if I were to make that crossing, I must pass for one.

Wandering through the waterfront, I came upon a building with words written in gilt on a dark red sign. Sailors and citizens passed in and out. Travelers with trunks and servants, ladies with maids carrying their hatboxes. Men loaded the trunks onto a cart to take to their ship.

Posted on a large board outside this building I saw a list of names, cities I recognized from the geography lessons Felix had given Safie. There, among the others, was the word *London*, followed by some numbers and the name of a ship. As I lurked at a corner, I heard a man and woman conversing, travelers about to depart, in French.

I wrapped the muffler around my lower face and pulled the hat low over my eyes. I let my black hair flow over my coat collar. I entered the building, approached the clerk behind the counter, and addressed him in French.

"My good man, I would like to book a passage to London."

The man looked at me warily and replied in Dutch. I shook my head. "Does no one here speak French?"

The clerk called over a second man. *"Bonjour."*

"Bonjour." I repeated my request for a ticket to London.

"The *Prince William* departs with the morning tide. Which class, monsieur?"

I did not understand. "Class?"

The clerk eyed me. "Do you wish a compartment, or will you share a space with the other passengers?"

The thought of sitting for a day or more in a public room terrified me. "A compartment, if you will."

"That will be ten guilders."

I pulled the purse from my pocket and opened it, grateful for the gloves that hid my hands. But I did not know the coins there. I placed a handful onto the counter and pushed them forward. "I am not familiar with your money," I said.

"That won't pay for more than third class," the man said, watching me. Something about the way I moved was strange to him. By this time half the others in the office were watching the huge cloaked man who spoke French and did not know a guilder from a cent.

I persevered. "Third class, then."

The clerk took half my money and wrote out a ticket, which he blotted and handed to me. "Your baggage?"

"No baggage," I said. I left the office and walked out to the pier. The great ship towered over me, its masts as tall as the tallest trees. It was full morning and the docks were busy with sailors, stevedores, and passengers. The longer I stayed abroad the more attention I would attract, but if I boarded, I would be confined in a space where I might elicit even more scrutiny and which I could not easily escape. There seemed to be no good choice. When a sailor stopped to stare at me, startled by my size, I turned and climbed the gangway.

The third-class passengers were in a large room below-decks in the forward part of the ship. The ceiling was not six feet above the deck. I stooped over and entered. The room had bunks on either side, little more than platforms with some mattress ticking, but better than any place I had ever slept. Down the narrow aisle between the bunks ran a long table with two benches. Two oil lamps hanging from the ceiling pro-vided dim light, and on either side of the room was a latticed unglazed window, with shutters that could be closed against bad weather.

There were already five people in the room: a husband, wife, and their child—a girl younger even than Victor's dead brother—and another woman and man who did not seem to be traveling together. The instant I entered, everyone went silent. Rather than sit on a bench and subject myself to their scru-tiny, I crawled onto one of the platforms and crouched in the shadows, curled up with my knees before my face, my arms encircling them.

The child clutched the folds of her mother's dress and stared at me with large eyes. Her mother said a few words to her in Dutch, steered her to the bench, and put a piece of biscuit before her. The father lay down on one of the pallets, and the exhausted mother sat beside him. The other woman watched me for a moment, then set her bag on the bench and opened it to search for something.

The other man pulled a printed paper from his coat—what I had learned, in my passage through the German towns, to be a newspaper. He spread it out on the table just below one of the lamps and bent over it. I watched his lips move as he read.

I began to think that I might carry off this masquerade, if I did not move quickly and was not called upon to speak.

The child continued to stare at me. She had finished but half her biscuit when she climbed onto the platform where I sat. She held the rest out to me. *"Heb je honger?"*

I did not know the words, but I could fathom her meaning, and my heart was moved. I held out my open palm and the girl put her biscuit into it.

"Je te remercie, enfant," I said as softly as I could. The first time in my existence I had occasion to use these words.

But my voice carried farther than I intended. The woman with the satchel turned to look, and the man at the newspaper lifted his head. The mother woke from her half doze. "Anki!" she called.

I tried to give the crumbs back to the girl, but the mother must have mistaken my reaching out as an attempt to seize the child. She yanked the girl's arm and the child began to cry.

The father awoke, but before he could move, the newspaper reader shouted and knocked over his bench in the effort to get to me. I was much quicker than he, but in the confined space I could not evade him, and when I tried to roll away, I hit my head on the ceiling. My hat came off, and the muffler fell from my face.

When he saw me, the man froze. The young woman and the mother screamed. "God save us!" the man said.

The young woman ran screaming for the hatchway. "Help us! Help! Captain!"

The mother huddled with her child and useless husband on their side of the cabin, but the other man stood between the hatchway and me. His expression of witless confusion enraged me. I grabbed my hat and scarf and with a swipe of my arm knocked him across the table. In a crouch I squeezed through the door and up the steps to the deck. The woman, screaming in English at a sailor who did not understand her, waved an arm at me as I crossed the deck in two steps and, seizing one of the lines that ran from the rail to the mast, leapt over the side of the ship onto the dock.

There came shouts from behind me as I ran through the smoke and bustle of the waterfront, my heart racing, and every astonished and horrified expression I encountered lies still imprinted on my mind, as does the sweet face of that little girl who thought I was hungry and offered me her food.

It was two days before I dared creep back to the waterfront. I had no other hope than to find my way onto a ship bound for England, and my experiment with purchasing passage was not one I was prepared to repeat. So I lurked and watched, discovered a cattle scow bound for London, and awaited my chance.

At twilight, in a downpour, the crew harried cattle up the ramp and into the hold. They did not see my huddled figure creeping among them. The hold was all gloom with a single lantern hanging beside the steps that led up the hatchway. Once inside I moved to the darkest corner.

The boat cast off and sailed down the river in the storm. Rain drummed on the deck above, and thunder rumbled. After a while the ship reached the sea and began to pitch as it fought the waves. The cattle stumbled about and threatened to crush me, so I crawled until I found a door in the floor that led to the bilge. I climbed inside and closed it over me.

So that was how I finally crossed the impassable ocean, in profound darkness, lying on a bed of ballast stones, sluiced by filthy waters, wet and cold and stinking. I tried to doze, but that was impossible. Instead I thought about Victor. Perhaps he believed that if he ran far away he could avoid keeping his promise. Or perhaps he only meant to draw me away from his family while he constructed my mate.

I had told him I would glut the maw of death with the blood of those he loved. Already I had murdered his brother and let Justine go to the gallows for it, but that had not been done in calculation so much as blind rage. I did not seek to become the fiend that he already thought me. It all depended on his keeping his promise—if he failed, or went back on it, how could I live? At times my fury burned so hot that I might wish the entire human race exterminated, but when I saw the comfort that these beings could offer one another, I longed to have a part in it. So as I lay there awash in the sewage at the keel of that cattle boat, I fervently wished that Victor had taken my threat seriously enough to keep to our bargain.

A man down here would drown or take sick. A man could not have lived through the things I had suffered. The cold, the heat, the hunger. I was stronger, more agile, smarter, more adaptable, able to eat things that would kill a human being, more able to recover from the physical injuries that humans had rained down on me. Stronger, too, in my mind. Lonelier.

He had so much, and I so little. When I thought of this

injustice, my mind ached. No more wretched creature could have walked the earth; certainly not one who was so aware of his wretchedness. I might have been a god, but I was nothing.

After two days of misery, the sound of the water against the hull changed, and the bilgewater no longer surged from side to side with the rolling of the sea. We had entered the estuary of the Thames. Hours later the crew stirred and the ship came to rest. I heard muffled voices and the moving of cargo above. I hid while all the cattle were driven from belowdecks. I waited until the daylight filtering down from above faded before I crept off the boat.

The waterfront here was like that in Rotterdam, down to the pens for the cattle and yards full of coal. Warehouses towered above the narrow streets. The air was thick with yellowish fog against which the wan light from streetlamps made little purchase.

Down an alley I found a rain barrel full of water clean enough to drink. I washed my filthy clothes as best I could, and cleaned my naked body. Then I broke into a warehouse, and, hidden among some bales of cotton, surrendered to sleep.

I was awakened by dockworkers arriving in the morning. Ravenous, I took to the streets. The cold, dank air reeked, and from every chimney rose a stream of coal smoke that soon made the day a second twilight. I wondered that humans would choose a place like this when they might live in the forest or mountains. The only benefit of this man-made darkness was that it enabled me to conceal my appearance more easily.

My education had proceeded to the point where I recognized the signs of dire poverty everywhere. Crowded, shabby buildings filled the neighborhoods near the dockyards, their facades blackened by the same soot that blackened the faces of their inhabitants out in the streets. My size and muffled face did not arouse notice here in the way they had on the *Prince William*, though I took no chances and kept out of the way.

I made my way toward the center of the city. I saw the tower fortress at the east of its heart. Businessmen and clerks hurried to and from their places of work. Here the clothes were finer, the faces cleaner, the bearing of the pedestrians more confident, though the streets were filled with mud and young boys with brooms attempted to extort a penny from passersby by sweeping it before them so that they might cross without soiling their boots.

When I passed a bakeshop, the aroma of cooking made me dizzy. On the street a costermonger sold pies for a penny; I gave him one of my remaining Dutch coins and he let me have one.

I retired to the neighborhood of a great domed church, a building as large as any I had seen on my journey down the Rhine, sat in a corner, and consumed my meal. I considered my prospects.

I had no idea where I might find Victor and Henry, I understood no English, and I had no British money. My attempt to buy passage, though it had ended badly, offered me hope: it was possible for me to pass among men for at least a short time, in the proper circumstances. Among the poor and downtrodden I might move without as much suspicion, and my frightening stature, rather than drawing trouble, might cause people to avoid me.

I would never find Victor as long as I could not speak the language, so my first task would be to teach myself English. In this I was aided by the fact that I was a superior mimic. I could imitate a sentence in an unknown tongue precisely enough to sound like a native speaker, even when I did not know what the words meant.

I spent that winter in this effort. I lurked in the corners of streets, hid in alleys where I listened to the boys hawking newspapers and men selling fruits, vegetables, and fish. I ate trash that had been thrown out as inedible by the poorest people in the city. I listened to these people argue with their wives and husbands, yell at their children, haggle with shopkeepers, and fend off constables. In shame, I robbed any number of men in order to put a few coins in my pocket. I listened outside pubs, and on occasion even entered them to buy a pint of ale. I heard desperate women offer their bodies to men in the streets for the price of a loaf of bread.

Every day in London brought a new astonishment. In the three months I lived in warehouses and alleys, I learned a great deal about the human race. What I learned was that most of the days of their short lives, the greater number of human beings were miserable.

How naive I had been that year and a half that I lived in a shed at the side of the De Laceys' cottage! Spying on them through a chink in the wall, I had thought they lived in paradise. They had fire. They had food. They had one another. The old blind man played guitar. The young women sang. They were beautiful, all of them, even the old man. I observed Safie touch Felix's wrist as they stooped over to put more wood on the fire, and his hand upon her back as he helped her to rise. Though I was no longer so innocent, I persisted in believing that these things were genuine.

Innocence was a treasure I no longer had. It had been spent—no, it had been stolen from me—by the blows Felix leveled on my back, by Agatha fainting dead away and Safie rushing from the room at the sight of me, and by the bullet in my shoulder shot by a man whose daughter I had saved from drowning.

I was alone. No woman would touch me, and I would touch no woman, unless Frankenstein kept his promise.

By February I had some command of the language, some knowledge of the city, and some confidence that I could pass among humans. I had become an accomplished thief. I waited in the alleys of the theater district, lurked along the Strand or Haymarket where prostitutes sauntered down the night streets with their skirts partly tucked up to advertise their wares. It was simple work to nudge one of their customers into an alley and rob him. Occasionally a soldier might put up a fight and I would have to knock him senseless, but I managed never to kill any of them. From the pockets of one of my victims, snagged while he was soliciting a prostitute, I gained not only money, but a Bible. Poring over this strange book, I learned the reading of English.

Then my search for Victor began in earnest. On the slim chance that he still remained in London, I haunted the inns of Mayfair and Bloomsbury. I went abroad mostly at night, when the guests went out to dine or attend the theater. I would set up on some corner or in some close and watch the entrances of the inns for hours at a time, hoping to spy Victor should he appear.

The Adelphi, the Crown and Anchor, the Golden Cross, Locket's, the Queen's Arms, the Bull and Gate, the Ram's

Head, the Red Lion, the Cross Keys. There were too many inns. Weeks passed. I might have concluded that Victor was no longer in London, but I needed to know for sure. At the pace I was setting, I could search forever and not know.

One night outside the Black Horse Inn I called from the alley to a street lad, "Here, boy!"

He peered at me in the darkness. I could see him consider flight. "Yes, I am large," I said. "If I wanted to wring your neck, it would already be wrung. So, do you speak?"

"Aye," the boy said. He had brushed his jacket and trousers, but his elbows were threadbare and his boots broken. His thick hair was almost as black as mine.

"How would you like to earn a pound?"

He kept his eye on the distance between us. "Doing what?"

"Come closer, boy."

"You come out of the alley."

"I like the alley. The lamplight does not suit me."

The boy smirked. "And you'll give a quid to the likes of me. You don't have thruppence."

I threw a coin at his feet. "There's thruppence."

Quick as a snake he snatched it up.

"I seek a certain gentleman," I said, "who stops in one of the inns about here. A Frenchman. His name is Victor Frankenstein. He travels with a companion, another man, named Clerval."

"Don't know no Frenchmen."

"*Quel dommage*," I said.

"Who is he? What do yer want with 'im?"

"Let's say he is a Bonapartist. He may look innocent enough, but he is a dangerous fellow."

"How do I know you'll pay?"

"There's thruppence on account. You find him for me and you'll have that pound."

"There's dozens of inns—I can't mind 'em all."

"You must know the other boys that work this part of town. I bet you know the slops boys of the inns, and the bootblacks, and the boys who hold the horses for gentlemen or fetch cabs for theatergoers. You can figure out how to spread your money around."

"When I find him, where'll I find you?"

"You know that alley that leads to the Blewitts Buildings off Fetter Lane? You have something to tell me, you stand by the gate there at seven o'clock at night. I'll find you, and you'll have your quid."

For the next week, every evening I scaled the rear of the building on the corner of the alley leading to the Blewitts Buildings. It was an easy enough climb for me. I lay between the chimney pots and watched the soot-stained facades of the buildings opposite, the passersby in the street, the lamplighters as they made their way in the deepening gloom. I pulled my cloak up around my neck against the late winter cold and waited.

A week to the day after I hired that boy, he came down Fetter Lane from High Holborn and waited at the entrance to Blewitts. I let him stand there in the dark for ten minutes while I made sure he had not been followed. Then, silently, I climbed down the side of the building and dropped to my feet not a yard from him.

He fell back against the gate. "Cor!"

"What do you have to tell me?"

The boy scrambled to his feet. "My—my money."

"Don't play with me, boy. Where is he?"

"He's staying at the Dorant's Hotel, near St. James's Street and Piccadilly."

"You know it to be him?"

"I know the yard boy there, and he knows the chamber-maids."

I fished a sovereign out of my pocket and laid it into his palm. "If you're lying, I will find you and kill you."

The boy peered up at me, trying to make me out in the dark. I turned my back on him, pulled the brim of my hat lower, and walked off. As I did so, a light rain began to fall.

Dorant's Hotel stood in a fine neighborhood of Piccadilly, between a saddler's and a pianoforte shop, across the street from a mansion so large that it might be a palace. In the early evening, despite the cold March weather and mist, the street was busy with cabs and people. The inn was brightly lit. Here Victor had resided for three months while I lived in a ware-house. If he was at work on creating a mate for me, this did not seem a likely place to do it. I stood on the edge of the street, wondering what next I might do, and was almost run down by a cab. I stepped back onto the sidewalk; men and ladies circled around me.

I crossed to the hotel entrance and stood there, ten feet from the door, prepared to loiter as long as it took until he might appear. As I watched, two men stepped out of the build-ing. One of them hailed a street lad and sent him to fetch a cab. The other man, I saw, was Victor.

They stood together, Victor and the other, who must be his friend Henry. They were elegantly dressed, in dove-gray pantaloons, polished boots, caped greatcoats with high collars, and beaver hats. Though they were dressed for an evening on the town, Victor did not look very pleased at the prospect, unlike Clerval, who chatted ebulliently with him.

My first impulse was to flee. But I checked myself, and instead stepped closer.

"I'm so pleased you have agreed to come along this evening," Clerval said in French. "We won't be in London much longer, and it has done you no good to isolate yourself in your room."

Victor, half-turned away from me, murmured some reply I could not hear. Then the boy came back down the street with a cab. When it pulled to a halt opposite them, Henry gave the boy a coin and began to climb inside. I stepped forward, intending to let Victor get a good look at me so that he might know that he could not escape his promise.

Before I could do so, Victor climbed into the cab and shut the door. I heard Henry say to the cabman, "Cavendish Square, number sixteen," and the cab rolled away down the crowded street.

I followed, but in seconds it had reached the end of the block and turned.

I stood stupidly in the misting rain on the corner of St. James's Street and Piccadilly, my satisfaction at finding him dissipated.

Where was Victor bound? What had he accomplished over the last months toward giving me an Eve to my misbegotten Adam? Within me anger swelled, and curiosity. I could do nothing to end my exile this night. I might return to the warehouse and try again tomorrow. I might wander the city streets.

I might rob some rich man to augment my dwindling store of money. I stood in the midst of a city of a million human beings, alone.

I struck north up Bond Street in the direction that the cab had gone. As I walked, shoulders hunched, I did not bother to avoid pedestrians on the sidewalk. Let them avoid me, if they hoped to survive the night. It took me some time to find Cavendish Square, but even before I saw the number, it was obvious which of the tall, imposing private town houses that surrounded it was number sixteen.

A party was in progress. The windows were brightly lit, and coaches and drivers were lined up before its portico. Whenever new guests arrived and the broad front door opened, music wafted from inside. The people who entered were clearly persons of importance: members of Parliament, merchants, government officials, noblemen and women of every rank. The women wore elaborate hats. The young women were beautiful, the young men well made; some wore the bright scarlet jackets of the military.

I walked around the square, my eyes fixed on the windows of number sixteen. The rain increased as the night wore on. This served at least to drive indoors or into their coaches any servants who might have taken notice of me.

I lingered there a long time, waiting to for Victor to leave, my rage increasing. I recalled a second passage from that book about man's creation, where Lucifer the fallen angel spies on Adam and Eve, his heart lacerated by envy:

> Sight hateful, sight tormenting! Thus these
> two,

Imparadised in one another's arms,
The happier Eden, shall enjoy their fill
Of bliss on bliss; while I to Hell am thrust,
Where neither joy nor love, but fierce desire,
Among our other torments not the least,
Still unfulfilled, with pain of longing pines!

After midnight the guests began to depart. The coachmen of the wealthy grew active, and one by one the chaises and landaus drew up to the door, the guests were helped into them, and they drove off. I could not approach any closer than the nearest corner, and I somehow missed when my creator and his friend left the party. I stood in the rain, a full-out downpour now, water streaming down my face like tears, unable to leave, watching the lovely women, protected by their parents, husbands, and lovers, pause beneath the portico, shivering against the cold, until a proffered hand took their own gloved hands, their privileged, slippered feet stepped up into their coaches, and they left.

THREE

Kitty had schemed for a week to visit the Egyptian Hall without a chaperone. Her argument was that she and Mary would attend at midday, and Mary would serve as chaperone. Mrs. Bennet was willing to grant the favor, but their aunt and uncle Gardiner, while acknowledging that the hall was one of London's most popular attractions, pointed out that it had gained the reputation of being frequented by the stylish and the vulgar. Mrs. Bennet reminded her daughters that Mr. Collins was visiting that evening, and that Jane and Bingley would be there as well. She wished to conserve her strength for this party and could not go with them. Aunt Gardiner decided to remain at home with her sister-in-law, but her husband agreed to go with Kitty and Mary.

And so Mr. Gardiner and his nieces found themselves on a cold Tuesday in March on their way to the celebrated hall. As their cab made its way down Fleet Street, Mary was excited at the prospect of seeing the Annings' ichthyosaur, said to be on display there. She did, however, wonder why Kitty wanted so badly to be unchaperoned. When they were girls, she would have understood it instantly as characteristic of Kitty's and Lydia's rebelliousness and therefore not in need of any explanation. But Kitty had sobered a great deal since then, and governed herself much better than she had at seventeen.

Bullock's hall had been constructed in the Egyptian style popularized in the last decade, with massive post-and-lintel arches over the doors and windows, two huge human figures in Pharaonic dress above the entrance, and hieroglyphics on the facade.

Though at first sullen about the presence of their uncle, Kitty brightened as they joined the crowd of people at the entrance. "Please, if you would, Mary, converse with Uncle while I peruse the exhibits? I do not have much conversation in me today, and you seem to know how to speak with him so much better than I."

It happened that Mary had a matter she wished to raise with their uncle, so she was glad to be able to speak with him while Kitty flitted ahead, hardly pausing to examine one exhibit before moving along to the next.

The sisters' reactions to being in London in these earliest days of the season could not have been more different. Kitty's spirits had risen every mile on the way from Lyme Regis to the city. Mary had suggested to her mother that she would be happy to return to Longbourn to tend to their father, who had not been well through the winter and had only recently resumed his station in his library, by his fireside, amid his books.

Woodleigh had written Mary upon his return to Exeter, a letter of apology for his questioning her faith, with a discussion of some new fossils that had been described in the latest number of the journal of the Geological Society. Mary did not know how much to weigh that final unpleasant evening against the interests they shared and the slim prospect of her ever meeting another man whom she might realistically imagine asking for her hand. His apology was well written and seemed sincere, even going so far as to moderate his opinion of Mary Anning and recommend that Mary take the time to see the ichthyosaur at the hall.

Mary supposed she could carry on a correspondence with him as well from the Gardiners' home in London as from Longbourn, but she would have preferred not to be compelled to attend the balls and card parties that occupied so much of people's time here. She had no desire to visit other ladies every morning or spend endless hours at the milliner's when she would much rather be in Lackington and Allen's bookshop. But Mrs. Bennet insisted that Mary remain in London, if only to provide a confidante for Kitty.

The citizens who had come to the hall on this day varied greatly in their deportment. Those few among them with the look of breeding were outnumbered by the common and the crass, by young men and women more interested in flirting than in the exhibits, by wits who demonstrated the truth that Londoners, in the public pursuit of indulgence, were no better than they ought to be.

Though he had made his fortune as a goldsmith, Mr. William Bullock fancied himself a naturalist. Among an excess of flummery, fraud, and bad taste, his hall offered some exhibits of natural history, including items collected by Captain Cook on his Pacific voyages. One room held a menagerie of exotic taxidermy: an elephant, two ostriches, and a zebra, beneath palm trees and tropical plants. Mary saw less to interest her there than in the side room that displayed the fossil that Mary Anning and her brother had discovered four years earlier. There, laid out on a table, were the four-foot-long skull of the creature and an almost complete skeleton, labeled CROCODILE IN A FOSSIL STATE. Mary examined it carefully, thinking of Anning standing in the street throughout the Lyme winter. She was probably at her table this very moment, seeking to sell some Dudley Locusts to tourists.

The vast majority of this day's visitors were drawn by the latest attraction, the subject of many drawing-room discussions: a hall full of wax figures fashioned by a Frenchwoman, Madame Tussaud. The likenesses were primarily of French notables whose names were known to the common Englishman, and whom Tussaud might actually have seen in person in Paris, among them the writers Rousseau and Voltaire and the American genius Benjamin Franklin.

But the chief allurement was her depiction of the Reign of Terror. Tussaud claimed she had been assigned by the regicides of the French Revolution to document the executions of the aristocracy, and so she had created death masks from the severed heads of both Louis XVI and Marie Antoinette. The tomblike Great Room of the Egyptian Hall displayed KING LOUIS XVI OF FRANCE AND HIS FAMILY AT DINNER. The king and his wife as they were in life, dressed in finery, sat at a table with their children.

Mary and her uncle stood amid the onlookers, reduced to some quiet as they considered the poignant scene: Antoinette, her older, dignified husband, their daughter, and their son, the unfortunate prince Louis-Charles, who, though he did not lose his head in the revolution, died in captivity at the age of ten—all of them so real that that they might almost be alive.

But not quite, Mary thought. Something of their skin, their glass eyes, their dead hair, made it impossible to mistake these creations for human. She was impressed by the skills of the artisan who had created them, but she wondered at the reports people had given that these models were indistinguishable from life. It showed that people could convince themselves of things that, in a sober moment, they would recognize were not true.

Mary found herself, with her uncle, in the sort of privacy one might enjoy in a room surrounded by strangers. Uncle Gardiner had made his fortune in importing and owned a warehouse not far from his home in Gracechurch Street, but as a young man he had read law. His knowledge of tariffs and his connections in government served him well, as did his reputation as a man whose word could be trusted.

His broad acquaintance with men of business and law in London went back many years. Mary took this opportunity to ask him if, in his dealings, he had ever encountered Mr. Woodleigh.

"Woodleigh? I believe I have heard this name."

As they strolled from the royal exhibit to one of the others, Mary said, "He worked in the exchequer's office in Mr. Pitt's first term."

"Ah, yes," said her uncle. "I recall hearing of him, though I never had any business with the gentleman. Mr. Woodleigh seemed more a politician than a man of the law. I do believe he made a goodly fortune for himself through some Irish business venture."

He cast a penetrating eye on Mary. "This is, I believe, the gentleman of whom your mother has spoken? You made his acquaintance in Lyme? He has written you, I believe?"

"He has."

"Well, I cannot judge his character, my dear, except as I have heard him spoken of by others. It is not unheard of for a politician to make his fortune based on the privileges available to one who holds office. In the case of Mr. Woodleigh, I do not know the details of his business arrangements, but I have never heard anything that would stamp him other than an honest man."

"But absence of a bad report is not the same as a good one."

"True enough." They had come to a likeness of Lord Nelson. Mr. Gardiner gazed at the wax figure, a handsome man in the uniform of an admiral emblazoned with decorations, a red sash crossing his breast. The right sleeve of the figure's blue jacket was pinned up, indicating his lost arm. "If you wish me to do so, I shall inquire among my acquaintances. I should be able to tell you more about his public reputation. But as for his personal qualities—that is something you must judge for yourself."

Mary did not know how to judge. Her mother, despite the rough seas of their dinner in Lyme, was happy to call him a match for her—whatever his failings as a suitor, Mary was lucky to attract any interest at all. Regardless of the name of the groom, Mrs. Bennet would be eager to consider what she might wear to Mary's wedding.

"Thank you, Uncle," said Mary. "If you would make such inquiries, I would be grateful."

"Nothing is easier," Mr. Gardiner said, smiling. "Now, let us move on from these sad scenes. I confess that the sight of so many people cut down before their time conjures up melancholy thoughts. Where has Kitty got to?"

Mary and Uncle Gardiner moved to the next room, and the one after, but did not find Kitty. Uncle Gardiner suggested that Mary might return to the main hall while he looked in at the smaller rooms.

Back in the chief exhibition hall, Mary wove between the groups gathered around each display of wax figures. As she circled around two dandies commiserating with two young women over the madness and cruelty of the French revolutionaries, she spied Kitty in a corner speaking with a gentleman. It was Jonathan Clarke, Kitty's suitor from eight years before.

A week earlier, the Bennets and Gardiners had been invited to a card party, and had been surprised to find when they arrived that Mr. Clarke and his wife, Margaret, were also in attendance. Kitty seemed to accept his presence with equanimity and had shared a table with Margaret Clarke during the evening with no sign of distress. Mary had been impressed by her aplomb. On the carriage ride back to Gracechurch Street, however, Kitty complained of not being warned of their attendance, and of the humiliation of having to pretend she felt nothing. She had given Mary the impression that Clarke would be the last person on earth she hoped to see again.

Mary stood at a distance, observing them. Clarke spoke

to Kitty with some urgency. Kitty's head was bowed, her back half-turned to Mary. Clarke's hand rested fleetingly on her forearm. She looked up into his face. He finished what he was saying, touched her cheek, and strode away.

Kitty watched him leave. After a moment she put her hand to her cheek, sighed, and turned. She saw Mary and went pale. She collected herself and approached.

"Wasn't that Mr. Clarke?" Mary asked.

Kitty looked Mary in the eyes. "Yes, it was."

"This is the height of recklessness. What possible reason might you have to speak with him that would require such an assignation?"

Kitty laughed shortly. "Assignation? I met him by chance. We merely talked."

"About what?"

"Good Lord, Mary. No one seeks to ruin my reputation."

"We must govern our impulses, Kitty."

"Govern our impulses? You sound like Lizzy. 'Be less impulsive,' she tells me. 'You don't wish to end up like Lydia.'"

"It is good advice."

"Lizzy has a husband; she can afford to sit back and judge the character of the men she thinks appropriate. In a month I will be thirty years old."

"There is no future in your keeping company with a married man."

"No. I suppose I must keep company with Mr. Collins," Kitty said. She tugged at the button on the wrist of her glove.

Mary was struck by the injustice of Kitty's words. At least Lizzy and Jane had taken an interest in Kitty; they had brought her into their homes for months at a time, and put her in the

way of any number of eligible men, while they were content to
let Mary live at Longbourn, the sole object upon which their
mother might inflict her nerves. As far as Jane and Lizzy were
concerned, Mary might retire into spinsterhood without a sigh.

"You think me a fool," Kitty said, more softly. Her eyes
were an appeal.

"You are my sister," Mary said. "And I understand how
lonely one can get."

Before Kitty could respond, Uncle Gardiner bustled up to
them.

"There you are," he said. "My lovely nieces. I don't know
how I would have explained to your mother had I misplaced
both of you!"

The rapidity with which Kitty composed herself made
Mary's head spin. Kitty took their uncle's arm. "I am sorry,
Uncle. There is no cause whatever for worry."

"No worry, my dear."

"We should go now," she said. "Mother will want us at
home."

"Have we seen a shilling's worth of wonders yet?" he asked.

"At least a shilling's worth," said Mary.

Lord Christopher Henry's ball was one of the first great dis-
plays of the season and would be attended by two hundred
persons of significance, including Robert Sidwich of Detling
Manor, who possessed a fortune of six thousand pounds a year,
and toward whom Mrs. Bennet directed Kitty's attentions as
Wellington had aimed his cannon against Napoléon's marshals
in the Peninsula.

The weather was not promising. The leaden skies pressed

down like a lid over London's coal smoke, with no hint of the coming spring. In the carriage from Aunt Gardiner's home, Mrs. Bennet insisted that Kitty take the lap robe against the chill. Despite the fact that it had begun to rain, they arrived at number 16 Cavendish Square at precisely the ideal fifteen minutes after the eight p.m. beginning of the ball.

A servant in livery took their coats, and Mrs. Bennet, accompanied by Kitty and Mary, entered the long drawing room on the second floor, where Lady Henry and her daughters greeted them. The carpets had been removed and the polished wood floors gleamed. Three large chandeliers hung festooned with candles. A fireplace with an ornate mantel of green marble centered one long wall. Around the perimeter of the floor, chairs were arranged. The orchestra of pianoforte, two violins, cello, and bass viol occupied a rear corner, partially screened by potted plants. Adjoining the ballroom were a sitting room for refreshments and a library for cards and other entertainments for the older guests.

Lady Henry's punctilious greeting gave no hint of the public wonder that Mrs. Bennet, who possessed neither elegance of manner nor a jot of sense, had come to be the mother by marriage of both Charles Bingley and Fitzwilliam Darcy. It was generally agreed that the credit for this achievement fell solely to her daughters Jane, who had inherited her mother's once great beauty, and Elizabeth, who had her father's wit.

In comparison, Kitty and Mary could only disappoint. Kitty, it was recognized, had gained a certain poise by association with the Darcys and at the brink of middle age remained a lovely if no longer young woman. But there were younger girls now who far outshone her.

Mary was more easily dismissed. Charles Woodleigh notwithstanding, the Bennets' tall, left-handed, wrong-footed daughter had long been assigned, in the minds of society, the role of old maid. In her youth Mary had approached such social challenges as tonight's ball with so much confidence yoked to so dim an understanding of human nature that it was likely she would commit some humiliating faux pas, yet remain unaware of the impression she created on others. That danger had passed. Now she expected little more than to sit in the corner for the entire night, convinced that she had rather be anywhere in England but at this party.

Kitty was alight with hectic energy, almost dancing on her toes. She had never looked more beautiful, Mary thought. She was determined not to return from this season without an offer of marriage, and that did not mean one from Mr. Collins.

Unfortunately, Collins was the first person to ask her to dance. As soon as they entered, he hurried over, as if he had been watching the door. He was dressed in a black tailcoat and black waistcoat, but his cravat was of bright green.

He bowed to Mrs. Bennet. "How good to see you, Mrs. Bennet. And your lovely daughters." He bowed to Mary, and more deeply to Kitty.

"We are surprised to see you here," Mrs. Bennet said. "We did not think that you were prepared to brave such a public gathering so soon."

Charlotte Collins had died six months earlier giving birth to Mr. Collins's second son, who had expired a week after his mother. The volume of Mr. Collins's grief was impressive, but its persistence left something to be desired. He had found occasion to visit the Bennets scant weeks after the funeral — for his living son's sake, he would say, the boy so sad to be without female comfort in the aftermath of his mother's passing—but in fact he seemed more interested in Kitty than in anyone else at Longbourn. Mrs. Bennet was not so chagrined by his unseemly haste in seeking a new wife as by his lack of interest in Mary, for she knew that if Kitty were to have any say in the matter, his prospects were dim indeed. Charlotte Collins's death was a great pity, to be sure, but this misfortune could be turned to some benefit if only Collins might marry one of her daughters and thereby save Longbourn.

Mr. Collins said gravely, "Though I might wear the gay apparel suitable to such a grand gathering"—he touched the cravat—"inside still remains a black ribbon tied about my heart. I shall indulge in a dance or two, but it is only the effort of an old widower to accord his actions with propriety. Excessive grief should not be indulged lest it seem we question the will of the Lord. My beloved Charlotte would not have had it any other way." He cast his gaze down upon his quite elegant shoes.

Kitty looked as if she would die on the spot, but she bore up. When Lord Henry and his eldest daughter opened the ball by taking the floor for the quadrille, she took a turn with Collins. Having pressed Kitty into his service, Collins was obliged to ask Mary for the second dance. He led her onto the floor and proceeded throughout the breaks in their cotillion to speak to Mary of Lady Catherine de Bourgh while studying every other woman in the room.

At twenty, Mary had mistaken Mr. Collins's moralism for a sincere belief in right and wrong, his obsequiousness for humility, and his self-regard for propriety. She recalled with embarrassment how unworldly she had been; back then, she did not grasp how people were capable of dissembling. It had been a hard thing for her to learn. If to present a false face was all that the world demanded, how could people live? It was a question whose implications were so distressing that she avoided it as much as possible. Though at thirty-two Mary knew more than that girl of twenty, she still read their actions with difficulty, and judgments that Elizabeth might come to instinctively, Mary could reach only through painstaking consideration.

Mr. Collins seemed only slightly more relieved to return Mary to her seat at the end of the dance than Mary was to be left alone to indulge her thoughts.

After Mr. Collins, she saw no other invitations. Kitty, however, had many partners. Mary could only observe others dancing for some time before excusing herself to her mother and aunt and going to the library. She ignored the noisy card players gathered there and examined the books on the shelves, among which she found several familiar volumes of sermons by John Wesley. She lingered over Wesley's curious *Desideratum; or, Electricity Made Plain and Useful*, which argued for the medical benefits of electrical shock. "This great Machine of the World requires some such constant, active, and powerful Principle," Wesley wrote, "constituted by its Creator, to . . . give Support, Life, and Increase to the various Inhabitants of the Earth."

Would that Mary had electrical stimulation to ameliorate tonight's tedium. Failing that, she returned to her family in time to observe Kitty brought breathlessly back at the conclusion of the fifth dance. A moment later Mr. Gardiner arrived from the smoking room, accompanied by two young men. They were dressed in dove-gray breeches, black jackets, and waistcoats, with white ties and gloves.

"My dear, Mrs. Bennet, and the Misses Bennet, let me introduce a visitor to our country, Mr. Henry Clerval, and his friend Mr. Victor Frankenstein."

Fair-haired Mr. Clerval bowed gracefully. "A pleasure to meet you," he said to Aunt Gardiner, then Mrs. Bennet, then Mary and Kitty.

Mr. Frankenstein bowed but said nothing. He had the darkest eyes Mary had ever encountered, and an air of being there only out of obligation. Mary had noticed Clerval on the dance floor earlier but had not seen his friend take a dance as yet. Pride, vanity, or shyness might account for it; there was no way to tell.

Mr. Gardiner explained how his friend Mr. Clegg had introduced him to Clerval at the offices of Clegg's import house in the City. Clerval spoke briefly about how he and Victor had arrived in London from Geneva, Switzerland, some months earlier.

Mr. Frankenstein mumbled a few words and, to her great surprise, turned to Mary. "Might I have the pleasure, if you are not occupied, of sharing the next dance with you?"

His eyes did not meet hers. She suspected he asked her only at the urging of Mr. Clerval. His diffident air intrigued her. His manners were faultless, as was his English—though he spoke with a slight French accent—but he conveyed an air of hesitance, as if he acted a part that was not comfortable. Not vanity, then, and not likely pride.

He took her hand and guided her to the floor. Through her glove and his she felt the pressure of his fingers; they entered the lines of women and men facing one another, prepared for the quadrille. Once the orchestra struck up, Frankenstein moved with some grace. Unlike Mr. Collins, his attention was on Mary, and she thought, despite herself, that she danced better than she had except at those times when she danced by herself in her room, safe from the world's observation. When she extended her hand, she did it with neither abruptness nor timidity. No trace of a smile crossed her partner's lips. He spoke not at all. They stood side by side as the line advanced, waiting to make them top couple, and Mary's discomfort increased. She cast about for something to say, but her mind was a humiliating blank.

At the end of the dance, Mr. Frankenstein broke the silence, asking whether Mary would like some refreshment. She might rather have been released, but she would not be rude. They crossed from the crowded ballroom to the sitting room, where Frankenstein procured for her a cup of negus. Away from the orchestra Mary could hear the rattle of windblown rain on the windows. She watched him retrieve the punch and bring it back, determined to make some conversation before she should retreat to the safety of her wallflower's chair.

"So, Monsieur Frankenstein, did you come to London as your friend Mr. Clerval did—on business?"

He sat across from her, his cup in his hands. Other couples in the room conversed with varying degrees of intimacy. Looking about as he spoke, in his excellent English he said, "I came to meet with certain natural philosophers here in London. Your country boasts some of the leading chemists of Europe."

"Oh. Have you met Mr. Davy?"

Frankenstein looked at her as if seeing her for the first time. "You are acquainted with Mr. Davy?"

"I am not acquainted with him, but I am, in my small way, an enthusiast of the sciences. Have you read his *Discourse Introductory to a Course of Lectures on Chemistry*?"

Frankenstein's eyebrows lifted. "I find myself astonished to meet a young woman who has read Humphry Davy. Is this the pastime of well-bred ladies in London society?"

For the first time in their evening he seemed to be animated by something other than duty. Mary felt unaccustomed daring. What did it matter what she said to a diffident foreigner whom she would never see again?

"The well-bred ladies of London are more interested in Mr. Davy's good looks than in his writings," Mary said. "The well-bred men, though they may attend his lectures, are for the most part less interested in his writings than in the well-bred ladies. You and I are likely the only man and woman here tonight who will speak of chemistry. So you have met Mr. Davy?"

"I attended one of his lectures on his recent return from Europe."

"Then you have seen more of him than I. My mother does not consider my attending such lectures a suitable way for me to pass my time. You are a natural philosopher?"

"Perhaps it is better to say that at one time I was. I studied at Ingolstadt with Mr. Krempe and Mr. Waldman. I confess that I can no longer countenance the subject."

"You no longer countenance the subject, yet you seek out Professor Davy."

A shadow swept over Frankenstein's face. "The subject is unsupportable to me, yet pursue it I must."

"A paradox."

"A paradox that I am unable to explain, Miss Bennet."

All this said in a voice so heavy as to almost sound despairing. Mary watched his sober black eyes and replied, "'The heart has its reasons of which reason knows nothing.'"

For the second time he gave her a look that suggested she had touched him. Mr. Frankenstein sipped from his cup, then spoke: "Avoid any pastime, Miss Bennet, that takes you out of the normal course of human contact. If the study to which you apply yourself has a tendency to weaken your affections and destroy your taste for simple pleasures, then that study is certainly unlawful."

The purport of this speech Mary was unable to fathom. "Surely there is no harm in seeking knowledge. The natural philosopher, Professor Davy suggests, should be as creative an artist as the poet, and combine together mechanical, chemical, and physiological knowledge. All knowledge, I believe, brings us closer to God."

"Would that it were always so, Miss Bennet."

"Why otherwise has he given us minds that reason, and hearts that question?"

"Why, indeed," Frankenstein said. He smiled. "Henry has urged me to go out into London society; had I known that I might meet such a thoughtful person as yourself, I would have done so long before now."

The isolation that he exuded touched something in Mary. She asked, "Have you not been able to confide in your friend Mr. Clerval?"

Frankenstein looked at her for a good five seconds before he spoke. "Henry thinks he knows my troubles, and it would not be politic for me to correct him."

"What does Henry know, then?"

"He knows that, on the eve of my return home from the university, my little brother William was murdered." Frankenstein's voice was low, and he studied the figures in the carpet. "That Justine Moritz, our family's ward, who was a sister to me, was accused of the deed, confessed, and was hanged."

Mary was shocked, but was called upon to make some response. She managed to say, "It's a wonder that you have the courage to be here at all."

Frankenstein lifted his head. "Courage," he said.

"You have my deepest sympathies. Thank God you find yourself in—what was it you called it?—the normal course of human contact. I would hope that this might present you an opportunity to leave your troubles aside for an evening and enjoy a few of the simple pleasures you recommend."

His smile now was more genuine. "I believe you are sent to save my evening, Miss Bennet." He sighed. "But I spy your uncle at the door. No doubt he has been dispatched to protect you. If you will promise me a dance later, I shall release you to your family. Then we may continue this discussion, and I promise in return that I will do so in a lighter mood. Here, give me your card."

She held out her dance card, embarrassed that it was blank. He took it, and the small pencil attached, and wrote in his name for the second dance after the supper.

He stood, took her hand, and led her to her waiting family.

"I must thank you for the dance, and even more for your conversation, Miss Bennet. In the midst of a foreign land, you have brought me a moment of understanding."

He returned to Clerval. Mary wondered at the nature of the study that had taken him away from his family. A man of sensibility, however guiltless, might feel some measure of responsibility had his pastimes drawn him away from home while such appalling losses occurred.

Escorting the ladies down to the supper, Uncle Gardiner commented on his conversation with Henry Clerval. "He is a charming fellow. It is his first opportunity to travel abroad. He intends to pursue a career in the East India trade, and is learning the language of Maharashtra and Bombay. I confess that I enjoyed telling him of my own experiences, and I offered to introduce him to Mr. Howland at the exchange."

Mary ate some of the ham and boiled eggs that were served, and took a glass of Madeira. Kitty coughed softly into her gloved hand.

"Stop coughing, Kitty," Mrs. Bennet said. "Have a care for my nerves." She turned to Aunt Gardiner. "They should not have put the supper at the end of this long hallway. The ladies, flushed from the dance, have to walk all that cold way."

Kitty took a sip of her own wine and leaned over to Mary. "I have never seen you so taken with a man. You were gone such a long time."

"We were talking."

"What did you talk about?" asked Aunt Gardiner.

"We spoke of natural philosophy. At first."

"At first?" Kitty said.

"Did he say nothing of the reasons he came to England?" Mrs. Bennet asked.

"That was his reason—to meet with some men of science.

But I think he is here to forget his grief. His little brother was murdered by the family ward."

"How terrible!" said Aunt Gardiner.

Mrs. Bennet asked in open astonishment, "Can this be true?"

"Would he tell such a tale to a complete stranger?" Kitty said. "It can't be true."

Kitty was right. It was not seemly for a stranger to speak of such things, and so much from the heart, to a woman he had just met. Yet her recollection of Frankenstein's manner, the tone of his voice and the cast of his face, left her no other conclusion than that he had been telling the truth. His appreciation for her responses had been genuine, she had no doubt. Yes, he had violated decorum, yet she could not find it in herself to condemn him.

"Why would he make up such a tale if it is not true?" Mary asked.

After a moment, Aunt Gardiner tentatively said, "It's not unknown for some men to tell dramatic tales in order to impress young women. Enough girls are attracted to a man suffering from a broken heart for some men to feign one."

Mary did not think she was the sort of woman on whom a stranger might practice such art. "A man should be what he seems," she said. "Mr. Frankenstein has asked to dance with me again after the supper. I will see what more I might draw from him on the matter."

Mary did not engage them for the rest of the supper, and the women returned to the ballroom silently. Mary was hurt that her family, even Aunt Gardiner, did not trust her judgment, as if she were the same purblind girl she had been at nineteen.

When the second half of the ball began, Kitty at last managed to dance with Mr. Sidwich. Mary surveyed the room, and eventually spotted Frankenstein standing near one of the windows. In the many-paned night-black glass, Mary saw reflections of the candles in the chandeliers and the ghostlike dancers. She caught Frankenstein's eye, and he inclined his head slightly. Feeling her face flush, Mary studied her dance card and his even, neat signature beside the second dance, a cotillion.

She watched the dancers. Kitty was smiling, her eyes bright, as she moved with energy across the floor with the dashing Mr. Sidwich. Mary knew what this evening meant to her, what this season meant. There was still the foolish girl in Kitty, the girl who loved a party and dreamed of romance, but she had been worn down by growing older with no prospects on the horizon. Still, she took a genuine pleasure in the ball, in being dressed well and feeling lovely and interesting to attractive, important men. Mary's heart went out to her, at the same time she felt envy for something she had never had.

She had never had a conversation, however brief, like that she'd had with Victor Frankenstein.

The orchestra finished the song with a flourish, and the ladies and gentlemen swirled to a stop, bowed to one another while catching their breath, and applauded. The gentlemen escorted the ladies to their seats. Conversation hummed. Mary looked back at where Frankenstein had stood, but he was no longer there.

The second dance was called, and couples moved onto the floor to take their positions. Mary still did not see Frankenstein. The musicians began to play, the couples to dance. It was too late to join now. Still he did not appear.

Mary was surprised how defeated this left her. Her emotions had been touched more than she could have imagined. She felt angry, but also worried. Had her prying into his sadness driven him away?

After the end of the dance, Mr. Clerval came through the crowd to where the Bennets sat. "Excuse me, Miss Bennet?" he said to Mary.

"Yes."

"You danced earlier with my friend Victor. Have you seen him about since then? Have any of you seen him?"

"He was there some minutes ago, before this dance," Mary said.

"Is something amiss?" Mrs. Bennet asked.

"I seem to have lost him. Perhaps he has gone to the card room. Thank you."

Clerval left.

The ball continued. Dance followed dance: quadrilles, reels, a minuet, the *Boulanger*. Though Kitty danced most of the dances, and spoke with several gentlemen, Mr. Sidwich paid her no additional attention; he seemed to be engaged in intimate conversation with a dark-haired young woman in a rich purple dress, a Miss Elphinstone from Bath.

Victor Frankenstein did not appear again, and Henry Clerval left shortly before the great clock at the end of the room struck twelve.

The cold March rain was still falling when, well after midnight, they left the ball. They waited under the portico while the coachman brought round the carriage. Kitty began coughing, her breath clouding the chilly air.

As they stood there, Mary noticed a hooded man, very tall, standing in the shadows at the corner of the lane. Full in the downpour, unmoving, he watched the town house and its guests without coming closer or going away, as if this observation were all his intention in life.

FOUR

Through the window of the town house, looking out on the storm, I saw him. He stood in the street at the end of the block, full in the rain, not much more than a shadow in the dim light. I could not see his face, but his size and his absolute stillness were unmistakable.

My mind was immediately out there, with him, while my body remained standing, well-dressed, at a ball in fashionable London. I hung suspended, the blood trickling through my veins, listening to the music of the orchestra behind me, the swish of dresses and tap of shoes on the dance floor, the buzz of conversations.

But only for a moment. While the music still played, I slipped quietly past the conversing men and women, the chaperones, the servants, the dancers, and out of the room. I found the cloakroom occupied by two chatting footmen. As I entered, the older one stood.

"May I help you, sir?"

"I would like my overcoat and hat."

While he went to retrieve my coat, I asked the other, "Is there a way out of the house other than the front door? One that does not give onto the square?"

"There's the servants' entrance, sir. But I don't believe—"

"Show me the way."

The other returned with my hat and coat. I followed the footman down a hall and two flights of stairs, through a door, a turn into a narrow passageway, past a busy kitchen, to an exterior door at the end of the hall. He unlatched it. "There's no cabs on the street at this hour, sir. Shall I go round to the front to fetch you one?"

"No." I gave him a shilling. "By no means say anything to anyone. You never saw me."

I opened the door on the pounding rain. Two stone steps led to a narrow, deserted street. I closed the door behind me and strode off, away from the square. The rain bounced off my shoulders and under my collar, glinting silver where it splattered on the cobblestones. Water flowed in the gutters.

How had he managed, with no allies or resources, to come all this way and find me in the midst of one of the largest cities in Europe? His capabilities were frightening.

It had been more than six months since I had agreed to create a mate for him, and in that time I had made no progress. I had scarcely addressed the matter.

During our months in London, I had managed to add some new chemicals and a Cruickshank battery to the equipment that I had brought from Geneva. But the longer I had gone without seeing the wretched thing, the easier it had been for me to fancy that he had drowned, or been killed or imprisoned somewhere on the long way from Geneva to Rotterdam.

One glimpse of his monstrous form had dispelled this delusion.

How long had he been observing me? Did he know where Clerval and I stayed? Perhaps if I hurried to the hotel, I might throw my clothing into a portmanteau and leave before he realized I was no longer at the ball. But even if I found a horse at midnight and stole away unseen, my leaving Henry risked exposing him to the Creature's rage. And where would I go?

I wandered the streets through most of the night, afraid to return to the inn, afraid to flee. Eventually the rain let up and a wind blew away the clouds. Down Oxford Street I could see the moon, a day or so past full, hanging above the buildings in the cold night air. The rain that washed the gutters and the wind that chilled my cheeks had for the moment carried away the stench of the city. The fine shops of New Bond Street were dark. No reputable person was abroad.

I circled over to Albemarle Street and stood in front of the Royal Institution, where, a month earlier, I had spoken with a number of prominent physiologists and chemists about Davy's *Chemical Agencies of Electricity*. Electricity: the fire of heaven, the spark that lit the mind. Davy had managed to create light by passing electricity through two carbon rods, but I knew from experience the union of electricity and light.

A blast of such light had started it all—a blinding glare that had changed my life. In the yard beside our house near Belrive had stood a huge old oak. Henry and I used to climb it when we were boys. We would pretend we were knights lost in Arabia, hiding from the Saracens, learning the secrets of the Eastern magical arts.

When I was fifteen, a violent thunderstorm came over the mountains. Even at a distance, the lightning and thunder of this storm were beyond any I had ever experienced. Bolts of fire shot between midnight-black clouds; when I closed my eyes, their blue image lingered. Wind whipped the leaves of the great oak, shaking its limbs, yet there came no rain. The storm exhilarated me. From the back door of the house I watched the spectacle, awestruck by the power of nature. As I stood there, a geyser of light surged out of the ground, meeting a torrent from above in an explosion that threw me from my feet.

The warm hand of my father on my breast called me back to my senses. "Victor. Victor," he repeated softly.

"Father."

He held me tightly. For the moment I was blind. My ears rang. When my eyes recovered, and my father helped me to my feet, I saw that, but for a blasted stump and some smoke that burned the charged air, the oak had vanished. In the morning, my father and I examined the site and found it strewn with thousands of narrow ribbons of wood six to ten inches long, no wider than two fingers.

When I asked my father the source of this almost unbelievable power, he replied, "Electricity."

Later he explained what little was known of this element. We repeated Franklin's experiment that drew electricity down from the skies. My imagination rushed ahead. Should a man ever control this power, he might someday hurl thunderbolts like Jove himself.

Thus I set my foot on the road that has led to my present misery.

The dawn rose between London's buildings. The air warmed, and the sky was spotlessly clear, promising the first truly springlike day of the year.

By this time I had found my way to the Mall and St. James's Park. The dripping trees were beginning to bud, and the breeze blew ripples across the surface of the canal. The city was waking. I looked across the Carlton House Gardens to the home of the British prince regent, famous for his debaucheries. Had he committed any crimes equal to mine?

But this self-recrimination served no purpose. My flight from the ball had been ill considered. To have it confirmed that the Creature followed me was a blow, but no matter how monstrous he was, how subject to passion, he was a reasoning being. If he killed me, he would never get what he wanted. To the degree then that he believed I would fulfill my promise, I had power over him.

His revealing himself in that way was not an accident. He wanted me to see him—as a reminder of my task, and as a threat. If the thing was to be believed, he had suffered a great deal with extreme patience, but I could not know how far that patience would extend, for he had also told me how much he hated humankind. To be rid of him I must apply myself to the work of fashioning him a mate.

I made my way back to Piccadilly and Dorant's Hotel. Shopkeepers were opening their establishments; servants swept the street before their masters' town houses, a brewer's cart made its way to the inn's stable yard.

When I entered our rooms, Clerval started up from the

chair where he had been dozing. "Thank God, Victor!" he said. "I've been worried to death."

"Not to death, I hope."

"Where have you been?"

"I've been walking," I said, taking off my sodden coat. I sat in an armchair and pulled off my boots. "I have had enough of London, Henry. There is work that I must attend to, studies I must pursue that I have let idle too long. It is time we moved on to Oxford."

"That's all you have to say? I turned the ball upside down looking for you. I made a fool of myself before any number of the other guests."

"Henry, since we've been here, you've been to dozens of plays, concerts, dinners, card parties, and balls. I'm sorry that I ruined this one for you, but I had a very good reason for leaving as I did."

"Did it have something to do with that woman you danced with—Miss Bennet? I can't say that she struck me as well favored."

"There is more to her than a pretty face." Miss Bennet had asked whether I had confided in Henry, as if she knew that I had not. She would no doubt have recommended I take this opportunity to unburden myself to him. "My leaving had nothing to do with her. It has to do with the fact that I am getting no work done. I need to visit Oxford."

"But I've made friends here." Henry studied me warily, watching for my reaction.

What were his friends to me? "You may correspond with your friends. We may stop in London on our way back home. If they are true friends, they may visit you in Geneva."

Henry looked wounded. He slumped back into his chair.

I mastered my exasperation. "Henry, I am sorry that I left the party without telling you. That was wrong of me, and I hope you will accept my sincere apology. You have been a brother to me since we were seven years old. You know that no man means more to me than you."

I rested my hand on his shoulder. He did not look up.

"You always knew that we would move on," I continued. "I say it is time to do so. Whether you are with me or not, I will not sleep another night in this hotel."

He looked up, and our eyes met for a moment. "I accept your apology. Yes, let us go. But only if we stop in Windsor along the way."

I agreed, and Henry wrote to our lodgings in Oxford to let them know that we would be arriving in four days. We bought tickets for the mail coach leaving at five that afternoon. I had the hotel porter retrieve my equipment from the hotel's storeroom. We packed our things. Henry begged my leave to say good-bye to some friend he had met at one of the parties. I encouraged him to do so, and he promised to return by three in the afternoon.

As he left the inn, and for some time afterward, I watched from our window, expecting to see the Creature. I paced the room, and then bestirred myself to write my father a letter full of pleasantries, telling him of our move to Oxford. I went down to a coffeehouse and ate a hasty meal. Henry returned in the afternoon. By the evening, our equipage was loaded onto the coach and we departed London with the driver, the liveried Royal Mail guard, and three other passengers—two inside with us and one riding above.

Henry's spirits had risen. I had always taken advantage of his good nature, and he had always offered it to me. However abruptly we were leaving London, he looked forward to our further travels.

The coach made its way through London's West End, past the former town house of the Duke of Buckingham and through the city's environs. Cobbled streets gave way to roads still sodden from the rains. Though the road was well kept, the lurching of the coach left no chance for me to doze after my sleepless night, but the evening breeze that came through the windows was a welcome relief from the fetid city air.

Henry's good mood did not endure past the setting of the sun. Despite the presence of the other passengers—Mr. and Mrs. Wilton, the man in a severe black coat and the woman in an unadorned bonnet—Henry said, in French, "Victor, I hope you will not mind my putting an observation to you."

I replied in the same tongue. "What is it?"

"I know the grief that William's death and Justine's loss have brought you. No man of feeling could easily put aside such tragedies. It was my fervent hope—and your father's, Ernest's, and Elizabeth's—that the change of scene might help you to lift your eyes from the past and open the future to you. Yet for the entirety of our time in London you stayed shut up in your room, when you were not buying some books, or some chemicals, or seeking out some dry professor."

"I have researches I wish to pursue."

"You called us brothers. We have not been so for a long time. Those bonds began to weaken on the day you went off to Ingolstadt. For two years we heard nothing of you. Your communications, when they came at all, varied from hysterical excitement to a few fatigued jottings. I worried. When I was finally sent to see you, I found you on the brink of the complete collapse that immediately followed."

"For your rescue of me, Henry, I will be grateful as long as I live."

"Why, then will you not let me rescue you now? This return to your scientific pursuits destroys your tranquility, rather than restoring it. You are descending into another abyss. I reach out my hand to pull you up. Won't you grasp it?"

I was moved, and ashamed of how little consideration I had devoted to Henry. I had seen him as engrossed in trivialities, happy in his optimism, and envied the bright future that doubtless awaited him.

"I am sorry, Henry. There is much in what you say."

"So tell me what it is that weighs upon you. And do not say it is the death of William. All this began before anything happened to William."

My mind cast about for something to say that was not a lie. "It is the way that William died that troubles me."

"That Justine murdered him? But here lies another mystery. I observed you throughout her trial. You insisted that she was innocent, despite the evidence against her."

"She was innocent. Do you think she could have strangled William for the bauble that hung around his neck? You knew her as well as I. It is inconceivable."

"We all believe her innocent. But your reaction was different. You were tortured by the accusations against her. It seemed to me that you protested her innocence so strongly because you knew something about the matter that none of the rest of us knew. I think that still. So—please, Victor—why won't you tell me, your oldest and dearest friend, the man who saved your life and nursed you back to health when you collapsed in Ingolstadt, what you know?"

By this time Mr. and Mrs. Wilton had become silent as mice.

"Henry, I don't wish to speak of any of this. Certainly not under these circumstances." I tilted my head slightly in the direction of our fellow passengers. "If we keep on speaking French, these people will think we are spies."

Henry peered at the Wiltons in the dim light. "You say this is scientific research," he continued in English. "We carry boxes of equipment with us, and still you purchase more. What do you hope to discover? Some new element? Some chemical device? A new battery?"

"It's not a matter that I can explain simply. And it has the gravest consequences. If you only knew the risks involved—"

"In a new battery?"

I drew back. In a clipped voice I said, "No. Not a new battery."

"Good. Because I must tell you that whatever it is you pursue, it does your mind, your soul—and your company, for that matter—no good. Solitude only deepens your melancholy. If you care at all for yourself, or for me, you will make more of an effort to engage with the world. You say yourself that this is what you need."

"I came with you to Lord Henry's ball."

"And ran away in the middle of it as if pursued by ghosts. I think Miss Bennet must have said something to you. I saw you in conversation with her. You were completely engaged—more than you have been with me at any time in the last two months."

"I should think you had enough company to occupy you."

"None that I would prefer to yours."

I sighed.

"Well, you have nothing to worry about, Henry. Your only rival for my attentions is, as you guessed, a new battery."

Henry retreated into silence. I looked out the window. The driver had lit the coach's lamps. Under the big moon I saw neat fields bound by hedges, and, in the distance, what must be the forests of Windsor.

Mr. Wilton said to his wife, "So, my love, shall we have some supper when the coach stops to change horses?"

We spent two days in Windsor and then moved on to Oxford, where we would remain for a month. Our itinerary was in one sense set, though subject to alteration should events require. From Oxford we would proceed to Matlock in Derbyshire, thence to Cumberland and Westmorland, and eventually to Scotland, where we had an invitation to stay with a friend, Dr. Marble, in Perth. It was my intention to separate from Henry there and continue to some remote place where I might set up my equipment and begin the delicate process of creating a bride for the monster.

My plan yet lacked two vital elements. The first I hoped to find at the Oxford colleges. I carried with me letters of introduction from my mentors Professors Waldman and Krempe. Although I spent some days in reading in the Radcliffe Camera's imposing science library, my chief aim was to speak with Cathcart Glover, a leading anatomist and physiologist.

During our first week in Oxford I went out of my way to

join Henry in his tours of the area. The weather had turned and we were favored with days of blossoming spring. Oxford's streets and ancient spires conveyed dignity and repose. The beauty of the surrounding countryside and the Isis River drew me out of myself. Henry was fascinated by how the English Revolution in its regicide had anticipated the French Revolution by a hundred and fifty years. As Swiss, we had not suffered such political upheavals. He wondered if, should Bonaparte finally be defeated after his recent escape from Elba, the history of France would follow that of England. Henry had many theories, and spoke of writing a book about them. For an hour or two each day, in his presence, I was able to put aside the knowledge of my promise and enjoy the moment, but every night I feared to find the Creature standing in the street outside our inn.

Henry spent his evenings with new friends he had made at the colleges, at some club or tavern or coffee shop, talking politics and literature. The presence of the university and its many students recalled my days at Ingolstadt, not so long past by the calendar, but an eon ago by the alteration of my heart. Henry was interested in the English radicals and asked these rowdy, privileged young scholars many questions about whether they had any lasting influence on the British government and society. I avoided these revels as much as possible.

Knowing now that the Creature was watching me, I worried when Henry was out without me, at the same time I was relieved by his absence, and the absence of his increasing questions about my research. I had resigned myself to the fact that I required the Creature to follow me, if only because he needed to see me fulfill my promise, take the female I created, and depart forever from my life. I told myself that as long as I progressed in this task, Henry would be safe. He would not dare harm Henry for fear of ending my commitment to creating his mate.

My letters secured me an introduction to Senior Fellow Glover, and he asked me to join him at his rooms for supper. At seven I arrived at Brasenose College, where Glover had his apartments. The porter ushered me to his rooms.

The professor greeted me heartily. He was a stout man of middle years, his hair thinning, his face open and good-natured, the very picture of the happy academic bachelor. The room was warmly lit by several oil lamps, and a small fire burned in the grate, but the latticed window was open to the cool night air. Over a meal of roast mutton and delicately prepared vegetables punctuated by full glasses of fine red wine — Professor Glover boasted his rights to the college's extensive cellars — I assumed a conviviality that I did not feel and answered his questions about Waldman, Krempe, and Ingolstadt.

Almost from the moment I had made my promise to the Creature, the question had occurred to me that, should the female I created not turn from him in disgust and terror, what might come of their union? The natural outcome of his coupling with a female would be offspring. I had fashioned the Creature to be exceptional in every way: he was stronger than a man, better able to endure pain, heat, and cold, and, as witnessed by his learning language and reading, and his eloquence in argument, brilliantly intelligent. Notwithstanding his promise that he and his mate would hie off to some distant corner of the world, a race of such beings would become a threat to all humanity—unless I could prevent such an outcome.

Glover had spent his career studying female human anatomy. I begged him to elaborate on his observations about the process of generation. He settled back over an after-dinner glass of malmsey, well satisfied to expound.

"The cornerstone of my understanding is William Harvey's assertion: *ex ovo omnia*. Everything originates in the egg! Certainly I honor van Leeuwenhoek for his discovery of the spermatozoon. It was a great achievement, the discovery of the spermatozoon. I believe in the spermatozoon—nonetheless, all mammalian creatures grow from an undifferentiated egg."

"Yes. I am interested—"

"Epigenesis, not preformation! A tiny man inside each spermatozoon—absurd!"

"I agree with you completely."

"I honor all our scientific forebears, mind you," Glover said, holding up an index finger. "Aristotle, Galen, de Graaf, Malpighi, the great Harvey—we are all Harvey's children, Mr. Frankenstein—but that does not mean we must tolerate, or worse still, perpetuate, their mistakes. We do not credit spontaneous generation, for example."

"But Darwin's experiment with vermicelli suggests that life may arise spontaneously."

"Nonsense. *Ex ovo omnia!* Even worms and maggots must originate in a living egg. There is no higher life without sex. And a good thing it is, eh?"

"Yes. No doubt sex is a good thing."

"Indeed! I should think a young man would agree with

that. You have read Harvey's *Exercitationes de Generatione Animalium*, have you not? Harvey did not believe in spontaneous generation."

I found it difficult to tolerate his dogmatism in an area where, by experience, I had proven him wrong. "A book written more than one hundred fifty years ago."

"Yes, but borne out by a century's worth of study."

"Life must at some point have originated from dead matter. Dr. Darwin—"

"Darwin? Darwin is moonshine. There is no such thing as spontaneous generation, Monsieur Frankenstein. Thirty years ago Spallanzani disproved Buffon and Needham. There are no 'vital atoms' responsible for life. Such notions are magic, not science."

I considered telling him that I was being stalked by a creature that proved that lifeless matter could be made to live. To kill. To discourse on justice. Even, perhaps, to have a soul. But this wrangling was not to my purpose. "I wonder if we might return to the matter of the ovum."

"Yes?"

"You have studied the causes of barrenness," I said. "The question I put to you is, could you, by manipulation of the female generative system, cause a woman to be barren?"

Glover swirled the sweet wine in his glass. "The cause or causes of barrenness have not been established. I speculate it is a matter of the ovaries not functioning. When and how they produce an egg, and precisely where in the body that egg meets the semen, and how the semen works on it, and how the undifferentiated egg grows to human form and why some are born male and others female—all these things are still not completely understood. Spallanzani—sadly, a preformationist, but still a natural philosopher of insight—demonstrated that filtered semen becomes less effective as filtration becomes more complete. So the active agent is the spermatozoon, not the seminal fluid. That suggests if one could prevent the sperm from reaching the egg, one would prevent conception. This is the principle, though none knew it, behind methods used for hundreds of years—pigs bladders, pessaries, and the like—with varying degrees of success."

"Might there be way to prevent conception by surgical means?"

"One might remove a woman's ovaries. As a possible cure for hysteria I have considered but never attempted this: given modern scruples, finding a subject for such an experiment is difficult. A woman without ovaries would doubtless not bear children. But we could hardly call her a woman then, could we? And such a surgery would likely be fatal."

"Do you know the specific place of generation within the woman's anatomy?"

"Well, this is still a matter of speculation." He pushed himself out of his chair, opened a cabinet, and drew from it a rolled-up chart. He moved some books from a worktable, unrolled it, and set a lamp down on one corner. I recognized the drawing as a diagram of the womb and associated organs, with Latin designations. Glover placed his thick finger on the center of the diagram. "I believe the semen meets the egg here, in the uterus."

"But the eggs must originate in the ovaries," I said.

"Yes. The egg I believe moves to the womb by way of one

of these channels. By what prompting, and at what time of the female monthly cycle—these and many other details of the process are obscure."

This was a more detailed diagram than any I had seen. "Did you create this yourself?"

"It is the work of thirty years."

"Remarkable," I said. "If one were somehow to block these tubes through surgery, would not the egg be bottled in the ovaries and never move to the womb? One might thus prevent a woman from ever conceiving a child."

"In theory. It's even possible this is something that happens in nature. But if so, the eggs, being confined to the ovaries with no escape, may rot and cause disease. The menstrual blood, with no possibility of discharge, might back up and clot the heart. And such surgery, though not so extreme as removing the ovaries, would be hazardous. One would be more likely to kill your patient. If you succeeded, your achievement would only be to make a woman barren. Such might be an advantage to a lady of the evening, I grant, but surely not to any wife or daughter."

"Surely."

Glover let go of the edge of his chart, and it rolled closed. "But why pursue this? What purpose would it serve?"

I had prepared a response to this question. "You are familiar with Malthus's *An Essay on the Principle of Population*?"

"Yes, of course. So you see this surgical treatment as a solution to the problem of an insupportable population?"

"Certainly for the poor. We might do away with almshouses and prisons if we could control the numbers of the unfit and criminal."

Glover returned to his armchair. "A rather utopian—if you will pardon my pun—*conception*." He winked.

"That may be. Still, the knowledge you have gathered would be invaluable to such a project. Would it be possible for me to copy your diagram? Do you have notes on the dissections? In anything I publish, I will, of course, give you full credit for these discoveries."

Glover smiled. "Ah, the ambitions of youth."

"What mysteries might be revealed if only we understood that first moment of life?" Though I said this only to distract him, it was a sentiment that two years ago had ruled my existence. Before my discovery of the secret of life, it had seemed the most desirable goal a man might seek: to know, and to control, the border between life and death. "To discover nature in her secret places, and expose her to the light," I said.

"Nature has concealed her mysteries for centuries," Glover said. "Yet we have learned more in the last one hundred years than men have discovered in the previous two thousand." He poured me another glass of Madeira. "As Newton said, if we see farther today, it is only because we stand on the shoulders of giants."

Glover agreed to let me have his dissection notes, drawings, and diagrams. I managed to continue in conversation with him for another hour while he plied me with ever rarer varieties of whiskey and snuff, more to give the appearance of engagement than out of any genuine wish to know him better. I had gained what I needed from him, enough at least to contemplate the distasteful task ahead of me.

As I left, my head spinning, three drunken young men staggered through the Brasenose gates, and outside, in the grand central square, a mob of their fellows passing by the Radcliffe Camera filled the night air with their revelry. I thought of Miss Bennet and her belief in the restorative effects of social interaction. Human contact. Companionship. Rather than as an example of acquiring knowledge through false pretenses, I might recast my visit with Cathcart Glover as an exercise in following her advice—but so far I had not felt its salutary effects. It seemed to me that as Miss Bennet had spoken, she was trying to convince herself as much as me. An empty dance card presented as good a spur to ineffectual rationalization as a need to create a sterile monster. Paradoxically, despite my perpetual dejection and Miss Bennet's questionable advice, during the moments I had spoken with her, I had forgotten the thing that followed me, and the burden on my heart had lifted.

What had she thought of the consolations of society when I did not return to dance with her as I had promised?

By the time I reached our inn, all my brooding had settled down on me again. The Creature was moved by the desire for physical affections that, thanks to Cathcart Glover, I would prevent from producing offspring. I would keep the evil that I created from spreading to destroy the human race. From a utilitarian perspective, my dissembling tonight was a moral act.

How would the monster react when he realized that his female would bear him no children? The thought that the wretched thing might aspire to fatherhood seemed both an absurdity and an abomination. More probably, lust was his sole motivation, which raised another thought: Once I gave him his bride, how would he treat her? Might he take out the abuse he had suffered on the one being who offered the affections he would never receive from a human being?

Even if so, such an evil could not rival the evil he might yet wreak upon everyone that I loved. I had better not waste my sympathies on a second, yet uncreated, monstrous thing, likely to be as soulless as the first.

I climbed up the stairs to the rooms I shared with Henry. He was not there. No doubt he was with some of his new friends, pursuing the carnal entertainments that my monster was willing to kill to experience — entertainments in which I had never indulged.

I lay in the dark. Below the window, a horse clopped by on the cobbled street. I heard distant music. I thought of Elizabeth, her long faithfulness to me, her beauty and goodness. I longed to be with her. I needed to be done with this, at home in her embrace. Thanks to Glover I now lacked only the second element vital to end the curse that had come on me the night I'd brought that vile thing to life: the body of a young woman, recently deceased.

FIVE

In the week after Lord Henry's ball, Kitty's cough worsened, to which were added a sore throat, fever, and chills. The apothecary summoned by the Gardiners pronounced it a bronchial catarrh and prescribed warm tea with lemon. Although Kitty received the best of care at the Gardiners' home in Gracechurch Street, Mrs. Bennet was not mollified. Had the Gardiners lived in Hanover Square, Mrs. Bennet might have rested easier, but from the vantage of Gracechurch Street, her daughter's illness seemed a grave matter.

So once Kitty had improved enough to rise from her bed, Mrs. Bennet insisted that they return to Longbourn. Despite Kitty's aphonial protests—her voice reduced to a whisper—Mrs. Bennet maintained that the country air would suit her better. Parental anxiety prevailed over filial aspiration, and by the third week of April, Kitty, Mary, and their mother were home again.

Mary would have been relieved to leave the city and its social engagements behind, had it not been for her dance and conversation with Victor Frankenstein. She did not imagine that she might encounter him again, and when she thought about how he had left her waiting by the side of the dance floor, she wondered why she would even want to, but still the evening lingered in her mind.

She ought properly to have put him out of her thoughts. She could not. He stood apart from every man she had ever met in ways that spoke to her heart so directly that it gave her pause. He did not take her interest in natural philosophy as some source of comedy. He spoke with her as an equal, a mind capable of understanding the rigors of science. Dare she conclude that he had been impressed with her?

And then there was the tragic tale of his lost brother. Mary had heard genuine grief in his voice, not some ballroom stratagem. He had been grateful for the comfort she brought him. There was in addition some mystery in his past that had driven him from his studies. She had the sense that he carried some great burden.

It did not detract from the impression he had made upon her that he was some years her junior, and very handsome, and that she, in his presence, had spoken with wit and confidence she had never mustered before. Had she been able to confront her reaction, Mary would have had to admit that she was smitten.

She did not trust such emotions. She was not some girl of sixteen. She was thirty-two years old. She set about making herself busy, studying a new piece for the pianoforte.

While Mary coped, nothing would raise Kitty's dampened spirits. Within a week she was feeling better and repining bitterly their remove from London. Mary pointed out that at home she was at least free of Mr. Collins, who would never forsake the city for the country during the social season. He left the duties of his parish to his curate, except when he had composed a particularly fine sermon or, of course, whenever Lady Catherine de Bourgh required his presence. Failing that, he seemed never to mind being absent from his parishioners. His son was left in the hands of what Collins let everyone understand was a superior governess.

None of this was consolation to Kitty for the loss of her season, as she did not fail to remind her mother and sister. Mr. Bennet remained in his study, emerging only at mealtimes. In recent years his sardonic comments about Mrs. Bennet's and Kitty's marital campaigns had gotten gentler, and then ceased. Though Kitty seemed to have given up thoughts of Mr. Sidwich, Mrs. Bennet still made daily reference to him.

"Perhaps," Mrs. Bennet remarked to her husband, "if you had moved yourself to venture into society and make Mr. Sidwich's acquaintance, we might have persuaded him to visit Longbourn after Parliament closed. You have no consideration for the prospects of your children."

"Perhaps you are right, my dear," Mr. Bennet replied wearily. "And had the Grand Armada met with better weather, we might be speaking Spanish right now. But we shall never know, shall we?"

At one time Mr. Bennet would never had said anything so unnecessarily cruel, and it made Mary uncomfortable that he had become so. Still, she wondered how her mother could live in a state of such perpetual dissatisfaction. No matter what felicity might befall the Bennet family, she would not let herself rest in the moment. Lacking the sympathetic ear of her husband, she inflicted her unsettled mind chiefly on her daughters.

Mary distracted herself by her daily practice and walks in the countryside, where she would stop beneath an oak and read. Some time after their return, she received a letter from Mr. Woodleigh.

Hartwell, Devonshire

My Dear Miss Bennet,

My good friend Mrs. Marigay Travers, wife of Mr. Joseph Travers, MP, for whom I worked when in Mr. Pitt's government, has informed me that Miss Catherine was taken ill some weeks ago, prompting your remove from London to Hertfordshire. You may imagine my immediate concern, and I write to send my best wishes for her renewed health and well-being, and for that of your mother and father. And yourself, certainly. Though our acquaintance is slender, the week we spent together in Lyme Regis shewed that your regard for your sister is such that, should she suffer any permanent debility, it would be as if it had happened to you as well. I fervently wish that that eventuality is not the case.

I thought I might inform you on a matter that, though it does not bear directly on your own situation, might be of interest to you. A collector of my acquaintance from Lincolnshire has announced that he will auction off all those fossils in his possession. I have seen his collection, and he has several specimens that I would dearly love to own. And I am afraid that it will cost me dearly to own them!

All jests aside, I will venture to say that I should be able to pay any likely bid without trouble. Should I succeed in obtaining any of the fossils in question, I will write you giving the particulars of each specimen, and accompany my descriptions with drawings that I will endeavor to make. But it would give me greater pleasure still should you find it possible to visit Hartwell, in the company of your mother, sister, or any guardian who may be appropriate, and allow me to show you these wonders in person, once I acquire them.

You may consider this a formal invitation.

Yours ever,
Charles Woodleigh

In the same post with Mr. Woodleigh's letter came one from her uncle.

My Dear Niece,

You may, I am sure, imagine how pleased and relieved your aunt and I were to hear that Kitty has recovered her health. I expect she regrets her removal from London but I hope her spirits have recovered as well, and that you will give her our best wishes.

But I write on another manner. After we spoke in the Egyptian Hall, I discreetly put out inquiries about Charles Woodleigh, in particular as regards his earning so much money in Ireland. From sources I am not at liberty to disclose, I have discovered the following:

Mr. Woodleigh was involved, in a small way, in
the drafting of the 1800 Acts of Union between England
and Ireland. He was also an acquaintance of Mr. George
McLennon of Belfast, a large landholder and owner of an
export house with offices in Belfast and Dublin. Article VI of
the Acts established a customs union eliminating the tariffs
on certain goods traded between the nations, but there was
a list of items on which the customs duties would remain for
a period of ten years. There was considerable debate in both
the British and Irish parliaments over which items should
be on this list. Mr. Woodleigh argued that certain items be
left off that list, and in the final draft of Article VI his party
prevailed. Mr. McLennon's enterprises have profited well in
the ensuing years.

My friends in banking tell me that Mr. Woodleigh owns
a substantial interest in Mr. McLennon's export firm.

I hasten to add that this sort of dealing is common in
government and business, niece, and that no charges of
impropriety have ever been raised against Mr. Woodleigh.
It may be that his success has as much to do with trade
restrictions caused by the recent wars in Europe as with
any stipulations of the Acts. All reports I have name him
as a respectable and diligent servant of His Majesty's
government for the time he was associated with it, though I
will say he was mocked a bit for his behavior, by all accounts
harmless, during a laughing gas evening of the Askesian
Society in 1801. Also for his fossil collecting. But this will,
perhaps, not be such an impediment to your association as it
might be for another.

Give my regards to your mother and father, and do not

hesitate to inform me if I can be of any further assistance in
any matter dear to your heart. I remain, as ever,

Your loving uncle,
Edward Gardiner

When Mary was forced, after repeated inquiry, to disclose the contents of Mr. Woodleigh's letter to her mother, Mrs. Bennet was eager to accompany her to Devon. Rather than tell her mother what her uncle had written, since she did not herself know what to make of it, Mary told her that she believed that neither her slender acquaintance with Mr. Woodleigh, nor the strictures of propriety, warranted such a visit, and suggested that Mr. Bennet's fragile health should prevent any precipitate departure.

It could be said that Mary's hesitance had less to do with Mr. Woodleigh than with the fact that, to her embarrassment, since the evening of Lord Henry's ball, hardly a day had passed that she had not thought of Mr. Frankenstein.

All this might not have convinced Mrs. Bennet, but when Kitty said that she would not go, and countered with the proposal that they visit Elizabeth and Darcy in Derbyshire, the matter of whether Mrs. Bennet should go north with one daughter, south with the other, or stay at home with her husband, became too confused for immediate resolution.

Kitty maintained that there was no reason for Mrs. Bennet to accompany her to Pemberley when Mr. Bennet and Mary both required her attention, and she became quite insistent on her desire. She used her London disappointment as an argument for her Pemberley hopes, and in the end, under the circumstances it seemed to both Mr. and Mrs. Bennet that remanding Kitty to the care of her older sister might be best. They agreed to let her go. Mr. Bennet wrote Lizzy, and she and Darcy agreed immediately.

Kitty's spirits improved. She ate better, went for walks, and began packing her clothes. Though the society of Derbyshire could not compare with that of London, the nearby town of Matlock was famous for its scenery and hot springs, and many people of distinction stopped there on their journeys to the Cumberland lakes and Scotland. Its society was far superior to that of sleepy Meryton.

On the Sunday before she was to leave, Kitty, Mary, and their parents rode to church for the morning service. In church Mrs. Bennet was careful of her appearance, aiming for elegance without ostentation. Her bonnet should not be too adorned with frills, but it should not indicate in any way that it had not cost very much.

Mr. Bennet took her arm and Mary and Kitty led them into the church. Their accustomed place was near the front, on the left. On the opening hymn, Mary sang harmony over Kitty's melody. She thought they sounded beautiful together. The music drew Mary away from the frustrations of their home into a world of contemplation. This was what she liked the best about church: it was a place where for an hour or two, while light streamed in the windows or rain drummed on the roof, she might consider her own relation to God without having to worry about other people.

Midway through the service, the Reverend Pottsworth stepped to the pulpit. "My text today is from the nineteenth Psalm:

"Who can understand his errors?
Cleanse thou me from secret faults.
Keep back thy servant also from presumptuous
    sins;
Let them not have dominion over me:
Then shall I be upright,
And I shall be innocent from the great transgres-
    sion."

The reverend launched into his sermon about the dangers of presumptuous sins, and how we must examine ourselves to try to discern our secret faults, faults that might look to us like virtues, or merely harmless habits. If we do not keep vigilance over these, we are subject to the greatest sin of all, the sin of confusing our own desires with those of God.

The nineteenth was one of Mary's favorite of the Psalms. Rather than the passage the reverend had selected, she liked best its beginning:

The heavens declare the glory of God;
And the firmament sheweth his handywork.
Day unto day uttereth speech,
And night unto night sheweth knowledge.
There is no speech nor language,
Where their voice is not heard.
Their line is gone out through all the earth,
And their words to the end of the world.

This spoke to her sense of the natural world as an expression of the mind of God. Everywhere men looked, if they looked closely, and were patient, and used the gifts that Providence had given them — Mary believed for exactly these purposes — they found order.

Day unto day uttereth speech, / And night unto night sheweth knowledge. When she contemplated these words, she felt herself very close to King David. He had seen what she saw: that the earth and heavens spoke to men, not in words, but in a language that all persons might understand if they took the time to listen. The psalm told her there was no conflict between her faith and her desire to uncover the mysteries of nature.

At the end of the service the four Bennets walked out of the church into the bright spring sunlight. As they strolled side by side to the carriage, Kitty surreptitiously reached for Mary's hand. Mary looked Kitty in the eye, smiled, and turned to their parents. "Father, might Kitty and I walk home today? The weather is so fine, and it's only a mile."

"I should walk with you," Mr. Bennet said. "It is a lovely day. But I believe I would only slow you down, so unless your mother objects, you may go."

Mrs. Bennet's eyes were on Mr. Bennet. His face was pale and he was short of breath. "Go on, girls. Have a care, and do not dawdle."

Their driver John helped Mr. and Mrs. Bennet into the carriage, climbed into his seat, took the reins, and they slowly rolled away. Mary and Kitty stood among the parishioners who lingered before the church speaking with one another or with the reverend. Some walked into the churchyard to visit the graves of loved ones.

"This was a good idea," Kitty told Mary as they began

down the lane that led out of Meryton toward Longbourn. "We have hardly spoken since we came home. I will miss you while I am at Pemberley."

"And I shall miss you," Mary said.

Mary did not look forward to Kitty's departure. This had been Mary's story for years: her sisters off pursuing their own lives while Mary remained at home caring for their parents. True, the absence of Mary's sisters caused their mother to attend to her more, but with Mrs. Bennet's attention came curbs upon Mary's interests. Mary had once suggested to her father that she might find work as a teacher or governess, but her mother would not countenance a daughter reduced to something little better than a servant. Such were the strictures of life at home. Mr. Woodleigh might offer an escape; much as he had occupied her thoughts in recent weeks, Mr. Frankenstein did not. Mary cast her mind forward to imagine herself a spinster, perhaps making a home with another such exile—Kitty, if she failed in her marital quest?—living together in a quiet town house in Bath, aunties to a score of nieces and nephews, taking meals together, reading books unbothered, inconveniencing no one.

Mary and Kitty idled along the lane and soon were outside the town. The weeks since their return from London had brought mild weather, and trees rustled in a breeze redolent of the fields' new growth. They passed an apple orchard where bluebells bloomed, and along the lane grew columbine, daisies, and buttercups. Mary stopped more than once to gather flowers. Kitty trailed her fingers along the hedgerows.

She drew a heavy sigh. "I should be in Kensington Gardens right now," she said.

"You will be at Pemberley soon," Mary said. "Many girls would consider that better than London."

"I am not a girl. In a week I shall be thirty years old."

Mary had said nothing to their parents about Kitty's meeting with Mr. Clarke. In truth she felt sympathy for Kitty. As a girl Mary had believed that the notion of following the heart was foolishness, but could one find happiness without following the heart? Lydia stood as a warning of the consequences of letting the passions of the moment overcome one's sense — but there must be some way to act in accord with one's soul less destructive of oneself and others. If there was life to be found in the world of sensibility, Mary could not condemn Kitty for seeking it.

She stood straight and held out her bouquet to Kitty. "Happy birthday, sister."

Kitty's smile was fleeting. "You and I have reached an age where we should perhaps stop counting our birthdays."

"Be of better cheer. One might think that you did not want to go to Derbyshire."

"I do wish to go. I may see Lydia. She and Wickham now live in Manchester, not so far from Pemberley."

"Mother might consider letting you visit Lydia, but I doubt that Lizzy will allow it."

"And who is Lizzy to rule over me?"

"Lizzy has done much for you," Mary said. "And Lydia is not the best judge of her pastimes."

"She is as much my sister as Lizzy, and as you."

Kitty did not question Darcy's contempt for Wickham, though it meant that she did not see her favorite sister as much as she would have liked, but when she spoke of Lydia, it was invariably with regret for the lost intimacy of their youth.

"Lydia sought to live, not be sewn into a sachet," Kitty said with some emotion. "Despite her wastrel husband, I would trade my place for hers in a second."

"Her marriage has not been an easy one," Mary said.

"At least she has felt something other than the pallid pleasure of a flirtation at a dance. Am I to marry Collins? He killed Charlotte as surely as if he had smothered her in her lonely bed."

"Kitty!"

Kitty sniffed the nosegay that Mary had made for her. "Do you really think that he is the father of their child?"

Mary shook her head. "Charlotte would not have violated her vows."

Still holding the flowers to her face, Kitty lifted her eyes to meet Mary's. "More's the pity. What did it get her?"

"We must not speak ill of the dead."

"I refuse to die alone," Kitty said with vehemence. "When I see what Lizzy has with Darcy, I am determined to find the like."

"There aren't eight men in England with ten thousand a year and an estate like Pemberley."

"You know that is not what I mean," Kitty said. "When Lydia and I chased the members of the regiment, all we wanted was to be admired and pursued. The men were dashing and some of them were going to die in the wars. Or we sought out men of property, those who were said to be in line to inherit a fortune. We would live in luxury. We would travel, meet great people, dress well, and be the envy of all who saw us.

"But all that means nothing—well, not nothing, but less

than it meant for me at seventeen. I don't want to be alone, Mary. I want to have a man who knows and understands me, who sees who I am and loves me. I want to look into his eyes and find a kindred soul."

It was Mary's own desire. "I fear you shall find it easier to get the man with ten thousand a year."

Kitty smiled. "Nevertheless, that is what I seek. I don't know how I shall survive without it."

"I hope you find this paragon," Mary said. "You deserve him." She remembered Mr. Clarke touching Kitty's cheek in the hall of wax figures.

"What about you?" Kitty asked. "What did Woodleigh say in his letter? He clearly keeps an interest in you."

"I shall not marry Mr. Woodleigh," Mary said.

"What?" Kitty said in surprise. "Has he asked you?"

"No."

"Women in our position do not have so many opportunities, Mary. I may tease you about his fossils, but I would not have you miss a chance to be happy. Why would you not marry him?"

"Well, for one thing, during the entire time of our visit to Lyme, whenever he was about to pronounce upon something I already knew, he pursed his lips like a fish. Because he makes such pronouncements very often, I would have to accustom myself to seeing that expression. And I do not like that expression."

Kitty laughed out loud. "Mary!"

"Well, he does," Mary said, and laughed too.

Kitty dissolved into giggles, to the point where she struggled to catch her breath. "Yes, he does!" she finally gasped. "When he spoke of the Jacobins at dinner, he looked like the haddock on the plate in front of him!"

They laughed together for a while, until they fell silent. Longbourn and the great oak trees at the end of its drive appeared ahead of them.

"I must get free of here," Kitty said. "At least at Pemberley I have a chance to meet someone who might save me."

"Must you be so dramatic?" Mary saw the carriage in front of the house where their parents had gone inside. John stood beside it, talking with one of the grooms. "Perhaps we don't need saving."

"Poor Mary."

"Don't pity me," Mary said. "I don't wish to be pitied."

"I'm sorry. That was unworthy of either of us. Yet I don't like to think of you here alone with Mother. I shall write you every day."

"Perhaps you should stay and I should go."

Kitty laughed as if nothing could be more absurd. Mary felt it.

"I'm sorry to burden you with my moods," Kitty said. "You have always listened to me with great patience, and been willing to discuss these things for as long as I have wanted— though perhaps you on occasion have bestowed moral instruction a little more than is compatible with lively conversation."

Mary sighed. "At one time it seemed to me that moral instruction *was* lively conversation."

"In that you are not what you once were," said Kitty. "See how we improve with age!"

"If only the male population of Britain were more clear-sighted," Mary said.

They approached their home. Kitty said, "We are a fine pair of spinsters, are we not? Come, take my hand. We shall give my birthday nosegay to Mother, a woman only slightly less foolish than I."

The next day, when Mrs. Bennet and Kitty had gone off in the chaise to Meryton to buy clothes for Kitty, Mary knocked on the door to the library. Her father's voice, tinged with a bit of annoyance, said, "Yes? Who is it?"

"It's Mary."

A pause. "Please come in."

Mary entered. While in the rest of the house the mark of Mrs. Bennet's taste was everywhere evident, the library was Mr. Bennet's domain. He sat in his chair by the hearth, marking his place in the book on his lap with his finger. He gestured toward a chair. "Sit down, my dear."

Mary sat. Her father's character comprised so odd a mixture of quick intelligence, sarcastic humor, and caprice that one never knew what one might get from him. Uncomfortably aware of her own hands, Mary clasped them in her lap.

Though the weather was warm, a fire burned in the grate. Mr. Bennet wore a flannel waistcoat with a knit cap pulled over his head, unkempt white hair sticking out beneath it. He was fastidious about keeping his gold-rimmed spectacles polished, and a carefully folded cloth for that purpose rested beside him on a copy of *The Quarterly Review*. Warm slippers covered his feet. In his library, nothing changed other than the signs of his increasing frailty. He was sixty-one years old.

As a girl Mary had always stood in awe of the library. None of her sisters, with the exception of Lizzy, spent much time reading. True, as girls Lydia and Kitty had found themselves in love with Young Werther, and for a while openly complained that none of the eligible young men in the neighborhood spoke German, but that passion did not inspire in them a desire to read other books. Mary, however, had always loved books, and the collections of sermons that lined one of the shelves were a result of her long study of human morality. She had copied passages out of them and made lists of apothegms that she shared with anyone who might conceivably benefit from her wisdom.

When Mary began to take an interest in natural philosophy, Mr. Bennet encouraged her, although he suggested she read more broadly. They occasionally discussed something she had encountered, though Mr. Bennet's own interests tended more toward Montaigne than Buffon. He warned her of the sad fate of the female bookworm: "Beware, Mary," he said impishly. "Too much learning makes a woman monstrous."

Yet he seemed to like the fact that she made herself available to be teased. Once, absent-mindedly, he had called her "Lizzy." Mary held that moment, sweet and bitter, in her heart for a long time.

"Father, I need to beg a favor," Mary said.

"Oh dear, this sounds serious," he said, with a trace of amusement. "What is it, daughter?"

"I wish to go with Kitty to Pemberley."

"Not Devon? I expected you to beg me to allow you to visit Mr. Woodleigh."

"No. Pemberley."

"Whatever for?"

"I wish to be with her."

"You needn't worry about Kitty; she will be well taken care

of. And if you go, who will occupy your mother?"

She swallowed the anger that rose in her. Yet when she recalled how in conversation with Victor Frankenstein she had put aside what was expected in order to speak what she felt, her tongue was loosened.

"I do not wish to spend all of my days occupying Mother," she said.

Mr. Bennet's eyebrows rose. He began to speak, but checked himself. He placed his book onto the side table. He held up his hand to her, then pushed himself from his chair and crossed to a cupboard, from which he drew a cut glass decanter and two glasses. He set the glasses beside the book and asked her, "Port?"

This had never happened before. "Please," Mary said.

He filled both glasses, handed one to her, then settled into his chair and sipped from his own.

"You are right, Mary. Occupying your mother is a task that should properly fall to me," he said. "A task in which I have failed. Your mother is not an easy person to live with."

The port was warm and sweet on Mary's tongue. "I do not say that."

"I'm sorry that I have left so much of her to you."

"You have lived with her a long time."

Mr. Bennet rested his hands on the arms of his chair and leaned back. His eyes got distant. "Your mother is yet a handsome woman. In the spring of 1777 she was the most beautiful I had ever seen. It was at a dance. She and her sister, your aunt Phillips, were visiting the Ayleworths, cousins of their father. Every squire in the county was smitten. Her laugh, her vivacity, her sense of fun. She was so innocent of the world, and so excited to be out in it. She was seventeen."

Mary had heard this story from her mother, but never her father. She had wondered more than once how two people so contrary in temperament and sensibility had come to be married to each other.

"I suppose she was vain, but it was not a vanity that went very deep. I had been home from Cambridge a year and had not a notion in the world what I would do with my life. When I saw her across the room I said, I am going to spend it making that woman happy."

He took up the glass of port and drained it. "In the event," he said, "my actions have not done justice to my intentions."

Mary would not have thought of asking a question that might be construed as criticism, but the extraordinary circumstances, and the port, led her to venture, "You must have seen her character clearly long before you married."

"Ah, Mary," her father said. "A young man—but why do I say that, the world is full of old fools, too—a man will forget everything in the pursuit of a woman. I've heard you speak of how, once lost, a woman's virtue is irretrievable. A man, too, may lose himself. Even if he break no law or violate no stricture of polite society, he will discard all that he knows, every sensible thing, falling into a kind of delirium, at the wave of a lady's fan, a certain light in her eyes . . . ."

Her father's voice faded. Mary was embarrassed, and yet could not escape the thought that no man had ever seen her in this way—the way that Wickham had seen Lydia, that her father had apparently seen her mother.

Mr. Bennet regained himself. "Eventually the delirium clears. Your mother is in many ways an excellent woman. No one is more aware of what the world expects of her. No woman understands better how lack of property will make one miserable. To our marriage I brought with me Longbourn and its income, which has enabled her to indulge her fancies to a degree that has offered her some satisfaction. It has allowed me to spend my life here in the library rather than the marketplace, to which in truth I was not suited. So we live in our separate rooms. In this one I have had many hours to regret that I married a person whom I could not, finally, respect. I have done some few things to make your mother happy, but I have, in the end, deprived her of my person and my heart."

These were terrible words. Mary was stunned to hear them from her father's lips.

"Aren't those the things that one gives in marriage?" she asked. "What more is there?"

"There should be more. The selection of a mate is perhaps the most important thing a person may do, yet mates are chosen for reasons as trivial, and with as little forethought, as a man may choose a new cravat.

"For a woman marriage serves two purposes. The first is to assure her comfort and security. The second is to propagate the race. But your comfort, Mary, is already assured, even after I am gone and Collins inherits Longbourn. The fact that your brothers by marriage are men of great fortune means you will never want for any material thing. As to the second, I do not know if you seek to have children, but you have never spoken of it."

"I don't."

"Then I do not see why you should marry."

"The things I would seek from marriage are not material."

"Those things that are not material are the hardest to find, and even harder to keep. When I was young, I believed in them. I am not certain that they exist."

"Mother thinks I should marry Charles Woodleigh."

"Has he asked you?"

"No. But with encouragement, I believe that he may."

Mr. Bennet sat silent for a moment. "And you are in some doubt as to whether you shall accept?"

"Do you think that it would be a good match?"

"I have not met the gentleman. Your uncle has written me of him. He seems to have friends of some standing. He would provide you a comfortable home. I gather he does not provide those immaterial gifts you seek. He's a dull man, and a little cold, perhaps?"

"A little."

"Well, consider this," Mr. Bennet said. "No man held warmer affections toward his bride than I did on the day that I married. Yet here I sit in my library while your mother shops, two people as opposite, and separate, as the left and right hand."

"So it doesn't matter if he is cold? If he does not care that much for me now, what will he be like in ten years?"

"His distance does not mean that he does not feel. The dullness—his regard for fossils—" Mr. Bennet caught himself. "But no, for you that is no impediment; it's rather an attraction."

"He is not so dull if one cares about the things he likes."

"Yet you seem not to have convinced yourself that he is the man for you."

Mary could not get past Woodleigh's treatment of Mary

Anning. "He has not asked, so the point is moot."

"I daresay Mr. Woodleigh will not take it as encouragement if you run off to Derbyshire."

"I need to go, Father. I don't know that anything will happen at Pemberley that could not happen here, but I am convinced that nothing will happen here. Will you let me go?"

Mr. Bennet poured himself another glass of port. "Yes," he said. He took a sip.

She came out of her chair and embraced him. "Thank you, Father!"

Mary's embrace almost caused him to spill his wine. He set it on the table. "You may not believe me, my dear, but I will miss you."

So it was that in the third week of May, Mr. and Mrs. Bennet tearfully loaded their last unmarried daughters into a coach for the long drive to Derbyshire. Mrs. Bennet's tears were shed because their absence would deprive Kitty and Mary of her attentions; Mr. Bennet's were shed because their absence would direct Mrs. Bennet's attentions toward him.

SIX

The town clerk of Matlock, a wizened man with a cast in one eye, told me, "We keep a record of property owners, but that is all. For births and deaths you'd be better served to speak with the Reverend Chatsworth at St. Giles Church. He knows more about the comings and goings in the parish than I do."

I decided to invent knowledge I did not have on the chance of drawing him out. "Didn't I hear about a recent decease? An unfortunate case?"

My arrow of speculation found a target. "Ah, you mean Nancy Brown. Dead two days now, drowned in the river not a mile from here."

"How sad," I said. "How old was she?"

"Just twenty," the clerk said. He leaned forward and lowered his voice. "Some say she perished by her own hand. The

Browns call that a vile lie, but I think they fear the Church won't let her be buried in hallowed ground."

"It is understandable that they might seek to hide their shame. Poor girl." I expressed my sympathies for the Browns and left.

In front of the town hall a crew of workmen was breaking up the cobblestone street, swinging pickaxes in the bright sun. Newly wedded couples leaned on one another's arms, whispering secrets. The streets, hotels, and inns of Matlock bustled with travelers there to take the waters. I had told Henry I was going to visit the cabinets of natural curiosities in the Matlock museum and circulating library, while he sought out the old stone bridge over the Derwent to enjoy views of the river.

It had been Henry's idea to visit Matlock. The village was proud of its setting and its long history, going back to Roman times, when it was a center for lead mining. The British seemed to believe that its scenery resembled Switzerland's, though nothing like an alpine mountain existed anywhere in this over-praised island. Henry must have thought Matlock would offer me some consolation after being so far from home for so long. Instead, it recalled the memory of William and Justine and drove me further into gloom—and annoyance at Henry.

I had been looking over my shoulder every day since we had left Oxford, fearing to find the Creature peering back at me from every shadow. Jesus said that he must be about his father's business. I was compelled to do the business of this misbegotten horror, my unnatural son.

Not ready to face Henry again so soon, I stopped in the library and museum. I was directed to a small, poorly lit room that contained several dusty glass-fronted cabinets displaying items unearthed in the mines. As I peered in the gloom at a fossil of a shell, a woman's voice called, "Mr. Frankenstein!"

Startled, I turned to find a rather plain woman, accompanied by a fair-haired boy of ten or eleven. I was taken aback: to an astonishing degree the boy resembled my brother William. And the woman was Mary Bennet.

I regained my composure. "Ah—Miss Bennet?"

She smiled. "Yes. How wonderful to find you here."

I made a slight bow. "It is good to see you as well. And this young man is . . . ?"

"This is my nephew William."

Nonplussed, for a moment I was unable to reply.

"Are you not well?" Miss Bennet asked.

"Forgive me. My brother was named William."

Miss Bennet's face paled. "I am sorry to bring up painful associations," she said.

In the awkward silence that followed, the boy asked if he might climb to the second floor to look down on the town square. "You may," she said. "But don't leave the building."

The boy ran off. Mary turned to examine the contents of the neighboring cabinet, leaving me to collect myself. I was grateful for her tact: although she had not mentioned my disappearance from the ball in London, I was acutely aware of it. She forbore no doubt in compassion for my dead brother. I might have bid her good day and left, but the wary quality of her sympathy—a certain awkward watchfulness, unlike the assumption that Henry and my family made that they understood what I felt, when they understood nothing—made me wonder what she actually thought. She was essentially a stranger.

My desire to avoid Henry as long as possible might also have had something to do with it.

I leaned over the case beside her. Beneath the glass was a stone plate, unearthed from a local mine, on which the skeleton of a fish stood in relief. The lettered card beside it read: BONES, RESEMBLING THOSE OF A PIKE, MADE OF LIMESTONE.

"I believe that it is I who should apologize," I said, not facing her. "I still owe you a dance."

She turned to me, and I lifted my head to meet her gaze. "I believe that you no more intended to hurt me than I to hurt you by mentioning the name of your brother." Her eyes were steady.

"You are very kind," I said. "Then we shall proceed as friends. How is it that you come to Matlock?"

"My sister Elizabeth is married to Mr. Fitzwilliam Darcy of Pemberley House. Kitty and I are visiting. Have you come to take the waters?"

"Clerval and I are on our way to Scotland. We stop here a week."

Mary watched me, the same guarded expression on her face. She gestured at the cabinet. "I take an interest in fossils."

"I suppose, given what you told me of your study of natural philosophy, I should not be surprised."

"It is an enthusiasm of mine," she said, her voice relaxing, "to fill the idle hours. Dr. Darwin has written of the source of such:

"Organic life beneath the shoreless waves
Was born and nurs'd in ocean's pearly caves;
First forms minute, unseen by spheric glass,

Move on the mud, or pierce the watery mass;
These, as successive generations bloom,
New powers acquire and larger limbs assume;
Whence countless groups of vegetation
    spring,
And breathing realms of fin and feet and
    wing."

Despite all that weighed upon me, I found this display charming. Her artlessness when she thought she was being artful was droll.

"Bravo, Miss Bennet," I said. "You declaim with authority. But I was recently informed, by an eminent man of science, that Darwin's work is moonshine."

"The moon shines on many things. Some say that finding the exuviae of such aquatic creatures hundreds of miles from the sea, in the midst of mountains, offers proof of the Great Flood—but the French naturalist Lamarck says it only proves the earth is immensely older than the five thousand years that Archbishop Ussher calculated. The faithful say the fact that none of these creatures exist any longer is further proof that God must have swept them away. Lamarck and Darwin argue their disappearance proves that they have changed into more modern forms. Which of these theories is moonshine?"

"I will take my stand with Monsieur Lamarck. The process that transforms bones to limestone must take eons. Anatomically, this creature here is more lizard than fish."

"You have studied anatomy?" Miss Bennet asked.

I tapped my fingers upon the glass. "Three years ago it was

one of my passions. I no longer pursue such matters."

"And yet you still meet with men of science."

"Only about moonshine. I am surprised that you remember our brief conversation, from more than two months ago."

"I have a good memory."

"As evidenced by your reciting Dr. Darwin by heart. Is science all you study?"

"Oh, you may rest assured that I have read my share of novels, Mr. Frankenstein. And even more, in my youth, of sermons. Kitty calls me a superior moralizer. 'Evil is easy,' I tell her, 'and has infinite forms.'"

Was this dart aimed at me? "Would that science had no need of moralizers."

"We spoke of this before. There is no evil in studying God's handiwork."

"A God-fearing Christian might take exception to Darwin's assertion that life arose spontaneously, no matter how poetically stated. Can a living soul be created without the hand of God?"

"The hand of God is everywhere present." Mary gestured toward the cabinet. "Even in the bones of this stony fish."

"You are a woman of faith."

Mary blushed. "I had faith that we might meet again—and see, it has come to pass. You may yet have the chance to grant me that promised dance."

We were interrupted by the entrance of Henry, accompanied by Miss Bennet's sister and another woman. "There you are!" said the younger Miss Bennet. "You see, Mr. Clerval, I told you we would find Mary poring over these heaps of bones!"

"And it is no surprise to find my friend here as well," said Clerval. He renewed his acquaintance with Mary Bennet, and she introduced the other woman as Mrs. Georgiana Golding, younger sister of Elizabeth's husband, Darcy.

Henry said, "I encountered Miss Catherine at the beginning of the riverside walk, quite scandalously unaccompanied."

"I was taking respite beneath the trees from this heat," said Kitty, fanning herself.

"So I served as her chaperone on the way back to the milliner's, where she introduced me to Mrs. Golding." Henry was at his most cheerful. "I propose that we assay the Lovers' Walk along the riverside to Matlock Bath. I am told we shall see some excellent prospects of the river, the High Tor, and the Heights of Abraham. These ladies can tell us of the history of the town."

Young William returned, and our party crossed the road and went down to the Derwent. The way was flat along the riverbank, but as we proceeded, the waters became swifter. The walls of the valley narrowed, and vast ramparts of limestone, clothed with yew trees, elms, and limes, rose up on either side. William ran ahead, and Kitty, Georgiana, and Clerval followed, leaving Miss Bennet and me behind.

Eventually we came in sight of the High Tor, a sheer cliff rearing its brow on the east bank of the Derwent. The lower part was covered with small trees and foliage. Massive boulders fallen from the cliff broke the riverbed below into foaming rapids. The noise of the waters left us, some yards behind the others, in the shade of an ancient oak, as isolated as if we had been in a separate room. I might have preferred to be about my business, but I could not deny the loveliness of the scenery, and the relief of Miss Bennet's company, and the provocation of her conversation.

"This does remind me of my home," I said. "Henry and I would climb such cliffs as these, chase goats around the meadows, and play at pirates. Father would walk me through the woods and name every tree and flower. I once saw a lightning bolt shiver an old oak, larger than this one, entirely to splinters."

"Whenever I come here," Mary said, "I realize how small I am, and how great time is. These rocks, this river, will long survive us. We are here for a breath, and then we are gone. And through it all we are alone."

Every time I thought I understood her to be simply an aging spinster, her reasoned frankness surprised me. "Surely you are not so lonely. You have your family, your sisters. Your mother and father."

"One may be alone in a crowded room. Kitty teases me for my 'heaps of bones.'"

She said this not with bitterness, but as objectively as one might observe some natural phenomenon.

"You might marry," I said.

She laughed merrily. "Come now! I am thirty-two years old, sir. I am no man's vision of a lover or wife."

I took some time before answering. The sound of the waters surrounded us. Ahead, Georgiana, William, and Clerval played in the grass by the riverbank, while Kitty Bennet stood pensive some distance away.

"Miss Bennet, I am sorry if I have made light of your situation. But your fine qualities should be apparent to anyone who took the trouble truly to make your acquaintance."

"You needn't flatter me," said Mary. "I am unused to it."

"I only speak my mind."

William came running up. "Aunt Mary! This would be an excellent place to fish! We should come here with Father!"

"We shall have to speak with him about that, Will. It's a long way from home, in a public place."

Henry and the two other women returned from the riverbank. He said, "I propose now that we adjourn to the coffee shop I spied next to the milliner's, to enjoy some strawberries and cream before you have to set off back to your home."

But Kitty Bennet objected to this. "I have a headache," she said to Mary. "I'm afraid I would not be very diverting company," she told Henry.

"Alas!" said Henry. "I'm heartbroken."

"I must return to the hotel, Henry," I said. "I need to see that new glassware properly packed before shipping it ahead. You needn't come."

"But at least we should escort these ladies to their carriage."

"Glassware?" Georgiana asked.

Henry chuckled. "Victor has been purchasing equipment at every stop along our tour—glassware, bottles of chemicals, lead and copper disks. The coachmen threaten to leave us behind if he does not ship these things separately."

Mary gave me a speculative look.

We did not exchange another word as our party walked back to the Crown Square. At the inn, a carriage and footman awaited the Bennets, Mrs. Golding, and William.

"Thank you for your company," Mary said. "It has made for a most pleasant afternoon."

"I hope we meet again, Miss Bennet," I said.

We helped them into the carriage, the footman shut the

door, and they rode away down the cobbled street. Mary's face was visible watching us, and then she settled back beside her sister.

It was quite warm on the pavements outside the inn. "I still desire some strawberries and cream," Henry told me.

"You may content yourself," I said. "But I must pack that equipment."

Henry gave me a sad smile and left for the coffee shop. As soon as he had departed, I set off to discover what more I could about the unfortunate, recently departed, very young Nancy Brown, including where she was buried.

SEVEN

During the hour's ride back to Pemberley, William prattled with Georgiana; Kitty, subdued, leaned back with her eyes closed; while Mary turned each word of her conversation with Victor Frankenstein in her hands so that she might view it in every light, and painted his every expression in her mind's eye.

Her own behavior in reaction to him was as much a source of wonder to her as the accident that had brought them together again. She did not banter this way with gentlemen. What had come over her, to speak to a man of her spinsterhood?

Reason told her that it mattered little what she said. There was no point in letting some hope of sympathy delude her into greater hopes. They had danced a single dance in London, and now they had spent an afternoon together in Matlock; soon Frankenstein would return to Switzerland and Mary would be left with her "heaps of bones."

Yet she could not leave it at that. Fate had brought them together again. Mary felt an affinity unlike any she had ever experienced. He was not an amiable man, or rather, he was passing through a time of his life that did not evoke the amiability of his nature. She could not doubt that his story of his brother's death was true—the way Victor had blanched at the sight of William Darcy had borne that out—but it seemed to her that beneath that true story lay some deeper trouble.

At supper that evening, Georgiana told Darcy and Elizabeth about their encounter with the handsome Swiss tourists. Mary was closemouthed about them at the table, but afterward, in the drawing room, she took Lizzy aside and asked her to invite Clerval and Frankenstein to dinner.

"This is new!" said Lizzy. "I expect as much from Kitty, but you have never before asked to have anyone come to Pemberley."

"I have never met someone quite like Mr. Frankenstein," Mary replied.

Elizabeth's place in the family relative to Mary's—and her other sisters'—was evident to all. She was the stable center of their emotional whirlwinds. Their father's favorite, she had his quick wit and sardonic view of society, but she also possessed a heart that could be moved. Unlike Kitty and Lydia, Lizzy had never been unkind to Mary, but at some point Mary had realized that Lizzy spent their time together stifling her annoyance at Mary's hopeless pomposity, her inability to get beyond her copybook morality, and her vanity at thinking herself wise.

Mary envied Lizzy's adroitness. Lizzy could say unexpected things and, though she might offend some people, always came out all right, whereas Mary, saying things in no way offensive,

drew sidelong glances. Lizzy had despised Darcy and then she
had married him, and yet no one in the family thought her a
poor judge of character. Mary had admired Mr. Collins and
then come to despise him, yet she got no credit for an increase
of sense.

Lizzy said, "I had heard about your meeting a Mr. Woodleigh in Lyme Regis, but who is this Monsieur Frankenstein?
How did you come to know him?"

"Mr. Frankenstein and I met at Lord Henry's ball in
Cavendish Square, before Kitty took ill and we had to return
to Longbourn. He is involved in some scientific researches,
though he and Mr. Clerval come here seeking recreation."

"Well, perhaps we may recreate them here. From Georgiana's description, I understand Mr. Clerval to be a charming
man. She said little about Frankenstein."

"Mr. Frankenstein is struggling with the aftermath of the
death of his brother William. When I introduced him to your
William, who it seems resembles Frankenstein's brother, he
went very pale."

"We shall do our best to put him at ease." Elizabeth took
a glance around the room, and seeing that they were alone in
this corner, said, "Mary, I am very grateful that you came to
Pemberley with Kitty. I must apologize for not inviting you
to visit more often. I have wanted to speak with you for some
time about a number of things that have weighed on my mind."

"What sort of things?"

"I must tell you how I regret the distance between us. I
blame myself for it. I have been quite happy to let you take care
of Mother while I went about my own life. In the beginning
you seemed to enjoy having her attention, and that was enough

for me to put the matter out of my mind. I never tried to help or understand you. I neglected to notice that you are not the person that you once were."

"I believe I am that same person."

"Your asking us to invite these gentlemen is a sign of how you have changed."

"The circumstances have changed. As I say, I have never met a person like Mr. Frankenstein. He listens to me. And I find that, when I speak to him, I have things to say that are worth hearing."

"I am glad of that," Lizzy said. She paused. She laid her hand upon Mary's forearm and leaned closer.

"This will perhaps sound strange coming from me, when it is clear to me that you have spent the better part of the last ten years protecting yourself, but I hope you will guard your heart. I remember that day at Netherfield. I believe you were completely unprotected that afternoon, and you have paid a price for that. I would not like to see you at risk for heartbreak. Something I never thought I would ever have to worry about—for which neglect I am sorry."

Lizzy looked her in the eyes, assessing. Mary discovered to her astonishment that, whatever Lizzy decided about her, she was not afraid of Lizzy's judgment.

They spoke for another ten minutes, the longest conversation they had enjoyed in five years. Lizzy had already planned a formal dinner to celebrate the coming visit of Jane and Bingley, who would arrive in a day for a fortnight's stay. At Mary's bidding she invited Frankenstein and Clerval to come for a period of days, and the Swiss gentlemen replied by return post that they would be happy to visit.

"Have you taken the Matlock waters?" Mary asked Clerval, seated opposite her at the dinner table. "People in the parish swear that they can raise the dead."

"I confess that I have not," Clerval said. "Victor does not credit their healing powers."

Mary turned to Frankenstein, hoping to draw him into discussion of the matter, but the startled expression on his face silenced her.

The table, covered with a white damask tablecloth, glittered with silver and crystal. A large epergne studded with candles dominated its center. In addition to the family members, and in order to even the number of guests and balance female with male, Darcy and Elizabeth had invited the vicar Mr. Chatsworth. Completing the dinner party were Bingley and Jane, Georgiana, and Kitty.

The footmen brought soup, followed by claret, turbot with lobster and Dutch sauce, oyster pâté, lamb cutlets with asparagus, peas, a *fricandeau à l'oseille*, venison, stewed beef *à la jardinière*, with various salads, beetroot, French and English mustard. Two ices, cherry water and pineapple cream, and a chocolate cream with strawberries. Champagne flowed throughout the dinner, and Madeira afterward.

Darcy asked how Mr. Clerval had come to be acquainted with Mr. Gardiner, of whom Darcy spoke with great fondness, and Clerval described his meetings with men of business in London and his interest in India. For their entertainment he spoke a few sentences in Hindi. Bingley told of his visit to Geneva when he was a child. Clerval spoke charmingly of the differences in manners between the Swiss and the English, with witty preference for English habits, except, he said, in the matter of boiled meats. The vicar spoke amusingly of his travels in Italy. Georgiana asked about women's dress in that country. Elizabeth allowed as how, if the threat of Napoléon Bonaparte could finally be settled, it would be good for William's education to tour the Continent. Kitty, who usually entertained the table with bright talk and jokes, was unaccustomedly quiet.

Through all of this, Frankenstein offered little in the way of comment. Mary had put such hopes on this dinner, and now she feared she had misread him. His voice warmed but once, when he spoke of his father, a counselor and syndic, renowned for his integrity. Only on inquiry would he speak of his years in Ingolstadt.

"And what did you study in the university?" Bingley asked.

"Matters of no interest," Frankenstein replied.

An uncomfortable silence followed. Clerval gently explained, "My friend devoted himself so single-mindedly to the study of natural philosophy that his health failed. I was fortunately able to bring him back to us, but it was a near thing."

"For which I will ever be grateful to you," Frankenstein mumbled.

Lizzy attempted to change the subject. "Mr. Chatsworth, what news is there of the parish?"

The vicar, unaccustomed to such volume and variety of drink, was in his cups, his face flushed and his voice rising to pulpit volume. "Well, I hope the ladies will not take it amiss," he said, "if I tell about a curious incident that occurred two nights ago."

"Pray do," said Darcy.

"So, then—that night I was troubled with sleeplessness—I think it was the trout I ate for supper, it was not right—Mrs. Croft vowed she had purchased it just that afternoon, but I wonder if perhaps it might have been from the previous day's catch. Be that as it may, lying awake some time after midnight, I heard a sound out my bedroom window—the weather has been so fine of late that I sleep with my window open. It is my opinion, Mr. Clerval, that nothing contributes to the health of the lungs more than fresh air, and I believe that is the opinion of the best continental thinkers, is it not? The air is exceedingly fresh in the alpine meadows, I am told?"

"Only in those meadows where the cows have not been feeding."

"The cows? Oh, yes, the cows—ha, ha!—very good! The cows, indeed! . . . So, where was I? Ah, yes. I rose from my bed and looked out the window, and what did I spy but a glimmer of light in the churchyard. I heard low voices in the distance, but was unable to make out what they said. I threw on my robe and slippers, took my good old walking staff from behind the door, and hurried out to see what might be the matter. I crept up, very quiet.

"As I approached the churchyard I saw the figures of two men, one of them—a great brute he was—wielding a spade. His back was to me, silhouetted by a lamp that rested beside Nancy Brown's grave. Poor Nancy, dead not a week now, so young, only twenty."

"Men?" said Kitty.

The vicar's round face grew serious. "You may imagine my shock. 'Halloo!' I shouted. At that the fellow threw down his spade, leapt out of the grave, and rushed toward me. I raised my staff. He was an immense man, yet he moved as quick as a panther.

"'No!' the other shouted. 'Let him be!' The brute, who I have no doubt meant to annihilate me, stopped dead in his tracks. He then turned, took two steps, and vaulted over the graveyard wall in a single leap. The other had seized the lantern and dashed round the back of the church. By the time I reached the corner he was out of sight. Back at the grave I saw that they had been on a fair way to unearthing poor Nancy's coffin."

"My goodness!" said Jane.

"Defiling a grave?" asked Bingley. "I am astonished."

Darcy said nothing, but his look demonstrated that he was not pleased by the vicar bringing such an uncouth matter to his dinner table. Frankenstein, next to Mary, put down his knife and took a long draught of Madeira.

The vicar lowered his voice, clearly enjoying himself. "I can only speculate on their motives. Might one of these men have been some lover of hers, overcome with grief?"

"Men don't weep over the graves of the women they have dishonored," Kitty said, "else every graveyard would be full of weeping men. That only happens in novels."

Darcy leaned back in his chair. "Gypsies have been seen in the woods about the quarry. They were no doubt seeking jewelry."

"Jewelry?" the vicar said. "The Browns had barely enough money to see her decently buried."

"Which proves that these were not local men."

Clerval spoke. "At home, fresh graves are sometimes defiled by men providing cadavers for doctors. Was there not a spate of such grave robbings in Ingolstadt, Victor?"

Frankenstein put down his glass. "Yes," he said. "Some anatomists, in seeking knowledge, abandon all human scruple."

"That is unlikely to be the cause in this instance," Darcy observed. "Here there is no university, no medical school. Dr. Montgomery in Lambton is no transgressor of civilized rules."

"He is scarcely a transgressor of his own threshold," said Lizzy. "One must call him a day in advance to get him to leave his parlor."

"Rest assured, there are such men," said Frankenstein. "I have known them. My illness, which Henry described to you, was my spirit's rebellion against the understanding that the pursuit of knowledge will lead some men into mortal peril."

Here was Mary's chance to speak of something she knew. "Surely there is a nobility in risking one's life to advance the claims of one's race. With how many things are we upon the brink of becoming acquainted, if cowardice or carelessness did not restrain our inquiries?"

"Thank God for cowardice, Miss Bennet," Frankenstein said. "One's life, perhaps, is worth risking, but not one's soul."

"True enough. But I believe that science may demand our relaxing the strictures of society."

"We have never heard this tone from you, Mary," Jane said.

Darcy said, "You are becoming quite modern, sister. What strictures are you prepared to abandon for us tonight?" His voice was full of the gentle condescension with which he treated Mary at all times.

How she wished to surprise them! How she longed to show Darcy and Lizzy, and Bingley and Jane, that she was not the simple old maid they thought her. "Anatomists in London have obtained the court's permission to dissect the bodies of criminals after execution. Is it unjust to use the body of a murderer, who has already forfeited his life, to save the lives of the innocent?"

"My uncle, who is on the bench, has overseen several such cases," Bingley said.

"Indeed," Mary said. "Some years ago at the Royal College of Surgeons, the Italian scientist Aldini used a powerful battery to animate portions of the body of a hanged man. According to the *Times*, the body's eyes opened, its hands clenched, and it moved its limbs. The spectators genuinely believed that it was about to come to life."

"Mary, please," said Lizzy.

"That's like something out of Mrs. Radcliffe's novels," Kitty said. "Life is hard enough without inventing new things to frighten us."

Their skepticism only made Mary more determined to force Frankenstein to take her part. "What do you say, sir? Will you come to my defense?"

Frankenstein folded his napkin and set it beside his plate. "Such attempts are not motivated by bravery, or even curiosity, but by ambition. The pursuit of knowledge can become a vice as deadly as any of the more common sins—worse still, because even the most noble of natures are susceptible to such temptations. None but he who has experienced them can conceive of the enticements of science."

The vicar nodded. "If I understand you aright, sir, you have spoken truth. The men who defiled poor Nancy's grave have placed themselves beyond the mercy of a forgiving God."

Mary felt charged with contradictory emotions. "You have experienced such enticements, Mr. Frankenstein?"

"Sadly, I have."

"But surely there is no sin that is beyond the reach of God's mercy? 'To know all is to forgive all.'"

The vicar turned to her. "My child, what know you of sin?"

"Very little, Reverend Chatsworth, except the sin of idleness. Yet I feel that even a wicked person may have the veil lifted from his eyes."

Frankenstein looked at her. "Here I must agree with Miss Bennet. I have to believe that even the most corrupted nature is susceptible to grace. If I did not think this were possible, I could not live."

"Enough of this," insisted Darcy. "Vicar, I suggest you mind your parishioners, including those in the churchyard, more carefully. But now I, for one, am eager to hear Georgiana play the pianoforte. And perhaps Mary and Catherine will join her. We must uphold the accomplishments of English maidenhood before our foreign guests."

The next morning, on Kitty's insistence, despite lowering clouds and a chill in the air that spoke more of March than June, she and Mary took a walk.

They walked north along the river toward the woods. Darcy's estate had one of the largest stands of forest in Derbyshire, a source of game that drew many well-born gentlemen for the hunting season, and numerous poachers the year round. Lizzy loved to walk in these woods, so Darcy's groundskeepers kept the paths through them free of underbrush and cleared the prospects of the river and valley that they opened upon.

If Kitty had something to tell Mary, she did not seem eager to say it; they walked in silence until they were well into the forest. Mary's thoughts turned to the wholly unsatisfying party of the previous night. The conversation in the parlor had gone no better than dinner. Mary had played the piano ill, showing herself to poor advantage next to Georgiana. Under Lizzy's gaze she felt the folly of her intemperate talk at the table. Frankenstein said next to nothing to her for the rest of the evening; he almost seemed wary of being in her presence.

She was wondering how he was spending this morning when, suddenly turning her face aside, Kitty burst into tears.

Mary touched her arm. "Whatever is the matter, Kitty?"

Without facing Mary, Kitty said, "Something you said last night kept me awake all night."

"What did I say?"

"That there is no sin beyond the reach of God's mercy. Do you believe it?"

"Of course I do. Why would you ask?"

"Because I have committed such a sin."

Mary thrust her own concerns aside and took Kitty's hand. After some coaxing, her sister unburdened herself. The previous summer, Kitty had renewed her acquaintance with Jonathan Clarke. On their recent rendezvous in London they had plotted to be together. In May, about the time that Kitty and Mary left Longbourn for Pemberley, Clarke, on the pretext of troubles in his business, had left his wife and children in London and returned to Matlock. Soon after Kitty and Mary's arrival, Kitty had begun meeting with him when she went into town on the pretext of shopping.

Though his butcher's shop supplied most of the tables of

Matlock with beef, lamb, and pork, and though he spent a month every season in London, Clarke was in no way a gentleman, and Kitty had vowed never to let her affections overwhelm her sense. But after no more than a week the couple had allowed their passion to get the better of them, and Kitty had given way to carnal love.

The two sisters sat on a fallen tree as Kitty poured out her tale.

"Lydia—Lydia told me about—about the act of love, how good Wickham makes her feel. She boasted of it! And I said, why should Lydia have this, and I waste my youth in conversation and embroidery, in listening to Mother's prattle and Father's mockery. Father thinks me a fool, unlikely ever to find a husband. And now he's right!" Kitty began to cry. "He's right. No man shall ever have me." Her tears ended in a fit of coughing.

"Oh, Kitty," Mary said.

"When Darcy spoke of English maidenhood last night, my heart stopped. I was a fool not to marry Jonathan when I had the chance." Her tears flowed readily. "I don't want to die an old maid!"

"No marriage awaits you at the end of this," Mary said. "You must end this affair."

Kitty buried her face in her hands, sobbing. Mary put her arm around her sister's shoulders. Kitty eventually caught her breath and continued.

"The other day, Jonathan asked me to meet him in Matlock. While you went off with William, I met him on the Lovers' Walk. When I tried to embrace him, he pushed me away. He told me he did not wish ever to see me again. He said he had tried my virtue, and found it lacking.

"I begged him not to forsake me. I threatened to tell his wife. He said he would deny everything. He warned me that if any reputation was ruined by my speaking, it would be my own."

A breeze had picked up, and thunder sounded in the distance. "He is not worth your tears," Mary said.

"He only speaks the truth. He is better than I. He told me how much pain my rejection caused him those years ago. There is no love between him and his wife, but he cares deeply for his children. Yet I threw myself at him. It is all my fault."

Mary held her sister. Kitty alternated between sobs and fits of coughing. Above them the thunder rumbled, and there came the sound of raindrops hitting the leaves. She felt Kitty's shivering body. She needed to calm her, to get her back to the house. How slender, how frail she was.

Once Mary might have condemned her, offering at best a dismissive pity. But Kitty's fear of dying alone was her own fear. As she searched for something to say, Mary heard the sound of a torrent of rain hitting the canopy of foliage.

"You have been foolish," Mary said, still embracing her. "He is a villain, but you must never speak of it."

Kitty trembled and spoke into Mary's shoulder. "Will you ever care for me again? If Father discovers, will he turn me out? What will I do then?"

The rain was falling through now. Mary felt her hair getting wet. "Calm yourself. Father loves you. I shall never forsake you. Jane would not, nor Lizzy. And no one need know of your indiscretion. Certainly Mr. Clarke will not speak of it."

"What if I should have a child!"

Mary pulled Kitty's shawl over her head. She looked past Kitty's shoulder to the dark woods. Something moved there. "You shan't have a child."

"You can't know! I may!"

The woods had become dark. Mary could not make out what lurked among the trees. "Come, let us go back. You must compose yourself. If it becomes necessary, we shall talk with Lizzy and Jane. They will know—"

A flash of lightning lit the forest, and Mary saw, beneath the trees not ten feet from them, the giant figure of a man. The lightning illuminated a face like a grotesque mask: long, thick, tangled black hair. Pale skin, milky, dead eyes beneath heavy brows. Worst of all, an expression hideous in its cold, inexpressible hunger. It was all the matter of a split second; then the light fell to shadow.

At first Mary thought it some scarecrow or grotesque pantomime doll, but it had moved. She gasped, and pulled Kitty toward her. A great peal of thunder rolled across the sky.

Kitty stopped crying. "What is it?"

"We must go. Now." Mary seized Kitty's arm. The rain pelted down on them, and the forest path was already turning to mud.

Mary pulled her toward the house, Kitty complaining. She could hear nothing over the drumming of the rain, but when she looked over her shoulder, she caught a glimpse of the inhuman figure, keeping to the trees, but swiftly, silently moving along behind them.

"Why must we run?" Kitty gasped.

"Because we are being followed!"

"By whom?"

"I don't know!"

Behind them, Mary thought she heard the man croak out some words: "*Arrêtez!* Stop!"

They had not reached the edge of the woods when figures appeared ahead, coming from Pemberley. "Miss Bennet! Mary! Kitty!"

The figures resolved themselves into Darcy and Mr. Frankenstein. Darcy carried a cloak, which he threw over them.

"Are you all right?" Frankenstein asked.

"Thank God!" Mary gasped. "A man. He's there"—she pointed—"following us."

Frankenstein took a few steps beyond them down the path. "Who was it?" Darcy asked.

"Some brute. Hideously ugly," Mary said.

Frankenstein came back. "No one is there."

"We saw him!"

Another lighting flash, and a crack of thunder. "It is dark, and we are in a storm," Frankenstein said.

"Come, we must get you back to the house," Darcy said. "You are wet to the bone."

The men helped them back to Pemberley, trying their best to keep the rain off the sisters.

Darcy went to find Bingley and Clerval, who had taken the opposite direction in their search. Lizzy saw that Mary and Kitty were made dry and warm. Kitty was unsteady on her feet, and her cough worsened; Lizzy insisted she must be put to bed. Mary sat with Kitty, whispered a promise to keep her secret, and waited until she slept. Then she went down to meet the others in the parlor.

"This chill shall do her no good," Jane said. She chided Mary for wandering off in such threatening weather. "I thought you had more sense, Mary. Mr. Frankenstein insisted he help to find you, when he realized you had gone out into the woods."

"I am sorry," Mary said. "You are right." She was distracted by Kitty's plight, wondering what she might do. If Kitty were indeed with child, there would be no helping her.

Mary recounted her story of the man in the woods. Darcy said he had seen no one, but allowed that some person might have been there. Frankenstein, rather than engage in the speculation, stood at the tall windows, staring toward the tree line through the rain.

"This intruder was some local come to snare game, or perhaps one of those Gypsies," said Darcy. "When the rain ends, I shall have Mr. Mowbray take some men to check the grounds. We shall also inform the constable in Lambton."

"I hope this foul weather will induce you to stay with us a few more days, Mr. Frankenstein," Lizzy ventured. "You have no pressing business in Matlock, do you?"

"No. But we were to travel north at the end of this week."

"Surely we might stay a while longer, Victor," said Clerval. "Your research can wait for you."

Frankenstein struggled with his answer. "I don't think we should prevail on these good people any longer."

"Nonsense," said Darcy. "We are fortunate for your company."

"Thank you," Frankenstein said uncertainly. But when the conversation moved elsewhere, Mary noticed him once again staring out the window. She moved to sit beside him. On an impulse, she said to him, sotto voce, "Did you know that man I saw in the woods?"

"I saw no one. Even if some person were there, how should I know some English vagabond?"

"I do not think he was English. When he first called after us, it was in French. Was this one of your countrymen?"

A look of impatience crossed Frankenstein's face, and he lowered his eyes. "Miss Bennet, I do not wish to contradict you, but you are mistaken. I saw no one in the woods."

EIGHT

I followed him to Oxford. I watched him take his meals in inns, tour the town with Clerval, wander along the banks of the river. Had he not occasionally purchased scientific equipment, I would have confronted him again.

I followed him to Matlock. The weather improved, and I was glad to be in the countryside, to hear songbirds and breathe fresh air, to drink pure water from the streams and feel the warmth of the spring sun. It was not easy to spy on him without being seen. In the towns I lurked in alleys and stables and climbed to the roofs of buildings.

It was there, peering down into the coach yard from the roof of the inn, that I saw him return that sunny afternoon with Henry, three women, and a boy. When first I saw the fair-haired boy, it thrust the memory of William Frankenstein before me. I pushed it down, buried it in some crypt at the back of my mind, hoping it would stay dead, knowing it would not. Two of the women—I could not be certain, as it had been the middle of the night, at a distance—two of the women I thought were among those I had seen leaving the ball in London.

Despite the noise of the street and the yard, my keen ears picked up their conversation. So I confirmed that he had been buying equipment that he meant to ship to Scotland. And that the name of one of the women was "Miss Bennet."

After the women left, Henry and Victor parted company and Victor moved off into the town.

I saw no point in spying upon his movements through the day: he would be back at the inn by evening, and at night I was better able to move in public. At night I might enter a tavern, sit in some gloomy corner, and buy a pint of ale. So, through the decline of the day, I found a spot on the back of the peaked roof, in the shadow of a chimney, and slept.

Nothing happened that night, but the next, well after midnight when the town was asleep, I saw Victor creep from the inn, moving with care that he not make a sound. He carried a shuttered lantern. Down the moonlit street I followed him.

Some distance from the inn stood a picturesque church on a hill, amid old oaks and elms, overlooking the river. The windows of the vicar's house were dark. A stone wall surrounded a graveyard; Victor slid past the iron gate in the wall. Silently I climbed the wall and from its top watched as he broke into the sexton's shed. A gleam from the doorway told me he had unshuttered his lamp. He emerged a moment later carrying a spade.

He prowled through the graveyard, the light from his lantern narrowed down to a beam, until he found a fresh grave with a simple wooden cross at its head. He set the lantern on the ground nearby and began to dig.

I hopped lightly from the wall and crept up on him. "Victor," I whispered.

To my great satisfaction he jumped a foot. He swung round, the spade clutched in his hands.

"Have a care, Victor! You'll wake the vicar."

He rested the blade on the ground. "How long have you been spying on me?"

"A very long time. I have kept myself invisible, in order to allow you to work with a calm mind."

"A calm mind! Better that I should never see you again."

"I am pleased that at last you act on my behalf. I had thought you might spend all your time with this woman you seem to have taken up with. Twice now have I spied you with her. Whose purposes does she serve?"

"That is none of your business."

"On the contrary, all that affects you affects me. I am here to help. Who is Miss Bennet?"

He stiffened. "How do you know her name?"

"That is none of your business."

"You shall not harm her. She is nothing to you."

"About that you are right. The question is, what is she to you? Does your Elizabeth know about her?"

He winced, as if I had laid a hot iron across his forearm. "God damn you," he said.

"God has already damned me," I said. "But we have no time to banter. We need to dig up . . . your materials. Give me the spade. I wonder how you expected to carry her out of this grave-yard, let alone through the town, when you can hardly carry yourself. Do you suffer from some nervous disorder, Victor?"

"I don't need your help."

"Yet I offer it. No one cares more for you than I. Do not forget that I am the reason you do this."

He laughed bitterly. "I cannot forget that."

I took the spade. "Hold the lantern high. She may not be buried in a coffin, and I would not wish to damage her."

He held the lantern while I set to work. The earth was loose, and the dirt flew. I enjoyed the working of my excellent body. I began to feel almost giddy with the thought that soon, very soon now, I would no longer be alone.

I was near to reaching the body, and had slowed down to take more care, when a voice called out, "Halloo! Who is there?"

Frankenstein ducked, raising his arm to cover his face. A big-bellied man in slippers and a robe stood there, hair wild from the pillow, brandishing a gnarled walking stick. I threw down the spade and rushed him, meaning to knock him insensible before he might wake the whole parish.

"No!" Victor cried. "Let him be!"

I stopped. The old man's face was rigid with fear, and the thought of striking him sickened me. I turned and ran for the churchyard wall, taking it in a single leap. I loped through the town, cursing myself for a coward. I had thrown away our chance.

By the inn I waited in an alley, hoping Victor had managed not to be apprehended. Finally he came down the street, walking rapidly, stiff-legged, the extinguished lantern clutched in his hand. I stepped out in front of him and he almost ran into me.

"Fool!" I said. "You'll never retrieve that body now. You should have let me silence him."

"I'll not have another death on my conscience."

"You'll have more than the death of some vicar on your conscience if you fail to keep your vow."

"Begone!" he hissed, and shouldered past me toward the inn.

It would not do for me to remain here this night, should the vicar alert the constables. I snuck out of town and made my bed in the woods near the river. I lay awake listening to the trickle of the waters, telling myself that Victor was wrong, that in silencing the old man I need not have killed him. It was some time before I was able to sleep.

An hour before sunrise, after slaking my thirst and eating some mushrooms I found, I crept back into the town and took up my watch. Our lost opportunity weighed on my mind. I considered trying to steal the body again, but I knew nothing of what Victor needed to complete his task and so could not act without him.

Two days later I watched as a chaise driven by liveried servants, the same carriage that had taken the women away, arrived at the inn, and Victor and Henry left in it. Each carried a single portmanteau, so I knew they were not leaving Derbyshire. They must be going to spend a short period of time at some estate. I did not know what Victor was about, but I suspected it had something to do with his connection to these women, this boy who looked so like his dead brother, and their family. Miss Bennet.

As quickly as I could without being seen, I escaped Matlock and followed the road the carriage had gone down. It hugged the course of the Derwent upstream, twisting through the woodlands. Once in the countryside, I began to run.

Frankenstein had given me an excellent body. I let myself go, stretching my legs, swinging my arms, head up, hair flying, breathing deeply and regularly. The blood thrummed in my ears. I raced along, each footfall lightly and precisely finding the exact, even place in the rutted road, and felt something akin to joy. When any traveler approached in the distance, I broke off into the woods, hardly slowing my pace.

It was not very long before I spied the chaise ahead of me. I swung off the road and kept pace with it, at a distance.

The chaise turned off the river road down a second, private road onto what I later learned was the estate of Mr. Fitzwilliam Darcy. It snaked up and down hills, then rose gradually for half a mile before opening on a prospect of the largest country house I had ever seen, set against a background of high, forested hills. The road descended to cross a stone bridge over the Derwent and circled gracefully, lined with great trees, around green lawns up to the great buff two-story, many-windowed stone mansion. I did not follow the carriage onto the open ground, but found a place of cover and watched as it climbed the slope before the house and stopped in front of the entrance. Henry and Victor were greeted by two men and a number of women; at this distance I could not tell if I had seen any of them before.

I waited through the afternoon. Once night had fallen, I crept up to the house and spied through windows upon a party of people, among them Victor, Henry, and the three women I had seen in Matlock, sitting at a great table laden with food. Miss Bennet sat beside Victor. To my astonishment, one of the other men was the vicar who had thwarted us two nights ago. What Victor made of his presence there, I could not imagine.

I dared not linger for fear of being seen, but later that night, after all had retired, I made a survey of the exterior of the house, its grounds, the stables, and the outbuildings. I stole a sack of oats from beneath the sleeping horses in the stable and carried it out to the woods, where I feasted.

I would never experience a dinner like the one I had seen. If I let it, envy as bitter as that of fallen Lucifer observing Adam and Eve would torment me. I did not need to live in a house like this—it seemed absurd even to call it a house. This Darcy was a rich man. He was a product of the world that had invented property only to divide and hoard it, the world of immense wealth and squalid poverty, of rank, descent, and noble blood. Two years ago I had envied the condemned and destitute De Laceys the miserable hut where they lived and the fire that warmed them. I would be content still to live as they, if only I had a companion for my loneliness, a sympathetic soul who might comfort me, and whom I would dedicate myself to making happy.

As I huddled beneath a tree and thought of the difference between my condition and that of the people in this mansion, rage grew in me. They ate of every fine thing nature might provide and civilization prepare; I ate fodder meant for beasts. I seized the sack of oats, swung it about me, and hurled it into the woods; I tore off a limb and dashed it against the boles of the trees, staggering in the dark, howling, until I fell to the earth again, holding myself in my arms. I wept and moaned like the animal I was.

For a moment in that graveyard, as I had dug away the

mould covering some dead girl, I had felt hope. I was unearthing my love; she was within reach, inches away—and then she
was stolen from me by cowardice and that fool vicar. I might
have torn him to pieces had I not, against every instinct to
do justice to myself, been held back by compassion—which
apparently, despite all that had been done to me, I still felt.

The next morning threatened rain. Though the weather
was much colder than it had been, I went down to the riverside and bathed myself. I scrubbed my face, rubbed my teeth
with a twig, combed out my hair with my fingers, and resumed
my shabby clothes, making myself as good a semblance of a
human being as I might. Just as I finished, I heard voices coming through the woods from the direction of the great house. I
hastened to hide myself beside the path.

Two women came along the pathway. They wore long
dresses, had shawls over their shoulders against the chilly
morning, and were deep in conversation. I recognized them:
they were two of the three women with whom Victor and Henry
had been in town, one of them Miss Bennet. They stopped and
sat on a fallen limb not twenty feet away. The other woman,
who seemed to me extraordinarily beautiful, and whom Miss
Bennet called Kitty, spoke with great emotion. I listened.

The one named Kitty told of a romance she had carried
on with a married man. She spoke with great feeling of her
desperate love, of the sexual favors they had exchanged, and
how, soon after it had begun, the man had rejected her. Now
she feared that her reputation would be ruined, and that she
might even be with child. My heart was moved to pity by her
plight, and to anger by his behavior. I could not understand
how a man, blessed by God with a wife, still further blessed to

receive the regard of this beautiful woman willing to surrender to him what all society said was her greatest possession, her maidenhood, and the pleasures that came with it, would spurn her so heartlessly once he had taken what he wanted.

It should not have surprised me. It was of a piece with every cruelty I had seen practiced by one human on another. I had seen the De Laceys persecuted. I had seen how Safie's father had used his daughter to escape imprisonment. The desire for those physical affections that draw men and women together against all barriers could be perverted to any use. Here was another example. How I would have bled, and fallen to my knees in grateful prayer, to be in that man's place. Kitty leaned on her sister's shoulder, sobbing, and Miss Bennet embraced her. Tears formed in my own eyes.

Above the treetops, thunder rumbled and it began to rain. Soon the trees were drenched and a downpour was falling on the women. The light had diminished until I could hardly see. Unconsciously, in the simple desire to protect them, I crept closer.

Lightning flashed and a great peal of thunder rolled across the sky. Miss Bennet, who had been facing me, gasped and pulled her sister closer.

She had seen me. I had forgotten myself, and was now brought brutally back to reality.

"What is it?" Kitty said.

"We must go. Now," said Miss Bennet, pulling her sister up by her arm. They stumbled away, back toward the manor house. I followed, not knowing what I did. I only knew that the drastically contrary emotions I had felt in the last days overwhelmed me, and that the pain this woman was undergoing was like my own. I longed to comfort her. *"Arrêtez!"* I croaked after them. "Stop!"

They ran from me. Despair washed over me like the rain, and my steps slowed. Ahead, some figures appeared out of the gray—two men hurrying to help the women. They threw a cloak over Kitty; Miss Bennet gestured toward where I stood stupidly in the rain.

One of the men broke away and took some steps toward me. I did not bother to run. It was Victor. He came within ten steps of me in the gloom. The sound of the rain battering the foliage drowned out all other sounds. His eyes locked on mine. A look of unutterable revulsion crossed his face, as if he were sick unto death and fatigued beyond speech. Then he turned and went back to the others. I could barely make out the words of his report over the din of the storm:

"No one is there," he said.

NINE

Kitty developed a fever and did not leave her bed for the rest of the day. Mary went back up to sit with her. When Kitty awoke, Mary tried, without bringing up the subject of Jonathan Clarke, to soothe her. Kitty, face flushed, looked as if she wanted to speak, but with Lizzy or Jane in the room, she kept her peace. Mary was not sure Kitty could have spoken coherently anyway.

By the late afternoon she had fallen back to sleep, and Mary went down to join some of the others in the saloon, including Darcy, Jane, Bingley, Lizzy, Clerval, and Frankenstein. The housekeeper, Mrs. Reynolds, had prepared tea with pastries and seasonal fruit. The conversation was subdued; Lizzy explained to Mr. Clerval how Kitty had always been susceptible to maladies of the lungs. Normally these were cured by rest, a good diet, and country air.

Victor Frankenstein looked up when Mary entered. Jane asked after Kitty, and Mary told them simply that she was sleeping. The maid poured Mary some tea, and she gratefully accepted it and sat on the seat before the window, gazing out on the hillside that rose to the forested hills. For a moment the rain had ended and the rag ends of clouds moved across the sky.

Mary pondered what she should do about Kitty's affair. If the world were just, Clarke would be publicly exposed, but of course that was out of the question. In the eyes of God his sin and Kitty's were equal, yet if it became known, he would be subject to gossip, but Kitty would be ruined. The world said one thing and did another. It had taken Mary years to learn that, and she felt a fool for believing differently for as long as she had—though she sympathized with the naive girl she had been and at some level still was. No matter how silly she had been, she had never wished anyone ill.

More important was what might be done to heal Kitty's heart. When she recovered, Mary would try to persuade her to let her feelings for Clarke go. Could Mary trust her own counsel? She considered telling Lizzy what she knew. Lizzy might not trust Mary's judgment, but she was a person of sense with a full understanding of the world, and to whatever degree was appropriate, an open heart. But it was not time to say anything yet.

Her thoughts turned to the man they had encountered in the woods. Though she had seen his face for only an instant, the impression it had made lingered. There was nothing malformed about his visage, but it had seemed somehow false, as if his face, however completely human, were not real. Yet it had borne an expression of deep, naked longing. She could not put together the two opposing impressions, other than to recognize the result as horrifying in a peculiarly disturbing way.

She would have appreciated the validation Frankenstein's testimony would have provided to prevent her looking like a fool. But it would not be fair to hold the fact that he had seen nothing against him. Had she been so wrong in her estimation of his regard for her? Upon his arrival he had seemed pleased to see her, but since last night's dinner he had treated her with reserve, if not wariness. If he were as indifferent as his current behavior indicated, why would he have accepted the invitation to come to Pemberley?

She decided to engage him in conversation. She moved to sit nearer him, but once she was there was miserably unable to think of a single thing to say.

Mary cradled her cup with its inch of lukewarm tea in her hands. At last, Frankenstein broke the uncomfortable silence.

"Mr. and Mrs. Darcy are gracious to ask Henry and me to stay, but I know that worry about your sister must weigh heavily on your mind. And let me apologize for the blunt way in which I contradicted your testimony about the man you saw in the woods. But I do believe you were mistaken, and I hope you will consider the possibility. There was no one there. Perhaps you heard some animal in the underbrush? Or the tossing of the tree limbs in the darkness of the storm may have misled you."

She was unable to read his intent. "Thank you for your sympathies, Mr. Frankenstein. However, I do not see how the tossing of branches in a storm might have called to us to stop, in French."

Frankenstein averted his eyes. "Perhaps, then, I was the

one mistaken. My thoughts were for your welfare, and that of Miss Catherine, and I did not search the woods. It is curious that this stranger spoke French."

"Curious indeed."

He cleared his throat as if about to speak, and then said nothing.

"I am sorry that your visit has not provided more in the way of entertainment," Mary said.

Frankenstein seized upon the change of subject. "Mr. Darcy suggests that should the weather clear tomorrow, we might try fishing. If your sister is still ailing, however, it would seem more a distraction than a pleasure. I think, despite your family's amiability, Henry's and my presence here may be *de trop*."

Mary studied the sullen ruins of her hopes in the dregs of her teacup. Although she protested that what Victor said was not true, and though they spoke idly for another few minutes, all Mary could draw from Frankenstein's manner was an overwhelming sense that he did not want to be there. Mary could tell herself that the change in his manner was because of Kitty's illness, but the evidence of his distance after last night's dinner suggested otherwise.

When, after a subdued supper, the party retired for the evening, Mary stopped in to see Kitty. She had managed to take some broth, after which she had fallen back asleep, and though her fever had not subsided, it had not increased. Her breathing was still labored. It was hoped that a night's rest would see her feeling better in the morning.

Rain still sounded outside the windows when Mary retired. Her maid had set a fire that threw gentle light about her darkened room. She lay awake wondering what dreams Kitty was experiencing at that moment, and she hoped they were peaceful ones. Eventually she slept.

In the middle of the night Mary was awakened by the opening of her door. She thought it might be Jane or Lizzy come to tell her some news about Kitty. But it was not Lizzy. She watched silently as a dark figure entered and closed the door softly. The remains of her fire threw faint light on the countenance of the man who approached her.

"Miss Bennet," he called softly.

Her heart was in her throat. "Yes, Mr. Frankenstein."

"Please do not take alarm. I must speak with you." His low voice was charged with emotion. He took two steps toward her bed. His handsome face was agitated.

"This is no place for polite conversation," she said. "Following on your denial of what I saw this afternoon, you are fortunate that I do not wake the servants and have you thrown out of Pemberley."

"I am afraid that nothing I have to say to you tonight shall qualify as polite conversation." Desperation sounded in his whisper. "You are right to chide me. My conscience chides me more than you ever could, and should I be banished from your family's company it would be only what I deserve."

Mary said, "Add another log to the fire."

He started to speak, then thought better of it and did as she asked. While he poked the coals into life, she drew on her robe and lit a candle. She made him sit in one of the chairs by the hearth. When she had settled herself in the other, she said, "Go on, then."

"Miss Bennet, please do not toy with me. You know why I am here."

"Know, sir? What do I know?"

He leaned forward earnestly, hands clasped and elbows on his knees. "I come to beg you to keep silent. The gravest consequences would follow your revealing my secret."

"Your secret," she said flatly.

"About—about the man you saw."

"You do know him!"

"Your mockery at dinner showed me that after hearing the vicar's story, you suspected. You played with me, offering every teasing sign of your surmise. Raising the dead, you said to Henry—and then you tormented me with your tale of Aldini and his College of Surgeons demonstration. Do not deny it."

"I don't pretend to know what you are talking about."

Frankenstein stood and began to pace the floor. "Please! I recognized your look of reproach when we found you in the forest. You saw that monstrous thing with your own eyes. Believe me when I tell you I intend to make right what I put wrong. But I will never be able to do so if you expose me to the world."

To Mary's astonishment, she saw that his eyes glistened with tears.

"Perhaps I will keep silent," she said. "But you must first tell me everything."

She sat back in an attitude of expectation. He stared at her, took his seat again, and began to speak.

"It began," he said, "when my mother died."

Over the next hour Frankenstein told her how his mother, the most loving of parents, had died on the eve of his leaving for the university. A reader of Cornelius Agrippa and Paracelsus, from childhood he had entertained fancies of alchemical powers; this tragedy only increased his forlorn wish that he might discover the elixir of life. At Ingolstadt he became the pupil of two distinguished scientists, M. Krempe and M. Waldman. They convinced him that alchemy was an outdated fantasy, but chemistry offered the chance for human beings to bend nature to their purposes. They set him to the study of the modern masters of natural philosophy and introduced him to the realm of the laboratory, the experiment, the minute observation of nature in all her works.

Having read some of the same thinkers that Frankenstein mentioned, Mary could see the attraction of the prospect, and how a person of strong enough imagination might seek to discover what Frankenstein after years of intense research claimed to have found: the secret of life. He told Mary how, emboldened and driven on by his solitary obsession to demonstrate his newfound power over life and death, he had formed a man from the tissues of corpses he had stolen from graveyards and purchased from resurrection men. Three years ago he had succeeded, through his science, in bringing this artificial being to life.

Only on the first vital motions of this new being did the monstrous horror of his accomplishment strike him.

"Nothing I can say can convey to you what I felt in that instant of triumph and sickening despair. One moment, heedless of my exhaustion, forgetful of the violations of common decency I had committed in the service of my obsession, I wanted nothing more than to see the result of my years of labor show signs of life. In the next, as the thing's fingers twitched and it opened its watery eye, the full horror of my actions, the godlike responsibility I had stolen and my presumption in stealing it, which until then I had ignored or pushed aside, transfixed me the way a pin fixes a moth in a box. My soul recoiled and my frame staggered under the weight of returning conscience."

In revulsion at this misbegotten parody of a human being, Frankenstein had fled his laboratory, and when he returned, his creation was gone. He fell ill, and months passed before he was well enough again to contemplate what he had done; by that time he assumed that the thing, without his care, had sickened and died. Fatal irresponsibility: the monster had survived. Two years later, it had somehow discovered Victor as its creator, made its way hundreds of miles to his home in Geneva, strangled his brother William, and caused his family's ward Justine to be blamed for the crime.

Mary did not know what to say. These were the ravings of a lunatic. But the earnestness with which Frankenstein spoke, his tears and desperate whispers, gave every proof that, at least in his mind, he had done these things. And she had indeed seen a horrifying man in the woods.

She considered all that he had said. "But if you knew that this monster had committed such awful crimes, why did you not intervene in Justine's trial?"

"I had no proof. Had I spoken, no one should have believed me."

"Yet I am to believe you now?"

Frankenstein's voice was choked. "You have seen the monster. You deduced, from your reading, that these things are possible. I come to you in remorse and penitence, asking only that you keep this secret." He fell to his knees, threw his head into her lap, and clutched at the sides of her gown.

Frankenstein had wholly mistaken what she knew. Yet if his story was true, it was no wonder that his judgment was disordered. And here he lay, trembling against her like a boy seeking forgiveness.

She tried to keep her senses. "Certainly the creature I saw was frightening, but he looked more wretched than menacing."

Frankenstein lifted his head. "Here I must warn you—his wretchedness is mere mask. He feigns humanity, and he is a superior mimic. Do not let your sympathy for him cause you ever to trust his nature. He is the vilest creature that has ever walked this earth. He has no conscience, no soul."

"Why then not alert the authorities, catch him, and bring him to justice?"

"He cannot be so easily caught. He is inhumanly strong, resourceful, and intelligent. If you should ever be so unlucky as to speak with him, I warn you not to listen to what he says, for he is eloquent and persuasive. Let me tell you a story about him to demonstrate his arrogance, his lack of conscience, and his derision:

"After he had killed William and Justine was hanged for his crime, I went to the top of a glacier to contemplate ending my life. He followed, and there confronted me. He accused me of abandoning him. I tried to reason with him and he told me he would keep no terms with his enemies. When in despair and rage I commanded him to relieve me from the sight of his detested form, he did this—" Frankenstein reached out and held his hands over Mary's eyes. "'Thus I relieve thee,' the fiend said, to show me that though I might not see him, he would ever be only an arm's distance away.

"He is brilliant and sardonic, and that makes his rage

against humanity more bitter still. He has told me in his own words that he has declared everlasting war against our species."

"All the more reason to see him apprehended."

"I am convinced that he can be dealt with only by myself." Frankenstein's eyes pleaded with her. "Miss Bennet—Mary—you must understand. He is in some ways my son. I gave him life. It is I he follows. His mind is fixed on me."

"And, it seems, yours is fixed on him."

Frankenstein looked surprised. "Do you wonder that is so?"

"Why does he follow you? Does he intend you harm?"

"He has vowed to glut the maw of death with the blood of my remaining loved ones, unless I make him happy."

"But how can you face this thing alone? Is there some-where you will flee? You are bound for Scotland—will he not follow?"

"I intend to travel, without Henry, to the remotest spot I can find. When he comes, I will deal with him away from the rest of humanity." Frankenstein's eyes glistened with tears. He rested his head again in her lap. He whispered, "Please, keep my secret."

Mary was touched, and in some obscure way aroused. She felt his trembling body, instinct with life. Tentatively, she rested her hand on his head. She stroked his hair. He was weeping. She was acutely aware of him as a physical being, a living ani-mal that would eventually, too soon, die. And all that was true for him was true of herself. How strange, frightening, sad. Yet in this moment she felt herself completely alive.

"I will keep your secret," she said.

He hugged her skirts. In the candle's light, she noted the

way his thick, dark hair curled away from his brow.

"I cannot tell you," he said softly, "what a relief it is to share my burden with another soul, and to have her accept me. I have been so completely alone. I am sorry to have come to you like this, so abjectly and improperly. Forgive me, and I will forever be in your debt."

He rose, kissed her forehead, and was gone.

The suddenness of his departure left her dizzy. Had she dreamed it? But she felt the lingering impress of his lips on her brow.

Mary paced her room, trying to grasp what had happened. A man who had conquered death? A monster fashioned from the flesh of corpses? Such things did not happen, not even in the novels she read. She climbed into bed and tried to sleep, but could not.

Mary remembered the weight of Frankenstein's head upon her lap.

The coals of the fire still illuminated the room, dimly. She felt stiflingly hot. She got up, stripped off her nightgown, and climbed back between the sheets, where she lay naked, listening to the occasional pop and crack of the dying fire.

The Creature had vowed to kill all whom Frankenstein loved.

Kitty's fever worsened in the night, and before dawn Darcy sent to Lambton for the doctor. Lizzy dispatched an express letter to their parents, and the sisters sat by Kitty's bedside through the morning, changing cold compresses from her brow while Kitty labored to breathe.

When Mary left the sickroom, Frankenstein approached

her. He looked calmer and more settled than he had the previous day. She would not have known that he had been in her
bedroom several hours ago. "How is your sister?"

"She is gravely ill."

"She is in some danger?"

Mary could only nod.

He touched her shoulder, lowered his voice. "I will pray for
her, Miss Bennet. I cannot thank you enough for the understanding you showed me last night. I have never told anyone —"

Just then Clerval appeared. He greeted Mary, inquired
after Kitty's condition, and then suggested to Frankenstein
that they return to their inn rather than add any burden to
the household and family. Frankenstein agreed. The gentlemen packed their belongings and Darcy had a chaise brought
round to drive them back to the Matlock inn.

As they gathered at the front entrance to Pemberley, Henry
and Victor thanked Darcy and Elizabeth for their hospitality.
Mary's thoughts were with Kitty upstairs, but Frankenstein
took a moment for one last word with her.

"I regret that circumstances will not allow us to better know
each other, Miss Bennet. My heartfelt wishes for your sister's
speedy recovery, and my sincere gratitude for your kindness."
He held her hand and looked her in the eyes.

"God bless you, Mr. Frankenstein."

With that they climbed into the carriage and were driven
away.

Dr. Montgomery arrived soon after Clerval and Frankenstein left. He listened to Kitty's breathing, measured her pulse,
felt her forehead, and examined her urine. He feared she might
have contracted a Boulogne sore throat, and recommended

that the immediate family members, and particularly any children, be kept from her room. He administered some medicines, and came away shaking his head. Should the fever continue, he said, they must bleed her.

Given how much thought she had spent on Frankenstein through the night, and how little on Kitty, Mary's conscience tormented her, and she was not about to leave Kitty's side despite the doctor's warnings of contagion. She spent the day in her sister's room. That night, after Jane had retired and Lizzy fallen asleep in her chair, she still sat up, holding Kitty's hot hand. She had matters to consider. Was Kitty indeed with child, and if so, should she tell the doctor? Yet even as she sat by Kitty's bedside, Mary's mind cast back to the touch of Frankenstein's lips on her forehead.

In the middle of the night, Kitty woke, bringing Mary from her doze. Kitty lifted her head from the pillow. "Mary," she whispered. "You must send for Jonathan. Tell him I accept. We must be married immediately."

Mary looked across the room at Lizzy. She was still asleep.

"Promise me," Kitty said. Her eyes were large and dark.

"I promise," Mary said.

"Prepare my wedding dress," Kitty said. "But don't tell Lizzy."

Lizzy awoke then. She came to the bedside and felt Kitty's forehead. "She's burning up. Get Dr. Montgomery."

Mary sought out the doctor, and then, while he went to Kitty's room, pondered what to do. Kitty was not in her right mind. If Mary sent one of the footmen to Matlock for Jonathan, no matter that Mary might swear her messenger to silence, the matter would soon be the talk of the servants, and eventually the town. The likelihood that Clarke would come was small, and what purpose would his coming serve? It would only arouse the speculation of scandal that Kitty had feared. Kitty's request ran contrary to both sense and propriety.

But Mary had promised.

It was the sort of dilemma that she would have had no trouble settling, to everyone's moral edification, when she was nineteen. She hurried to her room and took out paper and pen:

> *I write to inform you that one you love, residing at Pemberley House, is gravely ill. She urgently requests your presence. Simple human kindness, which from our acquaintance I know you possess, let alone the duty incumbent upon you owing to the compact that you have made with her through your actions, assures me that we shall see you here before the night is through.*
>
> *Miss Mary Bennet*

She folded and sealed the note and woke Benjamin, one of the footmen, whom she dispatched immediately with the instruction to put the letter into the hand of Jonathan Clarke, owner of the Matlock butcher's shop, at his home in Chesterfield Road. She asked him not to let on to the other servants that he had gone; if Mrs. Reynolds or even Mr. Darcy should discover he had been out, he should direct them to speak with Mary.

After he had left, Mary returned to Kitty's room. Kitty had dropped back into sleep, and her labored breath was audible in the stillness of the room. Dr. Montgomery was there, and Lizzy had woken Jane. The three were in whis-pered conversation, and Mary joined them.

"Her fever is very high," Montgomery said. "If we are going to do it, I believe it is time to bleed her."

"Shall we wait until Father and Mother arrive?" Jane asked.

"There is no way to know when they will arrive," said Lizzy. She rubbed the back of her hand across her brow. "I think we should proceed."

Mary said, "I would like to hold the basin."

"We can have one of the ladies' maids hold it," Dr. Mont-gomery said. "This is a difficult procedure to watch. I do not want to have to deal with a fainting sister."

"I shall not faint," Mary said.

Jane and Lizzy looked skeptical. Dr. Montgomery assessed her for a moment. "All right," he said.

From his bag he took a small enameled basin and a straight razor. "Bring the lamp here, if you would," he said to Lizzy. "Hold it steady."

Dr. Montgomery pulled back the counterpane, gently lifted Kitty's arm, and laid it on a towel at the side of the bed. He let her hand and wrist dangle over the edge. He directed Mary to hold the basin below Kitty's forearm, and then unfolded the razor. Jane looked away. Lizzy held the lamp. Kitty's breath-ing sounded rough in her throat.

Montgomery made an incision along the blue vein that showed beneath the pale skin of Kitty's forearm. Very slowly dark blood welled up and trickled over her arm into the basin. The flow was paltry. Montgomery held Kitty's arm with one hand while he felt for the pulse at her swollen throat with his other. Mary watched the blood drip from her sister's arm, compelling herself to breathe deeply and evenly as she caught every drop in the basin.

After some minutes, Montgomery said, "That's enough." He pressed a clean linen pad to Kitty's arm and wrapped a bandage around it from elbow to wrist. He took the basin from Mary. "Thank you," he said. "I see no reason why you ladies should not retire to get some sleep. I will wait here with her."

Jane extracted a promise that she should be called at any change in Kitty's condition. Lizzy and Mary insisted on remaining, but a half hour later Darcy entered and persuaded Lizzy that she could do nothing for anyone in the morning if she spent another sleepless night. "Mary is here; let her sit with her sister as she has for so many years." Mary was grateful for his words. Lizzy conceded; Darcy had a few words with Dr. Montgomery and bid Mary good night, and they left.

The doctor and Mary said little to each other. He settled back into a chair; soon his chin rested on his chest, and he gave a slight snore.

Mary was wide awake. She considered how she might deal with Lizzy and the others if Clarke did arrive. She decided to cross that bridge when she came to it.

She watched her sister's face. Kitty looked ten years older than she had in London. Mary could see the old woman she would become written in the faint lines at the corners of her eyes, the softness of her chin, the hollowness of her cheeks. Yet she was still beautiful. Her eyelashes were dark and fine. They fluttered as Kitty passed through some dream. Her brow furrowed. Her breathing came fast and shallow. Mary wondered what was happening in that dream.

Their temperaments were different, Kitty's and Mary's, but they had been yoked together for ten years. How many times had they whispered secrets to each other in their bedroom at Longbourn, speaking of things that they wished for, the difficulty of being alone? Kitty had teased Mary for her books and fossils, but begrudged her, Mary thought, just a little, the escape they gave her from the desert of spinsterhood. Kitty had even envied Mary the attentions of Mr. Woodleigh. Mary recalled the way they had both laughed when Mary swore she would not marry him.

Tears gathered in Mary's eyes. She reached out to hold the hand of Kitty's bandaged arm.

When Dr. Montgomery woke some time later, Mary asked him to watch Kitty while she stepped out of the room. The light was coming up in the east, and the clock in the hall told her it was six in the morning. She hurried to the servants' quarters and knocked on the door to Benjamin's room.

The footman was awake, and answered immediately. "Miss Bennet," he said in surprise.

"Did you give the note to Mr. Clarke?"

"Yes, ma'am."

"You put it in his hand?"

"I did, ma'am. The girl that answered said he was asleep, but I made her wake him. He was quite unhappy about it, Miss Bennet."

But Clarke was not here. "Thank you, Benjamin. Please do not say anything about this to anyone."

"Yes, ma'am. How is Miss Catherine?"

Mary swallowed her emotions. "Not well. Pray for her, if you will."

Walking back to Kitty's room through the still twilit mansion, climbing the marble stairs to the second floor, Mary, dizzy with sleeplessness, felt as if she were in a dream. This could not be real. Soon she would wake and Kitty would be there, complaining about their mother's moods, planning for the next dance at the assembly hall, speculating about some gentleman who had recently moved into the parish.

When she returned to Kitty's room, Darcy and Lizzy were there. Dr. Montgomery leaned over Kitty on the bed, his hand on her forehead.

"She has not improved," Lizzy whispered to Mary, her voice choked.

"I shall send for the priest," Darcy said.

There was nothing to do but to sit and wait, wait for Mr. and Mrs. Bennet, wait for Reverend Chatsworth, wait for whatever outcome lay ahead for Kitty. Mary had no doubt that they would not have to wait long. As they sat in the warm room, the only sounds were the crackle of the fire in the grate and Kitty's labored breathing. An occasional murmured word passed between Jane and Elizabeth. A soft knock came at the door, and Bingley entered to stand behind his wife with a troubled countenance.

To her shame, Mary found her thoughts slipping to Mr. Frankenstein. How excited she had been, despite telling herself not to have expectations, when Frankenstein had agreed to visit Pemberley. How long ago? Three days. It did not seem possible for such a revolution in circumstances to happen so quickly, yet here, in the person of her sister struggling to breathe, not five feet away from Mary, lay the simple proof. It was inexplicable. It was not just. It was the hard truth.

An hour and a half later Mr. Chatsworth arrived and hurried into the room, his cheeks flushed from his haste in riding the ten miles to the estate. It was a matter of minutes only for him to administer the last rites.

An hour later, at ten in the morning, Kitty died.

On the evening of the next day, Mr. and Mrs. Bennet arrived, exhausted and desperate, only to find they had come too late. The day after that brought Lydia and Wickham—the first time Darcy had allowed Wickham to cross the threshold of Pemberley since they had become brothers by marriage. In the midst of her mourning family, Mary felt lost. Jane and Lizzy supported each other in their grief. Darcy and Bingley exchanged quiet, sober conversation. Wickham and Lydia, who had grown stout with her four children, could not pass a word between them without sniping, but in their folly they were completely joined to each other.

Mrs. Bennet was beyond consoling, and the intensity of her mourning was exceeded only by the degree to which she sought to control every detail of Kitty's funeral. There ensued a long debate over where Kitty should be buried. When she was reminded that Mr. Collins would eventually inherit the estate back in Hertfordshire, Mrs. Bennet fell into despair: Who, when she was gone, would tend to her poor daughter's grave? Mr. Bennet suggested that Kitty be laid to rest in the churchyard at Lambton, a short distance from Pemberley, where she might be visited by Elizabeth and Darcy, and also by Jane and Bingley. But when Darcy offered the family vault at Pemberley, the matter was speedily settled to the satisfaction of both vanity and tender hearts.

Though it was no surprise to Mary, it was still a burden for her to witness that even in this gravest passage of their lives, her sisters and parents showed themselves to be exactly what they were. And yet this did not harden her heart toward them. The family was together in one place as it had not been for many years, and, she realized, as it should never be in future except on the occasion of further losses. Her father was grayer and quieter than she had ever seen him, and on the day of the funeral even her mother put aside her sobbing and exclamations long enough to show a face of profound grief, and a burden of age that Mary had never regarded before.

The night after Kitty was laid to rest, Mary sat up late with Jane and Lizzy and Lydia. They drank Madeira and Lydia told tales of the days she and Kitty had spent in flirtations with the regiment. When her turn came, Mary told a story of how Kitty, in order to impress a potential suitor, led him to believe that all of Mary's books on singing and harmony were her own, and that she was expert at playing the pianoforte. Then for two weeks she had twisted herself into agonies of furious practice while avoiding singing or playing in his presence, until her stratagem was exposed.

When Mary climbed into her bed late that night, her head swam with wine, laughter, and tears. She lay awake, the moonlight shining on the counterpane through the opened window, air carrying the smell of fresh fields and the rustle of trees beside the river. She drifted into a dreamless sleep. At some point in the night she was half awakened by the barking of the dogs in the kennel. But consciousness soon faded and she fell away.

In the morning it was discovered that the vault had been broken into and Kitty's body stolen from the crypt.

TEN

While the house was in turmoil and Mrs. Bennet being attended by the rest of the family, Mary went down to the stables. She found the stable master in the paddock with one of Darcy's riding horses. "Mr. Poole?" she called.

He dropped the horse's lead and walked over to her. "Yes, ma'am?"

"Mr. Darcy would like you prepare the gig. He and I must drive into Lambton to speak with the constable."

"Yes, ma'am." He said nothing about the theft of Kitty's body, though it must be the subject of every conversation between the servants.

Mary waited while Poole had the gig rolled out. "Fetch Cicero," he ordered one of the grooms. "He's the best in the stable," he told Mary.

Poole himself harnessed the horse into the traces. When

he had finished, she said, "I don't know what is keeping Mr. Darcy. Do you think you might go up to the house and ask after him? As you may imagine, everyone is terribly upset about what happened last night."

"It's no wonder, ma'am. I'll go directly."

As soon as he was out of sight, and the other stable hands occupied, she climbed into the gig, took the reins, tapped the horse's flank with the whip, and drove off across the bridge on her way to Matlock.

Cicero proved to be equable and fleet, and despite her slender experience of driving, Mary was able to reach Matlock in an hour. All the time, despite the splendid summer morning and the picturesque prospects that the valley of the Derwent continually unfolded before her, she could not keep her mind from whirling through a series of distressing images—Kitty lying dead, bandaged arm resting on her breast in her room at Pemberley, their father's face as he stepped down from the coach from Longbourn, Frankenstein's creature as she had seen him in the woods.

When she reached Matlock, she hurried to the inn and inquired after Frankenstein. The porter told her that he had not seen Mr. Frankenstein since dinner the previous evening, but that Mr. Clerval had told him that the gentlemen would leave Matlock later in the day. She left a note asking Frankenstein, should he return, to wait for her at the inn, and then went to the butcher's shop.

Mary had been there once before, with Lizzy, some years earlier. The shop was busy with servants purchasing joints of mutton and ham for the evening meal. Behind the counter one of Jonathan Clarke's workers, in white shirt, vest, and apron, was busy at his cutting board. Helping one of the women with a package was a tall young man with thick brown curls and green eyes. He flirted with the house servant as he shouldered her purchase, wrapped in brown paper, onto her cart.

On the way back into the shop, he spotted Mary standing unattended. He studied her for a moment before approaching. His manner held none of the teasing she had observed with the servant. Perhaps it was because she was a lady. Perhaps it was because Mary was not an attractive woman. She had experienced this indifference from men her whole life. "May I help you, ma'am?"

"I must speak with your master, Mr. Clarke. Where might I find him?"

"Mr. Clarke has left Matlock. He's gone to be with his wife in London."

"Could you tell me when he left?"

"Yesterday morning." The day of Kitty's funeral.

"He left Mr. Pike in charge," the young man continued. "Shall I fetch him for you?"

Mary shook her head. "No, that won't be necessary."

"I'd best be about my work, then. G'day, ma'am." And he moved on to his next flirtation.

Mary had seen enough to take Jonathan Clarke's depth. Her momentary fancy that he might defile a grave, in grief or guilt, had been absurd. He had not even bothered to send condolences. The distance between his petty intrigues and the love Kitty had wasted on him only deepened Mary's compassion for her lost sister. How desperate she must have been. How pathetic.

She went back to the inn. The barkeep led her into a small

ladies' parlor separated from the taproom by a glass partition. She ordered tea and through an opened window watched the people come and go in the street and courtyard, draymen with their Percherons and carts, passengers waiting for the next coach to Manchester, idlers sitting inside at tables with pints of ale. In the sunlit street a young bootblack accosted travelers, most of whom ignored him. All these people completely indifferent to Mary or her lost sister. Mary ought to be back with their mother, though the thought turned her heart cold. How could Kitty have left her alone? She felt herself near despair.

She was watching as two draymen struggled to load a large trunk onto their cart when the man directing them came from around the team of horses, and she saw it was Victor Frankenstein. She rose immediately and went out to the inn yard. She was at his shoulder before he noticed her.

"Miss Bennet!" he said, startled.

"Mr. Frankenstein. I am so glad that I found you. I feared that you had already left Matlock. Might we speak, in private?"

"Yes, of course," he said. To the draymen he said, "When you've finished loading my equipment, wait here.

"This is no place to converse," Frankenstein told her. "I saw a churchyard nearby. Let us retire there."

He walked Mary down the street to the St. Giles Church. They entered the rectory garden. In the distance, beams of afternoon sunlight shone through a cathedral of clouds above the Heights of Abraham. "Are you aware of what has happened?" she asked.

"I heard the reports of the death of your sister. I wrote you, conveying my condolences—"

"I received them."

"You have my deepest sympathies."

"Your creature! That monster you created—"

"I asked you to keep my secret."

"I have kept my promise—so far. But it has stolen Kitty's body."

He stood, hands behind his back, clear eyes fixed on her. "You find me astonished. Your sister's grave has been disturbed?"

"Last night someone broke into the family vault and stole her away."

"What draws you to the extraordinary conclusion that my creation did this?"

She was hurt by his diffidence. Was this the same man who had wept in her bedroom? "You spoke of his malice. Who else might do such a thing?"

"But why? This creature's enmity is reserved for me alone. Others feel its ire only to the extent that they are dear to me."

"You came to plead with me because you feared I knew he'd defiled that town girl's grave. Now Kitty's body has been stolen? Surely this is no coincidence."

"If the demon has stolen your sister's body, it can be for no reason I can fathom, or that any God-fearing person ought to pursue. You know I am determined to see this monster banished from the world of men. You may rest assured that I will not cease until I have seen this accomplished. It is best for you and your family to turn your thoughts to other matters." He touched a strand of ivy growing up the side of the garden wall, and plucked off a green leaf, which he twirled in his fingers.

She did not understand. She knew him to have a heart

capable of feeling. His denials opened a possibility that she had tried to keep herself from considering.

"Sir, I am not satisfied. You are keeping something from me. You told me of the grief you felt at the loss of your mother, how it moved you to your researches. If, as you say, you have uncovered the secret of life, might you—have you taken it upon yourself to restore Kitty?"

He sighed. "I wish I could do that, but I cannot." His voice was melancholy.

"Mr. Chatsworth said there were two men digging up Nancy Brown's grave. Were you the second man? Perhaps a fear of failure, or of the horror that many would feel at your trespassing against God's will, underlies your secrecy. If so, please do not keep the truth from me. I am not a child."

Frankenstein let the leaf fall from his fingers. He looked directly into her eyes. "I am sorry, Mary. To restore your sister is not in my power. The soulless creature I brought to life bears no relation to the man from whose body I fashioned him. Your sister has gone on to her reward. Nothing—nothing I can do would bring her back."

"So you know nothing about the theft of her corpse?"

"On that score, I can offer no consolation to you or your family."

"My mother, my father—they are inconsolable."

"Then they must content themselves with memories of your sister as she lived. As I must do with my dear, lost brother William, and the traduced and dishonored Justine. Had I such powers as you imagine, would I not have sought to bring them back long before now?"

"Yes, I believe that you would."

"I wish I could comfort you in your grief. Come, let us go back to the inn."

Mary began to cry. He held her to him and she wept on his breast. His hand pressed between her shoulder blades, and she felt the rise and fall of his chest. In her entire life, she had never felt her body against that of a man. She wept for Kitty, and for herself.

Eventually Mary pushed herself away. Frankenstein looked down on her, his eyes full of emotion. She allowed him to take her arm, and they slowly walked back down to the high street. She knew that when they reached the inn, Frankenstein would go. The warmth of his hand on hers almost made her beg him to stay, or better still, to take her with him.

But that was madness. They came to the busy courtyard. The dray loaded with Frankenstein's trunks and boxes stood there, but the cart men were not to be seen. Frankenstein let go Mary's arm and, agitated, strode into the taproom, where he found the men sitting with pints of ale. He upbraided them. "I thought I told you to keep those trunks out of the sun."

The older of the two men put down his pint and stood. "Sorry, guv'nor. We'll see to it directly."

"Do so now."

The men stumbled from their table and went to move their cart. As Frankenstein followed them out, the evening coach drew up before the inn. Victor and Mary stood outside the entrance.

"You and Mr. Clerval leave today?" Mary asked.

"As soon as Henry returns from the bank, we take this coach to the Lake District. And thence to Scotland to visit a Dr. Marble, a friend of Henry's father, in Perth."

"They say Scotland is very beautiful."

"I am afraid that its beauty will be lost on me. I carry the burden of my great transgression, not to be laid down until I have made things right."

She felt that she would burst if she did not speak her heart to him. "Victor. Will I never see you again?"

He avoided her gaze. "I am afraid, Miss Bennet, that our meeting again depends on events over which I have no control. My duty is to banish that vile creature from the world. Until that is done, to be linked with me would bring you only danger, and I could not answer to my conscience if I allowed that to happen."

Mary looked away. A mother was adjusting her son's collar before putting him on the coach.

"I will miss you," Mary said meekly.

Frankenstein pressed her hand. "Miss Bennet, you must forgive the liberties I have taken with you. You have given me more of friendship than I deserve. If there is any justice in God's creation, you will find the companion you seek, and live your days in happiness. I am afraid that I must leave you with no more than that fervent wish. Now, I must go."

"God be with you, Mr. Frankenstein." She twisted her gloved fingers into a knot.

He bowed deeply and hurried to have a few more words with the draymen. Henry Clerval arrived just as the men climbed onto their cart and drove the equipage away. Clerval, surprised to find Mary there, greeted her warmly. He expressed his great sorrow at the loss of her sister, and begged her to convey his condolences to her family.

Ten minutes later the two men climbed aboard the coach

and it left the inn, disappearing down the Matlock high street.

Mary lingered in the inn yard. Darcy's gig stood in the corner against the wall; Cicero, heavy-lidded, munched from a feed bag. She did not feel she could bear to go back to Pemberley and face her family, to endure the histrionics of her mother, to have nothing to contemplate but the death of Kitty and the endless days that stretched ahead of her. Instead she entered the inn. She made the barkeep seat her in the ladies' parlor and bring her a glass of port.

The sun declined and shadows stretched over the inn yard. The papers arrived from Nottingham. The yard boy lit the lamps. Still, Mary would not leave. Outside on the pavements, the bootblack sat in the growing darkness with his arms draped over his knees and head on his breast. She listened to the hooves of the occasional horse striking the cobbles. The innkeeper was solicitous. When she asked for something to eat, he brought her some bread, ham, and boiled eggs. When she asked for a third glass of port, he hesitated.

"I don't know, ma'am." He was a man of about fifty with a worried face, his thinning hair going gray. He rubbed his hands together nervously. "A lady like you don't belong in a place like this. Might I send for someone from your family to come take you home?"

"You do not know my family," she said.

"Yes, ma'am. I only thought—"

"Another port. Then leave me alone."

"Yes, ma'am." He went away. She was determined to become intoxicated. How many times had she piously warned against young women behaving as she had this day? *Virtue is her own reward.* She had an apothegm for every occasion, and had tediously produced them in place of thought. *Show me a liar, and I'll show thee a thief. Marry in haste, repent at leisure. Men should be what they seem.*

She did not fool herself into thinking that her current misbehavior would make any difference. Perhaps Bingley or Darcy had been dispatched to find her. Within an hour or two she would return to Pemberley, where her mother would scold her for giving them an anxious evening, and Lizzy would caution her about the risk to her reputation. Lydia might even ask her, not believing it possible, if she had an assignation with some man. The loss of Kitty would overshadow Mary's indiscretion, pitiful as it had been. Soon all would be as before, except Mary would be alive and Kitty dead. But even that would fade. The shadow of Kitty's death and her body's mysterious disappearance would hang over the family for some time, but nothing of significance would change.

As she lingered over her glass, she looked up and noticed, in the now empty taproom, a man sitting at the table farthest from the lamps. A huge man, he wore a greatcoat despite the warm weather, with a large hat shadowing his face. On the table in front of him were a tankard and a few coppers. Mary rose, left the parlor, and crossed toward him.

He looked up, and the faint light from the ceiling lamp caught his watery eyes, sunken beneath heavy brows. There was something wrong with his face. She thought to run. Instead she asked, "May I sit with you?"

"You may sit where you wish." The voice was deep, but swallowed, unable to project. It was almost a whisper.

Trembling only slightly, she sat. In the gloom his wrists and hands, resting on the table, stuck out past the ragged sleeves of his coat. His skin was yellowish, and the fingernails livid white. He did not move. "You have some business with me?"

"I have the most appalling business." Mary tried to look him in the eyes, but her gaze kept slipping. "I want to know why you defiled my sister's grave, why you have stolen her body, and what you have done with her."

"Better you should ask Victor. Did he not explain it to you?"

"Mr. Frankenstein explained who—what—you are. He did not know what had become of my sister."

The dark lips twitched in a sardonic smile. "Poor Victor. He has got things all topsy-turvy. Victor does not know what I am. He is incapable of knowing, no matter the labors I have undertaken to school him. But he does know what became, and is to become, of your sister." The Creature tucked his thick black hair behind his ear, a sudden unconscious gesture that made him seem completely human for the first time. He pulled the hat farther forward to hide his face.

"So tell me."

"Which answer do you want? Who I am, or what happened to your sister?"

"First, tell me what happened to—to Kitty."

"Victor and I broke into the vault and stole her away. He took the utmost care not to damage her. He washed her fair body in diluted carbolic acid, and replaced her blood with a chemical admixture of his own devising. Folded up, she fit neatly within a cedar trunk sealed with pitch, and is at present being shipped to Scotland. You witnessed her departure from this courtyard an hour ago."

Mary's senses rebelled. She covered her face with her hands. The Creature sat silent. Finally, without raising her head, she managed, "Victor warned me that you are a liar. Why should I believe you?"

"You have no reason to believe me."

"*You* took her!"

"Though I would not have scrupled to do so, I did not. Miss Bennet, I do not deny I have an interest in this matter. Victor did as I have told you at my bidding."

"At your bidding? Why?"

"Your sister—or not so much your sister, as her remains— is to become my wife."

"Your wife! This is insupportable! Monstrous!"

"Monstrous." Suddenly, with preternatural quickness, his hand flashed out and grabbed Mary's wrist.

Mary thought to call for help, but the taproom was empty and she had driven the innkeeper away. Yet the Creature's grip was not harsh. His hand was warm, instinct with life. "Look at me," he said. With his other hand he pushed back his hat.

She took a deep breath. She looked.

His noble forehead, high cheekbones, strong chin, and wide-set eyes might have made him handsome, despite his yellowish skin, were he a portrait of a man rather than a living thing. His pale eyes looked blind. He seemed like nothing so much as one of the wax effigies she had seen in London, come to life. Motionless he was tolerable, a statue, but when his lips or eyes moved, every fiber of her screamed that this thing was a sham, an animated corpse, a hideous parody of a human being.

The content of his expression made it worse. Every twitch

of eyebrow or lip revealed an extraordinary panoply of emotions, transitory as the flickering of a candle, but burning so intensely that she wanted to avert her eyes. This was a creature who had never learned to associate with civilized company, who had been thrust into adulthood with the passions of a wounded boy. Fear, self-disgust, anger. Desire.

The force of longing and rage in that face made her shrink. "Let me go," she whispered.

He let go her wrist. With bitter satisfaction, he said, "You see. If what I demand is insupportable, that is only because your kind has done nothing to support me. Once, I falsely hoped to meet with beings who, pardoning my outward form, would love me for the excellent qualities which I was capable of bringing forth. I was wrong. I am more alone than a starving man on a deserted isle, for he at least knows that others of his kind exist. I have no brother, sister, parents. I have only Victor, who, like so many fathers, recoiled from me the moment I first drew breath. I would obliterate him, were he not my only hope to find a companion. And so, I have commanded him from your sister to fashion my bride, or he and all he loves will die at my hand."

"I cannot believe he would commit this abomination."

"He has no choice. He is my slave."

"His conscience could not support it, even at the cost of his life."

"You give him too much credit. You all do. I have not seen him act other than according to impulse for the last three years. That is all I see in any of you."

Mary drew back, trying to make some sense of this horror. Kitty, to be brought back to life, only to be given to this fiend?

But would it be Kitty, or another agitated, hungry thing like this?

She still retained some scraps of skepticism. The Creature's manner did not bespeak the isolation that he claimed. "I am astonished at your grasp of language," Mary said. "You could not know so much without teachers."

"Oh, I have had many teachers." The Creature's mutter was rueful. "You might say that, since first my eyes opened, mankind has been all my study. Still, I have much yet to learn. There are certain words whose meaning has never been proved to me by experience. For example: 'happy.' Victor is to make me happy. Do you think he can do it?"

Mary thought of Frankenstein. Could he satisfy this creature? "I do not think it is in the power of any other person to make one happy."

"You jest with me. Every creature has its mate, save me. I have none."

She recoiled at his self-pity. "You put too much upon having a mate."

"Why? You know nothing of what I have endured."

"You think that having a female of your own kind will ensure that she will accept you?" Mary laughed. "Wait until you are rejected, for the most trivial of reasons, by one who ought to have been made for you."

Dismay crossed the Creature's face. "That shall not happen."

"It happens more often than not."

"The female that Victor creates shall find no other mate but me."

"Better you should worry if you are accepted: then you may truly begin to learn."

"Learn what?"

"You will learn to ask a new question: Which is worse, to be alone, or to be wretchedly mismatched?" Like Lydia and Wickham, Mary thought, like Collins and poor Charlotte. Like her parents.

The Creature's face spasmed with conflicting emotions. His voice gained volume. "Do not sport with me. I am not your toy."

"No. You only seek a toy of your own."

The Creature was not, apparently, accustomed to mockery. "Will you torment me as well?" He lurched upward, awkwardly, so suddenly that he upended the table. The tankard of ale skidded across and spilled on Mary, and she fell back.

At that moment the innkeeper entered the barroom with two other men. They saw the tableau and rushed forward. "Here! Let her be!" the innkeeper shouted.

One of the others grabbed the Creature by the arm. With a roar the thing flung him aside like an old coat. The men stared in horror at his face. The Creature's eyes met Mary's, and he whirled and with inhuman speed dashed out the inn-yard door.

The men gathered themselves together. The one whom the Creature had thrown aside grimaced, favoring his right arm. The innkeeper helped Mary to her feet. "Are you all right, ma'am?"

Mary felt dizzy. Was she all right? What did that mean?

"I believe so," she said.

The innkeeper set her overturned chair back on its legs, and Mary sat.

"Lord," the wincing man said, "I think 'e's broken my arm."

"Who *was* that?" the third asked.

"I dunno," said the innkeeper, "but I don't favor seeing 'im again."

"I wish I'd never seen 'im," said the man with the broken arm. "My wife's going to make me sleep outside when she finds out about this. We'll be livin' on the parish before I'm back to work."

The door opened and out of the night stepped Darcy and Bingley. They surveyed the poorly lit room and the four figures there.

"Mary," said Darcy, rushing forward. "Thank the Lord." His voice betrayed both surprise and relief.

Bingley was at her side. "What happened to you?"

Mary's mind was still spinning, struggling with the things the monster had told her. The notion that Kitty's body had been stolen in order to create a bride for that abominable creature was an impossibility so out of keeping with the world of Bingley and Darcy and their concerns that she could hardly speak.

Bingley asked the men what had happened and got their version of the story. Based on what Mr. Poole had told them, Darcy and Bingley had been in Lambton looking for Mary most of the day. Only when they had exhausted that possibility had they considered that she might have come to Matlock instead. Mary asked if Darcy might help the poor man who had been injured trying to help her, and Darcy spoke with him and the innkeeper for a moment before they took her outside. They arranged to leave Darcy's horse in the inn's stable. Bingley would ride on ahead back to Pemberley to report that Mary was safe, while Darcy drove Mary in the gig.

It was full night now. They drove in silence for some time. Darcy had lit the lamps on the gig, but they threw very little light and he was intent on the dark road. Mary could sense anger just beneath his gentlemanly surface, so very properly controlled. Darcy was a civilized man, a man who had enjoyed every advantage of education, of breeding, of loving care, of prosperity, and of social authority. He would never strike a woman who said something that upset him. He would never upend a table in a tavern. But she knew by their names and reputations men of his class who did these things and worse. Perhaps the Creature's turning to violence when frustrated might not be sufficient proof that he was so inhuman.

It was not until they had turned off the public road and were well along on the way to Pemberley that Darcy spoke.

"Sister, you will pardon me if I express astonishment at your behavior." His voice was calm, but Mary could tell he spoke from deep emotion. "I do not know who the brute was who assaulted you, but the very fact that you should find yourself in such a situation is almost beyond belief. We are all familiar with your mother's dramatic performances, but I tell you that at this very moment back at Pemberley she is legitimately ill, thinking that she has lost two daughters in the same week. Whatever did you think you were doing?"

"I needed to speak with Victor Frankenstein."

"And I find you intoxicated, reeking of ale, in a tavern with some monstrous stranger? What business did you have with Mr. Frankenstein that could not have been dealt with by civilized means?"

"It was about Kitty. I thought he might know something of what happened to her."

"How should he know anything?"

"He did not know anything. Then I came to the inn and ate

supper. I stayed longer than I intended. I drank three glasses of port. I was thinking about Kitty, and how I will never see her again."

They had reached the rise in the road and the break in the forest that opened upon the prospect of Pemberley House. Between them and the house ran the Derwent, the sound of whose waters reached them even here. The great stone mansion lay extraordinarily peaceful under the waning moon. All the many windows were dark, save for the two that belonged to the upstairs salon, where someone still stirred. To the left stood stone outbuildings and the stables, and behind the house, farther up the hill, the white ornamental wall that framed the garden that Darcy's father had built.

"And how is it," Darcy asked, "that your melancholy dinner in the tavern turned into an assault by some stranger?"

"The person I encountered there did not intend to assault me."

"I am not sure that I trust your testimony. Who is he? Where is he from? What is his name?"

Mary looked across the slope toward the house. To its right, in a little grove above the riverside, the family mausoleum gleamed in the moonlight.

"I do not believe he has a name," said Mary.

ELEVEN

On hearing of the death of Catherine Bennet, I felt at first a great sadness over the sudden loss of a person I had only so recently met, and of course sympathy for her sister and family. My second, less admirable reaction, was gratitude toward the Providence—or the workings of the devil—that presented me another chance to obtain a female body. Under the pressure of necessity I found in myself resources of strength and purpose that I had not imagined I possessed. I was not so sanguine about the guile it likewise revealed. How vigorously I could act despite my soul's rebellion against the criminality of my actions. The day after I heard the sad news, I searched out a deserted stone barn on the road to Lambton, where I secreted the materials I would need should I manage to acquire Kitty's body. As dusk fell that June evening I evaded Henry at the inn, rented a horse, and rode out to the Darcy estate.

It was little more than a week after I had failed to steal the body of Nancy Brown when, under a moon whose light threatened to expose me, I tied my horse within the verge of the woodlands and crept upon the Pemberley mausoleum. It stood a hundred yards down the slope from the mansion, amid a grove of elms. The structure was in the style of a Greek temple, of white granite, four fluted Doric columns holding up an architrave into which the name DARCY was incised. Below a barred window the iron door displayed a bas-relief of the Darcy arms.

I narrowed the beam of my lantern so that its light might not attract the attention of anyone in the house. It was difficult for me to assault the lock while striving not to make noise, and under those circumstances it was proof against anything that I brought to bear upon it. I was at the point of despair when around the corner of the mausoleum stepped the Creature.

"It seems you need my help again," he said.

This time I did not argue. "It seems I do."

"I am at your service," he said, giving a little mock bow.

The thing drew from beneath its greatcoat a pry bar. He set the thin edge of it into the crack between the door's lock and the masonry frame, and leaned into it. Had I not seen the muscles of his neck straining, I might have imagined he was hardly engaged, but in fact he was exerting superhuman force. I saw the iron of the lock compress, and the stone of the frame crumble. He deftly released the pressure he was exerting at just the correct moment to keep the door from being flung open. He placed the pry bar silently at his feet, seized a bar in the window, and pulled it open. The door's hinges squealed. From the kennels far away came the barking of dogs.

We froze in the shadows until the barking ceased. I watched the big house and its outbuildings for signs that anyone had taken alarm, but when no light appeared, I returned to the opened mausoleum. The Creature was already inside with the lantern. He stared at a fresh marble plaque on the wall:

CATHERINE MARIE BENNET

1785–1815

The mortar with which the plaque had been set into the wall was yet soft, and it was a simple matter to pull it down to reveal the coffin, still smelling of flowers. The Creature withdrew it from its chamber and we opened it to expose Kitty's body. In the lantern light the pale ivory of her dress was hardly distinguishable from the color of her skin. Dark curls haloed her drawn, powdered face.

"How did you expect to move her body from here?"

"I'll get my horse from the woods and lay her across the saddle."

The Creature slid his arms beneath her and lifted her out of the coffin. "I will carry her." His voice was quiet.

I led him from the mausoleum, across the turf of the well-kept lawn to the woods. I retrieved my horse, and the monster followed me all the way to the Lambton road. Neither of us spoke. The Creature did not struggle under the burden of Kitty's body, but followed me at a steady pace until we reached the barn.

"Lay her there," I said, gesturing toward a pallet of straw that I had prepared. As he leaned to set her down, in the light of my lamp I saw that his eyes glistened. He laid her down as gently as a mother setting her child in its cradle.

"You needn't remain," I said to him.

"Do your work," he said.

I removed Kitty's clothing. Her pale body gleamed, and from it came the faint odor of decay. Her skin was unmarked save for a wound in the right forearm where the provincial doctor must have tried bleeding her. I massaged the body to loosen its joints and promote the draining of its blood. I made an incision in her jugular vein and her femoral artery and drained what blood I could. Using a rubber bladder, I forced a chemical fluid I had prepared through her body. I washed her skin down with a solution of weak carbolic acid.

The Creature watched me silently. His eyes never moved from her naked body, so pale, so small in comparison to his own.

It was time to fold her into the trunk I had prepared. "Help me now," I told him.

Her joints were stiff, and it was only with difficulty that we were able to fold her, kneeling, inside the trunk. As I pressed the back of her head down to close the lid over her, he spoke. "Don't hurt her."

"She cannot be hurt," I told him. "She is dead."

"Let me," he said.

He put either of his huge hands on the sides of her torso and subtly adjusted her body so that there was more space to fold her forward. He held the back of her neck in one hand and adjusted it so that her chin lay close to her breast. "Now," he said.

The lid closed over her and I screwed it shut.

"Tomorrow I will return with some draymen to retrieve

this trunk and send it ahead to Edinburgh. I do not wish to see you again until my task is complete."

He stared at me with malevolence, then strode out of the barn. When I had packed my other equipment and came out after him, he was nowhere to be seen.

I rode back to the town, contemplating the recent events. The younger Miss Bennet's sudden demise would save my family, and by extension the human race, from the consequences of my mistakes: her body would become the armature on which I would construct the Creature's mate. I wished it could have come without bringing such grief to Mary Bennet and her family, but I could not but think it was fate that had brought us together again.

The next day I returned to the barn with two draymen. We had just gotten back to the inn, and I was directing them to load my additional equipment, when to my immense surprise Mary Bennet herself accosted me. The fact that she had driven from Pemberley alone indicated that she was in a desperate emotional state. She looked half-wild with agitation.

I hurried her away from the inn, worried that if she spoke with Henry she might discover that I had been absent that whole night. I was right to worry: the purpose of her coming was to charge the Creature with stealing Kitty's body. She looked so distraught that it was all I could do not to tell her the truth, but I was compelled to equivocate. I embraced her and she cried upon my shoulder.

How charming Mary had seemed when she had recited Erasmus Darwin's poem to me a week ago. How taken I had been by her earnestness, her attempts at a coquette's boldness that only exposed her innocence. And the longer I saw her, the more I recognized a certain slightly disproportionate beauty in her face, and began to have affection for her physical awkwardness. My heart had indulged for a moment the distraction she provided, and I had imagined a visit to her brother's estate might come as a welcome respite. Perhaps this had all been part of some grand design to bring me, not to her, but to Kitty. Seeing Mary in the company of her sisters and her distinguished brothers-in-law gave me a better sense of the life she had led. Men like Darcy formed the upright backbone of English society. Her sister Elizabeth was a sharp observer of this world, her sister Jane a deft mistress of it. They were the noblest expression of British womanhood, graceful and accomplished guardians of propriety.

The world of comfort and responsibility they lived in was not so different from the one in which I had grown up. Like my good father, they possessed a magnanimous willingness to relax the strictures of behavior for the ones they loved—provided no one overstepped the bounds that would make them unacceptable to polite society. This sphere I had ceased to live in the moment I had brought my Creature to life. I lived in a different world now. The grisly secrets I concealed, the unholy actions I had taken and must still take, would seem a deranged fancy in Darcy's sitting room; no wonder I could not speak them. They would never cross the mind of Bingley or Darcy or certainly of their wives—but Mary?

Perhaps. Mary was not so suited to the world she grew up in. She was an odd fish. She imagined things that her family thought outrageous, and cared for things that they thought silly, and to that one might add her unschooled, childlike moral vision. So she had in complete ignorance discomfited me with her account of Aldini and his experiment with the hanged man. It showed how the misery of my situation had disordered my judgment. I should never have told her my story. In retrospect it was clear that she had not surmised what I had been about. But the fact that I *had* told her made it imperative for me to put her curiosity to rest.

She was easy to lie to, and, I had discovered, I was a good liar. I regretted deceiving her. Her intellect was great, but her ability to see through sham was undeveloped, and a kiss on her forehead drove away every thought behind it.

I had solved the problem of Mary Bennet, but the problem of Henry Clerval remained.

Following our departure from Matlock, on his insistence Henry and I passed two months in the Lake District. We took a cottage in Grasmere, from which we made excursions upon the fells. In that summer season we climbed the highest peak in Britain, followed freshets of mountain streams, sailed on lakes the color of deep blue metal, circled herds of bleating sheep on hillsides, and picnicked in the picturesque ruins of old cottages shadowed by verdant green woods. Even more here than in Matlock, the landscape resembled that of our native country.

Though we were far from the city bustle that had engaged Henry in London, or from the clubs and colleges of Oxford, Henry was pleased to meet with the various poets and writers who had made this countryside famous: Romantics who wrote verses about Nature and the Soul and the Immaterial World, who took laudanum and theorized about the transcendental and practiced Socratic love. Aging litterateurs who in their youth had spoken of revolution and now hurled the word "Jacobin" as an epithet. Henry ingratiated himself to some of them, and we spent evenings in their homes discussing the poetic arts and the dispensations of nature. Henry was easy prey. He told me, "I could pass my life here, and among these mountains I should scarcely regret Switzerland and the Rhine."

With Henry I dawdled through the weeks in a kind of feverish distraction. Whenever we left the warm light of some home where we had spent the evening in idle speculation around the fire, the moment we were enveloped by the cool night and the sound of crickets in the field, I imagined the eyes of the Creature on my neck. It never left me for a second that the body of Catherine Bennet awaited me, decaying in a sealed cedar trunk in Edinburgh. Time would not stop. I was not so sure of my method that I could afford at this point to dawdle. Now that I had a body to work from, the Creature's desire to have his mate must burn like an uncontrollable fire. He would not harm me, but in a rage of impatience he might well kill Henry.

When these thoughts possessed me, I would not quit Henry for a moment, but followed him as his shadow to protect him from the fancied rage of his destroyer. I felt as if I had committed some great crime, the consciousness of which haunted me. I was guiltless, but I had drawn down a horrible curse upon my head.

As youths, in solitary hours one summer in the alpine meadows, we had spoken of love. Once or twice we had exchanged embraces that went beyond brotherly affection, and explored the pleasures of which our young bodies were capable. There was no shame in these idylls, for we truly loved each other. But for me these moments were the expression of a desire that had more to do with brotherhood than carnality, and when that magic summer ended, though I suspected Henry might have wished it, they were never renewed. As the years passed and our friendship deepened, I felt that I owed Henry a debt, and resented the fact that it could never be repaid. These thoughts had come to me more than once during our travels, and they were with me for those months in Cumberland.

At last in mid-August I reminded Henry that we were to meet with our friend in Perth in two weeks, and we needed to move on to Scotland. Henry reluctantly bid farewell to his new friends and we took the coach to Edinburgh.

We had arranged lodgings at a modern hotel located in the city's New Town, with its straight, broad, clean streets and fine buildings. As soon as we were shown our rooms, and before we had even unpacked, I left Henry to arrange for supper while I went to speak with the porter.

"I am Victor Frankenstein," I told him. "Some trunks and boxes should have been sent here in my name, from London, Oxford, and Matlock. Do you have them?"

"We are happy to see you, sir. They arrived some weeks ago. They have been stored in the basement."

"Show them to me."

The porter took his lamp and we wound our way down stone stairs to a dark basement. It was chilly down there, well suited for preservation. I examined the trunk. One corner was slightly damaged, but it was intact.

"I should like these boxes shipped to Thurso," I told the porter. "Can you direct me to a reliable carting company?"

"McMaster's will do the job for you, sir, at a fair price. But Thurso's a far way. It will cost you dearly."

"I shall pay whatever is necessary."

The next day I went to the shipping office and made arrangements for transporting my equipment.

Edinburgh and its university were noted for its men of science, but at this point I had no need to meet with any such luminaries. What few purchases I made were of women's clothing — Kitty's burial dress would not suit the creature I would fashion from her body. I bought servant's clothes: plain dresses of wool, a coat, and some sturdy shoes.

Henry had been uncommunicative on our journey from Grasmere to Edinburgh, but had brightened when we reached the city. We visited some of the notable sights: the Edinburgh Castle, the Parliament House, the royal palace and picturesque ruins of Holyrood Abbey. The day we visited Holyrood was overcast with occasional gusts of rain. Puddles stood on the worn stone pavements of the chapel floor, open to the elements. Water trickled down the ruined masonry, green with moss. My mind was not there, but drifted on thoughts of home.

As we left the ruined abbey, the sky cleared and sunlight broke through. Henry said, "The weather improves. Rather than return to the hotel, will you walk with me? We might climb to the summit of Arthur's Seat and take the prospect of the city and the landscape."

Arthur's Seat is a mount situated in Holyrood Park about a mile from Edinburgh Castle, and renowned for the view it gives of the region. In truth it is more a hill than a mountain, but Henry had enjoyed the Cumberland mountains so much that I decided to accompany him. Perhaps a climb together would help reduce the distance that had grown between us.

From the university the profile of the hill resembled that of a lion, couchant. For the most part the clouds had blown away, and the bright sun shone. Henry and I followed a gravel path up its flank, winding through folds of emerald turf, tall grass, thick bushes, and mossy boulders. In places the path broke into rough steps made of flat stones. The heather sported sprigs of purple flowers, and yellow wild iris lay scattered like fallen stars in beds of grass. Some few other people had come out onto the hill, but for the most part we were alone. We paused several times on our climb up to catch our breath, and the chilly air invigorated me.

The stark red stone Salisbury Crags, the shelf above covered with turf, looked down on the city. We could see the steeples of the town's churches, and the romantic pile of the castle with pennants flying above its tower. From the summit of the hill, some eight hundred feet above the surrounding plain, Edinburgh lay spread to the west and north where the land eventually ran down to Leith, Queensferry, and the Firth of Forth. The water lay silver with the reflection of the sun.

To the east, cows were visible in a field between lines of trees, pastures punctuated by stone houses and barns. Above us wind-torn clouds occasionally passed before the sun. Gulls swooped and hovered over our heads.

As I viewed this tranquil scene, I was startled to feel Henry's hand upon my shoulder. I turned to find him watching me with sober eyes, the faint smile upon his lips belied by his tragic mien. He did not let his hand drop. Instead he embraced me and held me tightly to his breast.

I submitted to his embrace, but did not return it.

He stepped back. "Victor," he said, "do you love Elizabeth?"

"Of course I love her."

"Yet you show no sign of wishing to return to her. I understand that sometimes we keep our true affections a secret even from ourselves. Whether with intention or not, I think you deceive her—deceive us all."

Henry had coaxed me up to this place only to make some claim on me. "The only deception I know is that you profess to travel with me in order to educate yourself for a career in diplomacy, when you are here simply to keep from taking up work in your father's business."

Henry looked wounded. "I came with you to help you."

"You might help me by leaving me to my thoughts."

"What else must I leave you to? Your grave robbing?"

My heart flipped. Henry stood very still. The wind blew back his hair.

"What do you mean?" I said feebly.

"I mean your absence from the inn on the night that the Reverend Chatsworth found the strangers in his graveyard. I saw you blanch as he told that story. I mean your absence on the night that Catherine Bennet's body was stolen. And your contracting the cart men to retrieve that new trunk the next morning, before we departed, and your hurrying to check on it the first thing when we arrived in Edinburgh. I am not blind, Victor, nor am I a fool."

"You have no faith in me."

"Had I no faith in you, I would have told someone about this. Instead I have kept silent. I thought, when we were in Cumberland, that you might have set aside this madness, but I see you are ready to resume whatever it might be. I do not look forward to what occurs next."

"What occurs next is that you will let this pass, or go back to Geneva without me."

"You jested of inventing some new battery. It's no battery you have sealed in that trunk. You met with that anatomist in Oxford. You have haunted graveyards. You are intent on pursuing the medical research that ruined your health in Ingolstadt—the obsession that has weighed on you ever since."

"What weighs on me is the death of William."

"William's murder does not drive you. I might accept that scientific research could distract you from your grief, but you act as if torn in two directions. One thing pushes you toward these researches, and something else makes you wish you could thrust them aside, as if a poisoned cup were being held to your lips."

"You have no right to ask me these things."

"I nursed you back to health through a German winter. No one has been more devoted to your well-being than I. But for the life of me I cannot understand what does drive you, and I fear where it will end. I worry for your sanity, Victor. Must I write your father? What promised achievement, what new discovery, could possibly justify your behavior?"

He was right to remind me of the trouble I had brought him, yet his hectoring tone pushed me past some limit, and I was suddenly furious. I had worried constantly that because of me he was in danger; I had hovered over him like a guardian angel—and it came to this.

"What promised achievement leads you into the private homes of these artistic older men?" I told him. "Or the younger men of Oxford? The clubs and dining rooms? On those evenings when you have been absent all night and come back to our rooms at dawn, whose graves have *you* been robbing, Henry?"

Henry crossed his arms over his chest. He looked at me for a moment, and then looked away. "You've been in half those clubs and dining rooms with me."

"Not of my own choosing, I assure you. And of late it seems to me that you have preferred that I not be there."

"Is it any wonder?" Henry could not look at me. He kicked at a stone and it skittered away on the path, landing amid some bluebells. "We were to be companions on this journey. It is almost a year now since we left home. I thought that time and a change of scene might foster the intimacy that we once had as boys, that you might open your soul to me as you once did — and as I did for you. But I realize that is not to be. So I have pursued other acquaintance."

"And amusement."

"Yes, Victor — amusement. What right have you to gainsay my doing so?"

Now I could not look at him. "No right."

"So," he said, an attorney summing up his case, "we come to a meeting of the minds after all. I have no right to ask you about your unsavory pastimes, and you have no right to ask me about mine."

He turned his back to me and looked to the west, where the summer sun glared off the Firth and turned the clouds silver. The birds still swooped overhead.

We stood a while in silence, and then, in silence, we descended the mount. The next day we left Edinburgh for Perth.

⌒⌒

In Perth we stayed at the home of Dr. Christopher Marble, who had lived in Geneva and done some business with Henry's father. He was very pleased at our arrival and proved the most generous of hosts. He and his family lived in a large town house in that busy municipality.

Dr. Marble was a tall, genial man with impressive side whiskers, whose distinguishing quirk was his insistence that everything in his home be kept spotlessly clean. Mrs. Marble was as sociable as her husband, and just as curious.

"And how fares your father?" Dr. Marble asked Henry in his soft burr. "Your dear mother? Does she still spend so much time tending the flowers in your garden?"

I was happy to let Henry occupy them with family tales, especially as, when Marble discovered that I had studied chemistry and anatomy, he became a fount of well-meaning but uncomfortable questions. I was at some difficulty to put him off, warily watching Henry out of the corner of my eye.

Marble had two children: a daughter of about our age and a younger son who had recently graduated from St. Andrews. The daughter, Julia, was a quiet young woman, but I could tell that she very much enjoyed having two young bachelors as guests. She and Dennis, the son, were eager to introduce us to Perth society, which was livelier, they said, than one might imagine thanks to the Perth Academy and the Queen's Barracks—to say nothing of the local distilling industry. Immediately we were scheduled for dinners, card parties, and balls.

I tolerated this for as long as I could—longer, really, than I might have, but the thought that Henry watched, expecting me sooner or later to take up my researches, was enough to trouble every moment. In the end my fate lay before me, not to be dispensed with by the wave of a lady's fan or the trepidations of a friend.

When I told him we must separate, Henry was unhappy. "Please do not go. I apologize for what I said that afternoon on Arthur's Seat."

"It is I who should apologize to you," I said. "I cannot explain what I have been about, but believe me when I say it is something I must attend to. Please forgive me. Do you enjoy yourself, and let this be our rendezvous. I may be absent a month or two. I entreat you to leave me in solitude for a short time. When I return, I hope it will be with a lighter heart."

"I had rather be with you than with these Scottish people, whom I do not know."

Without my having to reiterate my resolve, Henry saw that this last importunity would have no effect. He managed a rueful smile, at himself or at me, and continued, "Hasten then, my dear friend, to return, that I may again feel myself somewhat at home, which I cannot do in your absence."

And so I bid farewell to Perth, and with relief and dread, made my way in the most uncomfortable coach ride of my life to Thurso, on the northernmost Scottish coast. The northern scenery had its stark beauty, but I was not engaged. In Thurso I retrieved all the materials I had collected to essay my final task and hired a sloop to carry me to the tiny isle in the Orkneys, five miles from the mainland, that I had chosen as the site of my labors.

The island claimed only five inhabitants and three decaying huts, one of which I rented and had refurbished. It consisted of two rooms under a thatched roof. Workmen from the mainland replastered the walls, repaired the roof, laid down a plank floor, and constructed a shed attached to the house. I brought in simple furniture. One room became my living quarters and the other my laboratory.

The dull wretches who peopled the island scratched out a meager living fishing and tending the few scrawny sheep that cropped their barren pastures. All other fare had to be brought from the mainland; with a grocer in Thurso I established a weekly delivery of vegetables, bread, and meat; otherwise I had nothing to do with any person other than those I might occasionally encounter on my solitary walks along the beach. I listened to the endless churning of the surf, gazed at the swelling waters that ran from slate gray to deep green, and ducked the raucous seabirds that swooped over the waves.

When the improvements to my dwelling were completed, I set up my equipment and steeled myself to begin the task that I had delayed for so long. All illusions were sped. I was alone. Nothing now stood between me and the filthy work before me, only this time my eyes were not obscured by the enthusiasm that had blinded me in the months leading up to my bringing my tormenter to life.

My microscope and slides, the carboys of chemicals, the metal table, the large copper bath and electrical apparatus, all stood neatly arranged, awaiting use. I dragged the trunk containing Kitty Bennet's body to the center of the laboratory. When I unscrewed the lid and opened it, I gagged at the sweet stench that assaulted me. Struggling, I dragged her decaying corpse from its refuge and laid it out on the table where I was to fashion it into a bride for the fiend who had ruined my life.

TWELVE

Since Kitty's death Mr. Bennet's health had declined, and their return home to Longbourn had done little to recover it. Her absence hovered over every room of the house, every walk in the garden. Mary did her best to comfort both her parents.

Today was a splendid August afternoon, warm and bright with sun. Mary had arranged to have a place prepared outdoors for her father with an armchair, a small table, and tea. Mr. Bennet sat beneath one of the trees, a robe over his lap and a book open on it, but he was not reading. His head lay back against the chair, and his eyes were closed. He wore a black armband. Mary did not think he was sleeping. She wondered at the content of his thought, and hoped whatever it was comforted him.

The emerald turf lay thick beneath the elms, and the fine gravel of the path had been raked until it was as easy for her parents to traverse as Longbourn's second-floor hallway. The house, with its many-paned windows and ivy-covered walls, stood as lovely and inviting in the afternoon sun as any such residence in England. Mary sat with her mother on a bench some distance from Mr. Bennet, beside a low wall surrounding a bed of roses. Mrs. Bennet was silent. She had been more silent since their return than Mary had ever seen her.

From the vantage point of the garden at Longbourn, the events that had occurred at Pemberley seemed inconceivable, but Mary could not purge the disordered jumble of images from her memory: Kitty trembling in her arms as she confessed her indiscretion with Mr. Clarke, Victor Frankenstein's face in the light from the fireplace as he told his own impossible story, the voice of tipsy Reverend Chatsworth at dinner, Victor and Mary bantering over the fossils in the natural history cabinets, her conversation with the monster in the taproom of the Matlock inn, the blood running from Kitty's arm into the basin that Mary held on that last night of her sister's life.

In many ways nothing at Longbourn had changed but the banishment of color from their dress. Mrs. Hill, the housekeeper; Alice; and the other servants were the same, as were the daily round of pastimes, Father in his study, Mother writing to her grandchildren. Mary might have imagined that Kitty was simply away visiting Pemberley while she was consigned to stay at home. But of course everything was different. Kitty was dead. And the extraordinary memories in Mary's mind would not be wiped away.

"Mary, would you see that your father's tea is warm?" Mrs. Bennet asked her.

Mr. Bennet overheard her, lifted his head, and called

from across the lawn, "My tea is quite warm, my dear. Do not trouble yourself, Mary."

His voice piped like that of an old man.

"Very well, Mr. Bennet," her mother called, in a tone that would convince no one that all was well.

"What does Mr. Woodleigh write you about?" she asked Mary.

Mary folded the letter she had in her lap. "His sister has given birth to a son. Her second. The family is very pleased."

"I wish we had had a son," Mrs. Bennet said idly. She caught herself and looked at Mary with more purpose. "Please forgive me, Mary. Of course I would not have traded any of you for a son."

"You have done nothing that requires forgiveness, Mother."

"You are a good girl," Mrs. Bennet said. "You are all good girls."

She observed her husband for a space of seconds. Mr. Bennet adjusted his spectacles and took up his book. Mrs. Bennet could not rest easy, and stood. "Will you walk with me, Mary?"

"Certainly, Mother."

They took a turn around the garden. Lady Catherine De Bourgh had taken Elizabeth outside to walk along this same path while Mary, her sisters, and Mrs. Bennet had peered through the windows trying to surmise what they discussed, a prelude to Lizzy announcing her engagement to Mr. Darcy. Mrs. Bennet was not commonly a lover of strolls through nature. They walked in silence. Mary could see that her mother was working her way toward addressing some difficult subject. She was not a woman who long kept her thoughts to herself, and her reticence made Mary only more curious. Finally, without looking at Mary, she spoke.

"I have been thinking," Mrs. Bennet said slowly, "and I believe that Kitty died because of me."

Mary stopped. Her mother took a step beyond her, halted, and turned. Her eyes glistened.

"No, Mother," Mary replied. "That is not true. You were not even there."

"I let her go to Pemberley when I knew she was not well."

This sort of talk from her mother was new. It was perhaps in keeping with her character that she would see Kitty's death in the light of how it affected her, but not if that meant taking responsibility.

Mary said, "Mother, if you must blame someone, blame me. I went walking with her when I might have noted that it threatened rain."

"It was not your duty to care for her. It was mine."

"And you did care for her. You gave her every attention."

"I gave her the sort of attention that suited me. I sought to make sure she dressed so as to represent me well, and to get her a husband that would increase my importance in the world."

This was like nothing Mary had ever heard from her mother.

Mrs. Bennet resumed walking. After some moments she said, "Do you believe in Providence, Mary?"

"Yes. I do."

"I have heard this word my entire life, and I never gave it thought until now. I fear I have been a very vain woman. The world vexes me, and I blame your father, or the neighbors, or one of you, or the servants, or some other person. I have gone to church on the Lord's Day, sat in our pew, sang the words of the hymns, and never once considered what any of this meant. I might as well have been singing nursery rhymes. My prayers were no more serious than the wishes a little girl makes on a rainbow. I might as well be a little girl, for all the wisdom I have accumulated, all the virtue I have brought to our family. Your father stopped caring for me many years ago. Now God has stopped caring for me, as well."

Mary was frightened. "Mother, you mustn't speak this way. I know that you grieve, but the Lord does not wish you to take all this onto yourself."

"If the Lord wants anything, he wants sinners to admit their sins. I am finally ready to do that. He told me that when Kitty died. He told me again when she was stolen from her grave. Who would do such a thing?"

"Whoever did it," Mary said, "was certainly not doing the Lord's work."

They had come to the end of the grove, to the little wild hollow they called the hermitage, from which they could only see the very top of the house and chimneys. Mary and her sisters had played hide-and-seek here. Lydia and Kitty had come here to scheme about the brilliant marriages they would make.

Mrs. Bennet sighed. "I suppose to be vexed at God is another sin. And many have seen much more trouble than I." She pulled her shawl closer around her and looked about the place as if seeing it for the first time. "Why, this is a lovely spot. I don't know why I have never come here before."

Mary felt overcome with tenderness for her mother, and on an impulse embraced her. Mrs. Bennet stiffened, then relaxed and put her arms around Mary. Mary swallowed back tears. Her mother whispered into her ear, "I am so glad that you are still with me. You are my comfort."

They separated. Mary looked into her mother's aged eyes.

"We should go back and see after your father," Mrs. Bennet said. "And we must plan the dinner for Sir William Lucas and family, just you and I, together."

On the walk back, Mary considered what her mother had said. The great pity she felt for her mother was genuine, and to hear her call Mary her comfort was gratifying. But as they prepared for supper and Mrs. Bennet began to tell Mary all that they would have to do to prepare for their next social engagement, Mary felt less easy.

To be her mother's comfort was to be needed, but it was not what she had lived for. In fact, in the aftermath of Kitty's death and the encounter with Victor Frankenstein and his monster, Mary had come to wonder what it was for which she lived. Those moments confronting the Creature in the Matlock taproom had been the most frightening of her life, but they had also opened a view to a mode of existence that she had not imagined. Life and death lay very close beneath the surface of every earthly thing, and the door to them might be torn open at any moment, leaving no time to prepare the way one might prepare for a visit from Sir William.

One of the things they would certainly speak of at this dinner would be the deaths of Charlotte and Kitty. They would say the proper, polite things, and no one, not even her mother, would overstep the bounds of propriety. Mary could not imagine telling them what she knew of Kitty and Mr. Clarke. She could not tell them of Victor's visit to her room at night, or the nature of the Creature she had confronted. Or the kiss that Victor had given her. The feel of his body against hers in the St. Giles churchyard.

Not a day had gone by in the last month when these things had been far from her thoughts. Either Victor or the monster had lied to her. If the monster was to be believed, Kitty was to be brought back to life again to be his bride. Victor had insisted that such a being, if he were to create her, would not be Kitty, but Mary could not untangle truth from falsehood in all of this. Perhaps by some miracle Kitty might be restored. Even if that were impossible, it occurred to Mary that, if the burden that so obviously weighed Victor down was his vow to create a companion for his monster, once he had accomplished this task he would be free. Mary would give much to see his face untroubled by the torment of obligation to his demonic creation. In that happy moment, able at last to act in accordance with his best nature, to whom might his grateful attentions turn?

If there were a Providence, Mary believed that her role in it must go beyond providing comfort to her mother. Why otherwise would God have put Mary in the way of Victor Frankenstein and his Creature? Why otherwise would He have Kitty taken for their purposes? There had to be some sequel to these events. But she would never find it if she stayed in Longbourn. She would have to journey north, to Scotland, to fulfill whatever role destiny might have in store for her.

In his most recent letter to Mary, Mr. Woodleigh alluded to the sale of a fossil collection that was to take place at the University of Edinburgh. Mary showed her parents the announcement in the notes of the Geological Society. She told them that she wished to travel to Edinburgh to take part in the auction.

Mrs. Bennet said that she could not possibly spare Mary for such a purpose. Mary felt a twinge of conscience at the thought of abandoning her mother so soon after her revelations of her troubled conscience, but she also feared that if she did not get away now, no matter the outcome of her flight, she would never have the will to do so.

Mr. Bennet said that the distance was far too great, and suggested that Mary might bid on those items that interested her from their home. Mary maintained that she needed to see these fossils in person, and would need to know what other bidders there were, before she could make a sensible judgment. Mr. Bennet replied that, unfortunately, his health would not allow him to accompany her, so that should settle the matter.

Mary pointed out that she was not a girl but a woman of thirty-two years old. She proposed that they should send Alice along with her as a companion. Alice could serve in that capacity as well, probably better, than Mr. Bennet, if indeed a chaperone for someone as unexceptional as Mary might be required.

In the end, Mary's arguments carried the day, and it was arranged that she and Alice should leave by post coach in three days. They would stop briefly at Pemberley, and continue on to Edinburgh. Mr. Bennet prepared a letter of credit that Mary might use at the Bank of Scotland. Mrs. Bennet fussed, but in the end, clutching a handkerchief to manage her tears, she kissed Mary on both cheeks and released her to climb into the coach in front of the Meryton Assembly Rooms.

Alice was excited. She had seen London with Mrs. Bennet

and her daughters, but had never in her life traveled in the north, and was eager to see the sights of Scotland. They arrived at Pemberley in good time. The memory of Kitty's loss made for a melancholy visit, and Mary remained for only two days before continuing.

The journey from Derbyshire to Edinburgh was arduous, some two hundred fifty miles. Though the roads had recently seen great improvement, there were still long stretches where the coach jolted along ruts at a walking pace and any passengers perched on top had to hold on for dear life. The coaching inns along the way provided poor meals at a high price, and because the coach stopped for only twenty minutes to change horses, Mary and Alice often could not finish the meals they had paid for before they were obliged to climb back aboard for further sleepless hours of discomfort. At least they were not forced to ride on the top, exposed to the elements. For some stages of the trip there were as many as seven people up there. Yet the inside was frequently unpleasant and crowded, the conversation of their fellow travelers insipid, and the reek of their close quarters at times made Mary wish she were up top after all.

Alice's excitement at being away from Meryton faded rapidly. She did not spare Mary her complaints, ones she would not have voiced to Mrs. Bennet. "More than once I ask myself why you, miss, should trouble to make this journey for the sake of some curiosities," she sighed when they had spent a rainy day staring out the coach window at the dreary countryside, "but I suppose these rocks is vallable to those 'at knows them." In the end Alice recognized in Mary a milder mistress than her mother, and did not abuse the liberty Mary allowed her.

At last they arrived at the Two Swans in Edinburgh. If

the porter thought it untoward that Mary traveled with only a female companion, he showed no sign of his skepticism. Alice saw to unpacking their trunks and preparing their room at the inn. She was a shrewd woman when it came to dealing with servants and innkeepers, but she had been so long habituated to Mary's submission to the strictures of her family that she could not expect what Mary was planning.

Mary discovered that the mail coach to Perth left every Monday, Wednesday, and Friday at six in the morning. Without letting on to Alice, she arranged for her passage on the Friday coach. On Thursday she visited the Bank of Scotland and, using the letter of credit, obtained twenty pounds in banknotes and ten in coin. The bank clerk hesitated to disburse so large a sum, but Mary's far-from-girlish behavior did not offer him the opportunity to question her. On her return from the bank she stopped at the post office and mailed a letter to her parents. She packed a small case with those things she would need to continue her journey, and left it in the porter's keeping with the instructions that it should be loaded on the Friday morning coach, so that Mary might depart without having to alert Alice.

On that Friday morning, Mary rose early and, on the pretext of female indisposition, went down to the inn yard where, with little fuss or notice, she climbed into the coach. She waited in some anxiety over whether Alice might come down to breakfast and find her there, but the coach departed promptly at six and within minutes was rolling down Princes Street toward the Queensferry road.

It was fifty miles to Perth, and the coach should arrive there by late that evening.

Mary's heart was in her throat. She could imagine Alice's distress when she found the note that Mary had left.

> Alice,
>
> I have departed Edinburgh on a matter that need not concern you. I shall not return for at least a month. Do not attempt to follow me. Here is five pounds that I trust will see you safely back to Longbourn. I am sorry to abandon you in this way. I have written to my parents absolving you of responsibility for my actions.
>
> God keep you,
Mary Bennet

The letter that she had posted to her parents read:

> Dearest Father and Mother,
>
> I write to tell you that, having arrived safely in Edinburgh with Alice, I have since left her there. By the time you receive this, I will have traveled on to places elsewhere in Scotland.
>
> I know that you must consider this beyond anything you might have expected of me, and a source of great concern. It is beyond anything I might have expected of myself. I can only say that, in the wake of Kitty's death, and reflecting on certain knowledge I have obtained about the reasons for her remains being stolen, I have determined to pursue those who have done this with the hope of finding further explanation and, if God be willing, some justice for her and for our family. It may even be that, should what I surmise to be possible come to pass, I may bring home

with me a greater consolation than any of us might have imagined.

Please do not dispatch anyone to retrieve me, as it is unlikely that they will be able to find me until my goal has either been attained, or I shall have failed. In either case I shall return to you, I promise. I regret that I have had to resort to deception in order to follow this course, but it was clear to me that you would never have allowed me to leave on this quest had I revealed to you its nature. I regret even more the worry that I know this will cause you, dearest parents, and the rest of our family. If anyone should inquire after me, I suggest that you tell them that I have met with friends in Scotland and that they have invited me to stay with them in their country house until Michaelmas.

I will endeavor to communicate with you from time to time. If things go as I plan, I should return home by the beginning of October.

Please do not hold Alice responsible for my behavior. She did not know any of my plans, and if she has failed to prevent my slipping away, it is only because she trusted me, and not because of any neglect on her part.

I know that this will seem foolish if not mad to you. I am not mad, and if I am foolish, it is the foolishness of a person who seeks to live an honorable life in accord with her own nature. I love you both, and I remain always,

Your daughter,
Mary

Accompanying Mary in the coach were three men. Two of them, who introduced themselves as Mr. Craig and Mr.

Cromartie, were merchants headed for a meeting with distillers in Perth. They did not ask how it was that an Englishwoman came to be traveling alone in Scotland, and fell to debating each other about how much they could afford to pay per keg of the Scotch they intended to ship to London, and whether the recent end to the wars would open up new markets in the Continent.

The third man was Mr. Butterworth, who was traveling to Perth to take a position teaching history and philosophy at the Perth Academy. Mr. Butterworth had been educated at Cambridge and had studied at the university in Edinburgh.

Above them, perched on the seat behind the trunk containing the mail and in the seat behind the driver, were the guard for the Royal Mail and a husband and wife who could not afford to pay the premium to ride inside the coach.

It was perhaps nine in the evening, and the last light of a lingering sunset had faded. The expectation was that they would reach Perth in a little more than an hour. The driver had lit the coach lamps and the road lay along the winding path of the River Tay. Here, unlike on the heath they had earlier passed, trees overhung the road. The moon cast a little light through the branches.

Suddenly the coach lurched and halted. Mary was almost thrown from her seat, and above them the woman cried out. From outside came a shout, "Stand and deliver!"

They heard the crack of a rifle, and in return, two more reports. A thud on the coach roof, and past the window in the door fell the guard.

"Don't shoot!" the driver cried.

"Climb down!" demanded the first voice.

Mr. Cromartie fumbled inside his coat, withdrew some banknotes, and in great haste stuffed them into his stocking.

The door of the coach was jerked open and a man thrust his hand, holding a pistol, into their faces. "Out, now, all of ye." Mary cowered in the corner. Butterworth and the two others climbed out. The highwayman stuck his head in and saw Mary. "You, also."

THIRTEEN

Once I had helped him steal Kitty Bennet's body, it was difficult for me to remain patient. My senses were so charged it was as if my heart beat just below the surface of my skin. The sight of the poor woman's exposed form lay imprinted on my mind. So small, so frail. I felt the stirrings of desire, and imagined a future where I might take her hand and enfold her, living and breathing, in my arms. The sweetness of this prospect threatened to overwhelm me. Yet it did not happen—every time it seemed that Victor took a step forward, there inevitably ensued a long period of inaction. Two months—two months!—he and Henry went off to some picturesque backwater to commune with poets and poseurs.

I had eavesdropped at their Matlock inn and knew that they intended to continue eventually to Perth, Scotland, to stay with some friend of Henry's family.

I suppose that this served my purpose in one way. The coachmen I'd had to listen to for hours while spying on the inn courtyard had revealed that Edinburgh was two hundred and fifty miles from Matlock, and Perth farther still. If I were to follow Frankenstein, I must travel on foot. Those months gave me time to make my way there.

While I traveled, I had time to ponder many things. One of them was my conversation with Mary Bennet. Other than Victor, she was the one human being who had ever spoken with me in anything resembling common human intercourse. Whether through fear or anger she had trembled as she approached my table. She was clearly repulsed by my presence. It took all the bravery she could muster to look unflinching into my face. Yet she had confronted me as no one ever had and defended Victor against the truths I told her. When I contemplated this, it only increased my bitterness. She was a fool, another human being who upon seeing me quaked in unmotivated fear, a privileged, idle woman who could not see beyond the cage that society had fashioned for her.

It was not possible that a person like this could hurt me. Had I not received every sort of blow that a human being could level against another?

Then she charged me with seeking a mate only that I might have a slave to my desires. With contempt in her voice, she predicted that the companion Victor should fashion for me would reject me.

I had come all this way in the expectation that once Victor created my bride, my suffering would end. I had believed that my fate lay in the hands of Victor Frankenstein and no one else. If Mary Bennet was right, the world was more complicated

than that. My happiness depended upon a yet uncreated creature over whom I would have no control.

You only seek a toy of your own, she had told me.

Was that what I sought? I desperately needed this not-
yet-alive female to accept me. I had imagined that this conclusion was foregone. Would I wish her to have a choice, if
that left the chance that she would deny me? *Wait until you are
rejected, for the most trivial of reasons, by one who ought to have been
made for you.*

Miss Bennet's words hovered over me like a curse. And I
had fled her presence as if she had pronounced it over me.

It took me two months to reach Edinburgh. I traveled
mostly at night, and found my sustenance in the fields and
woods. Occasionally I would sneak into a farmyard to steal
some eggs. When I saw a human, I did my best to hide. I had
a few bad moments—one night when I stumbled upon a camp
of Gypsies who pursued me for a mile in the woods, another
when a farm boy found me sleeping in a shepherd's shack and
fled at the sight of me.

There were times as I made this slow journey that I wondered why I should even persist. Were it not for loneliness,
the life of a vagabond offered its consolations. From my first
moment of existence I had loved the natural world. Plants and
animals. The birds singing. The patterns that the wind wrote
on the rippling heads of grain in the fields. The taste of pure
water. The bitter sweetness of blackberries, the earthy taste
of mushrooms. All this was good, given without stint by the
world, without judgment or mockery. I might live in some
wood or vale for the rest of my days, feeling the sun on my
face, keeping a fire to warm me in the winter.

Had I not remembered Kitty's lovely figure, I might have stopped. In the light of it I knew that any respite nature offered me from the need of companionship would pall, only leaving me more isolated, alone, desperate for a human touch.

Once I arrived at Edinburgh, it took me a week to discover that Victor and Henry had been there and gone on the coach to Perth. Another delay came when I had to circle round the Firth of Forth to make my way north.

It was a night early in September when, on a winding road that followed the valley of the River Tay, I heard the sounds of a coach coming from behind me. I slipped into the trees and waited for it to pass.

Its lamps were lit, and I watched it approach for some distance. As it neared, I saw, in the faint moonlight, that it was a mail coach, its four horses moving at a steady but not strenuous pace. As it passed me, I saw the brightly liveried guard atop, head lolling as he slept with his rifle across his lap.

The coach was no more than twenty yards beyond me when a shout came from the woods and two men on horseback blocked the road. The driver hauled back on the reins and the coach rattled to a stop.

"Stand and deliver!" one of the horsemen called, a pistol in his hand. His partner had two pistols out. Both had pulled up their neck cloths until they obscured the lower half of their faces.

The guard came awake, raised the rifle to his shoulder, and fired.

His shot went wide of the highwaymen and both of them discharged their pistols at him. One at least hit home, for the guard tumbled off the top of the coach into the road.

"Don't shoot!" the driver yelled.

"Climb down," the first rider said.

Though I might easily have slipped away, I crept closer. The second of the highwaymen dismounted, came to the coach, ripped its door open, and thrust his pistoled fist inside.

The driver and the rooftop passengers climbed down, and from inside the coach came three men and a woman. The woman immediately knelt to examine the fallen guard.

"Is he breathing?" the first highwayman asked, dismounting.

The guard struggled to sit up, his left hand clamped onto his breast. The woman helped him to sit. I could hear his labored breathing.

"Here, you," the second highwayman said to the woman, "come away."

Reluctantly, the woman stood, staggering slightly. When light from the coach's lamp caught her face, I saw that it was Mary Bennet.

A chill ran through me. It was as if my thought had conjured her up. As if her words to me in the taproom were indeed a curse to follow me, and the curse was her.

"This man is seriously injured," she said. "He needs immediate medical attention."

"A scratch," the second man said. The smell of the gunpowder still lingered. The night was still.

"We'll have no more heroism tonight, shall we?" the first man said. "Let's see your purses."

The gentlemen from within the coach surrendered their purses. The robbers opened and emptied them in turn. "Hello, now," the first highwayman said. "You seem to be traveling light this evening, sir," he said to one of the men. "Turn out your pockets."

"I assure you, I have no more money."

The robber reached into the man's vest and pulled out a gold watch, which he studied in the light of the lamp, his gun still trained on the men. "Lovely timepiece for such an impoverished soul, i'n'it?"

The highwayman turned him around, poked his pistol square into the man's back, and pushed him against the coach. With his other hand he felt the man's legs. He stopped and, one-handed, plucked a wad of folded banknotes out of the man's stocking.

"Aren't we clever," the second thief said. He slammed the man's head against the coach. The passenger yelped and brought his arms up to protect himself.

"Any of the rest of you holding out?"

The other passengers emptied their pockets and purses.

"Madam," the first said to Mary Bennet. "I'll have your purse."

Miss Bennet handed it to him. He shook out a few coins. "Is this all the money you have? Which of these gentlemen do you travel with, madam?"

"I travel alone."

"A risky business for a fine lady like yourself. Where is your husband?"

"I am not married."

"Why am I not surprised? Yet clearly well-bred, and well-dressed. And six shillings in your purse. How is this possible?"

"I am to be met in Perth by family. They are to take care of me."

The thief shook his head sadly. "Ah, miss, if they cared for you, you would not be traveling alone. Until you see them again, *we* shall have to take care of you." He grabbed her by the wrist. "The rest of you, back onto the coach. You," he said to the passenger he had struck. "Help that guard up, and be on your way."

"What?" Mary Bennet said. "No! Let me go! What do you want with me?"

"Let her be," one of the passengers said.

The highwayman cuffed him with the back of his hand. The man fell to one knee. "Get in the bloody coach," the robber said. "Get the bloody guard inside and be off with you."

The curses hung in the silent air. Two men helped the guard, head lolling and blood glistening on his coat, into the coach, then climbed in after him. The others clambered up onto the roof, as did the driver, who took up his reins.

"Please, let me go!" Mary Bennet pleaded. "Why keep me?"

"I think, like that gentleman liar there, you carry about you more money than you admit. Take off that coat."

The driver cast a look down on her.

"Get on with ye!" the first highwayman said, and slapped the haunch of one of the coach horses. The horse jerked forward in its traces, and the driver took his whip and applied it. The coach rattled off into the darkness.

It left behind silence, the taste of dust, and the three fig- ures in the moonlit road. One of the men held the reins of their horses; the second said to Miss Bennet, "Off with your coat."

"It's cold," she said.

The man tore Mary's coat from her shoulders. She

stumbled. He went through her pockets but, finding nothing, tossed it back at her.

"Her shoes," the other man said. "Look in her shoes."

"There's nothing in my shoes."

"Then there's no harm removing them," the other robber said.

"I will not."

The man seized her arm. "Then I'll help ye."

Mary Bennet said, "Stop! I'll do it."

He released her. She bent over, removed her ankle-high half boot, and handed it to the man. From it he pulled some folded banknotes. "You little minx," he said. "Lying to us."

"I need that money," she said. "You mustn't take it."

"Hold your tongue," the highwayman said. He took her by the arm again. "You look like a lonely woman. Maybe you would enjoy some conversation before we send you on your way."

"Let me go!"

The man with the horses spoke. "Not that, Teddy."

"Why not? She's an ill-favored old maid, but I'm not particular."

Mary Bennet struggled in the man's grasp. The other highwayman stood, unwilling to help his partner.

The man pulled Miss Bennet's wrist behind her back. He pressed his masked face close to hers. She twisted her head away. "Be still, woman! I'll teach you to fight—"

She bit his cheek.

He knocked her to the ground and put his hand to his face. "You bloody bitch . . ."

I stepped out from the woods, took three strides, grabbed him by the collar and the seat of his pants, and flung him against a tree.

The other, still holding the horses, raised his pistol and fired. I felt a blow to my shoulder. I rushed him and knocked him into the ditch.

Their horses reared and ran off. The first highwayman struggled to his feet, hand to his ribs. Miss Bennet had her purse in hand and was seeking to pick up her boot. I scooped her into my arms and ran with her into the woods. Another shot went whizzing past us, tearing through the leaves.

"Who was that?" I heard from behind.

"The devil himself!"

"Here! The horses!" The sounds of commotion faded as I put distance between us and the road.

Miss Bennet struggled in my arms.

"Be still," I said. "Unless you'd rather be taken by those men."

She quieted. I carried her swiftly through the woods. She was not heavy. I felt a burning in my shoulder, but I kept on, spying a path among the trees. When the woods ran out at the edge of a field, I stopped and lowered her to the ground.

She shuddered and covered her face with her hands. I moved away from her and sat down to inspect my wound. I shrugged off my coat, unlaced my shirt, and slid my hand over my right shoulder. The ball had struck in the hollow below my collarbone and exited through my armpit. Blood seeped from the wound. The pain was tolerable. I unwound my neck scarf and tried to bind it around my shoulder, but I could not manage it with only one hand.

I had been fumbling for some time when Miss Bennet limped over to me.

"Give me that," she said. In the moonlight she could not

very likely see much, but she wound the scarf around my shoulder and under my armpit, covering the bullet wound. I hung my head as she did this, not looking at her. On her shoeless foot the heel of her pale stocking was dirty.

When she was done, she retreated. There was a fence around the field with a stile, and she sat on the step. "You— how are you here?" she asked.

I had expected her to flee by now. "I might ask the same of you."

"Do you follow me?" Her voice quavered.

"I follow Victor." With some difficulty I tugged on my greatcoat.

She remained silent for a moment. "So do I," she said.

"You know the reason I seek him," I said. "Why should you?"

"To warn him about you."

I laughed. "I have warned him about me in every conversation we have ever had. There is nothing you could tell him he hasn't heard."

She avoided looking at me. Occasionally she would peek at my face, and then her eyes would flit away.

"Thank you for saving me," she said.

"I didn't do it for you. I just did not fancy watching another act of human cruelty."

"You might have passed us by."

I did not wish to consider why I did not. "It's been two months since you saw Victor. Where do you expect to find him?"

"I knew that he intended to visit Perth. I hoped to find him there."

"Where are all the people who take care of you?"

"I don't need them."

"Those highwaymen might disagree." My shoulder was beginning to throb. I lay my forearm across my lap and winced at the pain. "How did you expect to find him in Perth?"

"I know who he was going to visit there."

"Who?"

She hesitated. "I won't tell you."

"You'll tell me or I will hurt you worse than those men intended."

"Does it count as an act of human cruelty if you do it?"

"A good question," I said. I crawled a little closer to her. "One that you may consider at length after I have made you tell me where he is."

She fixed her gaze on me. "I make you an offer," she said. "Help me to Perth, and when I discover where he has gone, I will tell you."

"I have followed him from Switzerland without anyone's aid. I don't require your help."

"You are a hulking brute with a wounded shoulder. You cannot show your face without causing a furor. I may pass down the streets of Perth in daylight without inciting alarm, can enter an inn and ask questions. I know the workings of human society far better than you. I am a lady."

She sat on the stile, an awkward woman with her hat awry, her face pale. "A lady missing a shoe," I said.

"A lady with"—she removed her remaining shoe, turned it over, and shook from it a handful of coins—"two pounds six shillings to her name." She tucked them into her pocket.

FOURTEEN

After a long, cold night Mary found herself, with Frankenstein's monstrous creature, at the verge of a stand of trees,
looking out on a farm in the predawn light. In the distance—it
must be several miles—the very top of a church steeple was
visible in the first gleam of sunlight.

"I need to rest," the Creature said. His voice was a rasp,
and he had been moving slowly for the last hour.

He sat down heavily at the foot of a tree and leaned back
against the trunk.

"I'm so hungry," Mary said. The stocking of her shoeless
foot was black with dirt and a hole had broken through at her
heel. "Rest here," she told the Creature. "I will stop at this
house for food and shelter. I shall go into Perth to find Victor
and return as soon as I may."

"They won't shelter you," he said. "At best they will drive

you from their door; at worst they will report you to the magistrate."

Mary avoided looking into his face. "It may take me a day or two to discover Victor's whereabouts. I will come back when I know."

The Creature breathed slowly. "Do not tell them of me," he finally said, "else I will find you and strangle you."

Mary set off across the field.

The simple stone house had a thatched roof, two trees on the side facing the road, a small barren yard, a barn that was little more than a stone shed. A thread of smoke rose from the nearer of its two chimneys.

Mary knocked on the door. After a moment it opened a crack and a man squinted at her. He opened the door wider. "What d'ye want?"

"Please excuse me, sir. My name is Mary Bennet. I was traveling on the coach from Edinburgh to Perth when we were beset by highwaymen. They robbed and abandoned me in the woods. I have been all night walking and yours is the first dwelling I have come to. Would you be so kind as to help me? Might I stay with you for a day until I can contact my friends in Perth?"

The stone-faced man was perhaps forty-five, though years of labor had taken a toll on him. His eyes were bright blue and his red hair shot with gray. He had not shaved in several days. He wore a dirty white shirt, rough trousers, and worn boots.

He looked her up and down. Despite the night spent in the woods, it was obvious her coat and dress, hat and gloves, were those of a lady.

A woman slightly older than he came up behind him, wiping her hands on her apron. She peered at Mary from around his shoulder.

"Where's yer shoe?" she asked.

Mary looked down at her feet, then back up. "I lost it in escaping from the highwaymen. I lost all my possessions, too. Please, I ask for one day. I shall depart by tomorrow morning."

The farmer scowled. "We should let some English vagabond stay wi' us?" His thick accent sounded rough on her ear.

"They stole most of my money," Mary said, "but I can pay you for food and a night's lodging."

The man's eyes narrowed. "How much?"

"Would a shilling be a fair price?"

"Three or be off with ye."

It was a week's rent for a Meryton tradesman. Mary took the coins from her pocket. "Here," she said, handing them to him.

He opened the door and let her in. "I've work to do. See to her," he said to his wife, and went out.

The woman took her in and gestured at a plank table.

"Porridge is all we can give ye," she said.

"Porridge will do."

The woman set out a wooden bowl and a pewter spoon.

"What's your name?" Mary asked her.

"Abigail Buchanan." She poured Mary a mug of water from a pitcher and sat opposite her in the only other chair. "How is it that you are come to Perth?"

The oatmeal was thick and congealed, but Mary was hungry enough that it tasted divine. She drank from the earthenware mug. "I am come to visit a friend of our family, a Dr. Marble. Do you know of him?"

The woman lifted her eyebrows. "Dr. Marble is physician to Mr. McKenna, who owns the land ye are sitting on, and half the county besides. He has a grand town house on Kinnoull Street." Mrs. Buchanan's voice lightened at the thought of Dr. Marble and his house. She was a small woman; she wore an apron over a plain gray homespun dress that matched her tired eyes.

"How far is that from here?"

"It's a mile or so to town, and maybe a mile more to his home."

"I shall walk there, then, after breakfast. Might I wash my face and hands, and have you a comb I may use?"

"I do." Mrs. Buchanan paused. "But it's a long walk for a lady with one shoe, and it will not do for you to knock on his door in such way."

"I intend to stop at the coaching inn and retrieve my portmanteau."

"And to walk to the inn? Ye cannot depend on the coachman to have left it." Mrs. Buchanan rose and went off to another part of the house. She returned with a package wrapped in old paper. She unwrapped it to reveal a pair of ladies' shoes. "You shall use mine. These is my best. I was married in them."

Her lips tightened for a moment in a wan smile. Mary realized that Mrs. Buchanan, instead of being near fifty as she had assumed, was no older than herself. She handed the shoes to Mary.

The shoes were old-fashioned high-heeled pumps of figured purple leather, cheaply made even when new. Mary's ankle-high boots of kid leather put them to shame. But one boot was worth nothing. "I should pay you."

"'Give to him that asketh thee, and from him that would borrow of thee, turn not thou away,'" Mrs. Buchanan said. Then she laughed, and looked positively girlish. "Donald took ten times what he should from you to stay a night. For both our sakes, best not to let him know I lent you these."

Mary reached across the table to touch her hand. "God bless you, Mrs. Buchanan."

Mrs. Buchanan showed Mary to the tiny loft room where she would sleep. "Give me your stocking and I will mend it. I'll have it done by the time you've washed up and combed your hair."

Within half an hour Mary had made her ablutions, donned her mended stocking and Mrs. Buchanan's shoes, and set off down the road toward the town.

It was a cloudy, dank day, and gave a strong intimation of the coming fall. There was not an ounce of sunlight, and a steady, cold wind blew from the west. Mary hoped that the sky would do no more than threaten rain.

Mrs. Buchanan's shoes were snug. She was weary. Had she been at home, she might have enjoyed this air, but she was uncomfortably aware, after the last night, of how vulnerable she was in the middle of this road alone, a stranger in a strange country, almost penniless, companioned with a creature that was not human.

When she reached the town, she found the streets busy with morning bustle. The smell of coffee wafted from a coffee shop, hams hung in a butcher-shop window, and wagons rattled over cobblestones. She found Kinnoull Street, and after inquiring of a costermonger, Dr. Marble's house. It was three stories with rows of windows, a great red door, and a brass door knocker in the form of a boar's head.

She lifted the knocker and rapped it against the plate.

Mr. Price, the butler who answered the door to Dr. Marble's home, did not know just what to make of Mary. She did not claim any acquaintance with Dr. or Mrs. Marble, but said she was there to pay her respects to their houseguests, Henry Clerval and Victor Frankenstein. She was a well-dressed lady, no longer young, and her accent marked her as English. She wore a pair of abominable shoes. Mr. Price took her coat — soiled about the hem with a loose seam in one shoulder — escorted her to the drawing room, and went to fetch Mrs. Marble.

While she waited, Mary examined the room. There was no fire in the grate. On the mantel stood two china statues, one of a shepherdess carrying a crook with two sheep looking up at her, and the second of a man wearing a kilt and carrying a pike. The furniture was new and uncomfortable. A large pendulum clock with a sylvan scene painted onto its face ticked ponderously. It was seventeen minutes past ten. After Mary had waited in the Marble drawing room for five minutes, the door opened and Henry Clerval entered, along with an older woman.

"Miss Bennet! I could not be more surprised to hear that you had come to see me. Mrs. Marble, this is Miss Mary Bennet, whose acquaintance Victor and I had the pleasure to make in London."

Mrs. Marble welcomed Mary. "Please allow me to express my deepest sympathies on the death of your sister, about which

Mr. Clerval has told me. What has brought you to Perth?"

"I have come in the hope of seeing Mr. Frankenstein, on a matter related to my sister's death."

Henry shook his head slowly. "I'm sorry, Mary, but Victor has left Perth. Could I perhaps answer your questions?"

Mary hesitated. "Mrs. Marble, I greatly appreciate your hospitality to a stranger, but might it be possible for me to speak with Mr. Clerval in confidence?"

Mrs. Marble looked very curious, and perhaps a little offended.

Henry said to their host, "Mrs. Marble, let us step out into the hall for a moment."

Mrs. Marble said to Mary, "Please let me know if there is anything that I might offer you," and followed Henry out of the room. Another three minutes ticked by on the clock before Henry came back into the room.

He sat, paused as if collecting himself, and then spoke. "Something is wrong," he said in quite a different tone from that he'd used when Mrs. Marble was in the room. He acted as if he knew more of her purpose than he ought. "Why come all this way to see Victor?"

"I need to know where he has gone."

"Why?"

"I believe that he is the person who stole Kitty's body."

Henry drummed his fingers on the arm of his chair and finally replied, "I believe you are right."

"Why did you not tell me this when I last saw you in Matlock?"

"At that time I was not sure."

"You are sure now?"

"I do not know it for a fact, but I have every reason to believe he has," Henry said. "But Miss Bennet, seeking justice in a matter like this is no task for a woman. Where is your father—or Darcy, or Bingley?"

"They don't know I am here. They have no idea about Victor."

"You should return home and tell them. No good will come of your pursuing Victor. He has defiled your sister's grave in service of his scientific research. It is the same madness that we spoke of at dinner at Pemberley—not something that you may remedy, and you are better to let it go."

"I cannot let it go."

Henry rose from his chair and moved toward the window. He idly parted the curtains with the back of his hand and looked out onto the street, then turned back to her. "I think you are in love with him."

He watched for her reaction. Mary's mind spun. "You are mistaken," she said.

"The air of tragedy that he wraps about himself is powerfully attractive to a person of sensibility," Henry said, "but he is not able, at least in his present state, to reciprocate any affections you might invest in him."

"You do me a grave injustice. That is not my purpose in being here."

"I should inform you, for I fear that he has not, that Victor is affianced to Elizabeth Lavenza, his cousin, who was reared in the same household. He has promised to wed her as soon as we return to Geneva."

Mary was shocked. She pulled a kerchief from her purse and held it to her lips.

Henry observed her discomfiture. "He did not tell you, did he?"

"No," she said. "He did not."

"Ah, Victor," Henry said softly, as much to himself as to Mary. "My friend is careless of others' hearts, Miss Bennet."

"He played upon my trust."

"I doubt he sees it that way. If it is any consolation, his engagement to Elizabeth has lasted six years and more. When asked he ardently expresses his love for her, but he shows little eagerness to wed. His affection for her is inconstant at best. When he was gone off to Ingolstadt and we heard so little from him, I wondered whether he might have formed an attachment to some person there of a different class or station, which he was embarrassed to admit. Perhaps he loves someone that none of us could imagine him loving."

Mary thought of the Creature lying wounded in the woods.

She put her kerchief back into her purse. "Thank you for telling me this, Mr. Clerval. I still need to know where he has gone."

"You will not return to your home?"

"I cannot until I see him, if only briefly. I have obligations of my own."

Henry lifted his hands in a gesture of surrender. "He has gone to the far northern town of Thurso. From there I believe he intends to live for a time—in complete solitude, he told me—on some isle in the Orkneys."

"How long ago did he leave?"

"A fortnight or more. I surmise that he means to resume his medical researches. But this is not something that you should witness. And how shall you travel all that way with no companion? It is not safe. I will go with you myself."

"If Victor wanted you there, he would have asked you to go with him."

"He specifically enjoined me from following. I am to meet him in two months. But this is all the more reason why you should return home.

"Victor is an unusual man, Mary. I have known him since childhood. He is brilliant, curious, high-minded, and eager to accomplish some great thing, but his fancies are so powerful that at times he cannot recognize anything beyond himself. He professes great love, yet I do not think he sees the people he professes to love."

Mary stood. "I thank you, Mr. Clerval, for your warning," she said. The chill in her voice as she said it was not something that she had intended.

"Please, forgive me for not conveying my misgivings about Victor back in Matlock. It seemed to me that in the immediate wake of your sister's death, my speculations about him, which were no more than surmise, would have done neither of you justice."

"You needn't apologize. I appreciate your candor."

"May I escort you to wherever you are staying?"

"I think not," she said.

Henry called for the butler and walked with Mary to the door. "If you will not be persuaded to give up this quest, Miss Bennet, let me then convey my sincere hope that when it is complete you return safely to your home. If you do find Victor, please tell him that he must treat you with respect or he will lose my friendship forever."

In the front hall, as the butler helped Mary on with her

coat, Mrs. Marble appeared. "I thank you for stopping to visit, Miss Bennet," she said, taking Mary's arm as she drew her away from Henry toward the front door.

She leaned close to speak in a low voice.

"I don't know you, Miss Bennet, but I cannot let you leave without lending you some advice. I speak only out of concern for you.

"Go home. You are too well-bred to chase after a man. You put at risk your reputation and that of every person in your family. You may suppose at your age that no one will care, but I assure you that your family will care a great deal."

Mary felt her face flush. She saw that Clerval lingered in the hall, watching them, and hoped that he could not hear.

"I know what I am about, Mrs. Marble," Mary managed to say.

Mrs. Marble opened the door. "Then may God keep you," she said, and ushered her out, closing the door behind her.

Mary stood on the doorstep. Across the way a portly man in fine clothes was helping an elderly woman in a white cap into the town house opposite.

Mary walked down the block only half-aware of the horses, carriages, and pedestrians. She felt humiliated, and angry, and confused. Why had discovering the existence of Victor's engagement startled her so? The image of Victor, holding a cup of negus in his hands, confiding in her at Lord Henry's ball; the delight with which he had listened to her recite Darwin's verse, rose to hearten her.

She sensed that Henry had spoken at least in part out of exasperation with Victor. It seemed clear that he did not know about Victor's monster, and that the creation of a second such creature was Victor's reason for isolating himself in such a remote location. But his assessment of Victor's character, from a man who had been his friend since childhood, necessarily gave her pause. It did not accord with her estimation of Victor. There was more to him than Henry knew. Henry did not share Victor's interest in the natural world. He could not imagine how a person might desire to know things simply to know them, to understand how nature works. Victor himself had warned against such ambition, but he could not be so insistent on the subject if his mind were completely convinced that it was wrong. How great a pleasure it would be to have such knowledge to oneself before telling—perhaps, if one chose to—the world and accepting its approbation.

The things she knew by now about Victor showed him to be a man who would test the limits of civilized behavior. But he was no devil. He was Prometheus, reaching for knowledge on behalf of all humanity. He simply had not taken proper care to anticipate the consequences of his actions, but his character was too noble to have left him incapable of understanding the moral responsibilities of a creator toward his creation. His current actions were evidence of that.

Henry might have given her pause, but Mrs. Marble's words were the ones that burned the most, because Mary could see the justice in them. It was not untrue that she had come to Scotland out of love. Certainly Victor had not asked her to follow him. But she knew there was more to it than that. There were things that she sought on this journey for her own purposes.

Despite these rationalizations, she saw herself reflected in Henry's—and Mrs. Marble's—eyes as a smitten, self-deluded, aging woman, prey as much to her own fantasies as to any deception on Victor's part.

Walking up Kinnoull Street, Mary realized that Lizzy would see her running off after Victor the same way she had seen Lydia's running off to be with Wickham—against every stricture of reason, of propriety, of self-preservation, of common sense—except that Lydia had done this as a foolish girl of sixteen, while Mary was a woman of thirty-two.

At this thought she stopped dead on the sidewalk. It was a hard truth, and it sat in the center of her mind like a stone. By this time her family must be in complete turmoil. Darcy must have been dispatched to Scotland the way he had tracked Lydia down in London a dozen years ago. When he found Mary— assuming he did—his displeasure would make that which he'd expressed to her on the night of her excursion to Matlock seem like a millpond compared to the Atlantic.

But what of the Creature? What of Kitty? If Victor could indeed create from Kitty's body the bride that the Creature sought, might there be some remnant of Kitty remaining in her revivified frame?

A passing gentleman saw her standing there and stopped. "May I help you, madam? Are you unwell?"

Mary came to herself and looked at him, a short man wearing a tall beaver hat. "I am quite well, thank you," she said.

The man looked her up and down, the matter of a second, and tipped his hat to her. "Good afternoon, then." He walked on.

Mary went to the coaching inn and asked after her portmanteau. The porter at the inn was surprised and grateful to see her well, but they had no portmanteau belonging to her.

He told her that it must have gone on with the coach to the next stage of the route. The innkeeper told of the confusion that had ensued when the coach had arrived with the bleeding mail guard.

The innkeeper offered to accompany her to the magistrate so that Mary might speak to him regarding the highwaymen. She told him that since she had escaped the men without harm, she did not seek to concern herself further with the matter except to regain her property. She asked if the company would reimburse her for her losses and inconvenience, to say nothing of the mortal danger she had experienced. The innkeeper said it was not his responsibility, and if she had objections she might take *that* up with the magistrate.

Mary left. Mrs. Buchanan's wedding shoes had begun to pinch. She might find a shoe store and buy some shoes for herself, but she was not eager to spend more of her dwindling resources just yet. She stopped at an apothecary's shop and purchased a poultice and a vial of laudanum. It took her some time to walk all the way back to the Buchanan farm. The day was already declining, the clouds gray as the slate cliffs at Lyme Regis. She recalled how cold the winds had been there.

Buchanan was in the fields when Mary returned, and his wife was washing clothes in a tin tub. She told Mary that she might join them for supper at six. They ate a meal of oats and boiled turnips with a scrap of smoked fish, and soon after retired for the night.

Mary sat at the tiny loft window that looked out over the side yard. The temperature had dropped since sunset; the wind ripped through the trees. She climbed onto the pallet they'd given her and tried to sleep. The humiliations she had suffered in the last day ran through her mind. How was she going to make it all the way to Thurso? What could she expect to come of it?

The rattling of the tree branches outside her window would not let her sleep. She turned from her own problems for a moment and imagined the Creature lying injured out in the woods in this cold. In the morning she would give him the medicine on which she had spent some of her scant resources. That was enough.

She could not stand to think of him; she could not avoid it. After an hour, she rose from the pallet, put on her coat, and descended the creaking stairs to the kitchen. From the pantry she took a turnip and the two most withered of a bunch of carrots. She found an empty bottle. Once outside she crept across the yard to a trough, filled the bottle with water, and corked it. She moved past the barn toward the woods. The moon was just a bright spot in the clouds; beneath the trees she got lost before she found the place where she had left the Creature.

He was not there. Her first reaction was relief. If he had gone on without her, she would not have to concern herself with him.

She had turned back toward the house and only taken a few steps when she heard his croak. "Miss Bennet." His voice was faint amid the rustle of the trees, and she wondered if he had been calling her without effect before now.

She found him huddled in the hollow of a great oak, half buried in leaves he had piled up to keep him warm. He looked like nothing so much as a discarded scarecrow, save that his watery eyes gleamed in the light. Mary knelt at his side.

She uncorked the bottle and held it to his lips. He steered

it with one hand but did not take it from her as he drank, and drank, until it was empty.

She offered him a turnip and carrots.

"Not hungry," he said, his voice a little stronger. He trembled.

"You are not well." She hesitated, afraid, then drew in a breath and held her hand against his livid forehead. He was very warm, but she could not tell if that was normal. "How does your shoulder feel?"

"It hurts."

Mary opened the vial of laudanum and gave it to him. He drank it in a single draft and let his hand fall to the forest floor beside him.

She helped him to remove his coat and unlaced his shirt. She unwrapped the bandage from around his shoulder. In the darkness she could not see the wound clearly. She touched it gently with her fingers. His flesh here was still warmer, and swollen around the edges of the bullet hole. Mary smeared the poultice onto his shoulder and pressed it into the wound, and then wrapped it in the fresh bandage she had brought.

Through all this he watched her like a mute animal. He might have been one of those wax figures in Bullock's Egyptian Hall, but for when an eyelid twitched as something she did caused him pain.

She had never touched a grown man like this. His sallow skin was perfectly smooth and hairless, as fine as that of a child, and he had no beard. Though he had lived in the outdoors for months, and his clothes were pungent, his body did not smell bad. He was as clean as a cat. She helped him lace up his shirt and, slowly, pull on his coat.

Embarrassed, Mary sat back onto the leaf mould of the forest floor.

After a moment, the Creature said, "I did not expect that you would come back."

"How will I get to Thurso without a companion?"

"What is Thurso?"

"It is a town in northernmost Scotland. Henry Clerval told me that Victor left for there a fortnight ago." She watched his face. It was still hard for her to keep her eyes on him. If she relaxed her self-control for a second, her mind recoiled, shouting, *This is a dead thing. It is an imitation, a diabolic counterfeit. Run.*

"I will return early in the morning," she said. "I hope you will be better then, and we can leave."

The Creature simply watched her. He gave a slight nod and closed his eyes.

Mary walked to the edge of the woods and across the harvested field of rye grass. When she entered the house through the kitchen door, she found Mrs. Buchanan waiting, sitting on a chair in the dark.

"You're a bold one, to come back," she said in a low voice. "Looking for something else to steal?"

"I've stolen nothing."

"The bottle that was in the pantry? My carrots and turnips?"

Mary could think of no answer. Finally she said, "Please don't tell your husband."

"He'd whip me as soon as he was done whipping you." Mrs. Buchanan's voice was tired. "I thought you was a lady, with your fine speech. Did you steal those clothes, too?"

"I'm sorry. I did not mean to—"

"Give me my shoes and get out."

Mary looked down. She lifted the hem of her coat to expose the cheap shoes. She was going to have to walk more than two hundred miles.

While she hesitated, Mrs. Buchanan reached for them. Mary pushed her away, knocking her from her chair, opened the door, and ran off across the field.

FIFTEEN

On the roadside north of Inverness stood a gibbet. The wood of its posts rose weathered and gray as old stone, the chains hanging from the crosspiece rusted red as a robin's breast. It did not look as if it had been used for a long time. Should we be caught, they would hang me from it without hesitation, food for crows and a warning to all such abominations of nature as I. But there are none such as I.

If they discovered that Miss Bennet had stolen the shoes she wore, they would perhaps even hang her, as the good citizens of Geneva had hanged Justine Moritz.

In the weeks after we left Perth, I learned a great deal from, and about, Miss Bennet. We were of necessity in each other's company every hour of every day. For the most part we traveled at night, safe from the view of human beings. Later, as we traversed counties as deserted as the surface of the moon, and just as spectrally haunted as the moon's counties must be, we took the risk of traveling during the day.

At first Miss Bennet was able to keep up with me only because I struggled under the effects of my wound and the fever it had brought. Within a fortnight I was returned to health, and after that I had to slow my pace so that she might keep up. I considered whether it might serve me better to leave her behind.

She was afraid of me but so intent on reaching Victor that she mastered that fear. I would catch her being brave. She seldom looked at me directly. Nine hours out of ten she kept her distance. But when she cleaned my wound, or when we huddled together against the cold of the evening, we were within an arm's length of each other. Sometimes closer. She was not so beautiful, nor young, as Victor's Elizabeth or Felix's Safie, or even as Justine had been. Lines creased the corners of her lips, and her hair was thin. Her jaw was heavy and her eyes small, and when she smiled—as she might at the sight of a field of foxglove or the song of a bird—her gray eyes squinted so they could hardly be seen.

Yet there were times that I could not help but be affected by her female presence, and angry that she seemed so afraid of me.

It was on one of those afternoon marches that we passed the gibbet, a day so overcast that one saw no direct sunlight until, in its last half hour, the sun descending below the clouds, the full force of its rays slantingly filled the landscape. The road ran through rolling moorlands, deep green, broken by outcroppings of rock that thrust out of the earth like hands from the grave, clumps of bushes in their lee. Not a tree in sight. A stream threaded its way through the folded moors.

"Might we stop for a while?" Miss Bennet asked. She held her hand to her brow and pointed. "Is that a shepherd's hut?"

It was. "We can shelter there," I said. "We need not continue tonight."

We crossed the moorland, boggy near the stream, and reached the hut. It was little more than a circle of stones piled high, with a broken thatched roof, but it would keep off the wind, and someone had stacked a pile of peat to dry outside.

"I shall build a fire," Miss Bennet said.

I carried two blocks of the dried peat into the hut while she tore up fistfuls of dead grass and broke twigs from the gorse for kindling. Miss Bennet took out the tinderbox she had become so expert at using. She struck steel against flint until sparks lit the tinder. Leaning forward on her knees, she held the flame to the grass and blew it until it caught and spread. She sat back.

"I will find food," I said, and crawled out.

I walked down to the stream. By now the sun was below the horizon and the land was darkening. I waded into the icy water, half to my knees, and peered down through the surface, waiting. It was not long before an unsuspecting trout darted by and I snatched it out of the stream. I tossed it onto the bank and sought another, which I had in a span of minutes.

When I took them up, they wriggled in my hand, so desperate to escape. Had I traveled alone, they would have lived on. Instead I beat their heads against a rock and brought them back to the hut.

Miss Bennet had taken off her bonnet and the stolen shoes and warmed her feet at the meager fire. I had to crawl to fit inside, leaving hardly room for her. The peat hissed as it burned, and tiny blue flames danced between its fibers. Miss Bennet rubbed her feet with her hands.

The shoes were falling apart, and her clothing had not worn well. Once it would have been obvious to anyone who saw her that she was what humans called a lady, but now her hands were raw and her hair unkempt. The Scots were wary of strangers. Whenever we came near a town, we were at risk of arrest. I would wait in the countryside while she went to ask directions: the roads were largely unmarked, and we had lost time by wandering from our way. On these forays Miss Bennet used what remained of her money to purchase food. But she was no lady now. The last time she had stopped in a town, she had been chased away by a grocer who accused her of thievery.

In truth, we had stolen food more than once. Outside Kingussie I had pilfered the tinderbox and a hooked knife. I used that knife now to scale, gut, and bone the trout, then spitted them to roast over the fire.

We did not speak. The smoke that collected in the tiny hut stung my eyes, which had of late become sensitive as never before. Whenever such changes occurred in my body, I wondered if they might be a sign of something going awry with it. Frankenstein's method for creating life might be imperfect, and his creations doomed. The sensations I felt at any moment might be the last I would ever feel. Dead, I would be nothing, for even if God indeed ruled the universe, there was no place in his afterlife for me.

All the more reason to live as well as I might, or, if my life became an insuperable misery, to end it. This would be decided when we next saw Victor.

It was peculiar to think of Miss Bennet and myself as "we." I wondered at my impulse to save her from the highwaymen, after she had been so scornful of me in our only encounter. Her stepping from the coach seemed an apparition, some sign that there might be an order behind the otherwise random events of my life. These thoughts would never have occurred to me before the journey to England forced me to enter the world of human beings. I saw them better now. Everything connected to everything else in ways that I could not fully understand.

Or perhaps this was just the fantasy of my overheated mind.

Miss Bennet had joined with me on this journey out of her need. That was one way to see it. Did she expect Frankenstein to bring her sister back? Did she love him? I pondered the nature of an emotion that would cause a person of her privilege to abandon all the rules that these people seemed to make for themselves and pursue a quest very unlikely to come to any happy conclusion.

I was surprised, when she fled the farm, that she bothered to find me. She came running across the shorn field of rye grass and stumbled between the trees. "We must run!" she gasped. "The farmer is coming!"

I pushed myself to my feet and stumbled with her into the woods. Weeks later we were still together.

Miss Bennet pulled two pieces of trout from the spit and offered one to me. I pushed her hand away and fumbled in my greatcoat pocket for the turnip I had dug up from a farmer's field.

"You don't eat animals," she said. She tore off the half-raw fragments of fish with her teeth, small, slow bites. Her shadowed eyes gleamed with the wan firelight.

"I have done so. I don't prefer to."

"Yet you killed these fish readily enough."

"Necessity compels such acts, at times. I think that this is what you call a 'sin.'"

"Killing in order to eat is not a sin," Miss Bennet said. "The Lord has given all the beasts of the field and the fowl of the air and the fish of the sea to men, to be used as they see fit."

"Am I a man?" I asked.

She hesitated. "There are many sorts of men."

"I was not made by your God."

She put aside her fish. "You are made in his image," she said. "Do you know the Bible?"

"I have read that book." I fumbled in my pocket and showed her my copy.

She smiled, and her eyes squinted. "Though Victor may think he created you, I suspect that the Lord guided your making."

I leaned on my elbow. My shoulder was well enough now that it no longer hurt. I gave what she said some thought.

"So I am allowed to sacrifice a fish," I said. "But murder? 'Thou shall not kill.'"

Miss Bennet did not reply.

"I murdered Victor's brother," I said.

"I know," Miss Bennet said. When she spoke, shadows deepened in the hollows of her cheeks. She was silent for some moments. "Why did you do that?"

"I could say that I did not mean to kill him, but the more time that passes, the less true that seems." Each night as I fell asleep, William's terrified face was never far from my thoughts.

"I had sought Victor for many months. After much pain and effort I reached the woods outside Geneva's walls. I had hardly arrived when, purely by chance, a beautiful boy came running into the hollow where I hid. It came to me that a child, unschooled in hatred, might learn to accept me as human. I could teach him to like me. But when I caught him, he called me a monster. He swore that if I stole him away, his father, Monsieur Frankenstein, would punish me.

"It was not simply that he bore the name of the person who had created and abandoned me. There was petulance in his voice—an unquestioned sense of privilege, an assumption that huge and monstrous as I was, I could not presume to harm him.

"I wanted to silence his presumption. He kicked and twisted in my arms. He screamed at me. Someone might hear. There was no thought in him now, only complete and utter terror. His revulsion fell like a knife in my breast. I had taken this boy, and as if I were a viper or a wolf, in three minutes turned him into a raving animal.

"I grasped his throat, and in a moment he lay dead at my feet."

I closed my eyes. It helped with the stinging of the smoke, but in my mind I could only see William more clearly. I opened them again, and watched the tiny flames amid the peat.

"I killed him as easily as I killed those trout," I said. I wiped my tears away with the back of my hand, and laughed. "I balk at killing fish, yet I murdered a reasoning being. You cannot absolve me of that sin."

"I cannot," Miss Bennet said. "But God can, if you repent."

"So? How does God regard what I did to Justine Moritz? I took the locket from around William's neck and, finding her asleep in the woods, placed it in her apron, knowing that when it was discovered that she possessed it, she would be accused of William's murder. She went to the gallows for it."

"Why did you do that? She had done nothing to harm you. She never even knew you were there."

"It was a leap forward in my learning to be human. An animal will respond with hostility when attacked. It takes a man to imagine a slight and then punish someone for something he has not done. Justine was a young woman. She was the sort of being who might have offered me the affections for which I long—but I knew that, were she to wake, she would recoil from me in horror. I punished her for a rejection she had no chance to inflict upon me.

"I confess also that this served as a test. I had grown cynical. I wished to see how the good citizens of Geneva would treat this girl: Would they be convinced that she had murdered William? My test was even more exacting than I had expected, as Justine turned out to be a ward of Monsieur Frankenstein and had taken care of William from his infancy. Could they actually believe, in the face of her denials, that she had committed such a crime? Not only did they do so, but with the weight of their accusations they convinced Justine herself that she had done it. So you see that I had willing, merciless collaborators in her destruction."

As I finished this narrative, I lifted my eyes from the fire to glance at Miss Bennet, four feet away. She watched me impassively.

Just as she had at the Matlock inn, she challenged me.

"These are terrible crimes," she said. "When you speak of them, your voice is full of scorn, not just for men, and not just for Victor."

"I have every reason to scorn men, and feel bitterness toward Victor."

"You have harmed yourself in these actions as much as you have harmed him."

"Victor collaborated in my crimes. He saw me in the woods outside Geneva. When Justine stood trial, he might have revealed my existence and my reasons for spite against him. Instead he let Justine hang."

"You blame everyone for your actions but yourself. I hear your self-pity. Yet I saw your tears as you spoke of William's death."

"This smoke stings my eyes."

"You will not be free until you take responsibility before God and ask for his forgiveness."

"Your God is convenient," I said. "Always prepared to forgive one sin so you may move on to the next. He seems to throw occasions for sin into my path with regularity—of all the boys in Geneva I might have met in the woods, I met Victor's brother. Of all the women who might fall asleep outside Geneva's gates on that very same night, I find Frankenstein's ward. Of all the women who might be accosted by highwaymen on a deserted Scottish road, I meet you. Given what happened to those who came before you, you should have a care."

"You might have left me to those men; instead you saved me. God gave you another opportunity."

"Our story is not ended yet. Who knows what God plans for its conclusion?"

"We make choices, and are responsible for them."

"Yet, if I understand aright, God knows what choice we shall make before we make it. He knew that Eve would eat of the apple before he created her, and that Adam would follow her to perdition even before he created the earth and the stars in the sky. What chance did they have?"

This talk of God and purposes, of dead fish and dead boys, tasted like bitter gall. Rather than wait for this woman's answer, I crawled out of the hut, and in the profound darkness went down to listen to the wordless murmur of the stream. Sitting there, forearms across my knees, my eyes still stinging, I addressed the sleeping moorland in a whisper that she could not hear.

"Better to thank your God for saving you from those highwaymen, Miss Bennet, and hope that he protects you in the future, for I shall not."

When we resumed our slow journey the next day, neither of us said anything of this conversation. It was a week or more later, as we moved up the desolate east coast of Scotland, that Miss Bennet said, "It is difficult for me to continue in your company without having a name for you. By what name shall I call you?"

"I have no name."

"So you are free to choose one to your liking."

I considered this. "You may call me Adam."

She said nothing for another mile. Then she ventured, "What do you expect to happen, Adam, if Victor should succeed in creating your bride?"

I resented this return to the subject of our Matlock conversation. "Do you seek to warn me again that I should not expect her to associate with me even if she is as horrifying as myself? Very well, then. You have warned me."

Traveling with Miss Bennet was unsettling. She showed many signs of distrust. She was repulsed by my physical presence. When I came into her field of vision unexpectedly, she would pull back. At times I caught her studying me, as if I were some sport of nature that did not fall into any category in which she might classify me. But what she did now was perhaps the most unnerving thing that she had done in the weeks we had been together. She apologized.

"I am sorry for what I said to you in Matlock," she said. "I still hope that Victor may bring my sister back to life. But if that is not possible, then I hope that the being he creates from her body will not reject your affections. Though I have never suffered the violence you have faced, I understand what it is to be alone."

I checked my annoyance at this presumptuous comparison. It was in keeping with Miss Bennet's fits of moralizing, and she did not realize her arrogance. I might have killed a less naive person.

"I have no experience of the physical affections you seek," she went on, "but I have observed that human beings will do many otherwise incomprehensible things in pursuit of them. This was the real cause of my sister's death. The emotions that the sexual instinct brings forth are, for some, overwhelming. Men, I have seen, will readily dishonor themselves for them, and many women, too. That highwayman from whom you saved me would have annihilated me for a moment's pleasure—though I cannot see how anyone might take pleasure in using another human being so."

The longer she spoke, the more difficult it was for me to listen. Miss Bennet grew more nervous as she rambled on. She was miserably awkward at such talk, and I sought to end this painful subject.

"Every animal seeks its mate," I said bluntly. "The birds of the air, the creatures of the forest."

"Men are not animals."

"I have more experience in this area than you," I said, "and my experience has not borne that out."

I lengthened my stride beyond her ability to keep up, and soon was twenty yards ahead of her. The narrow track, hardly worth calling a road, ran near the cliffs on the coast. No one lived here. Far below, gray ocean waves crashed on the rubble at the base of the precipice, and gulls hovered on the wind, scanning the water below them for prey. Nature showed her stark beauty. No matter how bleak the landscape, I felt more at home in these wilds than anywhere that men inhabited. Alone I might forget for moments how outcast I was. I might look up at the skies, watch the changing shapes of clouds, hear the cries of the birds, and enjoy the strength of my body.

I began to run. I felt the pleasure of my muscles working, felt the raw breeze on my face. My hair was blown back. I soon left Miss Bennet far behind. I thought I heard her voice call to me, but it might have been the sound of the gulls.

After some time I slowed and stopped. I sat on an outcropping of stone by the side of the track and waited. It took longer than I had imagined it would for Miss Bennet to reach me. I saw her approach for some time before she came abreast of me. Her head was fixed rigidly forward. Not acknowledging my existence she passed by, footsore but determined in her inadequate shoes, and continued down the road.

I might be well rid of her. But we were bound for the same place, and if I left her, she would not survive in this desolate land.

I followed and was soon walking at her side. Neither of us spoke, until she said, "The purpose of the sexual congress is of course procreation. Dr. Darwin observes that it is the power of reproduction that distinguishes organic beings from inanimate nature. You are alive, so naturally you will seek to reproduce. This explains your every action."

I held my tongue and let her continue her lecture.

"But Darwin also observes that there are two forms of reproduction: the simpler is the solitary, in which a living thing reproduces itself. More complex is sexual reproduction, and this method produces more robust and varied organisms. By bringing the male and female together, nature produces her finest forms.

"You, however, were not produced by sexual means. You were brought to life from inanimate matter without the intervention of parents. Or, you may say, like the budding yeast, you have a single parent: Victor Frankenstein. Offspring of an asexual gestation bear the disorders of the single parent without the ameliorating effect of the union of two separate natures that occurs when creatures reproduce sexually. As Darwin says:

> Where no new Sex with glands nutritious
> feeds,
> Nurs'd in her womb, the solitary breeds;

No Mother's care their early steps directs,
Warms in her bosom, with her wings protects;
The clime unkind, or noxious food instills
To embryon nerves hereditary ills;
The feeble births acquired diseases chase,
Till Death extinguish the degenerate race.

"I feel sorry for you, and for that reason I cannot hold you to the standards that I might expect from a complete human being."

If she knew in that moment how close she came to strangulation, she would have fainted. I decided that I need never concern myself with her anymore. I lengthened my stride again and left her to live or die by her own devices.

The feelings she inspired in me were different from those that I had felt the only other time that I had spent in the company of particular human beings for a long time, the year or more that I spent watching the De Laceys. There I had felt longing to be a part of their household, to feel the bonds of love that held them together and made their trials tolerable. When at last I tried to persuade them to befriend me and they attacked me as a fiend, my longing turned instantly to hate.

With Miss Bennet, my emotions reached neither extreme. I did not admire her beyond some envy for her ability to pass among other humans and be at least provisionally accepted, nor did I despise her. She had mastered her fear enough to pursue whatever advantage she might gain from our association. She cared for Victor, completely undeserving of her respect, far beyond any possible regard she might have for me. And instead of depending on her own observations, she judged me based on ideas that bore little relation to reality. I was done with her, and as much as I had longed for human contact before, happy to be free of her company.

It was a relatively warm fall day. Along that coast road are found few trees and fewer people. Far between were the villages, no more than a house or two, tiny sheep farms, raw fields producing a few straggling turnips. There was little risk of being seen. I came upon a narrow stream and stopped to drink some water. It was icy cold. As I crouched there in a little declivity, I heard men's voices. I lifted my head and saw two men crossing the moor carrying long fowling pieces in the crooks of their arms. A couple of dead partridges hung from the belt of one of them.

I ducked down, but one of them saw me. He pointed. "Who is that?"

I flattened myself to the earth.

"Where?" the other voice said.

"By the stream. Some stranger."

I heard the sound of their boots on the turf.

I saw them crest the top of the bank and turned my face away. "Here, now," one of them called. "Who are ye, and what do ye here?"

Head still turned, I said, "Only a poor vagabond, stopping to slake my thirst. Have pity on me, sirs."

I heard a rustle behind me, and I imagined the man raising his gun. "Let us see your face, man."

I got to my feet. Both of them stood frozen, trying to assess what it was they saw. Before they could act, I ran.

"Halt!" the man yelled.

I ran away from the road. A glance over my shoulder told

me one of them followed. I was sure that I could outrun him, but if he stopped running, he might shoot.

"Don't hurt him!" a voice cried. A woman's voice. I hazarded another glance. Miss Bennet had come upon the scene and was shouting, waving her arms. The men, nonplussed, turned to deal with her. I loped off across the moors and was soon lost amid the gorse.

I stayed out on the moors until twilight came on, then worked my way back to the road. Following it, before long I spied a few houses clustered among old trees. A couple of windows were dimly lit. Beyond lay the tiniest of villages.

I debated what to do, and at last moved off the road and circled around the village entirely, coming back as it left on the other side. There I found a hollow where I might not be seen but where I had a good vantage of anyone who might pass. I waited, half dozing, through a long, cold night.

In the first hour of morning, a person came along the road toward me. It was Miss Bennet, trudging wearily north. I unfolded myself from my crouch, stretched my limbs, and walked toward the road. She saw me immediately, and though she watched me as I approached, she did not alter her direction or pace.

I fell into step beside her. We walked for a while in silence. "What did they do to you?" I asked.

"They asked me who I was, and what I was doing here. They asked me who you were."

"What did you tell them?"

"I told them I was an Englishwoman and that I had lost all my money. I told them you were my half-witted brother, and that we were on our way to Thurso where our aunt Augusta

Sinclair lives. I said that you had gotten away from me on the road and I was trying to find you."

"And they believed you?"

"No. They insisted I tell the truth. They threatened me. They called me a Gypsy, a vagabond, a thief, and worse. When I did not change what I said, they said they would have me arrested. I cried. I begged them not to do so. They locked me in a cellar.

"In the morning they woke me up and gave me some bread. They prayed over me, and warned me never to show my face here again, and sent me on my way."

"Did you ask them how far it is to Thurso?"

"Forty miles."

We kept walking.

SIXTEEN

They spent the night in an abandoned barn. The land here was vacant to the horizon, but Mary thought that by now they must be close to Thurso. The circumspect thing would be not to risk drawing attention to themselves, yet the stack of dried wood in the corner of the roofless barn was too tempting, and they hazarded a fire. The river ran nearby, so they had clean water, and Adam managed to snag a salmon, so they had some food.

Now that they approached the end of their journey, both Mary and Adam had been avoiding talk of what they would do when they reached the town. They would have to discover where Victor was. Mary assumed that this was something that she would be better suited to find out, but she was afraid of facing these Scots in her shabby clothes and English accent.

Mary had never imagined that she might come to this,

eating half-raw fish under clouds that hid the stars, huddled beside a meager fire whose smoke permeated her clothes and hair and skin, in the company of a half-human monster that she was increasingly convinced was a man.

Adam was frighteningly intelligent. The fact that he had learned languages so readily, and could express himself so eloquently, astonished her. His memory was perfect. He was able to reason out a course of action with sureness and confidence. He could follow an argument, and when he chose to speak, could present one that showed he had thought deeply and reasoned his way to a logical conclusion. He was hard to gainsay.

Then, just when she had accepted that he was familiar with the world, he would exhibit a childlike ignorance that both surprised and, at times, made her want to laugh. He remembered every word he had ever learned, but those he had never heard spoken he would comically mispronounce.

He was immensely strong, inhumanly agile. While Mary had suffered for lack of food, he could eat almost anything.

In the countryside he seemed relaxed. He noticed everything. Once near the sea cliffs she had watched him chase away a flock of gulls, waving his arms as he ran among them like a six-year-old boy. His wax face lit up so that he almost looked alive. When they drew within the shadow of human habitation, he seemed to shrink into his coat, wary and quiet, as if willing himself to disappear. Since their contretemps and reunion he had said nothing of their disagreement, and he went out of his way to find her things to eat and to keep her warm even at the cost of covering her with his own greatcoat while she slept.

Among the many things Mary had done in the last month that she had never done before was to spend hours alone in the presence of this male creature. In order to survive and make her way to Victor, she had surrendered her modesty in a hundred ways. She was aware of Adam's body almost as well as she imagined a married woman might know her husband's. His form rivaled that of the statues of Greek gods she had seen, and in motion he was graceful and silent as a cat. On one freezing night, Adam had come close to embracing her to keep her from the cold.

Yet in the back of her mind always stood Victor's warning that his Creature's persuasive powers veiled a black heart. He was a confessed murderer, and when she had offended him, she had seen him struggle to control his rage.

Mary found a comfortable spot in the barn, leaning against the vertical post of what had once been a stall. "I never imagined that I might spend a night here," she said. Here: Scotland, the end of the world, this wrecked barn, penniless, beside a monster.

"This is far from the way you have lived," Adam said. When he sat cross-legged—the tails of his greatcoat spread around him, his long, tangled black hair shrouding his shoulders, his dead face reflecting the wan light of the fire—he looked like some savage pagan god.

"Indeed," Mary said.

"You have lost your privilege."

Mary considered this. "I suppose I had privilege, though it did not seem to me that it was undue, or excessive. I had good things to eat, and fine clothes, and a warm bed—and oh, many other things that I did not appreciate. But a spinster is not considered privileged in the world where I lived."

"What is a spinster?"

"A spinster is an old unmarried woman. People think spinsters are funny, and sad. If one has an income, one may live as one chooses, but a spinster is not doing the things that make a woman's life worthwhile—marrying, having children, taking care of her husband. It is a hollow existence, tedious in the extreme. The one use of a spinster is to take care of her parents as they age, but she is seldom given much credit for doing this by her siblings, who are wrapped up in their own marriages and children."

Adam set another fragment of the broken stall on the fire. "I know what I lack that has set me on the road to this place. What did you lack that brought you here?"

Mary thought over this question for some time before replying. "I lacked respect and attention. I was alone in the midst of my family. I am not beautiful, and the only man who has ever shown any interest in me as a possible wife is someone who behaves in ways that I find hard to tolerate."

"Did Victor show such interest?"

"He treated me as a person of intellect. Reflected in his eyes I saw myself perhaps better than I am. I thought that he might care for me, if it were not for—for the obligation he has to you. I thought if I saw him again I might discover . . . who he is. I wanted to protect him. I wanted to retrieve Kitty. I wanted . . . many things."

She sighed. "That was before I learned that he was engaged."

The fire crackled. A slender ribbon of smoke rose through the open roof to the sky. "If he fails me," Adam said, "you will not be able to protect him from my vengeance."

"I think," Mary said, "that as you continue in your career

on earth, you might consider finding some other means of persuasion than threats of death."

His eyes flashed with anger, and then his thin, dark lips split in a smile.

She could not help but smile in return.

"I should hope not to have to resort to violence," he said.

"Assuming that we ever find him, I would feel better about our next meeting with Victor if you should vow not to harm him. Despite all the suffering that you lay at Victor's feet, I urge you to find in yourself some sympathy for him."

"I have sympathy for you," he said. "I think someone should have protected you from him."

Mary had nothing to say to this. If Victor had hurt her, it was as much a matter of her pursuing the opportunity for him to do so as it was by any intention of his.

"I suppose," she said, "if I should survive this adventure, I shall spend the rest of my days reading books of sermons, collecting fossils, practicing the pianoforte, and studying thorough bass."

Adam lifted his head. "Thorough bass?"

"Music is one of the few studies considered appropriate for girls."

"I know what a pianoforte is, but what is thorough bass?"

Mary welcomed the chance to speak of something other than her foolishness. "It is a theory of music. In thorough bass, one marks the intervals between the notes. It is quite mathematical. Knowing which notes correspond with the notes of the melody allows one to sing harmony."

"What is harmony?"

"Harmony is the science of musical chords. One sings, for

instance, a single note. Let's say the note is C. Like this." Mary sang a C as clearly as she could. As a girl she had always been praised for having perfect pitch. Years later Kitty confessed that everyone in the family had told Mary that simply to make her feel better about being plain.

But she thought that this was a fair C. Good enough for a monster, at least. "Now, can you make that sound? Just breathe in deeply, open your mouth wide, and let the sound come from your throat. Here, I'll sing and you match my tone."

Adam looked skeptically at her. Mary sang another C.

Adam opened his mouth and emitted a hoarse cry. Mary stopped. She tried not to laugh.

"That's right. A little softer, though. You don't have to strain your vocal cords. Just a steady tone like mine."

She sang it again, and the monster joined in, and it was not half as bad.

She commended him and they practiced until he could hold the note fairly steadily. Despite his guttural speech, he sang in a baritone more pleasant than she would have imagined.

"Good," said Mary. "We'll call that note the melody. Now I want you to sing it again—here, I'll sing a little so you can imitate it—and then I'm going to sing a different note, an E, while you keep singing the C. Ready?"

Mary started in C, and when Adam had matched the note, she switched to E. The two notes, in totally different voices, created a chord that filled the night.

As soon as he heard this sound, Adam stopped singing. He looked at her in astonishment.

"That's harmony," Mary said.

"How do you know this?"

"I have studied it for many years. Have you never heard harmony?"

"I've heard human beings singing a few times, always at a distance. I listen to the birds. But never any sound like this."

"Let me teach you a song. I'll sing 'The Bailiff's Daughter of Islington.' It goes like this." She sang the ballad about the young squire who loved the bailiff's daughter, but whose disapproving family sent him away. The girl suffers because she thinks his love was shallow and once he is gone, he has forgotten her. Mary came to the final verses, when the young man, returning after seven years, meets the girl, in rags, on the road.

> "I prithee, sweetheart, canst thou tell me
> Whether thou dost know
> The bailiff's daughter of Islington?"
> "She's dead, sir, long ago."

> "Then will I sell my goodly steed,
> My saddle and my bow;
> I will into some far country,
> Where no man doth me know."

> "O stay, O stay, thou goodly youth!
> She's alive, she is not dead;
> Here she standeth by thy side,
> And is ready to be thy bride."

Mary taught him the words. It took some practice, but eventually Adam managed to carry the tune through a verse.

The next time they tried it, Mary wove a high harmony above Adam's melody. He closed his eyes and chanted the lyrics, struggling not to be distracted by Mary's harmony notes.

When they got to the end, he said, "May we sing it again?"

They sang it again, and once more for good measure, until Adam was hoarse. When he got to "She's alive, she is not dead" the last time, his voice broke and he stumbled through the final lines.

"That was wonderful," Mary said.

Adam studied her for a moment in silence. "This is hard. It makes me feel things, here." He touched his spread fingers to his chest. "It is sweet, yet painful. These are emotions that I do not understand."

Of course he had never felt such emotions, Mary told herself. He was three years old.

Mary found the grocer's on Sinclair Street in Thurso. She had done her best to clean her coat, and fortunately it was long enough to cover the ragged and filthy ends of her dress. Mary could do nothing about Mrs. Buchanan's shoes, broken by a month of walking on the poorest of roads. She raised her collar, held her head up, and swung open the door.

The shop was blessedly warm. A youth was stacking jars of fruit and vegetables on a shelf. Bushels of potatoes, onions, and turnips stood along one wall, with sacks of grain. Other shelves held dry goods, soap, and bottles of spirits. On the counter lay bundles of candles. The air smelled of tea and spices.

An older man, behind the counter, looked up as she entered. She approached him.

"Yes?" he said. He had red side-whiskers and wore gold-rimmed spectacles.

Mary launched into her appeal. "My name is Mary Frankenstein. I wonder if you might help me find someone who I believe is residing in the vicinity of your town."

"Ye don't wish to buy something?"

"Not at present. I—"

"Then ye have no business with me. Good day." He turned away.

"Sir . . ."

He stopped and turned, crossed his arms over his chest, and regarded her with eyes hard as flint. Out of the corner of her eye she could see the boy was watching. Her resolve wavered, but she pushed on.

"I beg your assistance. I am a stranger here, come all the way from England in search of my husband. He left me some months ago on business to Scotland. He is in the—he is a writer, and he came to the remote north to isolate himself and produce a new work. He said he would return in a month, but it has been three now since last I saw him, and he left me insufficient money to live. You see me now in the state to which I have been reduced by his abandonment."

"A sorry state indeed," the grocer said.

"Has there been a man living here—his name is Victor Frankenstein, and he is Swiss—anywhere in the parish? He would have selected some remote place, but I hazard he may have come here to buy groceries. Mayhap you have dealt with him and may know where he is?"

"And a sorry tale for a vagabond whore to purvey, ye pretend wife with nary a wedding ring to your hand. I know not yer true purpose, and I do not care." He pointed across the room. "Ye see the door, and outside it lies the street where ye belong. God help ye."

And with that he went about his business, leaving her standing there. She looked at the boy, who ducked his head and resumed stocking the shelf. There was nothing for her to do but leave.

Two months ago such a humiliation might have killed her, and the idea of persisting would have been beyond her capacities. She stored the experience somewhere inside her for inspection at some later date, unless further humiliations should make it so insignificant that she might never think of this one again.

Out in the cold Mary considered what she might try next. She walked to the end of the street, turned right and went down that one to the next, then again until she had gone round the block. The streets were not busy, but some of those she passed took note of her. She ignored them. When she had come round to the end of the grocer's street, she waited at the corner of a building.

It was not long before the young man came out of the shop carrying several bundles. He started in her direction. Mary let him reach her, then stepped into his way.

"You heard what I asked your master. In the name of mercy, I ask you if you know anything of Victor Frankenstein."

The boy met her eyes, then looked away. He tried to go around her, but she stepped into his way again. If anyone was watching, she did not care.

"What would ye have me do?" he asked.

"Just this, and you may be on your way and never think

of me again: if you know, tell me where Mr. Frankenstein is living."

The boy shifted the packages under his arm. "He's on Emray Isle, five mile off the coast. Once a week Mr. Lennox sends him a crate of vegetables and bread."

"You are telling the truth?"

"I brings the crates myself, and fetches them back."

"And how does one get to this isle?"

"It's due north of the river's mouth by boat. Nobody lives there but a handful of starving sheep men. Yer husband's picked himself a right lovely place to hide."

"So he has." Mary stepped out of the boy's way. "You may not think so, but you have done a good deed. God bless you."

The boy hurried off down the street.

By the time she reached Adam, who awaited her below the river bridge, it was four in the afternoon; the sunset was lighting everything in the hasty golden hour of the northern autumn. She told him what the grocer's boy had said, and they found a prospect from which they could make out the island in the distance.

"Now," Adam said, "we steal a boat."

It was not until well after midnight that Adam was able to slip away with a skiff, a small boat with a pointed prow and a sail. Adam rowed them past the breakers and they used the sail to direct themselves northward. The sky was lightening in the east when they came upon the barren island, surrounded by rocks and cliffs. They had to sail some distance around it until they were able to land on a stony beach in the first light of dawn.

Adam dragged the boat ashore, unstepped the mast, and hid it as best he could behind an outcropping of rock.

"Wait here," he told her. "I will discover where Victor lives."

Mary protested. "Promise me that you will not let him see you. I should be the person to reveal to Victor that we are here."

Adam said nothing.

"I know you place little trust in anyone," Mary told him, "But you must trust me to speak with him before he sees you. His abhorrence of you is the greatest obstacle between you and your desire."

Adam's face ran rapidly through expressions of anger, resentment, and calculation before he replied, "I shall do as you say."

Mary sheltered herself in the boat, in the lee of the rock that blocked the wind. The bleak landscape gradually became illuminated by a watery daylight. There was a tightness in her chest at the thought of seeing Victor again. What would he make of her, so out of her element, so sadly reduced? He had lied in more than one way. Better than she had in Matlock's St. Giles churchyard, she could see that powerful emotions overran his intellect, and that among those emotions was shame.

An hour later, Adam returned. "I have found the house where he lives. Come."

Though it was full day now, it was not difficult to keep away from the other two dwellings on the island, visible from a distance in this barren landscape. The only living things they saw were the ever-present seabirds and the few emaciated sheep that their owners left to crop the meager grass holding its place in the rocky soil. The house that Victor occupied was at the other end of the isle. Awkwardly constructed of plastered stone, it had but two small glazed windows and a thatched roof. Against one end stood a wooden shed that looked to be of newer provenance.

Adam said that he would not sit waiting on Victor's grace, and told Mary that if and when she had come to terms with Frankenstein, they could find him on the nearby beach. He did not wait for her reply but stalked off toward the sound of the rolling surf and the cries of gulls.

She knocked on the door. There was no answer. She knocked again, and it opened. Victor stood there in loose white shirt with an apron over it; his dark hair, longer than it had been, had not seen a comb in some time. He stared at her in incomprehension.

"Miss Bennet?" he said absently, as if calling her name up from the bottom of the sea.

Mary was startled by his physical presence. "May I come in?" she asked.

Victor stood dazed a moment, and then reluctantly opened the door wider. She entered and he closed it. He said, "I thought I would never see you again. How did you find me?"

"Mr. Clerval told me you had gone to Thurso." The degree to which he accepted her appearance as if he had expected it made her wary.

Moving slowly, he bade her to sit down, and offered her some tea that had not been hot since the day before. He said, "I have been starved for the company of another human soul. You are the answer to my prayers."

Mary would have welcomed this profession had Victor not seemed at once both nonchalant about and bewildered by her appearance on his doorstep. He was unshaven and clearly had not changed his clothes for a number of days.

She looked around, fearful of what she might discern. A small room, recently plastered, a fireplace in which the coals of last night's fire had not been stoked into today's. The single window let in enough light to relieve the gloom but not vanquish it. A wooden table, two chairs, two tallow candles in pewter holders, a crate of wilting vegetables, a small wheel of cheese and a knife on the table, a pot, some mugs, some bottles of spirits. In the corner stood a wooden bed frame with a flat pillow, mattress, and disordered blankets. Unlaundered clothing spilled from an open trunk. A closed rough wooden door, with a lock, led to a second room. Victor, seated in the other chair, leaned forward, hands clasped before him, as he had in her room at Pemberley an age ago.

Beneath the musty odor a slight chemical smell hovered in the air.

"You look so tired," he said, gradually coming to himself. "And your clothes. My Lord, what has happened to you?"

"It has been a difficult journey. I lost my money. But let's not speak of that now. Victor, I know that you stole Kitty's body. I know what you are here to do."

The concern he had shown vanished. "How do you know this?"

"I was forced into the company of the man you created. He has explained everything to me."

"Man?" Victor seemed to turn this word in his mind, and looked at her oddly. "Mary, I warned you. I am sure he told you of vast injustices he has suffered because of me. Remember, he murdered my brother William and sent Justine Moritz to the gallows."

"He did not hide that from me."

"It does him no credit to admit what he knows I told you already. All else is lies."

"So you did not steal Kitty's body?"

Victor's brow knit. He seemed to come out of his lethargy, as if preparing for battle. "For your own safety, Mary, you must not give the slightest credence to what he says."

Here was the crux of it. "Shall we go into the next room? I would like to see what you have there."

Victor stared at her. "We shall not."

"I have not come to accuse you, Victor, nor am I offended by your lying to me. In your circumstances I might have done the same. I have the greatest sympathy for you, and I hope that you will trust me. I only want to help. But you must tell me what you are about here."

He gave an exasperated sigh.

"Yes, I took Kitty's body. In order to prevent that demon's taking revenge on the world, I have agreed to create a female like him. He swore that if I did so, he and she would leave the world of human beings and never be seen again."

"I know this as well. He has told it to me."

"Perhaps I should remain silent, then, since that thing has revealed everything about me."

"Come, Victor, do not act aggrieved. I have left my family, traveled hundreds of miles, and suffered many indignities in order to speak with you. You say you are starved for company. I offer it, if you will treat with me as your friend."

His shoulders slumped. "I warn you—this is a grisly business, not fit for a person of your sensibilities. Every day my nature rebels at the work that monster compels me to. Must you insist?"

"I must."

He stood, took a key from his pocket, and unlocked the door to the other room. He gestured for her to enter ahead of him. Until this moment Mary had acted the part of cool reason, but as she passed through the doorway, her soul was awash with dread.

A single window admitted enough light for her to make out a room crowded with equipment. Along the wall were lined empty crates and several large bottles; on a bench above them Leyden jars, spools of copper wire, and cables. A microscope sat just below the window. Several voltaic piles, stacked disks of copper and zinc like those she had seen exhibited at the Royal Institution, stood on the floor. On another shelf were ranked a row of large ceramic jars. The room smelled acidic, but below that was a not unpleasant odor like that of yeast; the closest Mary could come to it was the odor of rising bread dough. This room was noticeably warmer than the other.

A low table with massive legs dominated the center of the room. Atop it rested a large copper tub, perhaps six feet long and two wide; its sides rose to two feet. It was filled with a cloudy fluid to within a few inches of its top. She stopped, not daring to draw nearer.

"This is my laboratory," Victor said. "It was with great difficulty that I was able to transport these materials here; the only virtue of these northern Scots is that, though they will gossip, they do not question the strangeness of my pastimes."

He moved to the side of the table. "Come closer."

Mary stepped to the side of the tub and peered into it. Beneath the surface of the milky liquid she could make out the figure of a woman. Her features were unclear, but long hair floated about her head. Mary's heart beat fast.

"This is the mate that you are creating for your Creature," Mary said. She blinked back tears. "This is Kitty Bennet."

"Kitty Bennet is gone," Victor said, "never to return."

"One of the reasons I came all this way was the chance that, despite what you told me, you might be able to bring her back."

"At one time I might have hoped to do that. What drove me on in the quest for the secret of life was the possibility of recovering those we have lost. I would give parents the chance to retrieve children dead too young, and husbands and wives their beloved spouses."

He took both of her hands in his. "Alas, Mary, I cannot do that." He gestured at the copper basin. "What you see here was once your sister but is no longer."

"What's become of her?"

"She is being transformed. Within each cell of every creature God has written a plan that causes it to function as it does. A myriad of different cells make up a human being. In the beginning I removed samples of these different cells from Kitty's body. Working upon them, I am able to bring some of them to a kind of incipient life, like a seed. I then plant these seeds back into chosen sites in her remains. These fertile cells consume and replace those dead cells surrounding them. Kitty's body thus supplies an armature around which a new being grows. This nascent creature is made of the same substance that made Kitty, but what results, though it will be born an adult, is a creature as new as an infant.

"Your sister's body has gestated in this chemical womb for three weeks. Little of what she was remains. Soon her transformation shall be complete. But she shall not be alive yet, merely reconstructed. It remains then to remove her from this bath and, using the voltaic charge that you have read of in the experiments of Galvani and Aldini, bring her to life."

"Will it look like Kitty?"

Frankenstein shook his head. "Though this creature will no doubt in some ways resemble your sister, it will be no more Kitty than the monster that you have met is the person whose body I used to form it. And I must warn you that it will be as appalling in appearance as that creature is. Once animated, this new thing's mockery of humanity will be evident in its every movement."

Mary's throat was dry. "Might I have some water?" she asked. She felt unutterably weary, and swayed on her feet.

"You are not well," Victor said. He helped her back into the other room. He led her to a chair and poured a cup of water from a pitcher. She held it in both hands and sipped, her eyes closed.

"I should have spared you this horror. It is not something that you need ever have seen, and I should not have allowed it, no matter how much you protested."

Mary could not have come here and been kept from knowing Kitty's fate. She drank until the cup was empty. She handed it back to Victor. "Thank you."

He put it on the table. "You must be famished. Would you eat?"

"Not yet," Mary said.

He sat across from her. "Miss Bennet, my conscience has troubled me from the moment in Matlock when I deceived you. I beg your forgiveness." He was silent for a moment. "But how is it that you arrived here? You say that the monster told you his story?"

"We traveled together from Perth."

"My God! How awful!" He contemplated the prospect, and his expression darkened. "Why, he must have abused you beyond belief. It is a miracle that you live. But . . . how is it that you were able to escape from him?"

"I did not escape," Mary said. "He awaits outside. He has been waiting all the time that I have been here with you." She felt stronger, more certain of what must happen next. "I need you, Victor, to let him remain here, in peace, with both of us, until your work is complete."

SEVENTEEN

When Mary Bennet told me that the monster waited outside the cottage, and had been waiting there all morning as we spoke, that she had not escaped but instead traveled willingly with him, that it was she who had discovered where I was and she who had brought him, and that she wanted me to let him live here until I brought his monstrous bride to life, I sat stunned.

From what conceivable perspective could she choose to do so many things dangerous and irresponsible beyond comprehension, and then so calmly relate them, as if I would accept her actions as sweet reason? Yet here Miss Bennet sat, offering me sympathy, her eyes an open appeal.

She might be versed in natural philosophy beyond most women's understanding, but it was clear that the demon had played upon her good heart in order to use her.

"You have entered a pact with your Creature to create a

spouse for him," she said. "I would not have wished you to use Kitty's body, but now that you have begun her transformation, I feel, despite my own dismay, Christian charity demands that I do what I might to see both of you fulfill your sides of the agreement. That is the right thing, and the moral thing, and the practical thing. I know, Victor, that once you see the matter in this light, you will agree that this is the only reasonable course."

Miss Bennet's mix of prim moralism with naïveté had charmed me, and I might yet have been amused but for the fact that she had brought with her that demon and was speaking on its behalf. I had expected the Creature to find me, of course, since he would have to claim his bride before I could be done with him. But how could I work with the monster himself waiting like a starving man outside a kitchen?

Like a starving man, he was ruled by his hunger. I had no illusions that his desire for a mate represented anything beyond lust untempered by any civilizing influence. The history of men in venery is not a happy one for the women who are the focus of their obsession. How much worse would it be for this bride I was creating? But of course, her nature would be no more noble than his. Perhaps they would be well suited to each other.

Thank God I had made sure they would produce no offspring.

The monster would have been here sooner or later anyway. If I rejected Miss Bennet's arrangement, she might tell someone about my situation, with disastrous results. And though keeping her here as long as the monster remained would not be safe, someone needed to care for her. Better to allow her to stay until we were done.

"It is not possible for me to take that thing into my house," I said.

"Perhaps he might sleep in the shed?"

"Let him live outdoors on the island. He is used to living outdoors."

"I gather that this is an inhospitable clime at best, and the weather worsens every day. If he is abroad on the island, there is more chance that the other islanders might encounter him."

This was true.

"Very well," I said. "He may sleep in the shed."

"I do not know if he will accept that, but I will propose it."

I bit back my exasperation. "You will take my bed," I told her. "I will make up a pallet for myself in the laboratory."

"You must promise me that you will not antagonize him, and I will make him promise the same."

I made this promise.

She stood. "It is better that I speak with him alone. You should prepare your pallet while I am gone. When we return, I will be pleased to help you in the laboratory in any way that I may be of use."

She left. I listened to the wind whistle around the corners of the cottage and speculated about how I might survive the week.

It was the better part of an hour before they returned. Miss Bennet entered first.

"He is just outside," she said. "Remember your promise."

She leaned out of the door. "You may enter."

The monster ducked to get under the lintel. He looked much as he had in Matlock. His slouch hat brushed the rafters. His eyes met mine.

"Show me," he said.

I led him into the laboratory. He stood motionless over the bath, peering down, and then lifted his gaze. "How much longer?"

"A week or more," I said.

To look into his face was painful. For months I had nurtured him, thinking I was creating a human being of such beauty that the world would fall worshipping at my feet. I had made myself sick with anticipation, so devoutly was that consummation to be wished. The second he came to life, I saw him as he was: a horrid mockery, in no way worth the years I had spent creating him. My passion had been like that of some virginal young men for the act of sex: how they plot and plan, spend hours in idle fantasy, build it up to be the supreme moment of their lives. Once they taste the hollow ecstasy, they flee in disgust.

My disgust for the product of my scientific lust was far beyond that of any disillusioned lover. "This is a delicate process, and I do not wish to be distracted. I would prefer if you went away and came back."

"I will be here every minute," the thing said.

"Then let me not see you."

"You shall see what you will." He turned his back and went out to examine the shed.

Miss Bennet stood at the laboratory door. "I know this is difficult for you—" she began.

"I have work to do," I told her, and addressed myself to my microscope.

So we constructed our misbegotten household. The Creature, whom Miss Bennet had taken to calling Adam, I kept out of the laboratory as much as I could. I gave Miss Bennet one of the cheap dresses I had purchased in Edinburgh and put her to work fashioning voltaic cells. I had several Cruickshank batteries, but I would need more electricity than they could offer. I explained to Miss Bennet my plans for the large ceramic jars I had purchased. I had her place a round copper plate, attached to an insulated wire that ran up the side, into the bottom of each jar. She filled the jar halfway with a copper sulfate solution, submerging the plate, and then carefully added a zinc sulfate solution to just below the brim. Because of its lesser density, the zinc sulfate formed a layer atop the copper sulfate. Finally, opposite the wire, from each jar's rim I had her fit a cast zinc piece that hung below the surface of the zinc sulfate. The result was a new sort of battery that would hold a charge longer than the Cruickshanks.

Other than assembling the electrical apparatus, the chief work was distributing coals to the tray below the gestational bath in order to maintain the temperature of the fluid at a steady 102 degrees, and daily harvesting a few cells for microscopic examination. At this point it was merely a matter of waiting until the body was ready.

Working on these things, I spent many hours with Miss Bennet. I compared the woman before me with that unworldly spinster I had met at a ball in London. Some changes had been wrought—how else could she have survived a month with the monster?—yet the moralism that she had imbibed from her books of sermons remained. She attempted to persuade me that the Creature was in control of his passions. She told me he had saved her from assault by highwaymen.

He was more subtle than I had imagined, to have taken her in so completely.

Despite her certitude she seemed to me a person lost, torn from her moorings and adrift in a treacherous world she little understood. She watched me with a transparent intensity. I could feel the pressure of her longing. One day, as I drew fluid from the bath to test, I asked how her parents fared.

"They are greatly troubled since Kitty's death."

"How is it that they allowed you to make this long journey? I cannot imagine your mother accepting it."

"I deceived them. They thought they were sending me to Edinburgh. From there I stole away from my servant. I wrote them to explain."

"What was your explanation?"

Miss Bennet lowered her eyes. "I said I had knowledge concerning the defilement of Kitty's grave."

I saw an opportunity to wean her away from the distorted vision of things that she had received under the Creature's influence. "Was that your only reason?"

"Adam threatened to annihilate you. I worried that even should you evade his ire, you were so near despair that you might take your own life."

"I am still near despair, doing this blasphemous work at the behest of a murderous demon." I applied a drop of fluid to a microscope slide and set aside the pipette. "I doubt you told your parents you came to save me."

"I needed to know which of you told me the truth. Had you indeed stolen Kitty's body? Was it possible to bring her back?"

"And now you see it is not. I told you so in Matlock."

"Oh, Victor. You lied. You swore you had no knowledge of what had happened to Kitty." She paused. "You never told me that you were affianced."

With this last remark much became clear. "I never swore to the former," I said. "As for the latter—"

"Clerval told me you've been engaged for six years yet show no eagerness to marry. Of course he does not know about the burden you carry. That alone might explain why you have not fulfilled your promise to your betrothed." Her hopeful tone spoke volumes.

"Keeping my engagement from you was wrong. My regard for you was never feigned, but my dear Mary, you would do better to invest your affections elsewhere."

She looked away. She took up a spool of copper wire, and turned it in her hands. She put it down again and looked me in the eye. "I shall not regret my concern for your welfare. Whatever becomes of our friendship, you must complete this task and free yourself of Adam's threats of revenge."

I brought this conversation to as cordial an end as the difficult emotions it revealed might allow. Knowing her affection for me at least let me hope that, if she ever had to decide between the monster and me, I might trust her. Yet in that final week, Miss Bennet spent much time with him. During the afternoons he would wander the desolate cliffs and beaches, and she would go out to speak with him. I told myself it was in the effort to keep him to his promise, but I could not know.

One evening, after Miss Bennet and I had shared a meager meal of white bean soup in the room that I had given over to her, I became aware of a presence in the next room. When I stepped through the door into the laboratory, I found the Creature standing beside the bench, staring down at the female in her cloudy bath.

I had caught him studying her like this more than once. An

expression of great longing would take over his dead face, on which it seemed a parody of human desire. But then I thought: a cat is not human, yet even in a cat's face one may read emotions. Was this Creature not infinitely more than a cat? If so, might his passions be true? And what did they portend?

And then I thought of the thing growing in the vat, which had once been the sister of the woman in the other room. What might it feel, once I gave it the power to feel things, and then put it into the hands of one whose sole motive was self-gratification?

When I entered the laboratory, the Creature looked up.

"You'll have her soon enough," I said.

He regarded me with distaste. When I stepped forward, he turned and left by the laboratory's rear door. Something in his silence charged my blood, and I followed him outside.

"I'll give you your bride!" I said. "You'll soon have the chance to inflict yourself on her rather than on poor Miss Bennet."

He stopped at the entrance to the shed.

"You know that Miss Bennet is in love with you," he said.

His words took me by surprise. "You know nothing of what is in Miss Bennet's heart," I said.

"I can see the effect your attentions have on one who has been alone. You owe her better than you have given."

She was in the room on the other side of this stone wall. Could she hear us?

The demon said, "It would be a sad thing if, while providing me a balm for my pain, you neglected the pain of someone who has done you none of the wrong I have."

He crawled into the shed, leaving me standing there.

I returned to my pallet and blew out the candle. In the dark, for the first time, I let my thoughts travel forward to ponder what I should do once I had freed myself of the Creature. It was true: once he and his bride had left, I would be obliged to deal with Miss Bennet and her forlorn hopes. It would not be pleasant, but I would do my best to be kind. Then, at last, I might return home and marry Elizabeth, in some confidence that my family would be safe from further threats. Henry and I might once again take pleasure in each other's company. I fell asleep thinking of the comfort I would bring my dear father by the simple act of uniting with my beloved.

Ten days after Miss Bennet and the monster had arrived, I judged that it was time to conclude my task. The preparations took all of the day; by the time we were ready, another cold night had begun, the waxing gibbous moon gliding noiselessly through the clouds. A gleam of its light shone through the window, augmenting the two candles and a lamp that dimly illuminated the laboratory. All three of us were tense with anticipation. Knowing how disturbing the first sight of this thing coming to life would be, contemplating that it had once been her sister, I implored Miss Bennet to wait in the other room. She would not. With a troubled conscience I pressed forward.

First it was necessary to remove the female from its bath. Using a linen hose, I siphoned off the generational fluid. When its surface had drained enough to expose the body, I climbed onto a bench beside the basin, slid my arms under the naked female, and lifted. The limp body was slimy. Its head lolled, hair dripping fluid, and the legs hung down. I struggled to raise it over the lip of the tank. I lost my balance and struck the head of the new female against the edge.

"Don't hurt her!" the Creature said. He stepped to the opposite side of the tank and took her from me. He held this naked thing, so much smaller than he, like some obscene parody of Michelangelo's *Pietà*.

Miss Bennet had averted her eyes. "Help me remove this tub," I told her.

She came to one end of the table and took hold of the copper tub. With the fluid drained, it was just light enough so that together she and I could wrestle it from the table to the floor.

"Lay the body on the table," I told the Creature.

With his help I rolled the body over so that we might drain the fluid from its lungs; milk white it bubbled up through the female's nose and leaked from its slack mouth. When that was accomplished, we laid the thing on its back. It smelled strongly, but not unpleasantly, of the fluids in which it had grown.

Now that she was exposed, it became apparent that the female's skin had not knit together properly: some areas were fair, but others were dark and discolored. Patches of dark hair grew on her thigh and abdomen. A dark purple stain like a birthmark, pebbled with knots of flesh, ran from her forehead, over one eye, her nose and mouth, and down her neck to her bosom.

"You may wash the body now," I told Mary.

Miss Bennet brought a basin of warm water and, with a sponge, carefully washed the female. When that was done, I began a minute examination.

First I moved the joints of the legs, hips, ankles, shoulders, elbows, and wrists. The female showed none of the rigidity of a body dead four months. Despite the areas of discoloration and the irregularity of the birthmark, there were no signs of decay. I palpated the abdomen, which had grown smooth over the incision where I had surgically sterilized her after removing the embryo I had found in her womb. The flesh was supple. The fingernails and toenails were soft and pink as a baby's.

Both Miss Bennet and my monster stared at the bride. Although the birthmark made it hard to judge, the shape of its face was that of Catherine Bennet, but the lips were much fuller, the ears larger. The teeth were of pearly whiteness, the forehead high and broad, the eyes widely separated. Where not blemished, the pores of its skin were so small as to be invisible, as smooth as a satin pillow, pale as a figure cut from marble. No event had been written on its vacant face.

"She looks like Kitty," Miss Bennet said.

The Creature hovered behind her. "She does not," he said.

In deference to Miss Bennet's sensibilities, and aware of the Creature's concupiscence, I drew a sheet up to its neck.

I hung my lamp above the face and pulled back the lids of its eyes. Unlike Kitty's blue, these were so pale and watery that the pupils were black beads. The whites glistened like the skin of a peeled egg.

I fastened copper bands to the body's wrists and ankles. A bracket held disks to its temples and a canvas strap bound similar disks to either side of the heart. Careful not to cross the positive and negative, I attached copper wires. These wires were connected to one side of a switch; wires from the other side ran to the batteries. I had previously wired the batteries, two by two in parallel, with each of these pairs wired to the others in series. From them I could call upon as strong a source of electrical current as any laboratory in Europe.

I forced a dowel wrapped in cloth between the jaws of the female. "When I close this switch," I said, "a powerful surge of electrical fluid will flow into the body. If nothing has gone awry in its preparation, it should be brought to life. I am sure there will be some spasms, but you must not assume that indicates that it has yet taken life. No matter what occurs, you must not touch the body while the switch is closed, and should refrain from touching it even after I have completed the infusion of electricity."

Miss Bennet moved away from the table. The Creature reached up to steady himself with a hand on one of the rafters. I closed the switch.

The legs and arms of the body went rigid. The jaw clenched. Beneath the sheet its back arched and its chin lifted as the head was thrown back. I let the electricity flow for a moment, then opened the switch. The body fell to the table, limp.

I leaned over and held a listening tube against its breast. There was no heartbeat. I stepped back. "Again."

I closed the circuit.

Once more the body went rigid. I let it run longer this time, fifteen, twenty, thirty seconds. A wisp of smoke rose from its forehead, carrying a scent of charred flesh. When I opened the circuit and listened, there was still no heartbeat.

If we were to keep trying, the power of the batteries would soon fade. I removed the connections to the wrist and ankle bands, and adjusted only the disks bracketing the heart.

This time, when I closed the circuit, the body did not twitch. But when I turned off the current, the thing suddenly convulsed. The bride jerked upright and coughed explosively, spitting the dowel across the room. She fell back, then gasped for air and coughed again. Her eyelids flew open and her pale eyes stared blindly. Her hands twitched. For the second time in my life I fell back, appalled at what I had accomplished.

Miss Bennet exclaimed, "She cannot breathe!"

"Help her," the Creature said.

Despite my warnings, they both converged on the table.

"Turn her over," I said. "She still has fluid in her lungs."

The Creature took the female by its shoulders and helped roll it to its side. It coughed up more fluid. Miss Bennet held its head, keeping the damp hair out of its face, and eventually it was able to breathe. When they laid it back onto the table, its eyes were open but unfocused. It lay there, unmoving but for the flutter of its eyelids.

Miss Bennet asked. "Does she feel anything?"

It was all I could do to bestir myself to respond. Now that it was clear that I had done it again, the experience of the first creation had come back to me strongly. Unlike that first time, when horror and revulsion so overwhelmed me, those emotions were second to my understanding that this was no accident. I indeed possessed the ability to create life, and with that knowledge came the conviction that this was as depraved an ambition as any human being had ever possessed in the history of our race. I was unworthy of such knowledge. I was not capable of wielding it wisely. And what was true for me was a thousand times over more true for the rest of humanity, whose vices and follies and unholy desire for power were all too evident to me.

I steeled myself, took a scalpel from my surgical kit, and ran its blunt end up the sole of the female's foot. It twitched, as did the other, and both of the hands when I tried them. "The nerves are functioning. I cannot say how well the muscles will respond."

When the bride had sat up, its sheet had slid to the floor. Mary said, "We must clothe her."

I unfastened the disks from its chest. Miss Bennet took one of the dresses I had purchased and, struggling to manipulate the bride's limbs, pulled it onto her body. The dress of a serving girl, the same dress that Miss Bennet wore. She buttoned it up the front. In it the female looked more vile than she had naked. Yet if Miss Bennet was repulsed by the thing's appearance, or by the enormity of the transgression against God and nature that had just transpired, she kept her reaction hidden.

The bride lay upon the table, limbs awry, breathing slowly, eyes unfocused, burn marks on her temples, face obscured by the disfiguring birthmark, fingers occasionally twitching. Her heart beat steady and strong.

The Creature looked down upon his hideous bride with eyes full almost to tears. Watching him and his mate, products of my own ingenuity, who would soon go out into the world to commit, in my name, I knew not what atrocities, tormented me beyond my capacity to express.

EIGHTEEN

At the north end of the island, above the sea cliffs, stood a circle of stones, remains of some ancient druidic ritual ground. Some of the stones were missing, others fallen, but one yet stood. Two days before the bride's birth Mary found Adam there.

As a way of understanding what they might expect from the bride once she was brought to life, she asked him about his first impressions of the world.

"My recollections are vague," Adam told her. "I remember feeling cold. I could not see well—my eyes reacted to light, but I had no understanding of the objects that I saw or of how they related to one another, no concepts of depth or distance. Sound and scent and touch affected me, but all senses seemed mixed together. My body obeyed to my desire to move, but I was terribly clumsy. Still, despite my having no more knowledge than a newborn infant, within hours after my awaking I had wandered out of Victor's apartments into the countryside. It may be that because I possessed the body of an adult I had by instinct that power of motion."

"Did you understand speech?"

"No. When I encountered human beings they made sounds, but those sounds meant nothing to me. I was sensitive to their emotions, however. I could tell if the speaker was afraid, or angry. Fear and anger: those were the first emotions I could distinguish, because they were the only emotions I aroused."

"We should make sure that the first voice your bride hears is not that of someone afraid or angry."

"A noble intention," Adam said slowly. "Perhaps you can sermonize to the rest of the human race about that." He sat staring down at the rocks, his dark lips compressed. With his livid, flawless skin he looked as cold as the ancient stone they sat on, fashioned by the hands of men dead a thousand years.

In the week leading up to the quickening of Victor's new creation, Mary's chief occupation had been to serve as go-between for Victor and Adam. The two seldom spoke to each other, and then only a few words. Victor never acknowledged that his creature had taken the name Adam, and Mary caught him looking at her with distaste when she used that name.

Their hostility to each other troubled Mary. She tried speaking with each about this, approaching the subject by means of other talk. In the evenings Mary would share her meal with Victor, and in the mornings with Adam—neither would eat in the other's presence, but each allowed Mary to join him as long as the other was not present.

Over those evening meals she was able to converse as she had never done with a man not related to her by family. Victor's professions of gratitude for her appearance at his door were borne out by his demeanor whenever he could be brought to forget the distasteful task they were about. He spoke with hope in his voice, as if, with the birth of the bride, he himself would be reborn. His face would open and the darkness lift from his eyes. Was it foolish for Mary to imagine there might be a place for her in Victor's new life? How ironic would it be if, with Adam's finding a mate of his own species, she might find one herself?

Mary worried that her happiness might come at the expense of Elizabeth Lavenza, but such situations occurred all the time in society, if under vastly different circumstances.

It gratified her that Victor trusted her to construct the batteries he would need. They spent much time together in his laboratory, and however distasteful he found the process, when Mary asked him questions he was the most patient of teachers. He showed her dead and living cells through his microscope and described their structures. He discoursed on the nature of positive and negative electrical fluids.

Three things impressed her most strongly about Victor in his laboratory: first, that his knowledge of science was vast. He understood nature's complex and subtle ways, and had an ability to leap from an observation to a sound conclusion without having to labor through the dozen intervening steps that he must explain to Mary to make his process clear. His was a brilliant and original mind, and in those few moments that he could forget the purpose to which all their work intended, she could see the delight he took in discovery.

Her second observation was that he seldom forgot that purpose, and it blighted what would otherwise be a happy nature.

Creating a bride for Adam harrowed him to the depths of his soul. He would give nearly anything to abandon the effort, and would do so instantly if there were any way he could without dooming himself and everyone around him to destruction. Under this aspect he hated his work, hated that his mind was capable of it, and hated Adam for forcing him, holding all that he loved hostage, to do this thing.

Mary's third observation was that Victor had given no thought to the female that he was creating other than as an object to appease Adam. Whether Adam thought of her as other than the focus of his desire was a question whose answer was less apparent. Mary attempted to move both of them to consider the being that was growing in the copper tub as a person, not some thing.

Mary pointed out to Victor that it would not be humane to thrust the female out the door as soon as she was created.

"It is not my responsibility what happens to her," he said. "The monster forces me to create her. Let him care for her."

"I will care for her until she is able to care for herself," Mary said. "She will share my room with me."

"Don't be a fool, Miss Bennet. Her only predecessor is that thing out there, who has chased a family from their home, burned it to the ground, strangled a ten-year-old boy, and implicated a young woman in that murder. This history does not recommend that you share a bed with his female counterpart."

"We must not abandon her into the world."

"I bought her a dress, and shoes."

"And I will see that she learns how to wear them."

"Cannot we leave her education to the care of the Creature?"

"I will not see her educated by the mercies of the cruel world, and without any notion of God."

Victor considered what she said. "You are a difficult woman, Miss Bennet. Very well. I shall watch over you, for your own sake. I could not bear to see you come to harm as a result of anything I have done."

As the time approached when his companion might be vivified, it became increasingly evident that Adam's spirit was wrought. The day before Victor decided he would bring the female to life, Adam said to Mary, "He works at creating her only out of compulsion. His every move shows his hatred of what he does. What can I do to assure that he completes his task?"

Mary did not think telling Adam of Victor's warnings would serve any purpose. "I will do all in my power to see that he completes her. Victor values my good opinion. He has brought your bride to the brink of life. Have patience. God has us in his hands, and with his guidance, by this time next week you will hold her hand in yours."

His voice was almost a whisper. "If she will have me."

"That will depend on your treatment of her. Do not let fear rule your heart."

On the day that Victor chose for the bride's birth, they spent the daytime preparing the electrical equipment. Night had come before Victor was ready to assay her awakening. He drained the bath of fluid, exposing her body. When he struggled to lift her, Adam took her in his arms, and Mary helped Victor clear the table.

She had prepared herself for cleaning the body, but in the event she found herself able to do so only by telling herself that this being was not Kitty. She washed it head to toe and dried it carefully. Only then did she allow herself to study its face. The large birthmark, ugly purple, made it hard to judge her features. The patches of coarse hair on her abdomen and thigh were repulsive, and other areas of her skin were raw and red. The unblemished portions were fairer and finer than Kitty's had ever been, as flawless as Adam's. The high forehead, the cheekbones, were familiar.

"She looks like Kitty," Mary said.

From behind her came Adam's voice. "She does not."

But he had not lived his life with Kitty. It unnerved Mary to see her lying naked there before these men. She supposed that modesty did not rule in the laboratory any more than it did in the surgery, but it gave her pause.

Victor affixed his disks and wires to the female's body. He warned Mary and Adam to keep away while the electricity was coursing through it, then closed the switch.

On the third try the body on the table jerked upright and coughed explosively, gasped for air, coughed again. Her eyelids flew open and her pale eyes stared.

"She cannot breathe!" Mary said.

Adam and Mary rushed to her. Victor at last came forward and, while Mary held her head, helped her to cough up the remaining fluid from her lungs. They laid her back on the table. Burn marks stood out on her chest where the electricity had entered her body. Victor stood by as if in a trance. When Mary glanced at his face, she saw a look of such dismay that she almost stopped and went to him. He was reluctant to touch the female until, at Mary's urging, he tested her reflexes and listened to her heart.

"We must clothe her," Mary said. Victor removed the disks, and Mary struggled to fit the female into a dress. Adam stood suspended, as if afraid to help. Victor busied himself in disconnecting the batteries. He had Adam carry equipment out to the shed. Adam did not want to leave the room, but he obeyed Victor's orders. His face held an expression of disbelief.

The female's progress toward physical self-control was swift. Her chest rose and fell regularly. Her fingers twitched. Within an hour, when Mary held her hand above the female's face her eyes adjusted to focus on it. She lifted a shaky hand to touch Mary's. She opened her mouth and made small sounds.

Victor moved himself to listen to her heart every hour, and warned them not to leave her alone, but otherwise seemed unnerved to be in the same room with her. At three in the morning he put on his greatcoat and told them he would be walking around the island until the dawn. Mary and Adam helped the female from the laboratory into Mary's room. With their aid, she was able to walk, shuffling, under her own control.

"May I sit here and watch her?" Adam asked.

"I think that it is better that we should have privacy," Mary said.

"I have gone through what she goes through now. I can tell you what she must be thinking."

"Tomorrow will be soon enough to begin."

"As you wish," Adam said. His eyes lingered on the female as he left the room.

The wind rattled the windowpanes and a draft shot in below the door. Mary fed the fire. The bride sat on Mary's bed and fixed her eyes on the flames.

Mary sat opposite her. The flickering firelight played

across the bride's discolored skin, her eyes that looked blind except that they darted about. The feeling that Mary was looking into the face of her dead sister made her look away.

"Sit there, now," Mary said. She felt the bride's hands. "You are cold. Here, let me warm you."

The bride's eyes watched Mary's face. Her slack mouth opened and closed soundlessly, imitating Mary's own. She looked brutally animalistic, as if a cow or fish had taken the shape of a woman. Mary felt nauseated, full of anxiety. What was she doing here, with this — this *thing*?

Mary pulled the blanket from the bed and wrapped it about the bride's shoulders. "There, that's better."

The bride moved toward the fire, overbalanced, and fell to one knee. Mary got down next to her and tried to help her up. The bride thrust her hands toward the flames.

"No!" Mary said, and pulled her back. They both fell clumsily to the floor.

Mary embraced her, holding her arms to her sides. She recalled holding Kitty in the woods on the day that she had told Mary of her affair. This same body.

"You mustn't put your hands into the fire," Mary said.

She did not fight, but let herself be guided back onto the bed. Mary made her lie down with her arms at her sides and covered her with the blanket, tucking it tightly around her to restrain her. The bride's eyes followed Mary's every movement.

Mary returned to her chair. The bride's depthless eyes remained open, but she did not try to move. Fatigue washed over Mary, the exhaustion of weeks of overstrained nerves. She wondered how her father and mother were, and felt a pang of regret for how she had abandoned them. As the bride lay quietly, Mary began to feel calmer. Perhaps she would survive this terrifying moment in her life and return at last to her home and her books.

After a while Mary looked up to see Adam peering in at the window, a ghastly grin wrinkling his dark lips. It sent a shiver down her spine, and she shook her head, waving him away. Adam's face withdrew, and a moment later Mary heard heated words between him and Victor outside the window. She could not make out what they said over the sound of the wind, but soon afterward the door to the laboratory opened and Victor poked his head into the room.

"Miss Bennet, are you all right?" he asked.

Mary looked up from her chair. "I am fine."

"I caught the demon spying on you. I told him to leave you in peace."

"Thank you."

"This one hasn't tried to harm you?"

"She is gentle as an infant," Mary said.

Victor shook his head slowly. "I beg you not to make that assumption."

"Thank you for your concern," Mary said. "You should go to sleep. It will be daylight soon enough. I shall take care."

"I will be in the next room," Victor said. "Call on me and I will come in an instant."

"Very well," Mary said.

Victor left and she heard him settle down on his pallet. She assumed that Adam was either roaming the seashore or had crawled into his shed. The image of his grinning face at the window lingered in her mind.

The bride lay without moving, and eventually her eyes

closed. Mary wondered what thoughts passed through her mind. Did she recognize anything of the world, or was she as blank as a newborn? She had already learned to walk, to use her hands, to focus her eyes on Mary's face. She did not seem afraid; if anything were evident in her eyes, it was of a mind trying to grasp what she was and where she found herself. Mary wondered if her dreams might be of things that had happened to Kitty. Might Mary appear in them? Might some echo of Kitty's soul linger?

Mary sat watching for a time, and then, quietly, crawled onto the bed beside her. She lay on her side and wrapped her arms around the bride, just as she had slept with Kitty many times, her face inches away from this uncanny, inhuman thing that had once been her sister. Eventually she slept.

The next day she taught the bride to sit, and stand, and practice walking. Mary sat her at the table and fed her porridge from a pewter spoon. The bride tasted it, and her eyes opened wide. Porridge dribbled from her lips, but soon she had learned to swallow. Her blemished, waxen face showed a type of pleasure.

Mary wiped the bride's mouth and chin. She helped her to drink water from a cup. The bride's ability to control her limbs progressed at an astonishing rate. By the end of the morning she could walk, sit, hold a cup, and drink without aid. In imitation of the conversation between Mary and Victor, she began making sounds.

Victor did not seem as eager to have her gone as he at first had been, but he did not help in any of this instruction. He repeatedly warned Mary not to lower her guard.

Adam, on the contrary, was eager to help, and in the afternoon Mary allowed him to join her in trying to teach the bride to speak. He seemed at first wary—perhaps fearing that the female might find him as repulsive as humans had. But the bride did not recoil from him. She watched him, and seemed fascinated with his appearance, his low voice, his bulk.

Mary and the Creature took turns speaking to her, pointing at objects, encouraging her to repeat the sounds they made. "Hand. Arm. Finger. Foot. Face. Nose. Mouth. Chin. Neck. Eye."

"Bed. Chair. Spoon. Cup. Table. Door. Hearth."

Adam's patience seemed infinite. Mary observed his expressions as all through the day into the evening he sat with the bride. She saw written there interest, amusement, surprise, wonder. He smiled. His attitude was one of awe that the bride attended so closely to everything he did and said.

Though she showed nothing that would indicate that any of the character of Kitty was written on her mind, she learned quickly. The sounds she produced were at first no more than nonsense, unbroken by distinction between one syllable and the next; by the end of the day she had spoken several intelligible words.

"Adam," the Creature said, touching his hand to his breast.

"A-dam," the bride said.

"Eve," he said, gesturing gently toward her.

"Eeef," she said.

"Eve," he said.

"Eeef."

Adam's dead face creased in a grin. "That's right," he said. "Eeef." He touched his own breast again. "Adam."

"Adam," she said.

Mary noted that, unlike Adam, Eve did not get to choose her own name. She considered the novelty of their situation: a woman created fully grown, innocent as a child, as the intended companion for the only other being of her kind. Though these circumstances were unlike any since the creation of the first Eve, destined to marry the first Adam, Mary had known women who were promised to men even before their births. It was not an unheard-of circumstance among the gentle families of England. Lady Catherine de Bourgh and Darcy's mother had vowed, while their children were yet infants, that Darcy and Lady de Bourgh's daughter Anne would marry when they came of age. In the end this had not come to pass, as Darcy fell in love with Lizzy, to Lady Catherine's chagrin.

Falling in love. Such a strange phrase. Mary supposed that "falling" most definitely applied to the Bible's Adam and Eve. From a higher state into a lower one, though to hear her mother and all the world speak, it was the opposite. Marriage was supposed to be an exaltation.

Eve in the Garden never considered not marrying Adam. They seemed to have a fundamental sympathy, which Mary supposed was a good thing. Although perhaps they were not so well mated as God had intended, else Eve would not have disobeyed Adam (to say nothing of God) and eaten of the apple. And then, worse, she had tempted Adam into eating of it, when she well knew what trouble this would bring him. That was not a very generous attitude to take toward one's husband.

But as far as Mary could tell, it was a common one. The Church said that such differences between husband and wife existed because we were born with original sin. Thus the necessity of religion and churches, to provide a hope of salvation in the next world and some rules of behavior for this one. Radicals like Byron and Godwin pointed out that this was a very convenient circumstance for churches and the kings they served, but to Mary history provided ample evidence that human beings should follow rules of morality rather than trust conscience—or whatever the German writers were calling it nowadays.

Here was another Eve, the first woman born since the Garden who might be said to face the original Eve's situation. Mary saw the Creature's naming himself Adam in a different light. Neither he nor Victor seemed to have considered how Eve might regard what was being asked of her, or what she was being offered.

The female was a child. Was it right to give a child into the keeping of the man who planned to marry her? Again, this was something Mary had seen done in her world and never questioned. How could those girls know what other possibilities life might offer? How could they ever become other than that thing their owner—for that was what he amounted to, even if one called him a guardian—wanted? And if, at some later period in their lives, these women understood the unfairness of their situation, would that promote a happy union?

Mary had seen some marriages of this sort, and based on the very little she had observed, she did not think them happy ones.

Yet she could not imagine Adam for a very long time forbearing from presenting his affections to Eve. There was no answer for it: Mary would have to teach Eve as much as she could in the few days before Eve and Adam left, and—if Adam was sincere in his professions—Eve never saw a human being again.

A day later Mary, having left the two of them while she spoke with Victor on the beach, returned to find them nowhere in the cottage. It was a blessedly mild day for October, the sky devoid of clouds, the wind more a breeze than a gale. Mary feared Adam might have drawn Eve away in order to take advantage of her; she searched this end of the island and came upon them sitting in the circle of stones near the brink of the cliff.

Unaware of Mary, they sat face-to-face in the slanting sunlight, their hair stirred by the light wind. Adam was saying something to her, holding his hand to her lips. Mary moved close enough to hear, hiding behind the one standing stone.

"Make this sound, like this," he said. He opened his mouth and sang a steady note, slightly off-key. It was a C.

Eve, eyes intent on him, sang a C. Her voice was steady and sweet.

Adam sang with her until she held the note, then switched to an E. The primitive harmony was carried off on the wind. They sang it until they ran out of breath; Adam coughed, and laughed. Eve laughed too. Mary was startled to hear how much her laugh sounded like Kitty's.

Adam saw Mary beside the standing stone, and stopped. "What do you want?"

"I was worried."

"There's nothing to worry about." Adam's voice was defensive. Then he paused, and looking at Eve said again, in an entirely different tone, "There's nothing to worry about." His face was solemn, but if anything, relaxed.

"Let me show you how it is with a third voice," Mary said.

Eve looked at Mary, a little uncertain. Her terrible skin shone in the sun. Mary sat beside her.

The three of them returned at sunset to find Victor waiting. As soon as Adam had left and Mary had laid Eve down on her bed to rest, Victor asked, "What were they about?"

"They were singing," Mary said.

Victor looked unhappy. "The fiend is a thing of appetites. I have seen him touch her, little caresses when he thinks no one is looking. He intends to use her in the most vile ways."

"When I found them together he was doing nothing untoward. He knows that she is little more than an infant."

"Once he takes her away, where no civilized person might object, he will make her his concubine. She'll have no choice—how might she have a choice, knowing no other man, and in complete ignorance of humane behavior?"

Having contemplated the same possibility, Mary could not with reason claim that it was impossible.

"We shall have to keep them here as long as we can," she said, "so that we might educate her—educate both of them, for he is as ignorant of the proprieties as she."

"No proprieties will exist between them the moment that they are away. And consider—one of the first results of those sympathies for which the demon thirsts will be children. A race of devils may be propagated upon the earth, who might make the very existence of man precarious and full of terror."

Mary had a troubling thought. "Victor, you have mastered every detail of human physiology. I would hazard that you know more about this than any man who has ever lived. When you performed your surgeries on Kitty's body, could you not have assured that she would never bear children?"

Victor was silent for a moment. "Unfortunately, I never thought of this possibility. Would that I had."

The question raised another in Mary's mind. "Might you . . . Did you by chance discover whether Kitty, when she died, was with child?"

"She was with child?" Victor studied her calmly.

"I don't think it likely, but it was a fear she expressed to me just before she died."

"Do not trouble your heart, Mary. No, I did not find her to be carrying a child. A good thing, else it be born to these devils."

"Must you call them devils? Why should they pursue evil once they are free and have each other for solace and mutual support?"

Victor shook his head.

"He has committed acts of monstrous evil, and felt himself justified in doing them. His is a bitter and vengeful spirit. Whether it comes by nature or usage, that's what he is. How may we be certain that the female won't inherit his temperament? Once their character is established, beings do not change. We are left, then, with the necessity of dealing with the world's dangerous inhabitants by any means available."

Victor spoke in a voice of reason, as calmly as he had at the Cavendish Square ballroom in London. He seemed not so much melancholy as exhausted, physically and mentally, sad and not angry. Mary had hoped that, once the burden of Eve's creation was lifted from his shoulders, he might turn to her with an open heart. She did not see it.

"It is a despairing picture you paint," Mary said. "I hope that you are wrong."

But what if Victor was right? Maybe the world was as he said. Mary remembered the highwayman, his grip on her arm, his breath sour with whiskey.

"Trust me," said Victor. "This will not end well."

Nineteen

On the evening that Victor chose for his attempt to bring my Eve to life, I felt such anxiety as I had not experienced in my short time on earth.

More than anything I wanted him to succeed. I knew that he hated me, felt revulsion for the process of creating my bride, and had the gravest misgivings regarding the consequences. He wanted us to leave, and I wanted just as much never to see him again. My hatred of him seemed woven into my flesh. But as the days passed, the uncomfortable realization was born in upon me that the moment my bride came to life, everything between Victor and me would change. I would owe him a debt of gratitude. I would be free to respect and honor him. Moreover, at that same moment, the guilt I already felt for the deaths of Justine and William would become a deadly burden. It would be up to me, with the help of Eve, to repay my debt.

I could not expect Victor ever to forgive my strangling his brother, but I could vow to be kind toward the human race for the rest of my existence.

Every time I passed by the bath in which she grew, I could not keep myself from staring into her blind, blank face. She was my sleeping princess. Studying her, I would slide into a reverie. I felt that the being growing to completion in that murky bath was already my wife. To her I would devote the rest of my life. In no way would I allow her to suffer any of the painful experiences that had been most of my contact with the human race.

More than once I came out of these spells to find Victor observing me with curiosity more than distaste. It was as if he saw in me not a horror but a mystery set for him to solve. Yet there was less intercourse between us now than when we argued in the ice cave on the Swiss glacier more than a year ago. He never spoke other than to order me out of the room.

What communications I had were with Miss Bennet. She would ask after my state of mind. When she realized that I would never speak to her of such things while Victor was there, she sought me out when I took my walks by the ocean.

On those days that the boat came from Thurso with his food and whatever letters might have arrived for him in the previous week, Victor would banish both Miss Bennet and me from the cottage. At the isle's north end, far enough away from the other islanders so that I might safely walk unseen to the verge of the cliffs, lay the ruins of an ancient stone circle. There I would retreat to contemplate my future.

I would watch the waves dash themselves upon the rocks below, draw back, and come again. The ocean was never still.

Farther out swells and rollers surged; seabirds swooped over them in search of fish, or floated in flocks on the surface. The sun gave no warmth, and the cold wind, as perpetual as the waves, buffeted my face. I felt the life in my body, the strength of it, its desire to taste and enjoy. I thought of how in a few days my Eve would experience this for the first time.

It made me uneasy.

Ten days after our arrival Victor gathered the instruments of life about the copper tub that was Eve's womb. Miss Bennet had prepared a basin with warm water with which she intended to bathe Eve after she had been brought to life. I brought the long hose that Victor used to siphon off the chemicals in which her body lay. It took a long time.

When Victor staggered trying to lift her body from the tank, I took her from him until they could clear the table. I laid her back down. Victor examined her body, and Mary bathed her, while all I could do was study her.

A large purple mark swept from her hairline to her neck and onto her breast. Miss Bennet said that Eve looked like Kitty, but she did not. It was clear to me even before Victor brought her to life that she bore no connection to Kitty Bennet. I knew Eve. I had been her. Three years earlier I had lain on just such a table as this, and awakened with a mind as unblemished as a drift of snow. Perhaps when she came to life she might retain some vague sense of floating in Victor's metal womb, but like me, she had experienced nothing of the world. She would begin as pure as the first Eve when morning awakened her in paradise. What would be written on her heart would be inscribed according to how she was treated from that moment when, on the third try, her heart began to beat and blood to circulate in her veins. She coughed explosively and her eyes flew open. Miss Bennet and I rushed to relieve her.

I held her shoulders. She moved and breathed. She was alive. I drank up every particle of her presence.

That first night Miss Bennet, rather than let me sit with my bride, chased me from the room. I could not abide pacing the tiny laboratory, and went outside. Victor had already fled—he had no taste for the outcome of his work, any more than when he had brought me to life—and so I was alone in the dark October night. The wind buffeted the small house beneath the light of the autumn moon. In the distance I heard the waves breaking on the seashore.

I circled the cottage several times, my mind so wrought up that what went through it could hardly be dignified with the term "thought." Elation surged through my chest like Victor's electrical charges, and disbelief through my mind.

This was the thing that elated me the most: the earth now contained a second person like me. I felt a bond to her that was no less real for the fact that it was based on our unwritten future. How much I could teach her! How much easier might I make the way for her! I had, thanks to Victor, a purpose for my life.

Miss Bennet's warning that she might reject me might still come to pass, but at the moment such a prospect did not seem possible. My eagerness simply to sit and observe her was almost more than I could stand. I felt like singing to the stars and the clouds and the sparse grass that covered the soil of this barren isle.

Instead I danced outside the rude cottage, her birthplace, just to express the joy overwhelming my heart. I leapt, I capered. I ran to the cliffs and shouted at the waves, my voice drowned in their crashing. I lost my breath, and, calming myself, walked back.

Candlelight still gleamed from the window of the room where I had left Miss Bennet with my bride. My Eve. I crept up to the window and, grinning with the effusions of my heart, peered inside. Eve lay on the narrow bed, her dark hair across the pillow; Miss Bennet sat beside her. I watched the firelight play across the features of my beloved. A thousand hopes contended in my fevered mind.

Miss Bennet looked up and saw me. She started. Her face twisted in dismay and she waved at me to go away. Abashed, still grinning, I stepped back from the window, only to stumble into Victor, returning from his own wanderings.

"What are you doing?" he asked. "Why do you spy on Miss Bennet?"

"I was not spying," I said. I towered over him; he fell back a step or two. The collar of his greatcoat fluttered in the wind. The air was raw on my cheek—how much more cold must it be to him, unused to such exposure?

I was so moved that rather than take offense I attempted to speak with him as I might to a friend. "It's cold out here," I said. "We should go inside and sit by the fire. I must explain to you how grateful I am for what you have done."

He stared at me. "I did not do this to earn your gratitude. I did it to prevent you from killing anyone else."

Nothing he had ever before said had caused me shame. Now I saw the face of his brother William, frightened into insanity a minute before I crushed his throat in my hands. I saw Justine as she lay asleep in the moonlight, so desirable, so impossible for me to imagine being with, that I drove her to despair and death. I truly was the demon he had called me. It did not matter how I had come to be a demon, or whom I might blame for it. I, not Victor or anyone else, was responsible for my actions.

Even in the dark I saw Victor's resentment.

"You are right to be angry," I said. "I forced you to this thing by the most dire threats, after having committed against you the most terrible crimes. I cannot ask your forgiveness. I only wish you to understand that I know what you have done for me."

"Oh, I doubt that either of us knows what I've done," Victor said. "I have only your word that the killing has stopped." He turned toward the laboratory door. "I do not think that we shall sit by the fire and talk."

He disappeared inside. I stood troubled for some moments, but then the thought of Eve and our future together came back, and the bad feelings Victor had evoked faded. I entered the shed and lay on my pallet, the wind whistling through gaps in the plank walls, thinking of Eve lying not ten feet away. Imagining a chain that linked her heart to mine, I fell asleep.

The next morning my only glimpse of her came when Miss Bennet fed her some of the same porridge she gave me to eat. Victor and Miss Bennet spoke for some time behind her closed door. Given my conversation with Victor the previous night, I did not wish to force myself upon him.

In the afternoon Miss Bennet asked me to help to teach my bride to speak. I sat on the floor and Eve sat opposite me on the wooden chair by the hearth. She had already learned to sit upright with her hands on her lap. In the light of day the rough surface of her birthmark stood out against the fineness of her other skin. Apparently the birthmark irritated her, as she kept raising her hand to her cheek to rub it. Miss Bennet noticed this as well, and asked Victor what might be done for her.

"Because of this Creature's impatience, I may have brought this female to life prematurely. Her body has not completely knit itself together. I will do what I can for her."

He prepared an ointment that Miss Bennet applied to Eve's skin every morning. It did little to lessen her irritation. To this he added a potion that he had her drink every night before going to sleep. After some initial hesitance, she took these ministrations without protest.

She was astonishingly acute, and learned many words rapidly. We soon exhausted all the objects in the small room and all the parts of the body. We stepped outside and taught her the words for house, sky, grass, stone, cloud, sea, bird, and a dozen more. Then came simple actions: walk, eat, touch, look, hear.

After that our language lessons took place every afternoon. Although the days were short and the weather inhospitable, Miss Bennet, Eve, and I took to walking outside for a time each day. Victor would take no part in these sessions, although he spoke with Miss Bennet in private. I did not attempt again to thank him for fulfilling his promise, though I still hoped to say something more to him before Eve and I departed.

Once while Miss Bennet and Victor were talking, I decided to take Eve to the cliff and the stone circle. She was fascinated by the seabirds. We sat on one of the stones and I attempted to explain to her that the gulls swooping over the waters sought fish below the surface to snatch up and eat. I explained that this war between bird and fish had been going on since the beginning of time.

"Bird," she said. "Eat."

"Yes," I said.

"Bird eat fish."

"Yes."

"Fish is alive."

"Yes. Birds kill and eat the fish."

"We eat fish," she said. "We kill fish."

"Yes."

She pondered that for a moment in silence, her brow furrowed. She was so much smaller than I. I wished to put my arms around her, envelop her and keep troubling thoughts away, to feel her head against my breast and to smell her hair. I could not tell whether this would be a welcome event to her; I held myself back. Eventually it would happen. We would have years together to discover these things. Despite my impatience, I would not impose my will on a creature no more than a child. I had seen the child whores of East London and Piccadilly.

To draw her thoughts to more pleasant discoveries, I attempted to reproduce Miss Bennet's lesson in harmony. I could in no way match Miss Bennet's voice, but Eve quickly grasped the idea of singing. Her voice was sweet, more beautiful than Miss Bennet's. Her pale eyes opened wide and she watched my mouth, forming a circle of her own open lips. She could hold a note much longer than I could, and when I ended one of my efforts with a cough and a descent into laughter, she laughed with me.

Then I spied Miss Bennet lurking behind the standing stone.

"What do you want?" I asked.

"I was worried."

"There's nothing to worry about."

Eve's eyes clouded at the tone of my voice. Though she might not know the meaning of the words we spoke, she was extraordinarily sensitive to the emotions of others. "There's nothing to worry about," I repeated to her, more softly.

"Let me show you how it is with a third voice," Miss Bennet said.

It was dark by the time we returned to the cottage. Victor had, ironically, prepared a supper from the herring that the grocer's man had brought the day before. I took my portion and turned to leave, as I had done every night since we had arrived. To my surprise, Eve spoke.

"Adam, stay," she said.

I turned back. Victor and Miss Bennet, their plates in their hands, looked at her, Miss Bennet in curiosity, Victor in what I can only call chagrin.

"Eat fish here," Eve said.

Miss Bennet nodded to me. The four of us sat uneasily in the crowded room, Miss Bennet and Eve on the two chairs, Victor on the edge of the bed, and I on the hearthstone. Few words were exchanged. Eve watched all of us, comparing our appearances, demeanors. I thought of myself peeking through the chink in the wall of the De Laceys' cottage, studying every detail of the family in hope of learning how one might live with other beings on terms of friendship and mutual respect. I suppose at that moment we were the queerest family on the face of the earth. I would not hazard to guess what Eve was learning behind her watery eyes.

So followed the days of another week. Every day Eve

learned more of what it was to be alive. She had complete control of her body now, and moved with a swiftness and balance that would mature, I was sure, into true grace. She treated Miss Bennet as a mother or older sister. I could see, at times, how Miss Bennet was startled by Eve, and at others looked upon her with inexpressible sadness. I imagined her thinking of her lost sister, and felt a great wave of sympathy. It was borne upon me how my present hope and future joy were built on the death of Kitty Bennet and my murder of William Frankenstein.

Finally, one evening after finishing one of these quiet suppers, a meal in which most of the talk was Miss Bennet or me answering Eve's childlike questions, I put to them the conclusion I had reached.

"It is time for us to go," I said.

"But Eve is not ready," Miss Bennet said. "She knows so little."

"She knows far more than I knew when I was cast into the world. She will have me as her companion, teacher, and protector. I will not let anyone harm her. I will keep her safe until we are able to leave Europe for some warmer clime, some place far from civilization where we may make our home and never cross paths with any human being. Perhaps in the New World."

Victor listened. He did not look happy, but he raised no objection.

Miss Bennet, however, was not satisfied. "Does Eve know enough to make a choice in this matter? I would not have her taken against her will."

"You may ask her," I said.

"Eve, do you wish to go away with Adam?"

"With Adam," she said.

"You may stay with Victor and me."

"Go away with Adam."

Miss Bennet looked troubled. "I do not think she knows enough to make such a decision."

"When will she know enough to satisfy you?" I asked her. "How long must we live here?"

"Some time longer. She knows so little of what it is to be a woman."

"She can never be a woman as you are. You have a place in the world. Eve can know nothing of human society—the very sight of her would cause any human being to flee or to attack her. That is what human beings do when confronted with the ugly or the strange. What will you teach her that will be of use to us?"

"She is too young to know what is best for herself."

"There is no way here for her to gain the experience you say she needs," I said.

At this point Victor intervened. "The Creature has reason on his side, Miss Bennet. He and she were not made for the human world, and would find no place in it. The only outcome of their contact with humanity would be deadly conflict. Their chance for happiness lies outside the sphere of human inter-course."

"He is right," I said. "To my regret."

"I feel that Eve should have a choice," Miss Bennet said.

"I go . . . with Adam," Eve said.

Miss Bennet was unpersuaded. "But how will you cross oceans, whole continents?"

"We shall survive," I said.

"I believe you shall," Victor said. "But I have one fear."

"Fear?"

"Your bride—your Eve—did not grow in precisely the manner that I anticipated. You see, for instance, the variegation and sensitivity of her skin. I have said that she was brought to life before her development was complete. I worry that further debilities may develop as time goes on, things that may seriously compromise her health."

"We cannot put her back into the bath. We will not wait here on the chance that something may happen that may not."

"I agree. But I have considered other options, and I have prepared a treatment that will, I believe, insure her continued existence."

"A treatment?" I said.

Eve looked at us, completely out of her depth. She watched my face, and Miss Bennet's.

"Kin to the medicine that I have given her every night. It contains the vital elements that I use to bring dead cells to life. It should act within her over the next weeks to correct those things that may have gone awry."

I tried to gauge his motives. "Why should you worry about this, when you would like nothing better than to see us disappear forever?"

"I have no desire to have to create for you a second mate, and I will not do so," Victor said. "She is all the companions you shall ever have."

The possibility of losing her struck terror in me. "Give us this potion, then."

"If you will come into the laboratory, I have prepared it."

Victor led us into the back room. He asked Eve to sit upon the edge of the table. Mary helped her up and began to fumble with the buttons of Eve's dress.

"There is no need for her to disrobe," Victor said.

On his worktable sat the alembic, which he had used to prepare her daily tonic; from its neck dripped a fluid into a china teacup. "I have brewed this medicine over the last day. It should be cool enough for her to drink."

Victor took the cup and swirled the potion within it. "I believe it is ready," he said. He handed it to Eve.

"The taste will be unpleasant, but she must drink it all down."

Eve's nose wrinkled at the smell, and she looked to me for reassurance. I nodded. "Drink," I said.

Eyes on mine, she brought the brew to her lips and drained it. She grimaced at the taste. She dropped the cup, which bounced off her lap, fell to the floor, and shattered.

Eve's eyes went wide. She swayed. I caught and steadied her. Her face was inches from mine. Her head trembled and she coughed, splattering saliva in my face. She heaved and choked. Her body convulsed in my arms.

"Eve!" I cried.

"What is it?" Miss Bennet said.

Victor stood watching, his face frozen. He turned away.

I carried Eve, spasming as she gasped for air, to the bed. She began to vomit, half of it blood, and I had to turn her over to keep her from choking. Still she gasped painfully for breath, a terrible rattling wheeze. Her eyes drooped and her head lolled. "Eve," I cried, holding her face in my hand. A thin line of white showed beneath her almost-closed eyelids.

She lay convulsing for several minutes, shuddering, and then she stopped breathing entirely. A bubble of blood burst on her lips.

On my knees beside the bed, I shook her, trying to rouse her. She was as limp as an empty coat. I laid my head on her breast and listened for her heart. It was still.

I must have let my head lie there, stunned, for some moments. I became aware of excited voices and lifted my eyes to see Miss Bennet arguing with Victor.

I stood. My head brushed the room's rafters. "Why?" I asked.

Miss Bennet turned her face to me. Tears showed on her cheeks.

Victor stood straighter and lifted his chin, the way, I had observed, men did when trying to convince themselves that they are brave.

"Shall I, in cool blood, set loose upon the earth a second demon, whose delight is death and wretchedness? Your semblance of humanity is deceit. You are indifferent to your own depravity. Your existence is wrong—the only cure for it is to do away with you. I only wish I had managed somehow to get you to share the healing draught."

Miss Bennet recoiled at his words, as if each were a physical blow.

"You could not recognize the beauty you had created," I said, "how simple and good she was. You had to annihilate her, lest by her very existence she point out the worthlessness of your entire race. How the thought of our marriage must have tormented you."

Miss Bennet stepped between Victor and me. "Do not kill him!"

"You think you must protect *him* from *me*?" I said.

"Don't trouble yourself, Miss Bennet," Victor said. "The hour of my weakness is past, and the end of his power is arrived."

"No—I will not kill you, Victor," I said. "But do not think you may be happy, while I grovel in the intensity of my wretchedness. You shall never be free of me. You, my tyrant and tormenter, shall curse the sun that gazes on your misery. I shall be with you on *your* wedding night."

"Villain! Before you sign my death warrant, be sure that you are yourself safe. I am no coward."

I looked down on Eve's body, lifeless for the second time. A cold rage burned in my heart. I laughed. "I have no doubt, my creator, that if you should survive to tell our tale, you will neglect to relate how you tricked me and poisoned Eve. You will give a report much kinder to your overwhelming vanity."

I gathered up Eve, shouldered past Victor's wrathful eye and trembling jaw, past Miss Bennet, and into the laboratory. In the corner stood the trunk. I kissed Eve's lips, bitter with the taste of poison. I folded her so that she might fit into the trunk, much as I had folded the body of Kitty Bennet to fit within it months earlier. I carried the trunk out of the cottage to the beach and loaded it into the stolen skiff.

TWENTY

The cup bounced off Eve's lap, fell to the floor, and shattered.

As Eve choked and went into spasms, Mary stepped toward her, then hesitated. Adam caught Eve up and carried her through the laboratory door to Mary's bed.

"What's happened?" she asked Victor. "Help her!"

Victor looked stricken. He did not move.

Mary followed the horrid sounds coming from next room. She found Adam kneeling over Eve on Mary's bed. Eve shook and gasped. Her mouth was red with blood. The sound of her tortured breath, a fearfully loud wheeze, sent shivers down Mary's spine. Eve vomited and Adam tried to clear her mouth. He held her face in his hand and spoke to her.

Mary heard Victor behind her. She turned on him. "Please, help her."

"She is beyond anyone's help," Victor said.

The end of Mary's confusion was like a physical blow. "How could you do this?"

"I had no choice," he said hoarsely.

"No choice!"

Victor tore his eyes from Adam and Eve and returned her gaze. His expression turned from horror to anger. "Mary, you are a fool. You are a fool twenty times over, and I a fool for drawing you into this. Look at them! They are not human, they are monsters. The idea that I could create a human being was a blasphemous presumption. Let no one else suffer because of my sin. Let it all fall onto me, his rage and hatred. I can bear it. I deserve it."

Mary could hardly speak. She was crying. "You had no reason!"

A few steps away from them, on the bed, Eve no longer gasped for air. She did not move. Adam's head lay on her breast. He lifted it and stood. His bulk filled the room.

"Why?" he said to Victor in a choked voice.

"Shall I, in cool blood, set loose upon the earth a second demon, whose delight is death and wretchedness?" Victor said.

Mary watched the rage swell in Adam; his voice trembled with it as he accused Victor of killing Eve out of envy. Mary stepped between them. "Do not kill him!" she said.

Adam looked at her in astonishment. "You think you must protect *him* from *me*?"

He threatened to make Victor miserable and vowed that he would be there on his wedding night. Then he picked up Eve and carried her into the laboratory. He fit her into the trunk that had contained Kitty's body and then, kicking the door open with his foot, carried it out of the cottage. The cold wind rushed in. He hoisted the trunk to his shoulder and walked toward the beach.

Mary turned on Victor. "How could you destroy an innocent like Eve?"

"I had every reason to destroy her. Her continued existence would have led to evil. I could see it happening—she was becoming an appendage of his will. Soon she would have seen humanity as he does, and acted out of his merciless hatred. His malice was evident in every move of his body, in the subtle manipulations by which he deceived you, in the lust revealed by every glance he cast upon his hideous bride."

"You are wrong. He had changed. He was changing every hour."

"Mary, you were made to be used. Have you never been told that you are a terrible judge of character?"

"I regarded you highly," she said.

"You erred in that as well. I committed an abomination. Out of cowardice I repeated the sin, but now I have mustered the courage to put it right. Like Prometheus, thinking I would benefit my race, I seized a godlike power, not realizing how inadequate we are to wield such power. Like Prometheus I shall be punished. You heard what the demon said."

Mary could not stand to remain. She ran out of the cottage.

She called aloud as she approached the beach. In the moonlight she saw the stolen skiff half in the water. Adam had loaded the trunk into it. He stooped over beside the skiff, tossing sea-smooth rocks from the beach into the bottom of the boat.

"Adam!" she called. "Please, stop."

He ignored her. He pushed the skiff into the waves and hoisted himself over the gunwale. Mary called out, "Wait! Please! Don't go!"

She ran into the water. A wave crashed against her and she staggered. The sea was icy. She gained her feet and pushed forward, the water rising to her waist. "Adam! Stop!"

He fitted an oar into the rowlock. She saw him turn and then another wave hit her and knocked her over. Her feet lost the seabed and she tumbled below the waters. The ocean was pitch-black. Her head broke the surface, but before she could draw breath, another wave pushed her under. Just as she realized that she was going to drown, something grabbed her arm and pulled her out of the water.

Her body scraped against the side of the skiff and Adam hauled her aboard.

Mary coughed and gasped, lying in the water that sloshed around the skiff's bottom. Her sodden dress weighed so much she struggled to move, and the wind on her exposed neck sent a chill down her back. She shivered.

Adam sat, took the oars, and rowed past the surf into smooth waters. His long, wet hair hung over the shoulders of his coat. He moved with rhythm and tremendous strength, and his eyes were dark pits.

Mary managed to pull herself up enough to lean against the trunk that contained Eve's body. The shoulder by which he had dragged her from the sea ached.

"I'm sorry," she said. "I'm so sorry. I didn't know what he was about to do. Had I known—"

"You know very little," he said.

She considered this a fair assessment. It seemed that Victor and Adam could at least agree on that.

He rowed steadily until they were well away from the island. The sea was calm and the stars bright. The waning moon created a glittering path on the water. Mary wished she could step out and follow it to the horizon, to escape this world of horror and blood.

After a while she said, "What will you do?"

"I shall desolate his life. I shall destroy his heart and mind. I shall make of his every moment a living hell. I shall torment him with the thought of the deaths . . . I shall take from him . . . I shall . . . I do not know all the things I shall do, but I shall never stop until he suffers as grievous a loss as I suffered tonight. I will burn, I will rage, I will—"

He pulled so hard on the oars that one of them popped out of the rowlock and he fell over backward. He struggled up, seized the offending oar, and hurled it end over end into the air. It splashed into the sea and floated some yards away.

He heaved a sigh and sat down on the thwart, his head hanging. Mary heard the sound of his weeping.

She sat shivering. After some time he stopped. He wiped his eyes. He scanned the sea. To the south a speck of light lay on the horizon.

Adam fished the discarded oar from the water. He crept toward her. The boat swayed. "Move," he said.

She fell back onto the seat that ran across the stern. She trembled with the cold. Looking at her feet, she saw that Mrs. Buchanan's wedding shoes were completely ruined.

Adam knelt beside the trunk and opened it. Mary could not see within, nor did she wish to. One by one Adam took up the stones he had tossed into the boat and set them carefully into the trunk. When he had finished, he closed it and sat staring at it.

He said to Mary, "Sit on one side."

She did so. On one knee, he picked up the trunk and, balancing against the boat's swaying, dropped it overboard. It made a slight splash and sank into the black water. He stared down, his hands on the gunwale, for some time. He turned. "I should throw you overboard too."

The boat rocked with the wind.

"You might have left me to drown back in the surf," Mary said. "But you chose not to."

"Why did you come after me?"

Mary asked herself the same question. "I could not stay with Victor. I wanted to console you."

"Console me!" His voice rose. "I have endured more than any being could abide. For a year now I have crept across Europe, England, and Scotland, living on the blasted heath, suffering cold and hunger, all the time waiting for him to give me the only consolation possible. And now he steals it from me! Worse, he took that poor creature's life. Console me. I should kill you for speaking the word."

"Adam, I know that—"

"Don't call me that name! I have no name!"

He stepped forward, rocking the boat so perilously that Mary had to clutch the seat to keep from falling overboard. Adam—the creature that had been, briefly, Adam—seized the mast that lay in the bottom of the skiff and mounted it in its socket in the boat's prow. He attached the yard and raised the sail, which caught the breeze and snapped full. The boat heeled over; Mary seized the rudder to keep it from capsizing.

Though Mary had sailed on a lake once or twice with Darcy, she knew little of guiding a boat. The Creature came back and managed to steer the skiff south toward the mainland. She wanted to reach out and touch him, but she feared he might respond with a blow.

He sat not three feet from her, leaning on the tiller, a huge black figure in the moonlight. He was gaunt in a way that she had not noticed before. The knob of the wrist that stuck out of the sleeve of his too-short coat stood out so starkly that it cast a shadow.

The moon was coming down, and soon the sun would begin to lighten the sea's horizon in the southeast.

Back at Pemberley she had watched Kitty die, lying in bed, her sisters around her, the focus of all the love—and understanding of her flaws and foolishness—that had grown between them over a lifetime together.

Now Mary had watched her, in Eve, die a second time. This death came from another realm. Mary had never seen and could hardly have imagined anything like it; her life could never have allowed her to come into a circumstance where she might witness such a barbarity. Horrors like this did not happen in the home of a gentleman, his foolish wife, and his family of girls.

Apparently they did happen in this other world. She sat a yard away from an artificial man who had sworn vengeance against all humanity. He had reason enough, in his heart, to kill Mary. But she had seen something in him on the road, and had most definitely seen it in the last week with Eve. He had a soul, a gravely tormented one, and that soul was at this very moment at risk. He knew right from wrong and cared about the difference. It was Mary's duty to try, with whatever means at her disposal, to help him save himself. He could only do that if he was able, with forbearance that Mary could not imagine, to turn the other cheek, battered and bruised as it was.

She would have to remain in his company. She would have to talk with him, listen to him, persuade him, if it came to that. For her to be here at this moment in this situation was so impossibly unlikely a circumstance that God must have had a hand in it.

She did nothing now but keep her eye out for that light in the south and search for the town. Soon the sky began to glimmer and with a piercing sliver of light the sun broke the horizon. They spotted the village, and the Creature steered toward it. Before reaching it he turned to the shore on the opposite side of the river's mouth. They ran aground on a deserted beach.

Mary did not attempt to climb out of the skiff. She said, "I know you have no reason to, but will you help me?"

"Help you," he said, his voice completely flat.

"I am cold. I am wet through. I have no money. I know no one here. I shall have to throw myself upon the mercy of the parish, if they will have me."

"Find the local church, then. That's their business, isn't it? Christian charity? Take this with you." He pulled the Bible from his pocket and held it out to her.

"You keep it. You may yet have need of it."

He looked at her with a face devoid of expression.

"What will you do?" Mary asked.

"What does it matter?"

"It matters. I beg you, Adam—"

"Have a care."

"I beg you to give up your quest for vengeance against Victor. Remember the regret you feel about killing William."

"I killed William. I killed Justine. Will I be more damned if I kill others—if I killed you here, on this beach? What difference would it make?"

"It would be an act of despair. It would not lessen your pain."

"I think it will. It is the only thing that will."

"You may yet repent and be saved."

"Saved? Saved from what? I am finished. Victor destroyed me. But I am not finished with him. I will desolate him. I will see that he will never know the acceptance and love he stole from me. I will kill all who love him. He will know that his cruelty to me is the cause of their deaths—if he is capable, which I doubt, of caring what happens to anyone but himself. If he had spent one moment caring for the life he made in me, I would hold back my wrath."

"I care for you," Mary said. As she said the words, she realized that the fear of him that she had never wholly abandoned was no longer in her heart.

The Creature's face twisted in agony. "Do not say that."

"I do," Mary insisted.

He sat in the skiff, his perfect, hideous sham face exposed to her study. It did not frighten her anymore. He said, "A year ago those words might have meant more to me than the air I breathe. It's too late."

"It is never too late."

"If you knew how bitter what you say makes me feel, you

would hold your tongue. The cup you offer me is as poisonous as that he gave Eve."

"Only if you cast it aside."

"What practical consequence does your caring have? Will it make me a man in the eyes of the human race? Will it cause the next person who sees me to give me succor? Will it change me from being what I am?"

"It can change you in here," Mary said, touching the sodden breast of her dress.

"It is easy for you to speak of changed hearts, who may return to her home and the arms of the family that loves her. And where shall I reside?"

"I will not abandon you."

"You will pardon my skepticism. Shall we now move to the wilds of South America together? Will you even touch my hand?"

Mary recalled when he had seized her wrist back in the inn in Matlock, the warmth of his grip, so alive. She reached forward and touched his hand. He snatched it away as if she had scalded him.

Whatever else this accomplished, she had caused him to think on something other than his desire to torment Victor. Victor had failed to take the opportunity to save himself. Perhaps here she might act to better effect.

The truth was, she did not know what would follow of her bold avowal. For the Creature was right: she had no power to change what the world would think and do. But that was the nature of love: one did not offer it with any assurance that it would change the world, even if in the end it was the only thing that could.

"Eve is dead," the Creature said. "How can you ask me to forget her, to forgive him?"

"I don't ask you to forget her. I cannot ask you to forgive him—if that comes, it must come from your own heart."

The Creature watched her as warily as a beaten dog offered food by a stranger. "What would you have me do, then?"

"I don't know. I think that you will need to keep out of sight of men, while I go into the town and seek some help. If I can write to my family, they will perhaps send some money."

"So I hide and wait for you, rather than Victor, to make my life whole. This does not alter my condition."

"I am sorry I cannot do more."

The Creature said, "You have done more than anyone has ever done, however little that may be, and however I doubt that you will be able to do more." He looked across the dawning beach. "We are exposed here; the fishermen will see us. You are cold. Take my coat, and I will sail up the coast until I find a place where I can hide."

"Whether I succeed or not," Mary said, "I will return to this place by the time the sun sets."

"I will be here," the Creature said.

St. Peter's Kirk was in the old part of the town, in the wedge of land bordered by the river on the east and the sea on the north and west. A somewhat dilapidated old stone structure, it stood just a short distance from the river and not far from the docks.

Mary entered through the porch door. The nave was empty; she knelt in one of the pews and tried to quiet her disordered mind. She was engulfed by the Creature's huge coat. Her dress was still wet, she smelled of salt and worse, hunger ground the pit of her stomach, and she felt cold and weary through to her bones. The experiences of the last month, Eve's horrifying death, Victor's actions, and her worry about what Adam might do left her overwhelmed with contradictory emotions. She bowed her head and sought some guidance.

She had never questioned that there was a moral order to the universe just as there was an order to nature. In the world of men, injustice was common, but that was because men were the authors of their own miseries. Evil occurred in nature—the hawk kills the starling, the starling kills the locust—but these savageries, seen through the eyes of faith, have a plan. Mary believed that even the terrible, inexplicable trials of innocent lives—the babes lost at birth, the lightning that struck Mary Anning when she was an infant—also fell according to some plan, difficult as it might be for mortals to understand it. She had always placed her faith in Providence, and it had comforted her on those occasions where injustice had seemed to prevail.

What she had experienced in the months since Kitty's death challenged this faith. She supposed she could explain all the evil that she had seen as resulting from the actions of men. She herself had lied repeatedly. She had stolen Mrs. Buchanan's shoes. God was not responsible for these things.

But the figure of Adam, hiding somewhere in the stolen skiff awaiting her return, increased her doubts. Yes, all the evil that had arisen could be laid at the feet of human beings. But was God indifferent to the death of Eve? Her mind told her that all could be explained, but her heart did not rest easy. She prayed that God might give her a sign to guide her through this thicket.

Kneeling there, her sleepless night soon caught up with

her, and she fell into a half slumber, her lips resting on her folded hands.

She did not know how much time had passed when she was awakened by a hand on her shoulder.

"Ye canna sleep here," a man's voice said.

Mary lifted her head, bleary eyed, her thoughts running slow. It was a man of middle years in a dark coat. "Who are ye?" he asked.

"I am sorry," Mary said. "My name is Mary Bennet."

"An Englishwoman, are ye? What do ye here?"

"I have no money. I need to write a letter to my family."

"A stranger in a shabby dress, wearing a man's coat. I doubt that yer family will be eager to see ye again. I'll not be played on by a vagabond."

"Please. You can tell by my speech that this is not the station to which I was born. My sister is married to Fitzwilliam Darcy of Pemberley, in Derbyshire."

"Ye may be sister to James MacLaine, for all I know. Away with ye, now. If ye must beg, come stand by the door on Sunday with yer head bowed, yer mouth shut, and yer hand out and maybe one of the Saved will have mercy on ye."

Mary got to her feet. The cleric followed her as she moved slowly toward the door.

On the porch she turned to him. "Would you tell me where I might find the magistrate? Perhaps he might be able to help me."

"He'll clap ye in gaol, if he knows his duty."

Mary looked into his eyes. He shifted one foot to the other and said, less abruptly, "The hall is on Traill Street in the New Town." He closed the door on her.

Mary sighed and leaned on one of the stones that filled the churchyard.

ALASDAIR FINDLAY, 1675–1737

ISOBEL, WIFE, 1687–1723

She walked to the high street. The pale sunlight was without warmth. Townspeople were up and about, in the streets and the shops she had passed when she had searched for Victor. The town hall was a square brick building that contained the office of the magistrate and the town gaol. As soon as Mary entered, a hard-faced old woman accosted her. "What want ye here?" she asked.

"I wish to speak with the magistrate."

"Mr. Kirwin is not here."

Mary was reluctant to go back out into the cold. Beside a battered table stood two wooden chairs. "May I sit here a while to recover myself?"

"Ye aren't from these parts," the woman said. "Unless ye state yer business, you'll have to go."

"I have been on the road for weeks now. I was robbed by highwaymen and lucky to escape with my life. I hoped that the magistrate might see his way to allowing me to write my family. My sister is married to Mr. Fitzwilliam Darcy of Pemberley, one of the richest men in Derbyshire. All I need is paper, pen, and—"

"And ye want to send a letter to Derbyshire, I don't know how many hundred mile from here?" She looked Mary up and down. "I doubt your sister, if ye have a sister, will want to pay the post on a letter come from so far, asking for money."

"My sister will be worried about me and would be grateful to know that I live."

"From the looks of ye, I'd not warrant you'll be alive when yer rescue comes."

"Will Mr. Kirwin be here later today?"

"I think it best that ye be on your way," the old woman said.

Mary was so weary, and faint from hunger, that she ignored her and slumped into one of the chairs.

"Here, now! I gave ye no leave to sit."

Mary rested her head in her hand. "I'm sorry. I have not eaten in a day."

Before the woman could reply, a man of about her age came into the room from the back of the building. A large ring of keys hung from his belt. "Who's this?" he asked.

"This woman comes here, bold as you please, to beg Mr. Kirwin for money and food."

"Not for myself alone. My friend, too, needs help."

"Go round to the church and beg there," the woman said. "On your feet, now." She took Mary's arm, the one by which the Creature had yanked her out of the water, and drew her to her feet.

"Wait," said the man.

"What is it now, John?" the woman said with irritation.

The man stepped out of the room and returned a moment later with a slice of hard brown bread, which he gave to Mary. "From yesterday's supper," he told the woman.

Mary thanked him. The woman scowled at the man and pushed her out the door. "And don't be coming back."

Mary stood in the street. She slipped the bread into the pocket of the Creature's greatcoat, and kept her hands in those pockets against the cold. She did not know what she might do next. Even had she been able to write home, no help would have come for weeks. She and the Creature would have to find some way to survive. She wondered if, in the hours since she had left him, his rage had lessened.

She realized that, after all her noble vows, she was relieved to be in a town full of ordinary people going about their days in something that she could comprehend as civilized life. That Scotswoman across the street at the butcher's shop might live modestly by the standards of Longbourn, but she was the kind of person Mary had known her entire life. Those idlers outside the inn, watching the courtyard for the arrival of some coach, were the like of the men who loitered about the inn in Meryton.

She stepped into the street and crossed before the inn yard. Just then the awaited coach arrived, trundling up the high street. It circled round and rocked to a halt. The driver hopped down, and from the inn a boy ran out to place a step below the coach door.

The door of the coach opened, and the first person who stepped down was Henry Clerval.

"Mr. Clerval!" she said.

He stopped. Seconds passed before he recognized her. "Miss Bennet?" He seemed nonplussed. "What a—what a happy accident that we meet again."

"Yes," she said. "A happy accident."

The other passengers stepped down from the coach while the porter and driver lifted down their baggage. The idlers clapped hands on the back of a young man who had arrived and headed for the taproom.

Henry stared at the vast, worn greatcoat that swamped Mary. "Mr. Clerval," she said. "I need your help."

Henry frowned. "I can see that. What has he done to you?"

"May we go somewhere to talk?"

"Come," he said. "Let me buy us both some dinner. You look starved."

He told the porter to have his bags placed in his room, and took Mary into the inn, where he ordered some cider and a meal for both of them. The smell of food from the kitchen made Mary dizzy.

"I confess myself astonished to see you, and, if you will excuse such frankness from one who has no claim to know you well, troubled by the condition in which I find you. What has happened to you the last months?" Henry asked. "Have you seen Victor?"

"I left him in his cottage in the Orkneys last night. You were right about many things, Henry. He is not well, and he greatly needs your friendship and attention. I fear he will do damage to himself. I am trying to see that he does not come to harm from others."

"Others?" Clerval paused. "Must you tell your family what he has done? Has he not given you satisfaction in the matter of your sister?"

"Victor has wronged others far more than he has me or my family."

The innkeeper came with two plates of mutton and potatoes. It was rude fare, but Mary fell to it.

She regretted saying anything to Henry about Victor being in danger from anyone other than himself. It became clear to Henry, however, that Mary's regard for Victor had changed.

"I cannot believe he drove you out in this condition," he said.

"I am well enough. If you could help me to write to my father, he will send me money to see me return home. And if you could spare even a little yourself so that I might survive until funds arrive—"

"Nothing is easier," Clerval said. "Do not worry."

"I cannot tell you how grateful I am." Mary took another sip of the cider. With her lack of sleep, even a little made her dizzy.

Henry asked her how she had been living. Mary told him about the cottage in the Orkneys and spoke of Victor's pursuit of scientific study, without telling him anything material about that study. She let him think her reticence was the result of shock at discovering Victor's use of Kitty's body.

"You were right, Henry. Victor is not well in his mind. His life is at risk, and the lives of those he loves. It would be best if you took him directly home, and took the utmost care for your own safety as well."

"This is mysterious. How am I to understand what you say?"

"I cannot explain—I would betray Victor's confidence if I spoke, even now—but perhaps he will tell you."

"I wrote to Victor telling of my arrival," Henry said. "I expect he will contact me here in the next day or so. I shall arrange a room at the inn for you."

"I would be eternally grateful." Mary's mind was already moving to how she might assure shelter and sustenance for Adam. Finding a way to turn him from vengeance would not be easy.

"If you would wait here," Henry said, "I will see that you have pen and paper. Your letter will go with the very next post."

Henry spoke with the innkeeper and returned to the table with pen, ink, and paper. He drew a newspaper out of his bag and made a show of reading it while Mary wrote a brief letter to her father, telling him where she was and imploring him to send her money so that she could return home.

When she finished the letter, she folded and sealed it with candle wax. She gave it to Henry. "Please tell the innkeeper that it should leave with the next coach," she said.

"I will speak to him now," said Henry. "And I will arrange for a room in your name."

The moment he had left her, Mary walked out of the inn.

It was late afternoon. The sky had clouded and shadows pooled in the gray streets and the lees of the buildings. Mary imagined Henry's consternation when he returned to find her gone; she hurried up the street and turned a corner down to the old stone bridge over the river. The farther she moved from the town's center, the fewer people were abroad.

She crossed the bridge and followed the road that ran along the other side of the river toward its mouth. This side was farms and fishing huts, widely scattered. It was a longer walk than she remembered, and by the time she came to the beach, it was dark. Aside from a light in a fisherman's house on the bluff, the shore lay outlined only by thin starlight; the late moon would not rise until midnight.

Mary stood on the deserted strand. Lines of white surf showed as the waves came in to break on the gravel and sea-washed stones. Although she had told Adam she would be back before now, she saw no sign of him or the skiff. Had he come and gone already, thinking her faithless?

Then she spied, away from the shore, a small sail. It tacked past her west, and then turned and ran before the wind toward the beach. As it came to the breakers, the man in it dropped the sail and took up an oar. He was tall and his hair fell over his shoulders.

Adam steered the skiff through the surf, leapt out, and dragged it onto the strand.

Mary came forward. "When I did not see you, I feared you might think I had abandoned you."

"There was no point in exposing myself. I waited offshore until I saw you. "

They stood facing each other. He said, in a different tone, "I will not expect you to live by the words you spoke this morning. I come only to say good-bye."

"No," said Mary. "I have written to my father. He will send money, and then you and I shall leave this place."

"To go where?"

"You tell me you lived in London for weeks. With a little money, we can find a place to live there, or better still, some large city on the Continent. Among many thousands you will not stand out, and if we mind our own affairs, we may live unmolested."

Adam laughed. "Miss Bennet, I think you do not understand what you say."

"You will nevertheless do me the courtesy to listen. I have lived among human beings longer than you."

"And I have been a monster my entire life."

"Which is three years. I believe I may know some things that you do not."

He shook his head slowly. "You are the best human being I have ever met. Yet still you flinch when I come upon you unawares, I see your eyes narrow when you inspect my face, I hear the uncertainty in your voice when you say, 'I am your friend.'"

Mary did not doubt that this was true, and it shamed her. But what was it to be Christian other than to master one's instincts? "Uncertainty. Can we not begin with that?"

"It is too slender a reed," he said, "and I am not some suitor. I am a murderer." He turned from her toward the skiff.

Mary came to the gunwale. She seized his hand in both of hers, raised it to her lips, and kissed it. She looked up into his face.

It was dark, but she saw him tremble and close his eyes.

"Miss Bennet!" a voice shouted above the sound of the surf. "Victor!"

Adam's head snapped up. Mary turned and saw a man striding across the beach toward them. Henry Clerval.

She still had hold of the Creature's hand. "Henry, no—"

When Henry came within a few steps of them he stopped. He stared. In the starlight Adam's livid face was that of a corpse.

"I am not Victor," he said.

Henry rushed forward, pulling Mary away. "Run!" he said. He seized the oar that lay across the bow of the skiff and swung it toward Adam's head.

"No!" Mary shouted.

Adam's hand flashed out and caught the oar in mid-swing. He ripped it from Henry's grasp.

Henry faltered, but then hurled himself at Adam.

Adam staggered at the force of Henry's assault, but he did not fall. He seized Henry by the throat.

"Adam, no!"

Adam lifted Henry by his neck. Henry kicked and struggled. Adam's face was set in a rictus of rage. He closed his hand on Henry's throat. Henry, writhing, tried to pry Adam's hand from his neck, to no avail. When he was still, Adam threw him down onto the beach.

Mary knelt over Henry. He was not breathing. Tears were in her eyes.

She looked up. Adam towered above her, looking down on them both, arms at his sides. His hands moved aimlessly, as if he had forgotten how to control them.

"Is he dead?" he said.

Mary nodded.

Adam poked at Henry with the toe of his boot. "It is my fate to kill them all."

Mary tried to speak, blinking away tears. She rubbed the back of her hand across her eyes and caught her breath. She should call him away from such thoughts. *You don't have to do these things,* she should tell him. *God will forgive you if you repent.*

She said nothing.

Adam pushed the skiff into the water, climbed aboard, and rowed away from the shore, leaving Mary standing with the body of Henry Clerval at her feet.

Numbly, Mary walked back from the beach into the town.

She needed to tell someone about Henry's murder. As a stranger and a beggar, she knew she would be suspect. If anyone had seen her with Henry at the inn, she would surely be questioned.

She had not slept for two days. She was so weary and heartsick that when she came upon a horse stall along the way, she crawled into it, curled into a corner, and fell unconscious. Her dreams were full of black terror, and in those moments where she lay half-awake, images of Eve dropping the cup, Henry's terrified and determined face as he assaulted Adam, and the warmth of Adam's hand against her lips.

The next morning it seemed that these things could not have happened. When she made her way to Traill Street, she found a grim-faced knot of people standing outside the town hall. They spoke to one another in low voices. Mary eavesdropped. Henry's body had been found by some fishermen coming ashore—it must have been not long after she had fled the beach—and failing to revive him, they had brought him to the gaol.

A stranger had sailed into the harbor with the dawn, in the kind of skiff that had been seen off the coast near where Henry's body had been found. The man had been arrested and was at this moment being interrogated by Mr. Kirwin.

No one said there was anything unusual about the accused, so it could not have been Adam. Whoever they had arrested was innocent. When Mary tried to enter the hall, she was turned away by the same woman who had dismissed her the day before.

She returned to the churchyard and sat on a stone bench among the graves. Idly putting her hands in the pockets of the greatcoat she still wore, she found the hard bread that the turnkey had given her. She gnawed at one end and considered what she must do. Her mind was not clear. She was a fool. She might have guessed that as soon as Henry missed her, thinking she had gone off to meet Victor, he would try to follow. By luring him to the beach, she had caused his death.

Eventually she walked back to the town hall and stood uncertainly among the people gathered. She drew a number of curious glances, but no one tried to speak with her. Then someone among the gawkers mentioned that the murderer was a foreigner, and Mary realized, cursing her blindness, that it had to be Victor.

She went to the door again. The woman saw her coming. "Didn't I tell ye yesterday to leave this town?"

Mary announced loudly, "I know who killed Henry Clerval."

"Who the devil's Henry Clerval?"

"The man they found on the beach."

The woman let her in. Inside were the fishermen who had discovered Henry's body and those who had apprehended Victor. "Where is Mr. Kirwin?" the woman asked.

"He's in back," one of the older men said. "He wants to see what this fella does when he sees the body."

A commotion arose somewhere in the back of the building, and a benevolent-featured man hurried into the room. "The fellow swooned," he told the woman. "Fetch the apothecary."

"Sir," Mary said, "if your suspect is Victor Frankenstein, I can tell you that he did not commit this crime."

Harried as the man appeared, he stopped. "And how do you know this?"

"Mr. Frankenstein was on an island five or more miles from here. He could not have killed Mr. Clerval."

"And who are you? How is it that you know these men?"

"My name is Mary Bennet. I came here yesterday but you

were not in. The turnkey and his wife met me, and can vouch for this."

"Come with me," Mr. Kirwin said.

He led Mary back to the room where Henry's body lay on a table. Henry's face was placid, but ugly bruises marred his throat. Mary had little attention to spare for him, for lying on the floor, writhing and muttering sporadic exclamations, was Victor. The turnkey had hold of his shoulders and was trying to get him to lie still.

"*Oh, Henri!*" Victor said. "*Henri, t'ai-je tué comme j'ai tué William?*"

Although his eyes were open, he did not seem aware of his surroundings. Mary tried to call him out of his fit, but he was oblivious.

Mr. Kirwin observed her attempts to bring Victor to his senses. He had Victor carried off to a cell and laid on a cot. The apothecary arrived and forced Victor to quaff a strong sleeping draught that at last subdued his mutterings.

Kirwin brought Mary to his office. He sat her down opposite him and closed the door. From a drawer in his desk he took a pipe and tobacco, prepared and lit it, and leaned back.

"You are exhausted," he said.

Mary rested her head in her hand. "This is undeniable."

"You know both the victim and the murderer. How is that?"

"Victor is not a—he did not kill Henry."

"So if this man did not commit the murder, who did?"

Mary hesitated. "I cannot say."

Mr. Kirwin studied her for some time. His gaze was not unkind. "It is clear to me that you have not always been this destitute. Tell me how it is that you find yourself here, and explain your connection to both of these unfortunate men. Beware: though I compassionate you, I ask in my official capacity, and will hold you accountable for whatever you say."

Mary rubbed her brow. She felt the hard chair she sat in, the weariness in her bones. What could she say to this good man that would not strike him as lunacy?

She took a deep breath and began: "I am a person who has always believed what people told me, and who could not see them well enough to know when they lied."

She related the story of a well-bred, naive woman who developed an unwise affection for a handsome and troubled man; how, against all her history and principles, she followed him to the remote north of Scotland. She told of Victor's despondency at the death of his brother, and how he and Henry had come to Britain so that he might recover himself.

She said nothing of the Creature, but she assured Mr. Kirwin that Victor had been on the island at the time that Henry had been killed.

"You cannot know that unless you were there," Kirwin said. "Mr. Frankenstein raves that he is responsible for his friend's death."

"You understood him," Mary said.

"Even in remotest Scotland there exist men who know French, madam. I heard what he said. I cannot say that I understood him."

"He is not in his right mind. The William he spoke of— that was his young brother, who was similarly strangled back in Switzerland. Mr. Frankenstein had isolated himself in the Orkneys so that he might drown his sorrows in scientific research. Your grocer will vouch for his presence on Emray Isle for many weeks. It was ill done. I arrived and, in the foolishness of my heart, thought I might draw him away from his obsession. I was wrong. Mr. Clerval came to meet Victor that they might return to Geneva. If you inquire at the inn, you will discover that he arrived only yesterday. Victor must blame himself for bringing Henry into a circumstance that has led to his death."

Mr. Kirwin was not satisfied with her tale. "No one here knows Mr. Clerval. Yet less than twenty-four hours after his arrival he is found strangled on the seashore. Witnesses say that a beggar woman was with him at the inn the last time that anyone observed him alive. I assume that woman was you."

"I knew that he was coming to meet Victor, and in my desperation I sought his help. The innkeeper will testify that Henry helped me to write to my family. When that help comes, if you will permit me to, I shall return to my home. Though I came all this way only to have Victor disappoint my hopes, I know that he cannot have killed Henry, his dearest friend. I would suggest that, before you settle on his fate, you write his father. He is a syndic in Geneva, Switzerland."

"The court will decide his fate. But I will write his father, and see that he is cared for until he recovers himself sufficiently to be tried."

"You are a generous man."

"As for you," he said gravely, "I believe that you are not telling me all that you know. You are a poor dissembler. It would be well for you to reveal everything. However, it is quite evident that you are not capable of strangling a man to death, and there is no indication that you have an accomplice. The person who was seen sailing away from the scene of the murder was a single man, in a skiff."

"Victor warned me that he had an enemy who would seek to harm those whom he loves. The murderer of his young brother still roams free."

"A convenient circumstance for Mr. Frankenstein. We shall discover whether he deceived you in that as he did in his regard for you. In the meanwhile, I will do my best to see that you are taken care of until your family is able to send you relief."

In the days after his swoon, Victor did not recover from his brain fever. Mary visited him more than once in the gaol, trying to bring him back to the world, but he only stared at her with blind eyes and muttered self-accusations in French.

Two weeks later Darcy arrived once again to save Mary from herself. He had become accustomed to this role with regard to his wife's sisters over the years, and though he was weary of it, he did not reprove Mary any more than she did herself. After meeting with Mr. Kirwin and offering to recompense him for his kindness to Mary—which Mr. Kirwin politely declined—Darcy and Mary left on the next coach back to Edinburgh.

Mary never saw Victor Frankenstein again.

TWENTY-ONE

When Mary entered the shop, Mary Anning's black-and-white terrier, Tray, lifted his head. His eyes brightened and he trotted over to sniff Mary's boots and push his head against her hand.

"Good dog," Mary said, and he circled back to his place beside the counter. He was as loyal a creature as had ever inhabited the earth, Mary Anning's constant companion when she went searching the Blue Lias cliffs for new fossils.

Despite the fact that the windows at the front were open, the air in the tiny shop lay heavy and motionless. The heat had been the beginning of every conversation for weeks. People fleeing London crowded the streets of Lyme Regis. The town bustled with visitors, the wealthy to country houses in the vicinity and the less wealthy filling the inns. A continual tide of curiosity seekers washed in and out of Anning's Fossil Depot.

Mrs. Anning stepped out from behind the door at the back.

"Good day, Miss Bennet," she said. "Mary is in her workshop. Shall I call her?"

"Don't bother. I'll go down, if I may."

"Certainly."

Mary stepped down the narrow stairs to the cellar. Here it was cooler, and the window to the street was open to let in daylight. Still, a lighted lantern hung above the table where Mary Anning bent over a slab of limestone. She held a small rock hammer and an awl, chipping away bits of stone. When she heard Mary on the creaking stair treads, she looked up.

"We sold the ammonite slab," she said in her blunt way.

"Wonderful," Mary said. She stood beside the younger woman, examining her recent find. "I have not seen this one."

"Center of a vertebra, I think, of a shark." She ran a finger over the disk that protruded from the stone. "Few and far between, such shark fossils."

Mary looked at the notebook lying nearby, where Mary Anning had made a drawing of the fossil. Mary loved to see the young woman so caught up in her work. She had the slightest education, and as Mr. Woodleigh had charged years before, could not pronounce ichthyosaurus to save her life, but she had laboriously copied word by word the scientific papers sent her by fossil-hunting correspondents. Her mind was keen and her ability to discern slight differences between even partial skeletons uncanny. From the shy girl she had been at sixteen, at twenty-two she demonstrated growing confidence in her abilities. She could be careless of social forms, and on occasion demonstrated a sharp tongue, but these things did not bother Mary as they once might have.

Mary said, "I came to ask whether you might wish to walk

on the Undercliff this Sunday. We might take a lunch and hunt for specimens."

The younger woman said, "I should be pleased—after church."

Mary Anning attended the Dissenters' church run by the Reverend Gleed, whereas Mary attended the Anglican service. "Will you come by the cottage, then? I'll have Alice prepare something for us."

"I shall be there at one."

This had become their habit on fine summer days. They took their baskets and hammers and a picnic lunch and lost themselves in the woods above the cliffs. In truth they did not so much hunt fossils—the fossils to be found were down on the beach—as the opportunity to be together away from the eyes of townspeople. Mary was that fossil-collecting old maid who had moved here from Hertfordshire, and Mary Anning was the queer girl who corresponded with important men half-mad for the bones of monsters dead thousands of years. Whatever gossip the two women stirred protected Mary Anning from worse gossip about her association with these strange men.

"At one, then." Mary kissed her on the cheek and climbed back up the stairs to the shop.

Anning's Fossil Depot might be said to be a product of Mary's intervention in the Annings' lives. She had observed the desperate hand-to-mouth existence Mary and her mother lived, dependent on Mrs. Anning's sewing and whether her daughter was able to find fossils to sell to tourists. Mary Anning's brother Joseph had given up fossil hunting and apprenticed as an upholsterer.

Not having the resources herself to save them, Mary called upon a connection she had forged with one of the wealthy enthusiasts who came to Lyme Regis. Lieutenant Colonel Thomas Birch had purchased many of the finer specimens that Joseph and Mary had found. Over the course of months Mary had gently drawn Colonel Birch to pay more than passing attention to the precarious living of the Annings. He recognized Mary Bennet's breeding and was familiar with her family connections. Mary put the notion into his head that perhaps something might be done to help the Annings, and from this came Birch's idea to auction off his collection and give the proceeds to them. It was a generous impulse. Mary praised him for his charity, contributed her own meager collection to the cause, and did everything she could to see that Birch garnered all the credit that might be had from it.

The auction drew bids from fossil collectors across Britain and raised more than four hundred pounds for the Annings. With that money they started their shop. Mary Anning recognized Mary's role in her good fortune, and though she was sixteen years her junior, over time the two women had become something more than close friends.

When Mary climbed to the front of the shop again, she found Mrs. Anning sitting on a stool behind the counter, stitching a piece on an embroidery frame. Tray rested with his head on his paws, eyes following a man who strolled around the tiny shop, examining the exhibits. He was finely dressed, perhaps thirty or thirty-five years old, and possessed an open and honest face.

Mary exchanged a few words with Mrs. Anning while idly watching the man. He leaned forward over the fossil of a fish cemented into a frame. As he did so, he clasped his hands behind his back, one of them holding his gloves, and Mary saw that he was missing the two smallest fingers of his right hand.

The door of the shop opened and a woman entered. It was Mrs. John Saville, a visitor to Lyme for the last weeks with her husband and two children. Mary had met her at the church and had enjoyed a pleasant conversation with her.

"Mrs. Saville," Mary said. "How good to see you."

"Miss Bennet. How are you?"

"Fine, thank you."

The man looked up. Mrs. Saville said, "Miss Bennet, this is my brother, Captain Robert Walton."

"Miss Bennet," he said, with a slight bow.

"Miss Bennet is a collector, Robert."

Walton raised an eyebrow. "Another lady fossil enthusiast? I shall have to snap up the bargains here, then, lest you anticipate me."

"Robert has a scientific temperament," Mrs. Saville said teasingly. She smiled at her brother, who smiled back.

"Not so much as in days gone by," Walton said.

Mary asked him, "You are a seaman and a scientist?"

"Some years ago I imagined myself an explorer destined to write his name in the history books."

Mrs. Saville said, "Robert had the mad fancy that the North Pole would be a region of beauty and delight! When he left England, I thought I would never see him again."

"But I came back to you, my dear Margaret."

"And I am grateful to God for your deliverance."

They chatted amiably while Captain Walton examined the fossils. Mary made a few comments and he ended up purchasing one that showed what looked like the small bones of some animal's foot.

On an impulse Mary invited them, if they were not too busy, to come to tea that afternoon. Living as she had in Lyme the year round, and having only herself to please, she had become bolder, and quite less formal, than she had ever been at Longbourn. Mrs. Saville and her brother agreed, and Mary went home to prepare.

Her cottage sat on a little knoll to the west of the town. Her garden had a fine view of the harbor and sea. It was not a home of any extravagance, but it proved an ideal dwelling for Mary and her lone servant. When she arrived, Mary found Alice and told her they would have guests for tea. She made sure the sitting room was in order, then retired to her room to change clothes.

When Darcy had brought her home from Scotland six years earlier, it was some time before her family treated Mary as anything other than a madwoman. Mary did not elaborate on the little she had told Darcy when he had found her in the care of Mr. Kirwin. Darcy was appalled at the fate of Clerval and the fact that Frankenstein, if he should ever recover his senses, was to be tried for Henry's murder. Every conversation Mary had with her mother back in Meryton was freighted with Mrs. Bennet's fear that Mary might say or do some new, terrifying thing. For her part, Mary brooded over her experiences. No detail was very far from her mind. In the midst of sitting in the garden, or during a church service, or while listening to William Darcy talk about his schoolwork, the desolation of her walk back from the beach where she had left Henry dead would sweep over her as if it had happened only moments before.

She sent Mrs. Buchanan's ruined wedding shoes back to her, along with a letter of apology and a sum of money that would replace them ten times over, but she knew that they were irreplaceable and that her betrayal of that good woman's trust could never be made right. Her conscience bothered her every time she opened her wardrobe and found her own many pairs of shoes lined up there.

Mary's distraction did not keep Mrs. Bennet from urging her in whatever way she might to present herself to the attentions of Mr. Collins. But Collins, who had never expressed an interest in Mary even in her youth, had decided that her Scottish exploits had cast a shadow over her character that put her quite beyond association with such a respected clergyman as he. Mrs. Bennet would never forgive Mary for spoiling her fantasies of saving Longbourn.

The year Mary spent at home after her return was a difficult one, and she devoted many hours to trying to understand what had happened to her. Victor and Adam were in her thoughts. She wondered what had happened to Victor when he recovered from his swoon—assuming he ever had. Had he been sent to the gallows for Henry's death? What an irony if he died for a murder he had not committed, which happened less than a day after he had committed one that would never be known to anyone.

And Adam? Mary's heart was torn in a dozen directions whenever she thought of him. He was a murderer three times over, yet she was tormented by her sight of his slumped shoulders as he climbed into the boat, by her image of him teaching Eve to sing, by her memory of the nights on the road when he had kept Mary warm, by her knowledge of the bullet he had taken in rescuing her. By the sound of his voice as he had spoken the last words he would ever say to her: *It is my fate to kill them all.*

Mr. Bennet had died three years ago, and Longbourn had passed into the hands of Collins, who by that time had remarried. He took possession of the estate with the smug sense of his worthiness that the family had come to expect of him. He even—as he told everyone—though not obligated in any way to do so, and despite the fact that her daughters were married to two of the most prosperous men of the midlands, set aside fifty pounds a year for Mrs. Bennet.

In tears Mrs. Bennet left the home where she had borne and raised her children. Where she was to reside was a difficult question. In the end, like King Lear, she was obliged to spend half the year with one daughter and half with the other, though it must be said that Jane and Elizabeth were more patient and more generous with their affections, despite whatever trials Mrs. Bennet might cause them, than Goneril and Regan.

Mary was invited to live at Pemberley, but she was not inclined to take Darcy and Elizabeth up on this offer. Besides the one thousand pounds of Mary's inheritance, Mr. Bennet, recognizing her to be unlikely ever to find a husband, had left her an income of one hundred pounds per annum. Darcy added another one hundred. With this money Mary took the cottage in Lyme Regis, bringing Alice with her as her maid-of-all-work.

Mrs. Saville and Captain Walton arrived promptly at four, and Alice ushered them into the sitting room where Mary waited. They chatted amiably for a while, and then Alice brought the tea, which Mary served.

"So, tell me about your expedition to the North Pole," Mary said. "When did this happen, and how did it end?"

"The expedition sailed from Archangel in the summer of 1816," Walton said. "Its end was ignominious. We never got north of the eightieth parallel. People call 1816 'the year without a summer': indeed, the bitter cold and the density of ice we encountered the farther we traveled north were extraordinary, though I suspect now that the arctic sea is impassable even in the best of conditions. Certainly I have had to surrender my belief that the apex of the globe hides a temperate hyperborean zone, and I am here to swear that those authorities who speak of such are purveying utter nonsense."

Captain Walton raised his teacup, held in the thumb and first two fingers—the only fingers that remained—of his right hand. "Frostbite," he said, and winked at Mary.

"Robert," said Mrs. Saville. "Must you?"

"But this is fascinating," Mary said. "Tell me what you sought?"

Walton was happy to tell his story, as it seemed he must have more than once before. He explained how his poetic nature had been attracted to the notion of discovering a land of eternal light, and the source of the power that commands the compass needle, at the pole. But in the event, the ship he had hired and crew he had assembled found themselves frozen tight in the arctic wasteland long before Walton had reached his goal.

"Here occurred something so remarkable, and unexpected, that it challenges the imagination, and has met with such disbelief, not to say ridicule, from men of science to whom I have told it that I have chosen not to publish the tale."

Mary was intrigued. Captain Walton's manner was so affable, his voice so full of mystery. Mrs. Saville, though she must have heard all of this before, listened indulgently to her brother. "Please, go on," Mary said.

"Our ship had been stuck in the ice, and the crew suffering the bitter frost, when in the glare of the unending, cold arctic sun we spied at a distance of half a mile or so a man of enormous size urging a sledge pulled by a team of dogs across the desolate, jumbled sheets of ice. He passed into the mists, giving no sign that he had seen us."

Mary stopped her teacup on its way to her lips, then carefully took a sip.

"A day later, when the ice had broken somewhat, we discovered another man stranded on a floe with his own sledge and team of dogs, all but one of them dead. I never encountered a soul in so wretched a condition. We brought him on board and over the next weeks, as he recovered his strength and faculties, he and I became friends. He was not some northern savage as I had surmised but a European, finely educated, a person of great melancholy, even despair, but also of a high and noble nature fit for a better fate than that which befell him. His name was Victor Frankenstein."

Mary put down her teacup. "An unusual name."

"He was a Swiss, educated in Germany, of about my age, though the tragedies and hard use he had endured left him enfeebled. He had spent some time in England and Scotland, and spoke excellent English."

"How did he come to be marooned on a shelf of ice in the Arctic Ocean?"

"He was in pursuit of the man—more accurately the

demon—we had seen the previous day. He had pursued this being across Europe since the day that the thing had strangled his wife."

"Robert," said Mrs. Saville. "See how you have upset Miss Bennet. She is as pale as a ghost. I should have stopped you as soon as you began this terrible story."

"No," said Mary. "Tell me more. Tell me what became of him."

"I shall. But first I must tell you his story, as he told it to me over the course of the next weeks, as he came to trust me and unburden himself of experiences that he had revealed to no one before we met. We may need more tea. It will be some time in the telling."

Captain Walton proceeded to relate the story that Mary had heard years before from both Victor and his Creature. Dramatically, Walton lingered over the extraordinary circumstance of Victor's discovery of the secret of life and his creation of a monster. He watched Mary's eyes, prepared for skepticism, but she was too troubled to feign astonishment at something she knew to be fact. Walton's narrative closely resembled what Mary already knew, but she appeared nowhere in it, nor any woman who might have been Mary. And there was nothing in the tale of bringing Eve to life, or of her death. To hear Walton tell it, Victor had earned the eternal enmity of his monster by dismembering his female before he had brought her to life.

Months after Mary had left Scotland with Darcy, Victor's father had arrived. Victor recovered his senses, and a grand jury determined that, despite his professions of guilt, he had been in the Orkneys when Henry Clerval was murdered. Victor and his father traveled back to Geneva, where Victor wed his cousin Elizabeth. That night, Elizabeth was strangled by the monster who had vowed to be with him on his wedding night.

Mary, agitated, could not help saying, "But if the Creature made such a vow of vengeance, why would Monsieur Frankenstein still marry?"

"This is just what I asked myself," Mrs. Saville said, "when Robert first told me this tale. It passes understanding."

"You did not know Victor Frankenstein, my dear," said Walton. "He would never have knowingly put his beloved into danger. He assumed that the monster's enmity was meant for him, and that, having refused to create a bride for it, it would kill him before he could enjoy the blessings of connubial companionship."

"Yet if the tale you tell is true," Mary said, "in all the time since his creation the Creature had not harmed Victor. He had destroyed his younger brother, his family's servant, and his best friend. How could he not have suspected that his wife, not himself, might be the target of the fiend's ire?"

"You should have heard the remorse in his voice as he upbraided himself for not understanding just this point," Walton said. "He accused himself more than anyone else could. Moreover, his father died in grief days after hearing that Victor's wife was murdered. Haunted by his guilt, he pursued the thing from Switzerland to the far north of Russia, and beyond across the polar ice. He was bound on a mission that was, I am convinced, the only reason he had survived as long as he had—although he did tell me that the demon, whenever it seemed Frankenstein was at risk of losing the trail or coming to grief, would slow his flight enough for him to follow, and leave food to keep him from starving."

The late afternoon sunlight was coming through the west windows of the sitting room. Mary rose to pull the muslin curtains and diffuse its force. The image of the Creature and Victor, pursued and pursuer, crossing a lifeless landscape of ice, haunted her. Out of his rage for vengeance the Creature plants markers to reveal his path, leaves food, and draws his creator on, keeping Victor alive so that he might follow his own rage for vengeance deeper into this suicidal whiteness. Each of them gives purpose to his life by this game. The two of them orbit about each other, so isolated that the rest of the human race might have vanished. It was a vision of hell more harrowing than any Mary had ever heard from the pulpit.

She returned to her seat. "When Monsieur Frankenstein recovered fully, did he give up this pursuit and return with you to Europe? Where is he now?"

Walton shook his head slowly. "Alas, though Frankenstein rallied for a time after his rescue, in the end exhaustion and the toll of his pursuit took him; he declined rapidly and died while we were still locked in ice."

"And did you believe his story?"

"Within hours of his death I had the terrible proof of it. Late that night, while I wrote an account of these events for Margaret, as had become my habit, I heard sounds from the cabin in which I had left Monsieur Frankenstein. When I investigated, I found the demon there lamenting over Franken-stein's body. Never have I beheld a vision more repulsive than his face, of such hideous strangeness, like and unlike that of a human being. He had the impudence to beg forgiveness over the corpse of the man whose life he had blighted, and whom he had lured to his death in this desolate place. Only now, after having destroyed beings who had done him no harm, did he feel the pangs of conscience. Although I was frightened, I charged him with his hypocrisy."

"Perhaps, if he was able to restrain himself under your accusation, he was not so monstrous as Monsieur Frankenstein portrayed him."

Walton raised an eyebrow. "I confess that I felt a moment of compassion for him. But Frankenstein had forewarned me about his eloquence and persuasiveness. Yet you never heard him—what causes you to feel sympathy for the wretched thing, Miss Bennet?"

"I only imagine what the world must have been like for a being abandoned at birth, and reviled at his every encounter with humanity."

"Your sympathy speaks well of you, though I hazard to say that if you had ever seen this monster, you would have run in terror."

"Perhaps. What ensued when you confronted him?"

"After expressing his hypocritical remorse and complaining of his treatment by Victor and the rest of humanity, he told me that with Frankenstein's death his life was without purpose. He said it was his intention to find land, build a funeral pyre, and put an end to his life amid its flames. Then he leapt out of the cabin onto a raft of ice, and I lost sight of him in the darkness and distance."

Mary said nothing. A silence stretched, broken finally by Mrs. Saville.

"Robert, I fear you have repaid Miss Bennet's gracious hospitality by giving her nothing but material for nightmares. I hope you will not trouble yourself over this story, Miss Bennett. We have long overstayed our welcome."

"No," said Mary. "I am glad to have heard your story, Captain Walton."

"I could tell that you were affected by it. I must say that, though I knew him for only a matter of days, and in him saw only a shadow of the man he must have been before the ordeals that he suffered, the loss of Victor Frankenstein still haunts me. He was a man of great qualities, a deep soul, and the noblest impulses, and deserved a better end."

"He was a remarkable person," Mary said.

She escorted her visitors to the door. Captain Walton and Mrs. Saville said their good-byes and left.

Mary closed the door on them and leaned her back against it. The ticking of the clock on her mantel reminded her of the one in the Perth home of Dr. Marble where she had waited for Henry Clerval. That was when she had learned that Victor was engaged to his Elizabeth. All three of them now dead.

It is my fate to kill them all.

Alice came into the parlor to retrieve the tea tray. Mary told her, "Alice, I will not be having supper tonight. Do not bother with it."

"But I have a roast I've been preparing all day."

"Keep it until tomorrow, if it will keep. I am going out."

She took shawl and bonnet and left the cottage.

The long summer day was declining, and the sun setting over the sea. The mild evening breeze from offshore, running up the lane, brushed Mary's face. With the coming of evening, people were returning to the busy town from a day at the seaside. There was to be a ball at the Assembly Rooms that evening; the front door of the hall was open and people bustled in and out, making preparations.

She walked down to the harbor, a woman alone in the gathering dusk. Even in a town as placid as Lyme Regis, even for an aging spinster as established as Mary, this was behavior that she would have questioned when she was a girl. It was not so much the danger of the world that Mary had been aware of, as the importance of propriety. She knew now that much of propriety consisted of a veil of hypocrisy over self-interest. The machine of society was prepared to grind those without money or powerful friends exceedingly fine if they should disregard the shibboleths of the righteous. It remained true that to discard propriety was to put oneself at risk, whether or not one ended up strangled.

But to lean on the promptings of the heart alone? That was what Victor had done, and Adam.

The longer she thought of Walton's story, the angrier Mary became. Victor and Adam had followed a direct path from the place she had left them, precisely the same course they had been on before she had entered their lives. For a time it had seemed to her that they might turn to a different, happier fate—though who could know where any path leads in the end? Still, there was little doubt where following the impulses of hatred and revenge led. In the case of Frankenstein and his creation, they had led exactly where they ought—to desolation and the grave.

Mary's intervention had been their last chance to avoid this. She had put herself between them expecting to keep them sane. It was a terribly foolish, dangerous thing for her to do.

She'd had no idea with what or whom she was dealing. How idiotic she had been, so blinded by her own hopes.

Yes, and still what she had told them to do was the right thing, the practical thing, the just thing. She had been a voice speaking from outside the drama that took place inside their heads. She had given them good counsel. And why should a woman have to do that, prevent men from killing each other? The true idiocy of their tragedy was that it did not have to happen. Victor and Adam had constructed it by their own choices, out of their inability to believe in the existence of anyone but themselves. William, Justine, Henry, Elizabeth, Victor's father. Eve. What about them? Hadn't they deserved better?

Mary came to the seaside and walked along the Marine Parade, stiff-legged in her anger, paying no attention to the others who lingered there at the decline of the day. The green bathing machines had all been drawn away from the water and stood in a row on the sandy beach. A flock of boats lay at anchor, sails furled, within the embrace of the Cobb. She continued until she reached the great breakwall and climbed to its top. The limb of the orange sun was just about to touch the sea's horizon, and its glare hit her full in the face.

> *In them hath he set a tabernacle for the sun . . . .*
> *His going forth is from the end of the heaven, and*
> *his circuit unto the ends of it: and there is nothing*
> *hid from the heat thereof.*

She held her hand up to shade her eyes and walked the sinuous masonry wall above the sea. She reached its end. Below her, waves broke on the rocks at the foot of the Cobb. The tide was running out: black algae and seaweed draped the wall's exposed foundations. The chill air brought with it the odor of the recent catch, sea wrack, and salt, pungent to her nostrils.

At the same time King David had told how God's truth was written in nature for men to read, he had also begged to be kept free from "the great transgression": doing wrong when one believes one is doing right. How easy, when one followed the promptings of the traitorous heart, to convince oneself that pure selfishness is the ultimate selflessness, that desire is fate, that murder is self-sacrifice.

By now Mary was furious. She had never been more enraged. She clenched her fists and squinted into the sun and shouted, at the limits of her voice, "The judgments of the LORD are true and righteous altogether!"

As soon as the words left her lips, the fury drained from her. Her heart raced. She looked back toward the town. Some people at the foot of the Cobb had turned toward her; they must have heard her shout, but they could not have heard what she had shouted. Behind them in the golden light of sunset the town rose from the harbor, streets twisting between homes and town houses where lights were coming on for the evening. In those homes young women excitedly prepared for the Assembly Ball. Worried about their dress, speculating about whether this lordling or that government minister's cousin would be in attendance, and who would dance with whom. The judgments of the Lord were far from their minds.

Perhaps there was no Lord. Perhaps he had started the world and gone away, leaving human beings to make what they would of it.

Mary turned her back on the sunset and slowly retraced

the Cobb toward the shore, then walked along the parade and up Coombe Street into town. By the time she reached Anning's Fossil Depot, it was full night. The shop's windows were dark, but through the opened cellar window Mary could see the lantern still alight over the workbench, and at it Mary Anning, intent over her notebook, Tray lying at her feet.

Mary Bennet came to the window and stuck her head inside. "Mary," she said. "Must you waste good lamp oil over another of your ridiculous fossils? Too much learning makes a woman monstrous."

Startled, Mary Anning looked up, saw it was her—and smiled.

It was the matter of a minute for her to climb up from the cellar and open the door to let Mary in.

AUTHOR'S NOTE

In crossing these two novels, I have done my best not to alter the facts as we are given them in Mary Shelley's *Frankenstein* and Jane Austen's *Pride and Prejudice*, but still it has been necessary for me to take many liberties. Chief among them is that I had to alter the chronology of the two novels to make them coincide.

Although the year in which *Pride and Prejudice* takes place is not stated in the novel, scholars have suggested that the most likely times for it are 1802 or 1811. I have chosen to assume that Austen's novel takes place in 1802. My novel takes place thirteen years after Ms. Austen's story, in 1815.

Frankenstein is set in the mid-1790s, but Mary Shelley herself must have been a little uncertain about this, since her characters refer to works of literature and social realities that did not exist until decades later. So I have pushed the events of *Frankenstein* forward twenty years.

In other regards I have striven to follow the chronology of Shelley's novel, though even there I had to improvise: on one page Victor tells us he and Henry arrived in England "at the beginning of October," although a page earlier he says, "It was on a clear morning, in the latter days of December, that I first saw the white cliffs of Britain." I have also shortened Victor's four-hundred-mile overnight sea voyage in a skiff from the Orkneys to Ireland so that he lands in northern Scotland instead.

I am comforted by the knowledge that adaptors of Austen and Shelley have taken the widest of liberties with these great novels, and the two seem to have emerged none the worse for wear. At least I hope Jane and Mary will forgive me my trespasses.

I have likewise rearranged a few genuine historical events, persons, and details of geography for the sake of my story.

I must acknowledge my debt to the great wealth of information that has been accumulated by readers and scholars of Jane Austen and Mary Shelley, including in particular Jane Austen's World (janeaustensworld.wordpress.com), Regency Reader (regrom.com), Jane Austen Society of North America (jasna.org/austen), and Jane Austen in Vermont (janeausten-invermont.wordpress.com).

Portions of this novel were written during a residency at the Virginia Center for the Creative Arts. Thanks to Antony Harrison and the department of English at North Carolina State University for administrative and other support. I must thank my readers Wilton Barnhardt, Karen Joy Fowler, Therese Anne Fowler, Edward James, James Patrick Kelly, and the 2016 Sycamore Hill workshop for comments, corrections, and advice. Friends and colleagues Belle Boggs, Richard Butner, Dorianne Laux, John Morillo, Leila May, and Lewis Shiner helped me with information, suggestions, and moral support.

I owe a great debt of gratitude to F. Brett Cox for the title.

Thanks to my agent, John Silbersack, and editor, Joe Monti, and the staff at Simon & Schuster for their enthusiastic support of this project from the beginning, and to Joe for his editorial suggestions and general good sense.

It is not possible for me to say how grateful I am for the emotional and literary support that Therese has, as always, offered throughout the writing of this book.

STARRING:

Mary Jekyll, Diana Hyde, Catherine Moreau, Beatrice Rappaccini, and Justine Frankenstein!

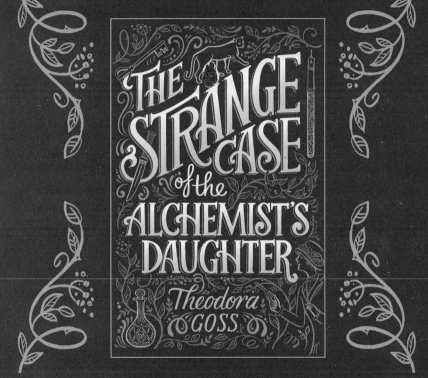

The daughters of literature's most famous mad scientists must come together to stop a murderer—and solve the mystery of their own creation.

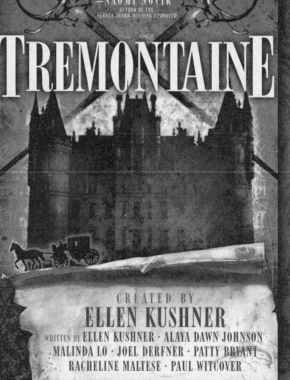

A MAGICAL REVENGE THRILLER.

AN
UNKINDNESS
OF
MAGICIANS

KAT HOWARD

PRINT AND EBOOK EDITIONS AVAILABLE
sagapress.com